SHOWDOWN

The noise that had halted Nevada came from the saloon. He strode to the nearest group of men. "What's happened?" he queried.

"We was playin' our caird games," spoke up the gambler, Ace Black, "when we heerd an awful row in the hall there. We all jumped up an' some one rushed out to see what it was. An' by Gawd—"

"Wal?" broke in Nevada, cool and grim, as Black choked.

"Lize Teller! She was layin' half naked, streamin' blood. Link Cawthorne had beat her over the head with his gun. She'll die!"

In three long bounds Nevada had reached and split the beaded door-curtain. His swift eye swept all.

"Cawthorne!" he yelled, in piercing voice that brought an instant breathless silence.

"Nevada"

ZANE GREY

BANTAM BOOKS · TORONTO · NEW YORK · LONDON

*This low-priced Bantam Book
has been completely reset in a type face
designed for easy reading, and was printed
from new plates. It contains the complete
text of the original hard-cover edition.*
NOT ONE WORD HAS BEEN OMITTED.

"NEVADA"

*A Bantam Book / published by arrangement with
Harper & Row, Publishers, Inc.*

PRINTING HISTORY

Serialized in AMERICAN MAGAZINE *1926–1927*

Harper edition published January 1928
2nd printing ... October 1929
3rd printing .. November 1929

Grosset & Dunlap edition published September 1929

Collier edition published 1931

*Walter J. Black (Black Reader's Service Company) edition
published June 1951*
9 printings through January 1957

Bantam edition / January 1946
17 printings through January 1975
18th printing .. January 1977

ISBN 0-553-10626-0

Published simultaneously in the United States and Canada

---

*Bantam Books are published by Bantam Books, Inc. Its trade-
mark, consisting of the words "Bantam Books" and the por-
trayal of a bantam, is registered in the United States Patent
Office and in other countries. Marca Registrada. Bantam
Books, Inc., 666 Fifth Avenue, New York, New York 10019.*

PRINTED IN THE UNITED STATES OF AMERICA

"NEVADA"

One

As his goaded horse plunged into the road, Nevada looked back over his shoulder. The lane he had plowed through the crowd let him see back into the circle where the three men lay prostrate. The blue smoke from his gun was rising slowly, floating away. Ben Ide's face shone white and convulsed in the sunlight.

"So long, Pard!" yelled Nevada, hoarsely, and stood in his stirrups to wave his sombrero high. That, he thought, was farewell forever to this friend who had saved and succored and uplifted him, whom he loved better than a brother.

Then Nevada faced the yellow road down which his horse was racing, and the grim and terrible mood returned to smother the heart-swelling emotion which had momentarily broken it.

There was something familiar and mocking about this precipitate flight on a swift horse, headed for the sage and the dark mountains. How often had he felt the wind sting his face on a run for his life! But it was not fear now, nor love of life, that made him a fugitive.

The last gate of the ranch was open, and Nevada flashed through it to turn off the road into the sage and go flying down the trail along the shore of the lake. The green water blurred on one side of him and the gray sage on the other. Even the winding trail was indistinct to eyes that still saw red. There was no need now for this breakneck ride. To be sure, the officers of the law would eventually get on his track, as they had been for years; but thought of them scarcely lingered a moment in his consciousness.

1

The action of a swift and powerful horse seemed to be necessary to the whirling of his mind. Thoughts, feelings, sensations regurgitated around that familiar cold and horrible sickness of soul which had always followed the spilling of human blood and which this time came back worse than ever.

The fierce running of the horse along the levels, around the bends of the trail, leaping washes, plunging up and down the gullies, brought into tense play all Nevada's muscular force. It seemed like a mad race away from himself. Burning and wet all over, he gradually surrendered to physical exertion.

Five miles brought horse and rider far around to the other side of the lake. Here the trail wound down upon the soft sand, where the horse slowed from run to trot, and along the edge of the lake, where the midday sun had thawed the ice. Nevada had a break in his strained mood. He saw the deep hoof tracks of horses along the shore, and the long cuts and scars on the ice, where he and Ben and the freed outlaws had run that grand wild stallion, California Red, to his last plunge and fall. Nevada could not help but think, as he passed that place, and thrill as he remembered the strange lucky catch of the wild horse Ben Ide loved so well. What a trick for fortune to play! How mad Ben had been—to bargain with the rustlers they had captured—to trade their freedom for the aid they gave in running down the red stallion! Yet mad as that act had been, Nevada could only love Ben the more. Ben was the true wild-horse hunter.

Nevada reached the bluff where Forlorn River lost itself in the lake, and climbed the sloping trail to the clump of trees and the cabin where he and Ben had lived in lonely happiness. Ben, the outcast son of a rich rancher of Tule Lake—and he, the wandering, fugitive, crippled gunman, whom Ben had taken in with only one question.

"Where you from?" Ben had asked.

"Nevada," had been the reply. And that had been the only name by which Ben had ever known him.

It was all over now. Nevada dismounted from his wet and heaving horse. "Wal, Baldy," he said, throwing the bridle, "heah we are. Reckon the runnin's aboot over." And he sank heavily upon the porch step, pushed his sombrero back to run a hand through his wet hair, smoothing it away from his heated brow. He gazed across the lake toward the dots on the far gray slope—the dots that were the cabins and barns of the Blaine ranch. With the wrench which shook him then, the last of that icy nausea—that cold grip from bowels to heart—released its cramping hold and yielded to the softening human element in Nevada. It would have been better for him if that sinister fixity of mind had not passed away, because with its passing came a slow-growing agony.

"Reckon I cain't set heah mopin' like an owl," soliloquized Nevada, getting up. "Shore, the thing's done. An' I wouldn't have it otherwise. . . . Dear old Ben!"

But he could not just yet enter the cabin where he had learned the glory of friendship.

"He was the only pard I ever had, except a hoss or two. . . . Wal, Ben's name is cleared now—thank God. Old Amos Ide knows the truth now an' he'll have to beg forgiveness of Ben. Gosh! how good that'll be! But Ben, he'll never rub it in on the old gent. He'll be soft an' easy. . . . Hart Blaine will know, too, an' he'll have to come round to the boy. They'll all have to crawl for callin' Ben a rustler. . . . Ben will marry Ina now—an' he'll be rich. He's got California Red, too, an' he'll be happy."

From the lake Nevada gazed away across Forlorn River, over the gray sage hills, so expressive of solitude, over the black ranges toward the back country, the wilderness whence he had come and to which he must return. To the hard life, the scant fare, the sordid intimacy of crooked men and women, to the border of Nevada, where he had a bad name, where he could never sleep in safety, or wear a glove on his gun-hand! But at that moment Nevada had not one regret. He was sustained and exalted by the splendid consciousness that he had paid his debt to his friend. He had saved Ben from prison, cleared his name of infamy, given him back to Ina Blaine, and killed his enemies. Whatever had been the evil of Nevada's life before he met Ben, whatever might be the loneliness and bitterness of the future, neither could change or mitigate the sweetness and glory of the service he had rendered.

Nevada went into the cabin. He had expected to find it as always, clean and neat and comfortable. The room, however, was in rude disorder. It had been ransacked by violent hands. The pseudo-sheriffs, who had come at the beck of Less Setter to arrest Ben, had not hesitated to stoop to thievery. They had evidently searched the cabin for money, or anything of value.

Nevada gazed ponderingly around on this disorder.

"Wal," he muttered, grimly, "I reckon Less Setter won't be rammin' around heah any more—or any other place short of hell!"

With that remark Nevada strode out and down the path to the corrals. There were horses in at the watering trough. He caught one, and securing packsaddle and packs, he returned to the cabin. Here he hurriedly gathered his belongings and food, blankets, ammunition. Then mounting his horse he drove the pack animal ahead of him, and rode down to the shallow ford across Forlorn River.

"Shore, Ben will always keep this ranch as we had it," he mused. "An' he'll come heah often."

Hot tears fell from Nevada's eyes, the first he had shed since his orphaned boyhood, so dim and far away. It was no use to turn his eyes again to the little gray cabin half hidden among the trees, for he could not see. But as he rode up the river his tears dried, and he saw the pasture where the horses he had owned with Ben raised their heads to look and to neigh. From a ridge top a mile or more up the lonely river, Nevada gazed back at the cabin for the last time. Something surer than his intelligence told him that he would never see it again. The moment was poignant. It opened a door

into his mind, which let in the fact he had so stubbornly resisted—that when he bade good-by to the little
cabin it was not only good-by to it and to his friend,
but to the most precious of all that had ever entered
his life—Hettie Ide.

Nevada made that farewell, and then rode on,
locked in thought which took no notice of the miles
and the hours. Sunset brought him to an awareness of
the proximity of night and the need of suitable camp
for himself and his animals. While crossing the river,
now a shallow rod-wide stream, he let the horses drink.
On the other side he dismounted to fill his waterbag
and canteen. Then he rode away from the river and
trail in search of a secluded spot. He knew the country, and before long reached a valley up which he
traveled some distance. There was no water and therefore an absence of trails. Riding through a thicket of
slender oaks, which crossed the narrowing valley, he
halted in a grassy dell to make his camp.

His well-trained horses would not stray beyond the
grass plot, and there was little chance of the eyes of
riders seeing his camp fire. How strange to be alone
again! Yet such loneliness had been a greater part of
his life before he chanced upon Ben Ide. From time to
time Nevada's hands fell idle and he stood or knelt
motionless while thought of the past held him. In spite
of this restlessness of spirit he was hungry and ate
heartily. By the time his few camp chores were done,
night had fallen, pitch black, without any stars.

Then came the hour he dreaded—that hour at the
camp fire when the silence and solitude fell oppressive-
ly upon him. Always in his lonely travels this had been
so, but now they were vastly greater and stranger.
Something incomprehensible had changed him, sharpened his intelligence, augmented his emotions. Something tremendous had entered his life. He felt it now.

The night was cold and still. A few lonesome insects
that had so far escaped the frost hummed sadly. He
heard the melancholy wail of coyotes. There were no
other sounds. The wind had not risen.

Nevada sat cross-legged, like an Indian, before his camp fire. It was small, but warm. The short pieces of dead hard oak burned red, like coal. Nevada spread his palms to the heat, an old habit of comfort and pleasure. He dreaded to go to the bed he had made, for he would fall asleep at once, then awake during the night, to lie in the loneliness and stillness. The longer he stayed awake the shorter that vigil in the after hours of the night. Besides, the camp fire was a companion. It glowed and sparkled. It was something alive that wanted to cheer him.

The moment came when Hettie Ide's face appeared clearly in the gold and red embers. It shone there, her youthful face crowned by fair hair, with its earnest gray eyes and firm sweet lips. It looked more mature than the face of a sixteen-year-old girl—brave and strong and enduring.

Strange and terrible to recall—Nevada had kissed those sweet lips and had been kissed by them! That face had lain upon his breast and the fair hair had caressed his cheek. They would haunt him now, always, down the trails of the future, shining from every camp fire.

"Hettie—Hettie," he whispered, brokenly, "you're only a kid an' shore you'll forget. I'm glad Ben never knew aboot us. It'll all come out now after my gunplay of to-day. An' you an' Ben will know I am Jim Lacy! . . . Oh, if only I could have kept it secret, so you'd never have known I was bad! An', oh—there'll never be any one to tell you I cain't be bad no more!"

Thus Nevada mourned to himself while the shadow face in the fire softened and glowed with sweetness and understanding. It was an hour when Nevada's love mounted to the greatness of sacrifice, when he cast forever from him any hope of possession, when he realized all that remained was the glory and the dream, and the changed soul which must be true to the girl who had loved him and believed in him.

Beside that first camp fire Nevada's courage failed. He had never, until now, realized the significance of that moment when Hettie and he, without knowing how it had come to pass, found themselves in each other's arms. What might have been! But that, too, had only been a dream. Still, Nevada knew he had dreamed it, believed in it, surrendered to it. And some day he might have buried the past, even his name, and grasped the happiness Hettie's arms had promised. Ben would have joyfully accepted him as a brother. But in hiding his real name, in living this character Nevada, could he have been true to the soul Ben and Hettie had uplifted in him? Nevada realized that he could no longer have lived a lie. And though he would not have cared so much about Ben, he had not wanted Hettie to learn that he had been Jim Lacy, notorious from Lineville across the desert wastes of Nevada clear to Tombstone.

"Reckon it's better so," muttered Nevada to the listening camp fire. "If only Hettie never learns aboot the real me!"

The loss of Hettie was insupportable. He had been happy without realizing it. On the steps of friendship and love and faith he had climbed out of hell. He had been transformed. Never could he go back, never minimize the bloody act through which he had saved his friend from the treachery of a ruthless and evil man. That act, as well, had saved the Blaines and the Ides from ruin, and no doubt Ina and Hettie from worse. For that crafty devil, Setter, had laid his plans well.

Nevada bowed his bare head over his camp fire, and a hard sob racked him.

"Shore—it's losin' her—that kills me!" he ground out between his teeth. "I cain't—bear it."

When he crawled into his blankets at midnight it was only because the conflict within him had exhausted his strength. Sleep mercifully brought him oblivion. But with the cold dawn his ordeal returned, and the knowledge that it would always abide with him. The agony was that he could not be happy without Hettie Ide's love—without sight of her, without her smile, her touch. He wanted to seek some hidden covert, like a crippled animal, and die. He wanted to plunge into the old raw life of the border, dealing death and meeting death among those lawless men who had ruined him.

But he could not make an end to it all, in any way. The infernal paradox was that in thought of Ben's happiness, which he had made, there was an ecstasy as great as the agony of his own loss. Furthermore, Hettie's love, her embraces, her faith had lifted him to some incredible height and fettered him there, forever to fight for the something she had created in himself. He owed himself a debt greater than that which he had owed Ben. Not a debt to love, but to faith! Hettie had made him believe in himself—in that newborn self which seemed now so all-compelling and so inscrutable.

"Baldy, I've shore got a fight on my hands," he said to his horse, as he threw on the saddle. "We've got to hit the back trails. We've got to eat an' sleep an' find some place where it's safe to hide. Maybe, after a long while, we can cross over the desert to Arizona an' find honest work. But, by Heaven! if I have to hide all my life, an' be Jim Lacy to the bloody end, I'll be true to this thing in my heart—to the name Ben Ide gave me —Nevada—the name an' the man Hettie Ide believed in!"

Nevada traveled far that day, winding along the cattle trails up the valleys and over the passes. He began to get into high country, into the cedars and piñons. Far above him the black timber belted the mountains, and above that gleamed the snow line. He avoided the few cattle ranches which nestled in the larger grass valleys. Well-trodden trails did not know the imprint of his tracks that day; and dusk found him camped in a lonely gulch, with high walls and grassy floor, where a murmuring stream made music.

Endless had been the hours and miles of the long day's ride. Camp was welcome to weary man and horses. The mourn of a wolf, terrible in its haunting prolonged sadness and wildness, greeted Nevada by his camp fire. A lone gray wolf hungering for a mate! The cry found an echo in the cry of Nevada's heart. He too was a lone wolf, one to whom nature had been even more cruel.

And once again a sweet face with gray questioning eyes gleamed and glowed and changed in the white-red heart of the camp fire.

On the following day Nevada climbed the divide that separated the sage and forest country from the desert beyond. It was a low wide pass through the range, easily surmountable on horseback, though the trail was winding and rough. The absence of cattle tracks brought a grim smile to Nevada's face. He knew why there were none here, and where, to the south through the rocky fastness of another and very rough pass, there were many. But few ranchers who bought or traded cattle ever crossed that divide.

From a grassy saddle, where autumn wild flowers still bloomed brightly, he gazed down the long uneven slope of the range, to the canyoned and cedared strip of California, and on to the border of Nevada, bleak, wild, and magnificent. The gray-and-yellow desert stretched away illimitably, with vast expanse of hazy levels and endless barren ranges. The prospect in some sense resembled Nevada's future, as he imagined it.

As he gazed mournfully out over this tremendous and monotonous wasteland a powerful antagonism to its nature and meaning swept over him. How he had learned to love the fragrant sage country behind him! But this desert was hard, bitter, cruel, like the men it developed. He hated to go back to it. Could he not find a refuge somewhere else—surely in far-off sunny Arizona? Yet strange to tell, this wild Nevada called to something deep in him, something raw and deadly and defiant.

"Reckon I'll hide out a while in some canyon," he reflected.

Then he began the descent from the divide, and soon

the great hollow and the upheaval of land beyond were
lost to his sight. The trail zigzagged down and up, under the brushy banks, through defiles of weathered
rock, over cedar ridges, on and on down out of the
heights.

Before Nevada reached the end of that long mountain slope he heard the dreamy hum of a tumbling
stream, and turning off the trail he picked his way over
the roughest of ground to the rim of a shallow canyon,
whence had come the sound of falling water. He
walked, leading his horses for a mile or more before he
found a break in the canyon wall where he could get
down.

Here indeed was a lonely retreat. Grass and wood
were abundant, and tracks of deer and other game
assured him he could kill meat. A narrow sheltered
reach of the canyon, where the cottonwood trees still
were green and gold and the grass grew rich along the
stream, appeared a most desirable place to camp.

So he unpacked his horses, leisurely and ponderingly, as if time were naught, and set about making a
habitation in the wilds. From earliest boyhood this
kind of work had possessed infinite charm. No time in
his life had he needed solitude as now.

Nevada did not count the days or nights. These
passed as in a dream. He roamed up and down the
canyon with his rifle, though he used it only when
he needed meat. He spent hours sitting in sunny spots,
absorbed in memory. His horses grew fat and lazy.
Days passed into weeks. The cottonwoods shed their
leaves to spread a golden carpet underneath. The
nights grew cold and the wind moaned in the trees.

The time came when solitude seemed no longer en-
durable. Nevada knew that if he lingered there he
would go mad. For there encroached upon his dream
of Hettie Ide and Ben, and that one short beautiful and
ennobling period of his life, a strange dark mood in
which the men he had killed came back to him. Nevada had experienced this before. The only cure was
drink, work, action, a mingling with humankind, the

sound of voices. Even a community of the most evil of men and women could save him from that haunting shadow in his mind.

Somberly he thought it all out. Though he had deemed he was self-sufficient, he found his limitations. He could no longer dwell alone in this utter solitude, starving his body, falling day by day deeper into melancholy and mental aberration. There seemed to be relief even in the thought of old associations. Yet Nevada shuddered in his soul at the inevitable which would force him back into the old life.

"Reckon now it's aboot time for me to declare myself," he muttered. "I cain't lie to myself, any more than I could to Hettie. I've changed. I change every day. Shore I don't know myself. An' this damned life I face staggers me. What am I goin' to do? I say find honest work somewhere far off. Arizona, perhaps, where I'd be least known. That's what Hettie would expect of me. She'd have faith I'd do it. . . . An', by Gawd! I *will* do it! . . . But for her sake an' Ben's, never mindin' my own, I've got to hole up till that last gun-throwin' of mine is forgotten. If I were found an' recognized as Jim Lacy it'd be bad. An' if anyone did, it'd throw the light on some things I'd rather die than have Hettie Ide know."

Two

It was a cold, bleak November day when Nevada rode into Lineville. Dust and leaves whipped up with the wind. Columns of blue wood smoke curled from the shacks and huts and houses of the straggling hamlet. Part of these habitations, those on one side of the road, lay in California, and those on the other belonged to Nevada. Many a bullet had been fired from one state to kill a man in the other.

Lineville had been a mining town of some pretensions during the early days of the gold rush. Deserted and weathered shacks were mute reminders of more populous times. High on the bleak drab foothill stood the ruins of an ore mill, with long chute and rusted pipes running down to the stream. Black holes in the cliffs opposite attested to bygone activity of prospectors. Gold was still to be mined in the rugged hills, though only in scant quantity. Prospectors arrived in Lineville, wandered around for a season, then left on their endless search, while other prospectors came. When Nevada had last been there it was possible to find a few honest men and women, but the percentage in the three hundred population was small.

Nevada halted before a gray cabin set well back in a large plot of ground just inside the limits of the town. The place had not changed. A brown sway-back horse, with the wind ruffling his deep fuzzy coat, huddled in the lee of an old squat barn. Nevada knew the horse. Corrals and sheds stood farther back at the foot of the rocky slope. Briers and brush surrounded a garden where some late greens showed bright against the red dug-up soil. Nevada remembered the rudely painted sign that had been nailed slantwise on the gate-post. Lodgings.

Dismounting, Nevada left his horses and entered, to go round to the back of the cabin. A wide low porch had been stacked to the roof with cut stove wood, handy to the door. Nevada hesitated a moment, then knocked. He heard a bustling inside, brisk footsteps, after which the door was opened by a buxom matron, with ruddy face, big frank eyes, and hair beginning to turn gray.

"Howdy, Mrs. Wood!" he greeted her.

The woman stared, then burst out: "Well, for goodness' sake, if it ain't Jim Lacy!"

"I reckon. Are you goin' to ask me in? I'm aboot froze."

"Jim, you know you never had to ask to come in my house," she replied, and drew him into a cozy little kitchen where a hot stove and the pleasant odor of baking bread appealed powerfully to Nevada.

"Thanks. I'm glad to hear that. Shore seems like home to me. I've been layin' out in the cold an' starvin' for a long time."

"Son, you look it," she returned, nodding her head disapprovingly at him. "Never saw you like this. Jim, you used to be a handsome lad. How lanky you are! An' you're as bushy-haired as a miner. . . . What've you been up to?"

"Wal, Mrs. Wood," he drawled, coolly, "shore you've heard aboot me lately?" And his gaze studied her face. Much might depend upon her reply, but she gave no sign.

"Nary a word, Jim. Not lately or ever since you left."

"No? Wal, I am surprised, an' glad, too," replied Nevada, smiling his relief. "Reckon you couldn't give me a job? Helpin' around, like I used to, for my board."

"Jim, I jest could, an' I will," she declared. "You won't have to sleep in the barn, either."

"Now, I'm dog-gone lucky, Mrs. Wood," replied Nevada, gratefully.

"Humph! I don't know about that, Jim. Comin' back to Lineville can't be lucky. . . . Ah, boy, I'd hoped if you was alive you'd turned over a new leaf."

"It was good of you to think of me kind like that," he said, moving away from the warm stove. "I'll go out an' look after my pack an' horses."

"Fetch your pack right in. An' I'll not forget you're starved."

Nevada went out thoughtfully, and slowly led his horses out to the barn. There, while he unpacked, his mind dwelt on the singular effect that Mrs. Wood's words had upon him. Perhaps speech from anyone in Lineville would have affected him similarly. He had been brought back by word of mouth to actualities. This kindly woman had hoped he would never return. He took so long about caring for his horses and unpacking part of his outfit that presently Mrs. Wood called him. Then shouldering his bed-roll and carrying a small pack, he returned to the kitchen. She had a hot meal prepared. Nevada indeed showed his need of good and wholesome food.

"You poor boy!" she said once, sadly and curiously. But she did not ask any questions.

Nevada ate until he was ashamed of himself. "Shore I know what to call myself. But it tasted so good."

"Ahuh. Well, Jim, you take some hot water an' shave your woolly face," she returned. "You can have the end room, right off the hall. There's a stove an' a box of wood."

Nevada carried his pack into the room designated, then returned for the hot water, soap, and towel. Perhaps it was the dim and scarred mirror that gave his face such an unsightly appearance. He was to find out presently that shaving and clean clothes and a vastly improved appearance meant nothing to him, because Hettie had gone out of his life forever. What did he care how he looked? Yet he remembered with a twinge that she would care. When an hour later he strode into the kitchen to confront Mrs. Wood, she studied him with eyes as speculative as kind.

"Jim, I notice your gun has the same old swing, low down. Now that's queer, ain't it?" she said, ironically.

"Wal, it shore feels queer," he responded. "For, honest, Mrs. Wood, I haven't packed it at all for a long time."

"An' you haven't been lookin' at red liquor, either?" she went on.

"Reckon not."

"An' you haven't been lookin' at women, either?"

"Gosh, no. I always was scared of them," he laughed, easily. But he could not deceive her.

"Boy, somethin' has happened to you," she declared, seriously. "You're older. Your eyes aren't like daggers any more. They've got shadows. . . . Jim, I once saw Billy the Kid in New Mexico. You used to look like him, not in face or body or walk, but jest in some way, some *look* I can't describe. But now it's gone."

"Ahuh. Wal, I don't know whether or not you're complimentin' me," drawled Nevada. "Billy the Kid was a pretty wild *hombre,* wasn't he?"

"Humph! You'd have thought so if you'd gone through that Lincoln County cattle war with me an' my husband. They killed three hundred men, and my Jack was one of them."

"Lincoln County war?" mused Nevada. "Shore I've heard of that, too. An' how many of the three hundred did Billy the Kid kill?"

"Lord only knows," she returned, fervently. "Billy had twenty-one men to his gun before the war, an' that wasn't countin' Greasers or Injuns. They said he was death on them. . . . Yes, Jim, you had the look of Billy, an' if you'd kept on you'd been another like him. But somethin' has happened to you. I ain't inquisitive, but have you lost your nerve? Gunmen do that sometimes, you know."

"Shore, that's it, Mrs. Wood. I've no more nerve than a chicken," drawled Nevada, with all his old easy coolness. It was good for him to hear her voice and to exercise his own.

"Shoo! An' I'll bet that's all you tell me about yourself," she said. "Jim Lacy, you left here a boy an' you've come back a man. Wonder what Lize Teller will think of you now. She was moony about you, the hussy!"

"Lize Teller," echoed Nevada, ponderingly. "Shore I remember now. Is she heah?"

"She about bosses Lineville, Jim. She doesn't live with my humble self any more, but hangs out at the Gold Mine."

Nevada found a seat on a low bench between the stove and the corner, a place that had been a favorite with him and into which he dropped instinctively, and settled himself for a talk. This woman held an unique position in the little border hamlet, in that she possessed the confidence of gamblers, miners, rustlers, everybody. She was a good soul, always ready to help anyone in sickness or trouble. Whatever her life had been in the past—and Nevada guessed it had been one with her outlaw husband—she was an honest and hard-working woman now. In the wild days of his former association with Lineville he had not appreciated her. She probably had some other idler or fugitive like himself doing the very odd jobs about the place that he had applied for. Nevada remembered that her kindliness for him had been sort of motherly, no doubt owing to the fact that he had been the youngest of the notorious characters of Lineville.

"Lize married yet?" began Nevada, casually.

"No indeed, an' she never will be now," replied Mrs. Wood, forcibly. "She had her chance, a decent cattleman named Holder, from Eureka. Reckon he knew he was buyin' stolen cattle. But for all that he was a mighty fine sort for Lineville. Much too good for that black-eyed wench. She was taken with him, too. Her one chance to get away from Lineville! Then Cash Burridge rode in one day—after a long absence. 'Most as long as yours. Cash had been in somethin' big,

south somewhere. An' he came back to lie low an'
gamble. He had plenty of money, as usual. Lost it,
as usual. Lize was clerk at the Gold Mine. She got
thick with Cash. He an' Holder had a mixup over the
girl, an' that settled her. Maybe I didn't give her a
piece of my mind. But I might as well have shouted to
the hills. She went from bad to worse. You'll see."

"Cash Burridge back," rejoined Nevada, somberly,
and he dropped his head. That name had power to
make him want to hide the sudden fire in his eyes.
"Reckon I'd plumb forgot Cash."

"Ha! Ha! Yes, you did, Jim Lacy," replied the
woman, knowingly. "No one would ever forget Cash,
much less you. . . . Dear me, I hope you an' he don't
meet again."

"Wal, of course we'll meet," said Nevada. "I cain't
hang round your kitchen all the while, much as I
like it."

"Jim, I didn't mean meet him on the street, or in
the store, or anywhere. You know what I meant."

"Don't worry, Mother Wood. Reckon Cash an' I
won't clash. Because I'm not lookin' for trouble."

"You never did, my boy, I'll swear to that. But you
never run from it. An' you know Cash Burridge. He's
bad medicine sober, an' hell when he's drunk."

"Ahuh, I reckon, now you remind me. Has Cash
been up to his old tricks lately?"

"I haven't heard much, Jim," she returned, thoughtfully. "Mostly just Lineville gossip. No truth in it,
likely."

Nevada knew it would do no good to press her
further in this direction, which reticence was proof that
Cash Burridge had been adding to his reputation one
way or another. Nevada had a curious reaction—a
scorn for his own strange, vague eagerness to know.
Old submerged or forgotten feelings were regurgitating
in him. A slow heat ran along his veins.

"Lineville shore looks daid," he said, tentatively.

"It *is* dead, Jim. But you know it's comin' on winter.
An' this Lineville outfit is like a lot of groundhogs.

They hole up when the snow flies. There's more travel along the road than ever before. Three stages a week now, an' lots of people stop here for a night. I get a good many; been busy all summer an' fall."

"Travel on the road? Wal, that's a new one for Lineville. Prospectors always came along. But travel. What you mean, Mother Wood?"

"Jim, where have you been for so long?" she asked, curiously. "Sure you must have been buried somewhere. There's a new minin' town—Salisbar. An' travel from north has been comin' through here, in spite of the awful road."

"Salisbar? Never heard aboot it. An' stagecoaches—goin' through Lineville. By golly!"

"Jim, there's been only couple of hold-ups. None of this outfit, though. We hear the stage line will stop runnin' soon, till spring."

"You mentioned aboot a cattleman named Holder buyin' heah since I've been away. Shore he's not the only one?"

"No. But cattle deals have been low this summer. Last bunch of cattle come over in June."

"Wal, you don't say! Lineville is daid, shore enough."

"Jim, that sort of thing has got to stop sometime, even if it is only a lot of two-bit rustlin'."

"Two-bit? Ha! Ha!"

"Jim, I've seen thousands of longhorns rustled in my day."

"Ahuh! Reckon you have, I'm sorry to say," responded Nevada, looking up at her ruddy face again. "Shore you never took me for a rustler, did you, Mother?"

"Goodness, no! You was only a gun-packin' kid, run off the ranges. But, Jim, you'll fall into it some day, sure as shootin'. You'll be in bad company at the wrong time. Now I'm from Texas an' I always loved a good clean hard-shootin' gunman, like Jack was. There wasn't nothin' crooked about Jack for years an' years. But he fell into it. An' so will you, Jim. I want you to go so far away from Lineville that you can't never come back."

"I'll go in the spring. Shore I'm not hankerin' for the grabline ride these next few months."

"Fine. That's a promise, my boy. I'll not let you forget it. An' meanwhile it'll be just as well for you to be snug an' hid right here. Till spring, huh?"

"Mother Wood, you said you wasn't inquisitive," laughed Nevada, parrying her question. Then he grew serious. "When was Hall heah last?"

"In June, with the last cattle that come over the divide. An', Jim, the right queer fact is he's never been back."

"Wal, I reckon that's not so queer to me. Maybe he has shook the dust of Lineville. He rode in heah sudden, so I was told. An' why not ride off that way? To new pastures, Mother Wood?"

"No reason a-tall," she said, reflectively. "Only I jest don't feel that way about Hall."

"An' that high-flyin' Less Setter from the Snake River country. Did he ever come again?"

"No. That time you clashed with Setter was the only time he ever hit Lineville. No wonder! They said you'd kill him if he did. I remember, Jim, how that night after the row you talked a lot. It was the drink. You'd had trouble with Setter before you come to these parts. I never told it, but I remember."

"Wal, Mother, I came from the Snake River country, too," replied Nevada, with slow dark smile.

"It was said here that Less Setter was too big a man to fiddle around Lineville," returned the woman, passing by Nevada's cryptic remark, though it was not lost upon her. "Hall said Setter had many brandin' irons in the fire. His game, though, was to wheedle rich cattlemen an' ranchers into speculations. He was a cunnin' swindler, low-down enough for any deal. An' he had a weakness for women. If nothin' else ever was his downfall, that sure would be. He tried to take Lize Teller away with him."

"Wal, you don't say!" ejaculated Nevada, trying to

affect interest and surprise that were impossible for
him to feel. Again he casually averted his face to hide
his eyes. For that cold, sickening something had shuddered through his soul. Less Setter would never have
a weakness for women again. He would never weave
his evil machinations around Ben and Hettie Ide, or
anyone else, for he and two of his arch conspirators
had lain dead there in the courtyard before Hart
Baine's cabins on the shores of Wild Goose Lake
Ranch. Dead by Nevada's hand! That was the deed
that had saved Ben Ide, and Hettie, too. It seemed
long past, yet how vivid the memory! The crowd that
had melted before his charging horse! The terror of
the stricken Setter! Revenge and retribution and death!
Those villains lay prone under the drafting gunsmoke,
before the onlookers. Nevada saw himself leap back
to the saddle and spur his horse away. One look back!
"So long, pard!" One look at Ben's white, convulsed
face, which would abide with him forever.

"Lineville has had its day," the woman was saying,
as if with satisfaction at the fact. "Setter saw that, if
he ever had any idea of operatin' here. Hall saw it,
too, for he's never come back. Cash Burridge knows it.
He has been away to the south—Arizona somewhere
—lookin' up a place where outside travel hasn't struck,
He'll leave when the snow melts next spring, an' he'll
not go alone. Then decent people won't be afraid to
walk down to the store."

"Good luck for Lineville, but bad for Arizona somewhere," returned Nevada, dryly. "Shore, I feel sorry
for the ranchers over there."

"Humph! I don't know. There are wilder outfits in
Arizona than this country ever saw," rejoined the woman, contemptuously. "Take that Texas gang in Pleasant Valley, an' the Hash Knife outfit on the Tonto
Rim, not to speak of the Mexican border. Cash Burridge isn't the caliber to last long in Arizona. Waters
an' Blink Miller are tough nuts to crack, I'll admit. I
suppose Hardy Rue will trail after Burridge, an' of
course that loud-mouthed Link Cawthorne. But there's

only one of the whole Lineville outfit that could ever last in Arizona. An' you know who he is, Jim Lacy."

"Wal, now, Mother, I shore haven't the least idee," drawled Nevada.

"Go 'long with you," she replied, almost with affection. "But, Jim, I'd rather think of you gettin' away from this life than lastin' out the whole crew. I've heard my husband say that gunmen get a mind disease. The gunman is obsessed to kill. An' if another great killer looms on the horizon the disease forces him to go out to meet this one. Jest to see if he can kill him! Isn't that terrible? But it was so in Texas in the old frontier days there."

"It shore is terrible," responded Nevada, gloomily. "I can understand a man learnin' to throw a gun quick for self-defense. Shore that was my own excuse. But for the sake of killin'! Reckon I don't know what to call that."

During the hour Mrs. Wood, who had a gift for learning and dispensing information of all sort, acquainted Nevada with all that had happened in Lineville since his departure. She did not confine herself to the affairs of the outlaw element who made of Lineville a rendezvous. The few children Nevada had known and played with, the new babies that had arrived in the interim, the addition of several more families to the community, the talk of having a school, and the possibilities of a post office eventually—these things she discussed in detail, with a pleasure and satisfaction that had been absent in her gossip about Lineville's hard characters.

But it was that gossip which lingered in Nevada's mind. Later when he went into his little room he performed an act almost unconsciously. It was an act he had repeated a thousand times in such privacy as was his on the moment, but not of late. The act of drawing his gun! There it was, as if by magic, level, low down in his clutching hand. Sight of it so gave Nevada a grim surprise. How thoughtlessly and naturally the fact had come to pass! And Nevada pondered over the singular action. Why had he done that? What was it significant of? He sheathed the long blue gun.

"Reckon Mrs. Wood's talk about Cawthorne an' the rest of that outfit accounts for me throwin' my gun," he muttered to himself. "Funny. . . . No—not so damn funny, after all."

He had returned to an environment where proficiency with a gun was the law. Self-preservation was the only law among those lawless men with whom misfortune had thrown him. He could not avoid them without incurring their hatred and distrust. He must mingle with them as in the past, though it seemed his whole nature had changed. And mingling with these outlaws was never free from risk. The unexpected always happened. There were always newcomers, always drunken ruffians, always some would-be killer like Cawthorne, who yearned for fame among his evil kind. There must now always be the chance of some friend or ally of Setter, who would draw on him at sight. Lastly, owing to the reputation he had attained and hated, there was always the possibility of meeting such a gunman as Mrs. Wood had spoken of—that strange product of frontier life, the victim of his own blood lust, who would want to kill him solely because of his reputation.

Nevada was not in love with life, yet he felt a tremendous antagonism toward men who would wantonly destroy him.

"Reckon I'd better forget my dreamin' heah," he soliloquized. "An' when I'm out be like I used to be. Shore it goes against the grain. I'm two men in one— Nevada an' Jim Lacy. . . . Reckon Jim better take a hunch."

Whereupon he deliberately set about ascertaining just how much of his old incomparable swiftness on the draw remained with him after the long lack of exercise. During more than one period of his career he had practiced drawing his gun until he had worn the skin of his hand to the quick, and then to callousness.

The thing had become a habit for his private hours, wherever he might be.

"Slower'n molasses, as Ben used to say aboot me," he muttered. "But I've the feel, an' I can get it all back."

The leather holster on his belt was hard and stiff. He oiled it and worked it soft with strong hands. The little room, which had only one window, began to grow dark as the short afternoon waned.

It was still daylight, however, when Nevada went out, to walk leisurely down the road into town. How well he remembered the wide bare street, with its lines of deserted and old buildings, many falling to ruin, and the high board fronts where the painted signs had been so obliterated by weathering that they were no longer decipherable! He came at length to the narrow block where there were a few horses and vehicles along the hitching-rails, and people passing to and fro. There were several stores and shops, a saloon, and a restaurant, that appeared precisely as they had always been. A Chinaman, standing in a doorway, stared keenly at Nevada. His little black eyes showed recognition. Then Nevada arrived at a corner store, where he entered.

The place had the smell of general mechandise, groceries, and tobacco combined. To Jones' credit, he had never sold liquor. There was a boy clerk waiting on a woman customer, and Jones, a long lanky Westerner, who had seen range days himself.

"Howdy, Mr. Jones!" said Nevada, stepping forward.

"Howdy yourself, stranger!" replied the storekeeper. "You got the best of me."

"Wal, it's a little dark in heah or your eyes are failin'," returned Nevada, with a grin.

Whereupon the other took a stride and bent over to peer into Nevada's face.

"I'm a son-of-a-gun," he declared. "Jim Lacy! Back in Lineville! I've seen fellers come back I liked less."

He shook hands heartily with Nevada. "Where you been, boy? You sure look well an' fine to me."

"Oh, I've been all over, knockin' aboot, lookin' for a job," drawled Nevada, easily.

"An' you come back to Lineville in winter, lookin' for a job?" laughed Jones.

"Shore," drawled Nevada.

"Jim, I'll bet if I offered you work you'd shy like a colt. Fact is, though, I could do it. I'm not doin' so bad here. There's a lumber company cuttin' up in the foothills. It's a long haul to Salisbar, but they pass through here. Heard about Salisbar?"

"Yes. Reckon I'll have to take a look at it. How far away?"

"Eighty miles or so," returned Jones. "Some miners struck it rich, an' that started Salisbar off as a minin' town. But it's growin' otherwise. Besides mineral, there are timber an' water, some good farmland, an' miles of grazin'. All this is wakin' Lineville up. There's business goin' on an' more comin'."

"Shore I'm glad, Mr. Jones," said Nevada. "Lineville has some good people I'd like to see prosper."

From the store Nevada dropped into a couple of places, where he renewed acquaintance with men who were glad to see him; and then he crossed to the other side of the wide street and went down to the Gold Mine. Dark had fallen and lamps were being lighted. The front of the wide two-story structure appeared quite plain and business-like, deceiving to the traveler. It looked like a respectable hotel. But the Gold Mine was a tavern for the outlaw elect, a gambling hell and a drinking dive that could not have been equaled short of the Mexican border.

Nevada turned the corner to take the side entrance, which led into the long dingily-lighted barroom. A half-dozen men stood drinking and talking at the bar. They noted Nevada's entrance, but did not recognize him, nor did he them. The bartender, too, was strange to Nevada. A wide portal, with curtain of strung beads, opened into a larger room, which was almost sumptu-

ously furnished for such a remote settlement as Lineville. The red hangings were new to Nevada, and some
of the furniture. He remembered the gaudy and ob-
scene pictures on the wall, and the card and roulette
tables, and particularly the large open fireplace, where
some billets of wood burned ruddily. Six men sat
around one table, and of those whose faces were visible
to Nevada he recognized only one, that of a gambler
called Ace Black. His cold eyes glinted on Nevada,
then returned to his game.

Nevada took the seat on the far side of the fire,
where he could see both entrances to the large room.
At the moment there was something akin to bitter re-
volt at the fact of his presence there. Certainly no one
had driven him. No logical reason existed for his visit-
ing the Gold Mine. He would never drink again; he
had but little money to gamble with, even had he been
so inclined; he rather felt repugnance at the thought of
seeing Lize Teller, or any other girl likely to come in.
But something restless and keen within him accounted
for his desire to meet old acquaintances there. Trying
to analyze and understand it, Nevada got to the point of
dismay. Foremost of all was a significant motive—he
did not care to have Cash Burridge or his followers,
especially Link Cawthorne, or anyone ever associated
with Setter, think he would avoid them. Yet that was
exactly what Nevada wanted to do. The mocking
thing about it was the certainty that some kind of
conflict would surely result. He could not avoid this.
Deep in him was a feeling that belied his reluctance.
Could it be a rebirth of old recklessness? He would
have to fight that as something untrue to Hettie Ide.
And as a wave of sweet and bitter emotion went over
him, a musical rattling of the beaded-curtain door attracted his attention.

A girl entered. She had a pale face, and very large
black eyes that seemed to blaze at Nevada.

Three

She came slowly toward him, with the undulating movement of her lissome form that he remembered even better than her tragic face. Life had evidently been harsher than ever to Lize Teller.

Nevada rose and, doffing his sombrero, shook hands with her.

"Jim Lacy!" she ejaculated, with stress of feeling that seemed neither regret nor gladness.

"Howdy, Lize!" drawled Nevada. "Reckon you're sort of surprised to see me heah."

"Surprised? Yes. I thought you had more sense," she returned.

"Wal, now Lize, that's not kind of you," he said, somewhat taken back. "An' I reckon I just don't get your hunch."

"Sit down, Jim," she rejoined, and as he complied she seated herself on the arm of his chair and leaned close. "I've been looking for you all afternoon. Lorenzo saw you ride in and stop at Mrs. Wood's."

"Ahuh! Wal, no wonder you wasn't surprised."

"But I am, Jim. Surprised at your nerve and more surprised at the look of you. What's happened? You've improved so I don't know you."

She leaned against him with the old coquetry that was a part of her and which Nevada had once found pleasing, though he had never encouraged it.

"Thanks, Lize. Wal, there was shore room for improvement. Nothin' much happened, except I've been workin' an' I quit the bottle."

"That's a lot, Jim, and I'm downright glad. I'll fall in love with you all over again."

"Please don't, Lize," he laughed. "I've quit throwin'

26

guns, too. An' I reckon it'd be unhealthy for me, if you did."

"Probably will be, boy. You sure have me guessing," she replied, and she smoothed his hair and his scarf, while she gazed at him with deep, burning, inquisitive eyes. "But don't try to lie to me about your gun tricks, sonny. You forget I'm the only one around Lineville who had you figured."

"Lize, I don't know as I remember that," he said, dubiously. He found she embarrassed him less than in former times. He had always feared Lize's overtures. But that dread was gone.

"Jim, you forget easily," she rejoined, with a touch of bitterness. "But God knows there was no reason for you to remember *me*. It was natural for me to miss you. For you were the only decent man I knew. But you treated me like you were a brother. And that made me hate you."

"Lize, you didn't hate me," he said. "That was temper. Maybe you got a little miffed because you couldn't make a fool of me like you did the others. Shore I cain't believe you'd be mean enough to hate me."

"Jim, you don't know women," she replied, bitterly. "I can do anything. . . . Where'd you say you'd been— workin'—all this long while?"

"Wal, now, Lize, I don't recollect sayin'," he drawled. "Shore never liked to talk aboot myself. What have you been doin'?"

"Me! Aw, hell! Can't you see? If I live another year I'll be in the street. . . . I hate this damned life, Jim. But what can I do? . . . Of course Mrs. Wood told you all she knew about me."

"Wal, she told me—some," replied Nevada, hesitatingly. "Wish I'd been heah when you made such a darn fool of yourself.

"I wish to God you had," she flashed, with terrible passion. "You'd have shot Cash Burridge. He doublecrossed me, Jim. Oh, I know I'm no good, but I'm honest. Cash actually made me believe *he* would marry me. I told Holder I was not a good girl. He seemed

willing to take me, anyhow. But Cash told him a lot
of vile lies about me, and it fell through. . . . I'm working here at the Gold Mine now—everything from book-
keeper to bartender."

"Lize, I heah you're thick with Link Cawthorne,"
said Nevada.

"Bah! You can call it thick, if you like," she returned, scornfully. "But I call it thin. He's a jealous
tight-fisted brag. He's as mean as a coyote. I was half
drunk, I guess, when I took up with him. And now he
thinks he owns me."

"Wal, Lize, wouldn't it be interestin' for me right
now—if Link happened in?" drawled Nevada.

"Ha! Ha! More so for me, Jim," she trilled. "I'll
give him something to be jealous about. But Link
could never be interesting to you. He's a bluff."

"All the same, Lize, if you'll excuse me I'll stand
up an' let you have the chair," replied Nevada, coolly,
as he extricated himself and arose.

She swore her amaze. "What the devil's come over
you, Jim Lacy?" she demanded. "Why, two years ago,
if Link Cawthorne had come roaring in here with
two guns you'd have laughed and turned your back."

"Two years ago! Lize, I've learned a lot in that
long time."

With sudden change of manner and lowering of
voice she queried, sharply, "Jim, did you kill Less
Setter?"

Nevada had braced himself for anything from this
girl, so at the point-blank question he did not betray
himself.

"Setter! . . . Is he daid?"

"Yes, he's daid," she replied, flippantly mimicking
his Southern accent. "And a damn good thing. . . .
Jim Lacy, I lay that to you."

"Wal, Lize, I cain't stop the wonderin's of your
mind, but you're shore takin' a lot upon yourself," he
returned, coldly.

She caught his hand.

"Jim, I didn't mean to offend," she said, hastily. "I

remember you were queer about—you know—when you'd had some gunplay."

"Ahuh? Wal, there's no offense. Reckon I'm sort of hurt that you accuse me."

"Jim, I notice you don't *deny* it," she retorted, with her brilliant searching eyes on him. "But listen. Only a few people in Lineville have heard Setter is dead. You know how we keep mum about that sort of thing. I heard it from a chance traveler who stayed here overnight. Setter had been shot by a wild-horse hunter over in California. That was all. That reminded me of something else. Last summer Steve Elkins saw you in a saloon in Hammell. He used to come through here occasionally and he'd seen you. So when I remembered that, I remembered you had a grudge on Setter, also that you loved wild-horse hunting, and I put two and two together and figured *you* had done for Setter. But I've never mentioned my suspicions to anyone. I'm not sure, but I don't believe anyone here has connected you with that little gunplay. Cash Burridge was glad enough to hear the news, you can bet. He had been sent to Arizona by Setter on some deal only the two of them were in. Cash had a roll of money big enough to stop up a stovepipe. He went to Arizona. And he never saw Setter again. That I know, for he told me so. Well, he didn't tell me how he'd benefited by Setter's death. I figured that, too."

"Lize, you're shore a clever girl," said Nevada, admiringly. "Reckon you hit most deals right on the haid. But shore I'd rather you didn't give me credit for removin' so many undesirable citizens from the world. You used to do that. I'm not Billy the Kid, or Plummer, or Wess Hardin."

"Have it your own way, Jim," she returned, with a sly laugh. "And now for what I was coming to. Did you ever hear of Hardy Rue?"

"Wal, yes, somewhere or other that name struck me. Never saw the man, though."

"He wasn't here during your time. But he's here now, and he's the man for you to watch. I think he was Setter's right hand man and came to Lineville to check up on Cash Burridge. They don't get along. I'd say Rue is a dangerous man. Deep sort of chap, seldom talks, never drinks, hates women, and has an eye like a hawk. He's . . . Hello! Somebody calling me. I forgot I have to work. I'll see you later. You bet I want to be around when Link strolls in."

She ran from the room, leaving Nevada with plenty to think about. Yet he was considerably relieved that his name had not been openly used in connection with Setter's death. That would have made his position less secure in Lineville. Not that security in this border town was possible for him or any other of its desperate men!

Gradually the gaming tables filled up. More than one keen-eyed player gave Nevada a curt nod of recognition. Probably everybody in Lineville now knew of his return. There was nothing unusual about that. All of these men were absent now and then. Nevada felt that he labored with an unreasonable desire to be somebody else, thus to avoid the complications sure to be woven around the name Jim Lacy.

He was approached presently by two newcomers, one of whom, a little alert man, no longer young, with a face like that of a weasel, and eyes that had a trick of opening and shutting quickly, he recognized as Blink Miller.

"Howdy, Blink!" he replied to the other's greeting.

"You're lookin' fust-rate, Lacy," replied Miller. "Shake hands with my friend, Hardy Rue."

Nevada found himself under the surveillance of a quiet, penetrating gray gaze. This man Rue was matured, a stalwart type of miner rather than the rangy rider. He had a hard lined face, with prominent chin and set thin lips.

"Care to drink with me, Lacy?" he inquired.

"No, thanks," replied Nevada. "Reckon I'm not fixed to buy drinks, so I'm not acceptin' any."

"Ain't you grown awful particular since you've been away so long?" queried Miller, with a smile.

"Wal, Blink, come to think aboot it, I have," drawled Nevada, with all his old cool carelessness. "Particular aboot not owin' anybody favors an' particular aboot who I drink with."

Nevada, despite his calculations beforehand, could not help giving that tart answer. If it was anything it was an instinct of antagonism, quick to grasp antagonism in others.

Miller blinked at Nevada. "Reckon that's particular nice of you, Lacy. Nobody wants to buy drinks for a feller who's broke."

Then Rue gave Nevada an inscrutable look, more deceiving for the pleasant voice with which he accompanied it.

"But you're not particular about throwin' a gun on —anybody?" he queried.

Nevada's cool bright stare was not so deceptive. And then he drawled: "Not at all—not at all, Mr. Rue. Shore it's just a habit. I never mean anythin' uncivil."

The two men passed on to a gaming table, where seats evidently awaited them. Nevada turned on his heel, muttering: "Damn them anyhow. They just cain't let me alone."

Among others who entered presently was Cash Burridge. He was a tall man nearing forty, but he looked younger. He had the build of a horseman, a fine figure in top-boots and spurs. Nevada was quick to see where he packed his gun, and that was significant. Burridge was a handsome, dissolute man, blond, with a curling mustache, almost gold, and light, gleaming, restless blue eyes.

Nevada knew that Burridge had seen him the instant of entrance, if not before, and he wondered what the outcome would be. It did not matter one way or another to Nevada. Burridge had been the ringleader in the stage hold-up to which Nevada had been a party. The one deed to which he owned with shame!

At length Burridge disengaged himself from his companions and deliberately walked around between the tables to get to Nevada.

"Jim, I'm dog-gone glad to see you!" he said, extending his hand, and his handsome face corroborated his words.

"Howdy, Cash!" replied Nevada, meeting the outstretched hand. "Reckon I'm glad you're glad to see me."

"It's good you blew in. I've often wondered what'd become of you. I'll tell you, Jim, I'm not curious about where you've been or what you've been doin', but I'm plumb interested in what you're goin' to do."

"Why so?" asked Nevada, not without surprise. He was not wholly proof against Burridge's warm welcome.

"Are you goin' to hole up here this winter, same as the rest of us?" queried Burridge.

"Reckon I am, as far as I know," returned Nevada, slowly feeling his way.

"Broke?" queried Burridge, with a knowing look.

"Shore am."

"I'm not so well heeled myself, but I can stake you to a roll."

"Thanks, Cash. But I cain't borrow. I don't like borrowin', an' maybe I never could pay back. I'll get a job for my keep heah. An' the cairds an' drinks won't bother me."

"Jim, what'll you do after the snow flies?"

"I'll be hanged if I know," replied Nevada, truthfully enough.

"That's all I wanted to hear," spoke up Burridge, with great satisfaction. "I've got a deal on—the biggest I ever handled. It's——"

"Cash, reckon you're not goin' to ask me to rustle cattle with you?" interrupted Nevada, severely.

"No. I swear I'm not," hastily returned Burridge, and if he was not sincere, he surely was a splendid actor. "By Heaven! it's an honest deal, Jim."

"Wal, I'm glad to heah you say that. An' I'll listen to you."

"This ain't the place for us to talk. Besides, I've a poker game on. The deal I'm in is big; it's cattle, an' it's honest. I've got to have a hard-shootin' outfit, an' a leader with a reputation like yours."

"But, Cash, I heard you say this deal was honest," protested Nevada.

"If it ain't then I don't know what honesty is," declared Burridge, forcibly. "Sure my talk is plumb misleadin'. But you wait till I tell you all about the deal."

"Wal, Cash, I'll shore try to be patient waitin'," drawled Nevada.

"I'm givin' you a hunch," rejoined Burridge. "Keep it to yourself."

Burridge withdrew then to his card game, while Nevada returned to his chair by the fire. "What the devil is Cash up to now?" pondered Nevada. "Honest deal? Cattle? Hard-shootin' outfit . . . I'll be darned."

Nevada discovered that the word honest inhibited all his deductive powers in relation to what Cash Burridge might be engaged in. Cash's deliberate assertion was a poser. Nevada could not solve it. But he grasped one significant fact at once, and that was a motive for Burridge's warm greeting. He had never before shown any kindliness to Nevada. Where Burridge had any special interest he could be agreeable, and, if the case required, most persuasive and dominating. These traits, however, had never before been exercised upon Nevada.

Meanwhile the saloon and gambling room filled up. In the former there was raucous noise and in the latter a contrasting silence, broken by the low voice of a gamester now and then, and a clink of coin, or the whir and rattle of the roulette wheel. During this period Nevada sat beside the fire, glancing at it occasionally, but seeing always those who came in and went out. The glowing embers of any fire cast a spell upon Nevada, always bringing the face which haunted his waking and sleeping hours.

A little later Lize Teller returned, and before he could get up to offer her the chair she had plumped herself over the arm.

"You sit still or I'll jump into your lap," she threatened, half petulantly and half merrily. She would have done it, too; therefore Nevada decided he had better be quiet. What had once been shyness in him had now become aloofness.

"But, Lize, shore if you want to make a show of yourself, you don't need to pick on me," mildly protested Nevada.

"Jim Lacy, there isn't a man in this room, except you, who wouldn't put his arm around me if I sat like this on his chair."

"Wal, suppose you let me see some of them do it."

"Aha, you're the smart one. Listen! If you want to make me your friend—I say *friend*—forever, just be lover-like for a few minutes. Or if you can't be that, make a bluff at it."

Nevada laughed at her in spite of the annoyance he could scarcely conceal. "What're you up to, Lize?"

"Link Cawthorne just came in," she replied, tossing her black head defiantly.

She still had some of the charms of girlhood left. With what pity in his heart did Nevada recognize this, and contrast the havoc of her face with the semblance of the thing she momentarily felt!

"So I reckoned," replied he. "Wal, Lize, it may be fun for you to use me in your little tricks, but it mightn't be funny for me. An' it might turn out bad for Link."

"That's why. He makes me sick. I'm so tired of him I ache. . . . He's in there drinking. I want him to come in and find me with you. He was up all last night, in a card game, and he doesn't know you're here."

"Lize, it strikes me you don't want very much a-tall," returned Nevada. "I hate to be rude to a lady, but *I* want to get up."

"I'll make it worse," she almost hissed, with the somber fire in her eyes leaping to a blaze. "You know me."

"All right." I reckon it's bad enough without you makin' it worse," he said, with a forced resignation.

"Bad? Bah! I can handle Link Cawthorne. All I

want is for the conceited lout to *see* I can like some other man."

"Lize, I reckon you must have given Link some reason for bein' so conceited. Now didn't you?"

"I suppose I did. I thought I was mad about him, but I guess I was only mad at Cash Burridge. . . . Women are strange, Jim."

"Wal, you cain't prove it by me," answered Nevada.

"There he comes," she whispered, in fiendish glee, and then leaned over Nevada, radiant with some feeling quite beyond his comprehension.

Nevada looked up, not without a stir in his veins. Link Cawthorne stood with the bead curtain parted. How well Nevada remembered the heated face, the beady little eyes too close together, the reckless, weak, leering lips, the choice and manner of garb that inclined to dandyism. Indeed, he had been called the dandy outlaw, an epithet far from displeasing to him.

Nevada doubted Lize's assertion that Link had been unaware of his return to Lineville. He certainly did not start, nor change his expression materially. But he looked steadily at Lize, while she babbled to Nevada, apparently oblivious to her lover's advent.

Nevada's feeling, in that moment, changed from a good-natured contempt for Link and a vexation at his own part in this little farce to something vastly different. It seemed to be premonition that amounted to shock. He saw something, as a dream might foreshadow a future event—something that moved gray, cold, sickening across the swift stream of his consciousness. The sensation was so sudden and dismaying that Nevada heard nothing of Lize's whispered pretenses. It took violent effort of will, which was effected with Cawthorne's stalking across the room, to return to his cool, keen self.

A year and more did not set lightly upon Link Cawthorne's features. Nevada judged all these men by the changes that had risen in himself. Cawthorne halted before Lize and Nevada, bending his lean, hawk-like head, with his elbows crooked and his hands at his hips. His right hand covered the butt of a gun belted high. Whatever he had intended to say or do manifestly yielded to the passion which arose at close range. His gimlet-eyes fastened first upon Lize, who did not turn her face away from Nevada for a long moment. Then Lize's glance traveled from Cawthorne's boots slowly upward, at last to meet his piercing gaze with surprise that seemed as genuine as insolent.

"Oh, you here?" she said. "Link, have you ever met my old friend, Jim Lacy?"

"Cat!" he spat out, fiercely, and his body jerked with the liberation of something in the word.

"Howdy, Link!" interposed Nevada, thinking to pour oil on the troubled waters. "Reckon Lize has forgotten you an' me was acquainted."

"Forget—hell!" responded Cawthorne, in hard scorn. "Never mind Lize. I'll settle with her. I'm ad-dressin' you, Jim Lacy."

Nevada seemed a long moment in replying, during which he looked steadily up at Cawthorne.

"Ahuh. Wal, strikes me you're not very civil aboot it."

"Strikes me you're too familiar with Lize," flashed Cawthorne, hotly.

"Familiar? Say, you're out of your haid. If it's any of your business, we're old acquaintances. Shore I never had nothin' but a brotherly feelin' for her. An' if she wants to sit on the arm of my chair—"

"Guff!" interrupted the other. "She was sittin' on your lap. An' that won't go with me."

"Link, look for yourself," returned Nevada, quietly. "There's where she's been all the time. Shore that isn't anythin' to raise a row, even if you an' she are en-gaged."

"Pooh!" burst out Lize, airily.

That word must have been a blow to Cawthorne, and his whole body leaped with a muscular violence.

"Jim Lacy, you're a liar!" he burst out, stridently.

Lize, swift as a panther, slid off Nevada's chair, to spring erect like a released willow bough. Nevada could not see her. He heard her panting breaths. He was gazing hard up at Cawthorne's face, which had suddenly turned white. In his ungovernable fury he had said what had not been calculated upon. A sudden cessation of all sound from the gamesters was proof that they had heard him denounce Nevada. Cawthorne stood a moment as one transfixed, if not with terror, then with the inevitableness of catastrophe.

"Now, Link, I'm not a liar an' you know it," replied Nevada, without evident stress. "Reckon I can make allowance for your feelin's."

The young outlaw's face lost its pallor and rigidity. It waved red, and all at once his hair appeared to bristle. His youth, his fury, his conceit, not to define his lack of penetration, misled him into mistaking Nevada's reply.

"I'll have no allowances from you," he shouted. "I'm invitin' you for a little walk outdoors."

Four

Nevada calmly rose to his feet and stepped aside from the chair. He did not believe that Cawthorne would attempt to draw on him, but as there was no certainty, he wanted to be on his feet. Even at the moment he seemed strange to himself. Yet after that first flash he felt coolly master of himself.

Cawthorne, more emboldened every instant, shouted the louder:

"I'm invitin' you outdoors."

"What for?" queried Nevada.

"You know what for."

"I haven't an idee, Link," went on Nevada. "Shore I see you're r'iled. But I reckon there's no call for me to get r'iled, too, aboot your mistake. It's cold outdoors. An' I like this warm fire. If you've any more to say, why, go ahaid."

Cawthorne expanded under this wholly unprecedented experience. A few drinks had addled his brains and an unreasonable jealousy had set them on fire. To realize Jim Lacy had refused the challange born of wild haste had set him on the pinnacle of his dream of fame.

"Say?" he demanded, with hoarse and pompous contempt. "I've no more to say. I've called you, an' you're yellow. That's all."

Whereupon he turned to the amazed and discomfited Lize and, half leading, half dragging her, left the room. The business of the gamblers was resumed, with a loud laugh here and caustic remarks there. Nevada heard the content of some of them: "What the hell's got into Lacy?" . . . "He always was a decent chap." . . . "Reckon he couldn't kill thet durn fool right before the girl's eyes." . . . "You're wrong, gentlemen," said a cold-voiced gambler. "That was a little by-play between a real gunman and a would-be. I've seen it often."

As Nevada resumed his chair and drew it closer to the fire these and other remarks did not escape him, and that of the gambler lingered with him moodily. Gradually his momentary depression passed away. He saw Hettie Ide's face in the golden glow of the fire. How he quivered in heart and body! He had been put to the test and he had been true to what she would have expected of him.

Nevada went early to his lodgings and his sleep was untroubled. When he awoke in the morning he was glad to face the sun.

There was plenty of work for him to do, which he set about with a will. He found tasks that Mrs. Wood did not think of. Thus, with most of the daylight hours passed in manual labor, Nevada began his winter in Lineville.

For nearly a week he stayed away from the Gold Mine. Then one night at supper Mrs. Wood spoke up seriously:

"Jim, that big-mouthed Link Cawthorne is braggin' around you're afraid to come downtown."

"Wal, you don't say," drawled Nevada.

"Yes, I do say. I don't like it at all, Jim. You can't let him keep that up."

"Shore, I don't care what Link says."

"Son, that's not the way of the West," she went on, gravely. "I've lived all my life on the frontier. No man can afford to lose the respect of his associates, even if they are mostly a worthless outfit of gamblers, rustlers, an' sech. They can't understand it. Least of all Link Cawthorne can't. He's likely to shoot you from behind a corner an' swear he met you on an even break."

"But, Mother Wood, what can I do?" queried Nevada, robbed of his imperturbability.

"Well, as long as you're here in Lineville be Jim Lacy as *they* used to know him," she declared, forcefully. "If you let this towhead run amuck with his brag, pretty soon he'll get the nerve actually to draw on you. Now, Jim, you don't want to have to kill him. Lize was fond of him. An' if she's fond of anyone it keeps her straight. You go downtown an' slap Link's face. Take his gun away from him an' stick it down the back of his pants!"

Nevada laughed mirthlessly. "Wal, maybe you're right," he said, with a sigh. "By gosh; I wish spring would come, so I could hit the trail."

"Mark my words, son," she replied, earnestly, "the best way for you to make sure of spring an' summer an' fall is to be yourself!"

Nevada went back to the Gold Mine, dubious in mind, once more doubtful that he could ever escape the inevitable consequences of his name.

It chanced that Link Cawthorne was sober and deeply involved in a card game, where he was having a remarkable run of good luck. He merely sneered when Nevada strolled in.

Cash Burridge, however, made at once for Nevada, with all show of friendliness.

"Where you been, Lacy?" he inquired, disapprovingly. "We've certainly looked for you here."

"Aw, been workin' hard an' goin' to bed early," replied Nevada. "Then, Cash, I reckon I wanted to avoid meetin' Cawthorne."

"Bah!" snorted Burridge. "You'll have to shoot that damned brag, an' the sooner you do it the better we'll all be pleased."

"Wal, we won't argue aboot it, Cash, but I'm not seein' it that way."

"I'll bet you five to one Link will nag you to draw. I've seen a hundred four-flushers like him. An' they all got the same."

"Wal, I cain't bet with you, that's shore," returned Nevada, in good humor.

"Let's go up to my room, where we can have a

quiet talk," said the other, and led the way through the hall and upstairs.

"Shore, you're comfortable heah," remarked Nevada, gazing around the room.

"I like it nice when I'm not in the saddle," returned Burridge. "Take a seat, an' if you won't drink have a smoke. . . . One more word about this Link Cawthorne. He was harmless enough until Lize made him a snake in the grass. That girl is a hell's rattler. My advice is for you to beat the daylights out of Link or call his bluff an' kill him."

"Reckon I'm some worried, Cash," admitted Nevada.

"A man like you must always worry," rejoined Burridge, with evident sympathy. "You can't ever be free unless you hide your name. It's bad enough to have sheriffs after you, an' natural enemies, but it must be hell to know there're men who want to kill you just because of your reputation."

"Wal, I hope I don't get sore an' go back to drinkin'," said Nevada, gloomily.

"Jim, I want to talk serious to you now," went on Burridge, with change of voice.

"Wal, fire away. You'll shore get my honest opinion, anyway."

"Lineville is gettin' a little too much travel to suit me. In another year it won't be any place for me, let alone you. Agree with me?"

"Shore do. When spring comes I go for good."

"Exactly. Same here. Now I want to tell you about my deal. I'll tell you straight. An' if you don't want to go in with me, it'll be all right, only I want you to respect my confidence here in Lineville. Will you do it?"

"I reckon," replied Nevada, soberly.

Burridge showed satisfaction at that assurance, but he plainly hesitated over the next disclosure. Little flecks of light danced in his eyes, suddenly to coalesce in a set, cold gleam.

"Jim, you knew Setter was shot over in California?" he queried, sharply.

"I heard it from Lize," rejoined Nevada, matter-of-factly.

"Killed by a wild-hoss hunter," went on Burridge, with emotion. "Jim, there are men who connect you with that gun-play."

"Shore. I get blamed for a lot of things," returned Nevada, imperturbably.

"Well, that's none of my business," spoke up Burridge, with more relief, "only I want to say that whoever killed Setter did me a good turn."

"Me too. Setter did me dirt once, over on the Snake River."

Burridge drew a long breath and laid aside his cigar.

"Listen," he began, with tenseness. "I was in on several deals with Setter. After he left here he sent for me to meet him at Klamath Falls. I did it. He had gotten in with big cattlemen an' had more money than he knew how to spend. He told me he wouldn't risk settlin' down in Oregon. He'd sell out there pretty soon, an' he wanted a new an' safe place. No more rustlin' or sharp speculation with other ranchers' money. He might marry. Anyway, he was goin' in for honest ranchin', an' wanted me as a partner. Well, the upshot was that he gave me a hundred thousand dollars to buy a well-stocked ranch in Arizona. I was to own half, an' to help him develop cattle an' horses on a big scale. He had never been in Arizona an' only knew it by hearsay. He left the choice of place to me, makin' the provision that I find a wild an' unsettled range, where money would develop water."

Burridge halted in his narrative, the recital of which manifestly stirred him deeply, and picking up his cigar he puffed on it a moment, and leaned back in his chair, with his light hard eyes intent upon his listener.

"Well," he resumed, "I went to Arizona an' rode hossback from the New Mexico border clear to the

White Mountains. Talk about wild an' beautiful country! Arizona has everythin' beat. I bought out a rancher
who wasn't keen to sell. He owned a big ranch, had
miles of grazin' range, an' ten thousand head of stock.
I ain't tellin' you the location until you decide to accept my offer. After the deal was settled an' property
turned over to me I began to get a few hunches. But I
hustled back here an' sent word to Setter. He hadn't
consummated his deals over there. I waited. No word
came from him. I went back to Arizona—that was
early last summer. Then I had my eyes opened. It
was funny. Such a joke on *me,* an' especially Setter.
Well, I had been huntin' for wild country, an' you
can gamble I'd hit on it. Our cattle were bein' rustled
right an' left. I suspected the very cowmen I'd taken
over with the property. It was a grand big country—
desert, canyon, plateau. There were many more ranchers an' cattle than I'd suspected. Some of these ranchers
were rustlers, thick with the worst of the outfits. You've
heard of the Hash Knife gang an' the Pine Tree outfit.
But nobody seemed to know just *who* belonged to
them an' *who* didn't. Then there were some hard nuts
known to everybody. This country around Lineville
even in gold-rush days couldn't hold a candle to that
neck of the woods in Arizona."

Burridge made a final flourish with the cigar he had
let go out.

"Now when I got back here a few weeks ago I
sent word to Setter an' waited. No reply. Then we
heard Setter was dead. Hardy Rue brought the news.
I've a hunch he's got somethin' up his sleeve. Anyway,
he knew Setter, an' I'm not worryin'. That property in
Arizona is mine. An' my job is to get back there to
run it. Here's where you come in. Jim Lacy! That
wouldn't sound so pleasant to those outfits. I'll make
you foreman an' give you an interest. It'll take some
fightin' to keep my cattle. I want a bunch of the hard-
est-ridin' an' hardest-shootin' boys that can be hired.
An' you to lead them! . . . An' now a last word, Jim.

You know that many an honest an' prosperous rancher was once a rustler. . . . What do you think an' what do you say?"

"Wal, Cash, reckon I'll think more'n I say," returned Nevada, ponderingly. "You shore talked straight. I savvy when a man's tellin' me the truth. It's a darn interestin' story. What the courts might say aboot it I cain't guess. But I reckon half that hundred thousand Setter gave you is honestly yours. Maybe the other half, too. Nobody could tell just how much money Setter earned an' what he got speculatin'. He was always careful to get the other fellow to take the risks. Yes, sir, I reckon the Arizona ranch is yours, all right."

"Good. I'm glad you see the deal that way," replied Burridge, rubbing his hands together. "An' you'll accept my offer?"

"Cash, I cain't promise that yet," responded Nevada, slowly. "Reckon to be honest, the day might come when I'd be glad to take you up. But now I want time to think aboot it."

"Take all the time you want," spoke up Burridge, heartily.

"Wal, I might need a lot. There's a couple of points that'll shore be hard to get over."

"What are they, Jim? I might help you."

"Wal, the first is—your past deals might crop up any day."

"I thought long about that," returned Burridge, earnestly. "An' at last I figured myself free of any worry. I'm not known in Arizona. Idaho never knew me as Cash Burridge. An' what do any two-bit deals here amount to? They'll be forgotten after I've gone."

"Reckon you don't miss it far," replied Nevada. "But my second point is the serious an' important one. That is, so far as I am concerned."

"Shoot!" replied Burridge, with good-natured impatience.

"Wal, Cash, I don't mean any offense, but I'm just plain doubtful that you can *ever* go straight."

Burridge threw his cigar at the stove and the dark blood waved over his face in a tide. "By Heaven! that sticks in my craw, too! I wonder. But I'm no damn fool an' I'm not without some brains."

"Shore. I admit that. But, Cash, you've asked my opinion an' heah it is. You've a weakness for women an' red liquor. An' the crux of the deal is—can you stand prosperity?"

"Ha! I never had a chance to find out," replied Burridge, clenching his fist. "I've got it now. We'll see. I swear I want to make the best of it. An' I'd do better with my chance if I had you beside me. That's all."

"Wal, I appreciate that, Cash, an' I'll think it over. What I hate aboot it is livin' up to my name."

Nevada went downstairs with Burridge and amused himself by standing and walking in front of Cawthorne for a while. Lize did not put in an appearance. It was mid-week and business was slack. Nevada left the Gold Mine early, not forgetful that Mrs. Wood surely would wait up for him. The night was dark and cold, with a hint of snow in the air. The wind whistled through the leafless trees. Excitement and distraction had somehow been good for him. He found his landlady waiting up beside the kitchen fire.

"Wal, Mother Wood, heah I am, standin' on both feet an' without any hole in my haid," he said, cheerily.

"So I see, Mr. Lacy," she returned. "But that might be only a matter of luck. Did you run into Link?"

"Shore. I stood around hours, but nothin' happened. So I reckon you got me all scared for nothin'."

"Scared! Pooh! I wish I could put the fear of the Lord in you," she replied.

"Wal, I'll agree to let you, if you will give me a piece of pie an' a mug of milk."

The short days passed, the snow fell, adding to Nevada's work. In the evenings, if the weather was not stormy, he would drop in at the Gold Mine. Burridge had made another strong plea for Nevada to join him, and then had left for Arizona, intending to make a wide detour through Oregon and California to avoid the snow.

Lize Teller had passed from jest to earnest in her mood toward Nevada. She was vain, willful, and malignant when under the influence of drink. Her life worked daily toward some final tragedy. During the early part of the winter she had made love to Nevada, more, he thought, to inflame Cawthorne than for any other reason. But the time came, which was coincident with Cawthorne's further bold attempt to force or aggravate Nevada into a fight, when she ceased wholly her flirting with Nevada. Soon after that she broke her engagement with Cawthorne and took to wild flirtations and drinking bouts with the gamblers. She lost all restraint and began to fail in health.

When Nevada at length took her to task, as if indeed he were a brother, he received an impression that gave him concern.

"No decent man wants me and I'm slated for hell," she told him, bitterly.

From this speech Nevada conceived the idea that somehow he had failed the girl. It could not have been otherwise, yet the fact hurt him. Another side of the situation was the peril she had incurred by jilting Cawthorne. There was, however, no use in talking to Lize about that. Whenever Cawthorne accosted her, whether humbly or harshly, or in a maudlin way, she flouted him as she would have a repulsive dog.

Days and weeks went by, and this situation wore on, growing toward its climax.

Nevada resisted his premonition of its outcome. Almost he yielded to the urge to leave Lineville even in the dead of winter. But the side of him that was Jim Lacy, brooding, augmenting, always in conflict with Nevada, would not let him run from a cheap bully and from a worthless girl whom he yet might help. Something held Nevada back from the easiest escape out of that dilemma.

Always there was encroaching upon his gentle kindly mood, eating like a poison lichen into the sorrow and dream of his love for Hettie Ide, lost to him forever, that dark instinctive fire of spirit, that antagonism of the gunman.

Nevada acquitted himself of any responsibility for what he had become. As a mere boy he had been thrown among brutal and evil men. He had worked himself above their influence time and time again, only to be thrown back, by accident, by chivalry in him to redress a wrong done some one, by passion to survive, into that character which fate had fastened upon him and to which he seemed unfortunately and wonderfully fitted.

"Reckon it'll always be so for me," he soliloquized, somberly. "I cain't get away from myself. . . . I wonder if Hettie would believe me false to her faith. No! No! . . . I'll always know, even if I'm forced to be Jim Lacy again, that I'm true to her."

One afternoon Nevada, actuated by an impulse beyond his ken, bent his steps toward the Gold Mine. All night an oppression had persisted through his slumbers, and all morning he had been restless, brooding.

He entered the place by the side door, and paused in the hall before the entrance to the gambling room. The usual quiet of that den had been disrupted.

With his left hand Nevada quickly opened the door and entered sidewise, his right arm crooked. The room was full of men, all standing. Cards, coins, chips, glasses on the tables showed evidence of having been violently abandoned. There followed whispers, a cough, shuffling of feet. The noise that had halted Nevada came from the saloon. Suddenly it augmented to a banging on the bar accompanied by the bellow of a harsh voice.

"Rum! Hand it out—er I'll bust your head, too!"

Nevada strode to the nearest group of men. Something terrible had happened. He saw it in their faces.

Immediately he connected it with the raucous voice in the saloon.

"What's happened?" he queried.

"There's been a hell of a mess," replied one, wiping a moist face.

"Jim, we was playin' our card games, quiet as usual," spoke up the gambler, Ace Black, "when we heerd an awful row in the hall there. Then a woman's screams, quick hushed, I'll tell you. An' after that a heavy fall. We all jumped up an' some one rushed out to see what it was. An' by Gawd—"

"Wal?" broke in Nevada, cool and grim, as Black choked.

"Lize Teller! She was layin' half naked, streamin' blood. Link Cawthorne had beat her over the head with his gun. She'll die! . . . An' listen to him!"

In three long bounds Nevada had reached and split the beaded door-curtain. His swift eye swept all.

"*Cawthorne!*" he yelled, in piercing voice that brought an instant breathless silence.

Five

It was springtime in northern California. Old Mt. Shasta stood up grandly and took the morning light, his vast snowslopes beginning to be ridged by black. From the Tule Lake depression the land waved upward in wide belts, brown and gray, and at last green as emerald.

Honk! Honk! Honk! The wild geese were coming from the south. Great flocks in triangle formation, led by huge old honking ganders, came flying over the sage hills, to circle the grain fields and drop down among their fellows.

The wide acres of the Ide ranch, mostly lake-bottom land that the draining of Tule Lake had made available, spread rich and fertile along the southern shore. The squares of brown soil but recently ploughed, the fields beginning to show a tinge of green, the pasture lands, running far up on the gray sage slopes, the droves of horses and herds of cattle, the hedge fences, the orchards, young and old, the neat sheds and the rambling red-roofed barn, and the white house half hidden in a grove of maples and pines—all these amply testified to the prosperity of the Ides.

Hettie Ide had awakened this morning twenty years old. The wild geese that she had loved since childhood had come back from their pilgrimage to the south, and were honking as if they knew it was her birthday and that on this beautiful May day she must be joyous with young life.

But Hettie had a secret sorrow, which she hid deep in her heart, while she ministered to her ailing mother, and shared with her brother Ben the one bitter drop in his cup of happiness.

49

It wanted an hour yet before breakfast. As Hettie tripped down the stairs she heard Ina shrieking with laughter, no doubt at little Blaine's pranks. How happy they were and how blessed by God! But Hettie had no envy in her heart this birthday morning. She was closer to Ben than ever, and she loved Ina and the child as if indeed they were her own flesh and blood.

Hettie went outdoors. What a glorious morning! Bright and warm was the sun; the birds were singing in the maples; violets lifted their sweet faces out of the green; the wild-lilac buds were bursting into pink.

She knew where to find Ben. Down in the hedge-lined lane to the corrals she strolled, her heart full, yet with the old pang keener, listening to the hum of bees and the honk of wild geese, the bawl of calves and the twittering of the swallows.

Above all these sounds, so sweet to her listening ears, she heard the shrill whistle of Ben's great wild stallion, California Red. He was trooping across the pasture in defiance of Ben, or venting his displeasure at the corral bars.

Hettie found Ben sitting on top of the corral fence. California Red was inside, and indeed he did not like it. Hettie halted to peep through at him. She loved this wonderful horse, too, for his beauty, his spirit, and for another reason which only Ben would ever have suspected.

California Red had been in captivity four years. He had been broken, yet never had lost his spirit. It took a halter to make him lower his ears and stop rolling his fine dark eyes. Red was never gentle, but, on the other hand, he had not one mean trait. He shone red, glossy, silken, beautiful, and his long mane was a flame. He was a big horse, yet so perfectly proportioned that most observers would not have judged his size. High and rangy, with body round as a barrel, a wonderful deep wide chest, legs powerful, yet not heavy, and an arching neck and noble head, he looked indeed what he had been for years, the wild stallion king of the sage hills of northern California.

Hettie climbed to a seat beside her brother.

"Mawnin', pard," she drawled, mimicking the Southern accent of one neither of them ever forgot.

Ben gave a little start. He had been gazing out over the red stallion, over the corrals and fields and the sage slopes, to something beyond. Hettie did not often take such liberty with her brother. But this was her birthday and she meant to recall something of the past that might hurt them both.

"Wal, howdy there, old girl!" replied Ben, surprising her with his answering drawl. Beneath the humor in his voice lay deep feeling. But as he reached for her with his gloved hand he did not look at her.

"What're you doing, Ben?" she asked, brightly, as she took his hand in both hers.

"I was just coaxing that red son-of-a-gun," he replied, nodding at the stallion.

"Red doesn't seem to obey you very well."

"I'd have to rope him before he'd lay down those ears."

"Ben, you mustn't expect him to grow tame."

"Tame? No, I only want him to love me."

"Perhaps love was left out of Red's makeup," laughed Hettie. "Or perhaps he can't forgive you for taking him from his sage hills. I certainly wouldn't love you, if I were Red."

"It's four years now," said Ben, thoughtfully. "What a long time! I couldn't ask a finer, gamer horse. Sure there isn't one in all California that can touch him. But I—I always seem to want something from Red—I never get."

"Ben dear," replied Hettie, pressing his hand, "what you want is something—some one to tame Red."

"I reckon. . . . The only man who ever could tame Red," muttered Ben, more to himself than to her.

"Your old pard, Nevada," she whispered, leaning closer.

Ben dropped his head, and his gloved hand closed tight on Hettie's.

Not for a long time had Hettie dared to broach this subject and now that she had, she meant to follow it up in a way to help her, and perhaps Ben, too.

"Ben, this is my birthday," she spoke up, softly.

"Well, so it is," replied her brother, starting out of his reverie. "I plumb forgot. But I reckon I can dig you up a present of some kind. . . . Let's see, you must be eighteen—nineteen."

"Twenty," she added, gravely.

"How time flies! Why, you're a grown woman, and a darned fine handsome one, too. But you always seem my kid sister."

And as he turned to kiss her cheek she saw tears in his dark eyes. There were threads of gray, too, in the hair over Ben's temples. That shocked Hettie. He, so young and strong and virile! But Ben, all those long years exiled from his home, outcast and wild-horse hunter, had led a lonely and hard life. It was Nevada who had saved him. And now, as so often in the past, she prayed God to bless Nevada, and keep him good and clean and brave as when she had known him.

"Ben," she spoke up, "I don't want any present on my twentieth birthday. But I ask this. If I'm a woman now I'm old enough to be listened to. Let me talk to you as I want—as I need to."

"Hettie, I'm sorry you had to ask me that," he returned, contritely. "But you hurt so. . . . And I thought you just a—a sentimental girl—that you'd forget."

"Forget *him?* Never," she whispered. "Have you forgotten?"

"If I ever do may God forgive me," replied Ben, poignantly.

"Ben, I know your secret, and I think Ina knows, too," went on Hettie, earnestly. "We are dear friends —nay, we're sisters. She's so good—so lovable. . . . We have talked often. You remember when Ina came home from college—when you were a poor wild-horse hunter of the hills and father almost hated you—remember how Ina and I plotted for you and Nevada. How we fought for you!"

"Ah, Hettie—I do remember," said Ben, dreamily.

"Well, Ina and I know what ails you. It's loss of your pard, Nevada!"

"No, Hettie dear, *not* all loss of mine," burst out Ben, passionately. "I'm not so selfish as that. I could stand loss. But what has grieved and shamed me—and, well, broken my heart—is that Nevada saved me, made all my good fortune, my happiness, possible, by sacrificing himself. Father forgave me, took me back home to mother and you. Hart Blaine was proud to give me—*me,* the lonely wild-horse hunter—his talented and beautiful daughter, the richest girl in all this valley of rich ranchers. I had fame, family, home, love, happiness beyond belief. Then father died, leaving me rich. I should say leaving us rich, for half of all this wonderful ranch is yours, Hettie. Next little Blaine came to bless me—my boy! . . . And Nevada went back to where he came from. God only knows where that is. I've spent a lot of money searching the West for a lean-faced rider who drawled his Texas accent—and answered to the name Nevada. And I can't find him."

"Some day you will, Ben," she whispered, thrillingly.

"Always I believed I would," went on Ben, whose tongue, once loosed, seemed in haste to unburden itself. "I lived on that hope. But it's four years now. Four years. And that Forlorn River Ranch of ours is now worth a fortune. Half of that is Nevada's. Half of the Mule Deer Flat Ranch is Nevada's. He's worth money. . . . Why didn't he come back? The whole country rose up to bless him for killing Less Setter and his two accomplices. Why didn't he ever write? Just a line—a word to let me know he was alive and hadn't forgotten. Oh, damn him—damn him!"

"Hush—Ben," returned Hettie, almost faltering. "You don't mean to damn Nevada. . . . Don't you understand that the reason he disappeared like that, and became as one dead to you, was not because he feared the law might hold him for killing those wicked men who had trapped you. No! But because he feared we would find out who he really was. Oh, I know, Ben. That was it. Nevada had been bad. How bad I dare not imagine. . . . Don't you remember that day when he rode so furiously into the crowd to face Setter? How the mere sight of him froze them with terror. . . . . Oh, Ben, I fear Nevada had been some great and terrible gunman. . . . That gentle, soft-voiced boy who was afraid to touch me with his little finger! Oh, the mystery, the pity of it!"

"Gunman?" queried Ben, almost harshly. "I reckon so. I think I guessed it, he was so strange with guns. He handled a gun so marvelously. But what was that to me? . . . He could be Billy the Kid, or Plummer, or Wess Hardin, or Kingfisher, or Jim Lacy, or any other desperado I ever heard the name of—and what would I care?"

"Ben, dear, you quite overlooked something," rejoined Hettie, bravely, while she felt the hot blood mount to cheek and temple. "Nevada loved not only you—but me too . . . and I—I loved him."

"Well, now, Hettie," replied Ben, strangely softened, "I reckon that's no news, though you never declared it so—so openly. But even though that was true, why should it make such a difference?"

"The boy came of a good family," replied Hettie. "He had fine instincts. And one of them was as instinct to disappear when there was danger of my learning who he really was. There can be no other reason. He had pride. And he loved me so—so well, he couldn't bear to shame me."

"Damn him, anyway!" burst out Ben, again. "He's broken your heart, too."

"Not yet," replied Hettie, in strong vibrating tones.

"Hettie, did that son-of-a-gun make love to you?" queried Ben, struggling with his resentment and remorse.

"Did—he?" murmured she, with a little broken laugh. "Ben, when he found out I cared—he—he made the most terrible love to me. . . . Oh, I can never forget—never get over it!"

"Well!" ejaculated her brother, amazed out of his own pain. "How and when did he ever get the chance?"

"Wouldn't you like to know?" asked Hettie, archly.

"And you—my little sixteen-year-old sister! . . . Who can ever tell about a girl?"

"Ben, didn't Ina Blaine love *you* when she was five years old—and ten—and fourteen?" queried Hettie. "And at eighteen after she'd been away from you four years?"

"Thank the Lord, she did. I've never begun to understand it. But it's beautiful, wonderful. . . . Did my pard, Nevada, ever know you, too, had that strange, glorious thing—woman's love—for him?"

"Yes, Nevada knew," replied Hettie, eloquently. "He knew he had my faith, too. . . . And, Ben, *that* is why I've never lost him. I know. It's the way a woman feels. Nevada is not dead. He is not false to me—to what I believed he had become. And somewhere, somehow, he will come back to me—to us."

"My God! that's good to hear!" exclaimed Ben, with fervent emotion. "You strike me right in the heart, Hettie."

"I'm glad. I've wanted to speak for long," replied Hettie, simply. "And there's another thing that touches us closely."

"What's that?" he asked, anxiously, as she gazed solemnly up at him, and hesitated.

"Mother is failing. Haven't you noticed it?"

Ben nodded his head sorrowfully. "I reckon I try not to see, but I do."

"She has brightened up since spring came," went on Hettie. "Mother loves the sun, the trees, the flowers, the birds. She likes to be outdoors. Winter is long and cold here. It rains and snows and sleets. She dreads the icy wind. Honestly, Ben, I don't think it's grief for father. She has gotten over that. I believe this valley is bad for her. It's bad for me, too, in winter."

"I've been afraid of that very thing," declared her brother, thoughtfully. "But there's a possibility of some organic disease."

"Mother's not old," said Hettie. "She ought to live many years yet. But we must do something to help her. Ben, I suggest you take her to San Francisco. Get the opinion and advice of some up-to-date physician. Take Ina with you. Blaine will be safe with me. I'll run the ranch, never fear."

"By George! it's a great idea," declared Ben, with amazing enthusiasm. He leaped down off the corral fence, then turned to help Hettie. "Ina will be tickled. She'll get her brother Marvie to stay with you."

"Ben, I actually believe you've decided already," replied Hettie, suddenly feeling radiant.

"Reckon I have, and I'll bet you Ina squeals with joy. Let's go tell her this minute."

Hettie peeped through the corral fence at California Red.

"Good-by, you beautiful, stand-off wild thing!" she cried. "Some day some one will come and he'll tame you to eat out of my hand."

With arms locked, Hettie and Ben hurried down the lane, eager with the import of new hopes, happier than they had been for a long time. It was Ben now who talked, while Hettie kept silent. She thrilled with the consciousness that she had roused Ben from a creeping sad abstraction that had grown more noticeable of late. Ben not only missed his old friend, Nevada, but also the wild-horse-hunting life which had been his sole occupation for years before his marriage, and which had been the cause of the alienation from his father.

Ina was in the yard, gathering violets, which certainly matched the blue of her spring dress and the color of her eyes. Little Blaine babbled at sight of his father and ran as fast as his short fat legs could carry him.

"Well, good-mawnin', you-all!" said Ina, gayly. "Say, you look excited." . . . Then she kissed Hettie and continued, "Many happy, happy returns of the day."

Ben snatched the boy up and, holding him on his arm, he confronted Ina with a smile that held great portent.

"How soon can you get ready for a trip to San Francisco?" he asked, quite naturally, as if he were in the habit of speaking so every day.

"What! Oh, I knew something was up," she cried, the color flashing to her beautiful face. "How soon? . . . Fifteen minutes!"

"Ha! Ha! I thought you'd hit the saddle and ride that idea pronto," said Ben, happily. "But you needn't be so swift as that."

"Ben, are you really going to take me to Frisco?" asked Ina, eagerly.

"Yes. It's all settled. But—"

"You darling," she cried, kissing him. "I wanted to go somewhere. The winter has been so long, so confining. Klamath Falls was my hope. But San Francisco! Oh!"

"Ina, I'm sorry I don't think of such things," replied Ben, ruefully. "I guess I'd fallen into a rut. You must thank Hettie."

Whereupon Ina most heartily embarced Hettie, and then, coming down to earth, she said: "Let's go in to breakfast. You can tell me there all about this grand idea."

"We'll tell you now," said Ben. "The trip to Frisco is on mother's account and we mustn't discuss it before her. The fact is, Ina, mother is failing. Something wrong with her. Hettie suggested we take her to San Francisco to see a competent physician. Blaine will be safe with Hettie and so will the ranch. What do you say, dearest?"

"I say it's a happy and wise suggestion," returned Ina, with a nod of commendation toward Hettie. "This damp cold Tule Lake does not agree with mother."

The only hitch in the plans formulated by Ben and Hettie concerned the coming of Marvie Blaine to stay at the Ide ranch. Hart Blaine would not allow his son to go.

"That boy can't run a mowin' machine, let alone a ranch," old Blaine had said to Ben.

There was trouble between Marvie and his father, for which, in Ben's opinion, both were equally to blame.

"Sure reminds me of my scrap with dad," remarked Ben to Hettie. "Only *I* was right and dad was wrong. Marvie refused to go to college. Reckon he's not so different from me. He likes horses and the open country."

"Some day Marvie will run off just as you did, Ben Ide," Hettie had answered.

So Hettie was left alone in the Ide homestead with little Blaine and the two women servants. She rather welcomed the solitude. She found how much her mother had taken of time and thought. Part of the day she had the servants take care of Blaine while she devoted herself to the many set tasks at hand and the new ones always arising. After supper, when Blaine had been put to bed, she had hours to be alone and think before her own rest claimed her.

The running of the ranch had at first seemed something that would be pleasure, rather than work. She discovered presently that it was not only work, but an extremely embarrassing and exasperating task. There were eighteen hands employed on the lake ranch, and as many more out in the hills. Most of these employees were young men of the valley, unmarried, and very desirous of changing that state of single blessedness. Some had been schoolmates of Hettie's. And there were several riders, long, lean, rangy fellows from the South, with whom Hettie grew most annoyed. They continually found reasons to ride in to the ranch. Some of the excuses were ridiculous in the extreme. These droll boys of the open range paid court to her, wholly oblivious of her rebuffs. In two weeks' time the whole contingent was in love with Hettie or trying to make her believe so. And the plowing, the planting, the movement of stock, the hauling of supplies, the herding of cattle, in fact all tasks pertaining to the operation of Ben Ide's ranches, had to be talked over elaborately with the temporary mistress.

Hettie had fun out of it, except in the case of the several lean-faced, quiet-eyed riders from the hills. They made love to her. Moreover, they reminded her of Nevada, and that inflamed her lonely, hungry heart.

If Nevada had come to mind often in the past, what did he do now but haunt every hour? She saw him in every one of the range riders. Yet how incomparably he bestrode a horse! Hettie saw his lean, fine still face, so clean cut and brown, with the sleepy eyes that yet could wake to flame and also smile with a light she had never seen in any other. His old black sombrero, with bullet holes in the crown, when laid aside had appeared a disreputable thing, but on his head it had seemed picturesque and beautiful. His old silk scarf with the checks of red, the yellow vest with the string of a little tobacco pouch always hanging out of a pocket, the worn leather wristbands, the high top-boots with their scalloped edges, and their long bright jingling spurs—how well she remembered them, how vividly they were limned in the eye of her memory! Then, as something inevitable at the end of reminiscence, something that seemed an inseparable part of Nevada, she recalled the dark and heavy gun he had always worn. It had bumped against her as she walked beside him. When he had taken her in his arms, even in the sweet madness of that moment, she had felt the gun hard and cold against her.

The years had brought Hettie stronger and deeper love for Nevada. As she looked back now she remembered her open aversion to his gun, and to the something about him that hinted of its deadly use. She had been a callow, sentimental girl, sickened at the thought of bloodshed, hostile toward the spirit and skill that had eventually saved her brother from ruin and perhaps herself from the villainous Setter.

She had lived and suffered during the four years since Nevada had ridden away, leaving death and calamity behind him. She was a woman now. She saw differently. She divined what she had been to him—how her friendship and love had uplifted him. How great and enduring had her own love become! She was his alone. Separation could never change her.

"What did it matter who Nevada was or what he was before he came to Ben and me?" she mused, sitting by the open window in the dark, listening to the last sleepy honks of wild geese and the melancholy peep-peep of spring frogs. "But he could not see that. Yet he must have known it would not matter to me, so long as he kept himself the Nevada we knew and loved. . . . Would he ever fall to rustling cattle, if that had once been his crime? No! Would he ever drink again? No! Could he sink to the embrace of some bad woman? Never! . . . Will he use again that terrible gun? . . . Ah, he *will!* I feel it. If not for himself, then for some one. . . . He was flame and lightning to destroy!"

Six

Hettie's folk did not return from San Francisco on the date they had specified, nor did she receive any letter from them. Every day thereafter she expected them, only to be disappointed. This, added to the increasing perplexity of the duties that had been left to her, and the persistence of her admirers, wore her into such a nervous state that she failed to keep her boast about running the ranch.

One day several strangers from Klamath Falls called upon Hettie. They were business men, representing an Oregon syndicate, who were buying up land around Tule Lake Valley. There had been considerable speculation in that vicinity since the draining of the lake. The Ides had received offers before, but never anything like the one made by these men. Hettie was shrewd enough to grasp that some situation had arisen, such as the possibility of a railroad from Klamath Falls, to increase the value of the Ide property enormously. She neither refused nor accepted the offer, saying that control of the ranches was in her brother's hand. Her amazement and gratification, however, lingered after their departure. She scarcely ever thought of herself as sharing equally with Ben the fortune their father had left them.

Hettie happened to be out on the farm somewhere when her people returned; and upon coming back to the house, hot and dusty and weary, what was her surprise and joy to be waylaid in the hall by her mother and Ina. It took no second glance to see that the little trip had been happily beneficial, especially to her mother.

When they reached the sitting room, Hettie was on

the verge of tears. Sight of Ben then was too much for her, and she ran weeping into his outstretched arms.

"Oh—Ben," she cried, "I—I fell down on running the ranch! . . . The silly fools nagged me—to death!"

"Who?" queried Ben, suddenly aghast.

"The boys—and some of the men—too. They just —made my life—miserable."

"Well! The lazy sons-of-guns!" ejaculated Ben. "I'll fire the whole caboodle of them."

Ina's tender solicitude and Ben's anger at once calmed Hettie.

"Oh no, Ben. It's not so—so bad as that. They only hatched every pretense and excuse to approach me— just to make outrageous love."

Ben's haw-haw mingled with Ina's scream of laughter. Hettie had to accept that mirth with the best grace possible. Her troubles were over, at last, and she could not but forgive the suitors who had so besieged her. The high spirits of Ben and Ina and the certain evidence of her mother's improvement were sufficient to lift Hettie to the heights.

"What'd you bring me from Frisco?" she asked presently, with all a child's eagerness.

"Candy," replied Ben, with a smile.

"A new spring dress and hat—oh, adorable," replied Ina.

"Well, daughter, I fetched you somethin' too," added Mrs. Ide, beaming.

"I—I'm almost glad you went off and left me alone," responded Hettie, gratefully.

Nothing was said during supper about the main object of the journey to San Francisco. Ina told of their trips to the stores, and Ben of their jaunts to seashore and parks and theaters. Later, when Mrs. Ide had retired, Ben took Hettie into Ina's room, where the ecstatic Blaine gloated over his new toys.

"Well, Hettie, your sending us off on this trip means a great change in our lives," began Ben, gravely.

"Oh—Ben!" faltered Hettie.

Here Ina interposed to reprove Ben for his abruptness and lack of tact. Then she added, "Hettie dear, it's nothing to frighten you."

"Winter and spring are too damp and cold for mother," continued Ben. "To keep her here longer will endanger her life."

"Then we certainly won't keep her," replied Hettie, resolutely.

"Exactly. Ina and I got that far, anyway, in our decision."

"Will mother—be all right in some other climate?" queried Hettie, with hesitation.

"She'll get well," answered Ben. "She needs a mild, dry, warm climate in winter and a high, dry, bracing climate in summer."

"Where can we find them?"

"Easy enough. But the thing that stumps Ina and me is how to decide what's best to do."

"That's easy enough," returned Hettie. "I will go with mother and live with her."

"Sure you will. But that doesn't solve the problem."

"Surely we can afford it, Ben?"

"I reckon. However, the point is I don't want to be separated from mother and you. Neither does Ina. That much is settled. We won't be separated."

Hettie gazed with suddenly dim eyes at her brother. He and Ina felt what she had not spoken. They were both in dead earnest, and Ina's color had faded. Evidently they had talked this thing over, to a conclusion that was momentous.

"Ben, you can't imagine how happy you make me," said Hettie, feelingly. "Separation would be hard. I have only mother and you and yours to live for. . . . Then, if you won't let mother and me leave you . . ."

"We've sure got to go with you," interrupted Ben, forcibly. "But what to do is sure a sticker."

"Sell—out!" said Hettie, huskily.

"But we've lived here all our lives. This land has made us prosperous. It's home."

"Ben, it'd not be home without mother."

"No. And it wouldn't be the same if we were all

separated. But I'd hate to sacrifice the land just to get a quick sale. And we'll need money, wherever we go."

"Ben, I can sell this lake property of ours for two hundred thousand," declared Hettie.

Her brother stared at her. At length he spoke: "Hettie, don't make wild statements like that. It's hard enough on me to make decisions."

"I can sell for that *to-morrow,*" grandly added Hettie, conscious of a sudden tremendous importance.

"Now I know she's crazy," wailed Ben, turning to his wife.

"She looks pretty sure and sane to me, Bennie boy. You're only a wild-horse hunter, anyway. Hettie and I have the business brains."

"By George!" cried Ben, leaping up. "You're right. But I can't believe we could sell for that."

"It's true, Ben. Listen," said Hettie, and then briefly told about the offer of the Klamath Falls syndicate.

"Horses not included in the deal? Not California Red?" queried Ben, beginning to manifest signs of extreme excitement.

"Their offer embraced land and buildings on this ranch, and all the Ide cattle. But not horses."

"Girls, it's settled, it's done!" cried Ben, giving way to the force of something that had been impelling him. He kissed Ina and hugged Hettie. He tore up and down the room. He woke little Blaine, who had fallen asleep on the bed amid his toys.

"Ben, aren't you ashamed? All that show of gladness over selling our home!" exclaimed Ina, reproachfully.

Hettie did not voice her surprise and disapproval. She had not seen Ben show excitement like that for years. What did it mean?

Ben ceased his violent expressions and faced them, quite pale, with his dark eyes full of fire.

"Forgive me and try to understand," he said. "Remember I have not the tender associations with Tule Lake that actuate you girls. It is home and I reckon I love it, but not as you. Father was hard on me for years. He made me an outcast. For years more I lived over there across the sage hills, hunting wild horses, lonely and wretched. Then Nevada dropped into my life. Then, Ina, you came, too. . . . And so between you I was brought home again. But despite all, there has been something lacking. . . . This ranch country is too populated for me. It is too rich. There's not enough hard work for me. The sage hills and the valleys, once so wild, where the horses roamed free, are now ranches and farms. I'd be happier in a new country—say in Arizona, where the ranges are vast and ranches few. I'd do better, working as I used to. . . . That's why I'm glad to sell out here, to take mother where she'll get strong again, where you all will be the happier because of these things."

"Arizona? Ben, you didn't tell me you'd decided," expostulated Ina.

"I hadn't until now. Hettie settled it, bless her heart."

"Arizona!" murmured Hettie, thoughtfully. "We know so little about Arizona. Isn't it very wild?"

"Wild? I reckon," replied Ben. "Arizona is everything northern California used to be. Then it has vast grass and sage ranges, desert and valley, canyons and mountains, great forests, great rivers. There are thousands of wild horses in Arizona. Deer, bear, lion, turkey—wonderful hunting. It has minerals—gold, silver, copper. There's just been war between cattlemen and sheepmen. Oh, it is a wonderful country for the pioneer."

"Hettie," added Ina, "we met an Arizonian in Frisco, a grizzled old fellow. I wish you could have seen him. He surely was full of Arizona. But Ben didn't tell you all."

"What'd I forget?" inquired Ben, lamely.

"About the bad crews who live off the ranchers—Indians, Mexicans, rustlers, horse thieves, wild cowboys, gunmen—and I don't remember who else. That plan of Arizona worries me, Ben, if you must go there."

"It'd worry me, too, if I thought I'd fall into such company as the old Arizonian bragged about. But he was only blowing. . . . At that, though, I think I could stand a few wild cowboys. Couldn't you, Hettie?"

He spoke teasingly and laughed with something of his old boyishness. Verily this possibility of Arizona had stimulated him.

Hettie tried to smile, but her effort was a wan one. There had seemed to come a knocking at her heart.

"I'll keep Forlorn River Ranch and Mule Deer Flat," mused Ben, pacing the room. "I'd never part with them. We own them, Nevada and I, share and share alike. . . . Some day I'll come back to see them, and who knows?"

Hettie lay sleepless and distracted late into the hours of the night.

She could not tell whether she wanted to weep or rejoice. Ben's revelation had not been such a surprise, though the violence of his feeling dismayed her. Despite all that wealth, home, wife, child could give Ben, he yearned for the old free life in the open, for his lean-faced beloved friend, for the color of the sage and the movement of wild horses on the horizon. How he had welcomed this opportunity to get away from Tule Lake! And Ina was as wise as she was loving. Her home was where her heart abided. That night she had followed Hettie to her room to say: "Hettie, we didn't guess how it was with Ben. And I want to ask you, don't you think this change will be as good for Ben's soul as for mother's health?"

"I do indeed, Ina," Hettie had replied. "Ben was a strange boy, even when he was little. Father never understood him."

"Well, I'll be happy with Ben anywhere," returned Ina, simply. "My folks will make a fuss about this. They'll be shocked to hear we are going back to the pioneer life in far-away Arizona. Money has made snobs of my people, except Marvie. He's eighteen now, and as wild to hunt and fish and ride as when he used to run away to Forlorn River. He just worshiped Ben and Nevada. He and dad are at odds now. I wonder how our going will effect Marvie?"

"Ina, you needn't wonder," said Hettie. "That boy will go with us."

"Oh, if he only could!" sighed Ina. "But dad would rave at the very idea."

"Marvie will run off," declared Hettie, positively.

Whenever Hettie's thoughts wandered back to herself, she wanted to weep. There was regret, of course, mingled with the emotions roused by the thought of leaving Tule Lake, where she had lived all her life. But not regret was it that threatened to bring the tears. Rather a joy rising from the depths of her! The old oppressive certainty that Nevada would never come back to Forlorn River was now lifted from her heart. She would no longer eat her heart out in waiting. Over there in wild Arizona she might see him again. Ben would never cease to search for Nevada. Surely he would locate him some day. How Ben loved that comrade of his lonely Forlorn River days!

Ben was late at breakfast next morning. No one had to tell Hettie and Ina that he had been out to the corrals. He strode in more like his old self than for months, keen-eyed, virile, with the spring of a rider in his step.

"Say, girls, what do you think?" he declared, radiantly. "Red came to me this morning. The wild son-of-a-gun! He did, and it sure tickled me. And I said to him, 'Old boy, you're going back to the unfenced ranges.' He understood me, too. . . . Oh, Ina—Hettie, I'm another man this mawnin'!"

"You look it, Bennie," replied Ina, with her beautiful eyes warm and glad.

"But you and Hettie look as if you'd lain awake and cried all night."

"That's a way women have, sometimes," said Ina. "It's a break, of course. But we're happy for you, and, thank God, we've found the way to restore mother."

"Blaine, my boy," said Ben, leaning to the child in his highchair, "we're going to Arizona. Are you glad?"

"Papa happy?" replied Blaine, with big-eyed, questioning wonder.

"Well, there's a bright youngster," declared Ben, raising his head to smile at Ina.

Mrs. Ide came in at the moment, to take her place next to Hettie. "What's that I hear about Arizona?"

"Oh, nothing much, mother," laughed Ben. "I was teasing Blaine about Arizona."

"Reckon you're full of Arizona since you met that cattleman," rejoined Mrs. Ide, placidly. "I didn't think much of him. He was as rough as the country he bragged about."

"Nana, we's doan Ar-zoonie," chirped up little Blaine, with great importance.

Mrs. Ide had not until that moment been given any inkling of the secret.

"Land's sake!" she ejaculated. "So that's the mystery. . . . Ben Ide, you ain't goin' back to chasin' wild hosses? Your father would turn over in his grave."

Ben Ide was not noted for deception or beating round the bush. Despite warning glances from Hettie and a kick under the table from Ina he told his mother that he was thinking of selling out and moving to Arizona. Mrs. Ide declared she would never go or permit Hettie to leave home. Ben tried to expostulate with her and, failing that, tried to laugh it off. But when his mother asked him a deliberate question he maintained silence. Whereupon she rose from the table and, weeping, left the room.

"Blaine, I reckon you're not such a bright kid, after all," said Ben, ruefully.

"It was a shock, Ben," rejoined Ina. "You were so abrupt. But she'll come round to it all right."

"Leave mother to us," added Hettie.

They talked it over, and at the conclusion of breakfast both Ina and Hettie urged Ben, now that he had made the great decision, to proceed at once toward its fulfillment.

"I'll run over to tell mother and dad," said Ina. "They'd never forgive me if I didn't tell them first.

Maybe they'll not forgive me, anyway. . . . And Marvie! I'll bet he lets out a whoop."

"By George!" ejaculated Ben. "Marvie will want to come with us. Ina, it's a big chance for the boy."

"I believe it is, Ben," she replied.

"Well, there's something sort of tough about this deal," went on Ben. "Yet it's great, too. . . . I'll go to Klamath Falls today. Reckon the papers will require your signature, Hettie. Say, what're you going to do with all that money?"

"What money?" queried Hettie, blankly.

"Why, ninny, your share in the Ide property!"

"Goodness! I never thought of that in money. Ben, I'll want the same share in your Arizona ranch."

"Good. You're one sister in a million. I'll leave you to talk some sense into mother, and you, Ina, to do the same by your folks. Reckon that'll be leaving you a job, because you and Marvie have all the sense in the Blaine family."

Ben left early for Klamath and Hettie had her hands full, not only with her mother, but with the ranch boys and riders among whom the news spread like wildfire in dry grass. Ben had not been any more tactful than usual. But then, Hettie reflected, since everybody had to know, what difference did it make whether they were told sooner or later?

Hettie told nine boys, one after the other, that Ben had not been joking, and that the Ide ranch was to pass into strange hands. Each and every one of these ranch hands was visibly agitated at the news.

"Miss Hettie," said one, "I reckon we ain't carin' what becomes of Tule Lake Ranch, but we care an awful lot about what becomes of you an' the boss. You can't get along without us."

"Oh, I wish Ben would take you all," replied Hettie, half distracted.

Then she had a long and trying hour with her mother, who, of course, could not be told the most important reason for this breaking of old home ties. But

Hettie knew how to handle her mother, and with patience and common sense, and dwelling much on the need of a change for Ben, she at last won the victory.

"After all, Hettie, it doesn't—matter about me," concluded Mrs. Ide, weeping. "But you'll be marryin' one of them long-legged, long-haired Arizona jacks, like that terrible Nevada."

"Why, mother, what a happy thought!" exclaimed Hettie, with a divine blush. "I might be just that lucky."

Ina, however, did not have such success with her folks. She returned both with fire in her eyes and with traces of tears on her cheeks.

"Oh, Hettie, they were just horrid," she said. "Kate was there, too, and you know she hates me. Dad was idiot enough to suggest that I come back to live with him. And Kate said I'd never need any more pretty dresses and hats out in that wild, woolly Arizona. My clothes always stuck in Kate's craw. But Marvie. Oh, he was adorable! In front of dad he never batted an eye. Once outside, though, he nearly hugged the breath out of me. 'Come with you?' he shouted, so loud I was afraid they'd hear. 'By the great jumpin' horn of Jehosaphat, I'm comin'! Dad can't stop me. Nor ropes, nor jails! I'll ride for Ben, an' chase wild horses, an' hunt an' fish. . . . Who knows, I might see Nevada out there.' "

"Bless the boy's heart!" exclaimed Hettie, her eyes filling with tears.

"Strange how Ben and Marvie loved Nevada," mused Ina.

"Strange?" queried Hettie, smiling through her tears.

"No. I don't mean that. . . . I think I loved him, too."

"Well, Ina, we've broken the ice," rejoined Hettie, quickly changing the subject. "Mother made a fuss, but I won her over. Your folks will have to come round, whether they like it or not. Now we must get our heads together. Ben will think of taking you and Blaine, and us, and his horses. That's all. But you know there are many things he can't part with. What a job it will be! How will we travel?"

"Goodness! I hope Ben doesn't make us ride horseback or in tent-covered wagons," replied Ina. "That'd be just like him."

"It'd be fun, once we got started," said Hettie, dreamily.

Seven

Three days later the Ides stood on their front porch and watched a buckboard drawn by a spirited team of horses rapidly passing down the lane toward the main road. This vehicle contained Ben's lawyer and a representative of the Oregon syndicate. Ben held a certified check in his hand, for which he had signed away the broad fertile acres of Tule Lake Ranch. He had also agreed to turn over the property before the first of September.

"By George! it happened quick!" he exclaimed, breathing hard. "Ina—Hettie—we're homeless."

"Ben, if it hurts you to lose this ranch, how will you ever give up Forlorn River?" asked Hettie, wonderingly.

"I'm sure keeping Forlorn River," declared Ben, but he winced perceptibly. "That reminds me, I'll have to ride out there."

"I'll go with you," said Hettie.

"Me, too," added Ina. "Reckon you-all haven't any corner on love for old Forlorn River."

"Honest, girls, I'd rather go alone," returned Ben.

"We won't intrude on your grief, Bennie dear," smiled Ina.

"I stopped over in Hammell on my way back from Oregon," said Ben. "You remember Sheriff Strobel. He always was a friend of mine, even in those outcast days when I was suspected of being a rustler. Strobel knows a good deal about Arizona. I asked him to come out this afternoon. I'll sure take what he says pretty serious."

"Now that we've burned our bridges behind us, it's late to ask advice," said Hettie.

"Yes, as far as going is concerned," agreed Ben.

"But about *where* to go—that's another matter. Arizona is a big place."

No wonder, thought Hettie, that Ben wanted to consult some one who was familiar with Arizona. She had begun to realize the responsibility of their undertaking. Therefore she was quite as eager to hear Sheriff Strobel as Ben; and Ina, too, did not want to be excluded from the interview.

They sat out on the shady porch, and while little Blaine played on the grass they explained to Ben's old friend the exigencies of the case.

"Wal, if you've sold out an' have got to go, there ain't no use advisin' ag'in' it," replied Strobel. "I reckon it's a pity. Folks around will miss you-all. . . . But what'd you pick out Arizona for, of all places?"

"Arizona has the climate. The doctor recommended it," said Ben.

"Wal, Arizona sure has a lot of climate," admitted Strobel. "There ain't no gainsayin' that. But climate is the only *good* thing it has got. The rest is desert, rocks, cactus, Gila monsters, an' tarantulas, side-winders, bad varmints, greasers, rustlers, an' gun-throwers."

"That's the worst I've heard yet," returned Ben, regretfully. "Are you giving Arizona a square deal?"

"Wal, after all, it's a wonderful country," replied the sheriff, as if forced to make a concession. "I went there twice, first time in the early days of the Territory, an' second about two years ago. Outside of the Indians bein' quiet, I didn't see much difference. Of late, hard characters have slipped into Arizona from all over."

"I've heard that," said Ben, impatiently. "It's about all anyone seems to say. What I want help in is where to strike for."

"Reckon I don't know enough about Arizona to tell you that. I'm able, though, to give you some hunches about where *not* to go. Southern Arizona is too hot, an' in the north it's too cold. On the other hand, you want to steer clear of the Tonto Basin, the Sierra Ancas, the Mogollons, the Little Colorado country. Around Springerville an' Snowflake there's fine grazin' lands.

That's near the White Mountains. But Mormons mostly have settled in there. The Santa Fé Railroad has just
lately been laid across Arizona. An' all along the line
new ranches have been added to the few settlers that
were there. Anyone goin' into the cattle game on a big
scale, as of course you will, don't want to get too far
from the railroad. I'd say a hundred miles should be
the limit, an' that's too far, in Arizona. Roughest, wildest country on earth, I reckon. . . . Now, Ben, the
only advice I'll presume to give you is this. Have a
winter home in San Diego, California. There's the
mildest, most equable climate in all the world. That's
the place for your mother an' for all of you. San Diego
is not so far from southern and central Arizona. By
doin' so you can pick the best range land in Arizona,
an' needn't worry so much about winter climate. Some
of them high plateaus get plumb cold in winter, but are
grand all the rest of the year."

"By George! that's a good idea," exclaimed Ben, en-
thusiastically. "Never thought of that myself. I've heard
about San Diego. It's on the seashore near the Mexican
border. They say the sun shines there every day in the
year. By George!—it solves our problem, Ina."

"I like the idea very much indeed," replied Ina.

"How about you, Hettie?" queried Ben, eagerly.

"It would appeal to mother," said Hettie. "She's a
little hipped on this wild and woolly Arizona, as your
San Fransisco informant called it."

"Sheriff, you sure have given me a hunch," declared
Ben, turning to his friend. "Now, about my horses. You
know I'd never go anywhere without Red and some of
the others. But why not take the best of my stock?"

"Wal, by all means take them," replied the sheriff.
"That's a hoss country, an' also a hoss-*thief* country.
I'd send them overland by easy stages in care of some
reliable men. Send a chuck wagon, an' also another
wagon, so they can haul outfits an' plenty of grain. An',
Ben, I'd start them soon as possible. They'll need time.
They got to cross Nevada an' most of Utah. That de-
pends on the best route, which they'll have to find."

"Exactly. The main thing, though, is an objective point. Where shall my men go in Arizona?"

"Wal, that is a stumper," replied the other. "Here it's well along in May now. You said you'd agree to vacate this range in about two months."

"Yes. But, come to think of it, that's just prolonging the agony. . . . Girls, how about it? Couldn't you get out of here in two *weeks?*"

"Oh dear!" cried Hettie, helpless before this rush of events and the wonderful stir it roused.

"Yes, Ben, we could. The sooner the better," replied Ina, wide-eyed with the seriousness of this decision.

"Good!" ejaculated Ben. "Then I'll go with the horses. You can pack what you want to take, send it to Klamath to be freighted. Then you and Hettie can fetch Blaine and mother by way of Frisco."

"They can take the Santa Fé from Los Angeles," interposed the sheriff.

"And be landed somewhere in wild Arizona to wait weeks for you," asserted Ina.

"Ben, if you go overland I'm going with you," added Hettie, spiritedly.

"We'll *all* go with you," added Ina, a spot of red showing in each pearly cheek.

"Aw, girls, that'll never do," expostulated Ben. "It's —it's a crazy idea."

"We could stand it," returned Ina, gathering courage with the growing conception. "I think we'd have fun. Back to the pioneer days! Remember how our mothers used to brag about the wagon-team into Oregon?"

"It would be great," added Hettie, in low voice, and she felt her breast heave.

"Say, you're laying it on thick," declared Ben, at his wits' end. Plain it was he had at once set his heart upon riding overland. "You girls might do it, but think of Blaine and mother."

"Mother would not only like it, but she could go through with it," said Hettie, jumping up. "I'll ask her."

She ran in to lay the point before her mother.

"Well, daughter," came the reply, with unusual animation, "reckon that's the first sensible idea Ben has thought of, if it did come from him. It'd do me good. Work an' livin' outdoors is what I need."

Hettie rushed outside triumphantly to announce her mother's opinion, at which Ben threw up his hands.

"I'll have to give up that plan," he said, regretfully.

Whereupon he took the sheriff off for the corrals, leaving Hettie and Ina deep in a discussion of this important phase of their exodus into a new country. On Blaine's behalf, Ina could not see any reason why he should be a deterrent. And Hettie found innumerable arguments in favor of the overland journey.

"We can pack a wagonload of trunks and chests and boxes with the things most dear to us, and ship the rest," averred Ina. "It'd be a safer way."

Hettie agreed wholly with Ina on the economic and practical aspects of the matter, and did not slight the romance, or the adventure side. In the end they convinced each other that the overland journey was the one they wanted to take.

"Leave Ben to me," concluded Ina.

"Oh, what will Marvie say to this?" added Hettie, with shining eyes.

As Hettie had suspected, her brother was not so easy to persuade as Ina had confidently anticipated. During the two days of this deadlock the affairs of the ranch went topsy-turvy. What time Ben was not listening and gradually weakening to Ina's importunities he lounged around the corrals, not in a very approachable mood.

At daylight on the third morning Ben pounded on Hettie's door.

"Wake up!" he shouted, gayly. "You'll make a fine wife for a pioneer."

"Oh, Ben, what's the matter?" cried Hettie, sitting up in alarm.

"Roll out. There's work to do, young lady."

"Are you—have you——" faltered Hettie.

"I reckon. We leave June first," he replied, deep-voiced.

"Overland?"

"Sure. And Marvie goes with us. Ina's father was pretty decent, for him. Agreed to let Marvie come with us for a year, on trial. I had to give my word of honor I'd send him back if he went wild."

"Marvie won't go wild—that is, not much," replied Hettie. "Oh, I'm glad! Ina loves him best of all her family. . . . Ben, then we're—really going?"

"You bet, unless you girls four-flush on me," rejoined Ben, and then he thumped away down the hall with rapid stride.

Hettie gave a little gasp and fell back on her pillow. She seemed suddenly weak. What a wonderful prospect, yet terrifying for all its thrill! Before she recovered Ina came running in, fully dressed, with wild dark eyes of radiance.

"Get up, you lazy girl," she said, hugging and pulling at Hettie. "It's all settled. Ben was over home till late. I was asleep when he got back. He woke me at four o'clock and told me he'd decided. We're to go overland. We'll have a regular wagon-train. Oh, I'm so excited I'm silly. . . . I believe it was Marvie who turned the scales. He can do anything with Ben—he's so like Nevada. Wasn't it bright of me to enlist Marvie in our cause?"

"Bright? You're wonderful! The Ide outfit wouldn't be complete without Marvie."

That dawn was the beginning of excited, full, strenuous days. Hettie did not know where the hours flew. If anything inspired her more than her own secret longing that she might meet Nevada out in Arizona, it was the interest and enthusiasm shown by her mother. They wasted as much time in choosing what to take as they worked hard and late in packing. Ben sold most of the furniture almost over their heads. As the first of June drew swiftly and fearfully on, Hettie realized she must spare time to see a few old school friends before she left. As it turned out, however, they called to see her.

Ben bought several new, large, deep-bodied wagons, which he had covered with canvas stretched over high hoops. One for Hettie and her mother, and another for himself, Ina, and Blaine, he had fitted out so that they made comfortable little rooms. What tingling pleasure Hettie derived from climbing into her wagon, that must be her home for weeks, possibly months! It was almost like, when she had been a little girl, playing at keeping house.

Wherefore furnishing this wagon-house proved both a joy and problem. Hettie arranged curtains just behind the wide driver's seat in front. The two single cots had a narrow aisle between them, which was covered with a strip of carpet. Underneath the cots Hettie stowed bags and boxes. At the rear of the wagon was space enough for a low chair, a bureau with mirror, a tiny washstand, and an improvised cloth-curtained wardrobe in which to hang clothes.

The morning of departure was like a nightmare for Hettie. But after she had passed through Hammell, which passing was in the nature of a parade, Hettie began to recover. Her mother lay quietly on her cot, wearied, but not manifesting any signs of deep grief. Hettie parted the front curtains and got out on the high seat with the driver, one of the older men, who had worked for the Ides as long as Hattie could remember. She did not want to cry, and thought that outside she might better keep from it.

A string of horses, mostly bays and blacks, among which California Red shone like fire in the sun, led the cavalcade up the long hill road. They were in charge of three of Ben's best riders. Next came the chuck wagon, and after it the one containing extra supplies, both of which were drawn by four horses. Ben's wagon came third, and Hettie's last.

She had a powerful impulse to look back, but she resisted it until they had passed over the hill. When at last Hettie turned to look her eyes were so wet that she had to wipe them so she could see. How far they had already come! The cluster of houses that constituted the village of Hammell lay at the foot of the long hill. Beyond widened the green valley, for miles and miles, with its threads of bright water and its shining remnant of lake, and the great squares of grain, waving in the wind. She located the Ide ranch, the fields, the barns, the dark patch of maples, the white house. Home! She was leaving it, surely forever. Yet she whispered to herself that she was glad to go; her heart had almost broken there; she would never return unless—unless . . .

Hettie had overestimated her powers of resistance. That one lingering last look back at Tule Lake was her undoing. She crept through the curtains again and sought her couch, where she hid her face and let emotion have its sway. Following that, a relaxation from the weeks of excitement and work set in, and she was glad to rest and sleep. Late in the afternoon she awoke, refreshed and calm, soon to feel a lively interest in the present.

At this juncture a halt was made for the first camp. Hettie saw that wagons and horses had stopped off the road in a level place where gnarled oaks stood far apart and a trickling stream wound between green banks. She walked here and there to stretch her legs, conscious of the return of a vague delight. She had always loved camping out, of which she had experienced but little. This indeed was to be a real camping adventure. The horses were rolling on the ground, in all kinds of violent action to scratch and dust their sweaty backs. Some of the more spirited animals were being hobbled. Ben was coaxing California Red with a nosebag of grain. The driver of the chuck wagon, who was also the cook, staggered under a load of firewood. Rolls of bedding were being thrown from another wagon.

When Hettie got back to her wagon and Ben's, which were close together, she found her mother, Ina, and Blaine all out, smiling and interested. Just then Marvie Blaine strode up with an ax on his shoulder.

He was a tall, well-built youth, freckled and homely, with fine clear eyes. He wore overalls, high boots, long spurs, and he packed a gun. Ina espied this latter simultaneously with Hettie.

"Marvie Blaine!" cried Ina, pointing at the gun. "What's that?"

"Why, my six shooter, of course!" retorted Marvie, with importance.

"What're you going to do with it?" queried his sister, in consternation.

"Ina, I'm sure not wearing it for ornament," replied the lad.

"Gracious! It might go off and hurt somebody!"

"Ahuh! That's the whole idea of packing a gun," replied Marvie, and strode on.

"Hettie, did you hear him?" asked Ina, wide-eyed.

"I sure did," said Hettie, with a laugh. "Marvie's awakened to reality."

"And Ben swore to dad he'd keep that boy from going wild," ejaculated Ina.

Ben, who approached on the moment, heard his wife's exclamation, and he picked up little Blaine to toss him up and catch him. "Ha! Ha! reckon here's another gunman in the making."

"There's nothing funny about that remark," said Ina, reproachfully.

Just then the cook came shuffling up to Ben, manifestly in a high state of dudgeon.

"Boss, your mother says she's a-goin' to do the cookin', an' thet I can wait on table an' wash dishes," he asserted.

"By George! I forgot about mother," rejoined Ben, struggling with his mirth. "Now, Hank, that's nonsense, of course. But you must use some tact. Mother wants to help along. Can't you let her putter around?"

"Putter, hell!" sputtered Hank. "She calls me dirty an' greasy—throws out my sour dough—an' snooks into everythin'. .... Now, boss, I'm a-goin' to quit."

"Hank, you wouldn't go back on me," returned Ben, in alarm. "Come, I'll talk to mother."

When Ben had gone with the irate cook, Ina and Hettie burst into merry peals of laughter.

"Hettie, I wouldn't have—missed this trip—for the world," said Ina.

"Neither would I. But I've begun to have glimmerings."

"Of what?" asked Ina, curiously.

"Of lots besides fun," replied Hettie, soberly.

Presently Ben returned, somewhat crestfallen. "By George!" he said, throwing off his sombrero and pulling at his dark locks. "I fixed it up, but I'm scared stiff. I reckon all camp cooks are more or less rough and not very particular. It's sure fire mother won't stand for dirt. She knows, too. I forgot she used to travel with dad years ago. She wouldn't even consider the plan Hank and I had agreed on—that we'd eat first, then the men. No, says mother. Waste of time and work. We'll all eat together."

"That's sensible," replied Ina.

"I am reminded that I'm starved," interposed Hettie.

"I's hungry," chirped up little Blaine, from the grass.

"We all are, son," agreed Ben.

Presently they were called to supper. The picturesque significance of that scene was vividly impressed upon Hettie—the smoking fire, and smell of burnt wood, the steaming pots, the new white tarpaulin spread under an oak, the hot biscuits, and sizzling bacon with its savoury fragrance; the tall, lean, dark-faced young riders, still in chaps and spurs; her mother, bustling and happy as Hettie had not seen her in years; young Marvie with his shining freckled face and conscious air; Ina, with violent eyes alight; and the tumbling, disheveled Blaine, at last in his element, and Ben, both gay with the zest of this journey and thoughtful with its responsibility.

Then after supper came the hour beside the camp fire. As dusk settled down and the night wind arose there were comfort and pleasant sensation in the heat from the red logs.

Hettie watched and listened, conscious of a mounting interest in all that pertained to this overland journey. The men talked with Ben about the practical details of travel, the need of shoeing a certain horse, the greasing of a wagon wheel, the night-watches, and especially of the road ahead.

"We'll have fust-rate goin' fer a couple of days," said Raidy, one of Ben's older hands. "I've been over this hyar road lots of times, far as Jefferson. We turn off, howsomever, about day after to-morrer. An' that road used to be a terror for a wagon. Over the foothills into Nevada. But I heerd in Hammell thet it's been improved by travel. There's new minin' towns sprung up, Salisbar is quite a town."

"How about that thar border place, Lineville?" asked one of the riders.

"I ain't never been there," replied Raidy. "All I know is hearsay. Reckon it's growed, too, along with the booms. But she shore was a wide-open town once. Not so long ago, either, as time goes. We'll hit Lineville along late the fourth day from hyar, if my figgerin' is correct an' we have any kind of travelin' luck."

"Boss, do you aim to go through Salt Lake City?" queried another.

"No. We'll strike Utah far south of Salt Lake," replied Ben.

"Then we don't hit Tombstone?"

"I'm not sure. How about that, Raidy?"

"We don't run into Tombstone," returned Raidy, "an' thet's jest as well. Our trail zigzags across Nevada, workin' down. Bad road, but passable. We go into Marysville, Utah. Thet burg is pretty far across the line an' pretty far south. Thar's a road from Marysville down over the line into Arizona, an' way around to a crossin' of the Colorado called Lee's Ferry. Mormons have been comin' across the head of the Grand Canyon thar fer years. Reckon we can travel whar any Mormons go, though thet country is said to be the grandest an' roughest in all the West. It'll save us a thousand miles."

When Hettie retired to her wagon that night she had

a clearer realization of the tremendous task of travel Ben had set himself. Almost it daunted her. But there came a strengthening and enduring memory.

Her little tent room was as cozy and comfortable as she could have wished. Evidently her mother had found it likewise, for she was fast asleep. Hettie prepared herself for bed, put out the lamp, and slipped into her blankets. The novelty and strangeness of the situation precluded sleep for the time being. She lay wide-eyed, staring at the flickering shadows on the canvas. After a while the low voices of the men ceased and the firelight faded. Black night and deep silence enfolded her. What had become of the horses? The wind swept through the oaks, now softly and again with a rush. She felt it blow cold through the curtains, fanning her cheek. Then lonely sharp wild barks made her flesh creep. Coyotes! She was on the edge of the wilderness.

Ben's cheery call seemed to rend Hettie's slumbers. To her dismay, she saw the sunlight gilding the canvas and that her mother had arisen without awakening her. Hettie made such haste that she was not late for breakfast. The men had eaten earlier, despite the law laid down by Mrs. Ide.

It was a wonderful moment when the horses came trooping in behind the yelling riders. After that all seemed action and noise, color and life. Breakfast over, Hettie helped in what few tasks she could find, then made her bed and was ready for the long day's ride. She found she had to kill time, however, while the horses were hitched and the chuck wagon packed. So she gathered wild flowers until Marvie rode up on her, proud as a peacock in his chaps and mounted on one of Ben's spirited horses.

"Hettie, you don't want to get left, do you?" he asked, gruffly.

"I should smile not, Marvie," she replied, secretly amused at him.

"Well, rustle to your wagon," he replied, and spurred his horse away.

Hettie watched the lad. He could ride. "I wonder," she mused. "Some Arizona girl will fall in love with him."

"Men, here's the deal," Ben was saying as Hettie reached the wagons. "We're in no hurry. Save the horses and stick close together. About mid-afternoon look for water and grass."

Then followed days that held increasing interest for Hettie. Once off the main road, swift progress would have been impossible, even had Ben desired it. The road was not merely rough, but narrow and dangerous. Yet it showed signs of considerable travel. But they met not a wagon or horseman going or coming.

The third day, while climbing the foothills Hettie grew tired of dust and heat and the brush that continually obstructed her view, and she sought the comfort and security of the inside of their little canvas home. Camp was made so late that darkness had intervened. The next day was hard, a long jolting ride downhill, with nothing to see but rough slopes, gullies, and dust.

They expected to reach Lineville in time to pitch camp early, but sunset had come and gone before they rode into a wide street lined by strange old houses, which constituted the border town. Hettie would have been more curious had she been less fatigued. As it was, the place gave her a queer sensation and she would far rather have gone on to camp in the open.

The wagons halted. Rough-looking men, some with picks and packs over their shoulders, passed by with bold eyes seeking out Hettie and Ina. Also she saw Chinamen peep from dark portals, and tall white-faced men in black garb and high hats stare fixedly at her. So she sought her tent.

Presently Ben poked his head between the curtains at the back of the wagon and said:

"There's a hotel here, but I reckon we'll dodge it.

It's called the Gold Mine. Raidy said it was a terrible dive once, an' it's pretty raw yet. But there's a woman has a nice place near the edge of town. We can drive in her yard and get our supper there. It'll be a little change and save waiting. The men will go on to a farm outside town and make camp."

Hettie peeped out to take a look at the Gold Mine. It was a drab low building, with vacant eye-like windows, the blinds of which seemed to hide secrets. Dark faces peered from a wide doorway.

"Ben, I'd rather not stay in this town," said Hettie.

"Reckon I'm not keen on that myself," replied Ben, with a laugh. "After supper we'll drive on to where the boys make camp."

Hettie did not look out again. The driver called, "Getdap" to his tired horses, and again the wagon rolled on. It relieved Hettie that some distance was traveled before they made another halt.

Darkness had fallen when again Ben called: "Come, mother and Hettie. Supper is ready. And I'll bet it'll be good, for I was in the kitchen. The woman's name is Mrs. Wood. She's a Westerner, all right, and likes to talk."

Ina was beside Ben, and he held the sleepy Blaine in his arms. The house apparently stood back in a large lot, surrounded by trees through which the wind roared. Ben led the way round to the side, where a bright light shone. They were ushered into a clean, warm kitchen, where in the light Hettie saw a stout, ruddy-faced woman who appeared most agreeable and kind. She had keen eyes that did not miss anything. Hettie liked her, particularly her solicitude for the weary little Blaine, who did not thoroughly awake until he was being fed. Hettie sat at the table, aware of the ample and appetizing supper, and hungry enough to do justice to it. But for some reason she could not eat much. She attributed her inhibition to a nervousness roused on the entrance into this border town. Yet she was seldom nervous.

Ben and Ida enjoyed the meal, and were not in the

least affected by any unaccountable something in Lineville. Ben particularly found the woman interesting. He kept asking questions. Hettie noted that, though Mrs. Wood appeared talkative in the extreme, she never made one query or showed any curiosity whatever.

"How long have you lived here?" asked Ben.

"Nigh on to six years now," she replied.

"Then you must have seen Lineville in its heyday?"

"I seen it when it was bad, if that's what you mean. Course Lineville ain't no Sunday school to-day, but, shucks! it's nothin' to what I've seen it. Lineville is a growin' town. We've got a school, post office, church, new stores, an' people comin', mostly people connected with minin' interests."

"Any cattle?" asked Ben.

"No. The cattle went with the rustlers," she replied, smiling.

"That's lucky for your town and for the ranchers over the range," laughed Ben.

"Yes, I guess so. But some rustlers weren't so bad, when you come to know them. All cattlemen on the open range are rustlers, if you know what I mean. I've met a pile of Westerners in my day, an' I've knowed worse men than rustlers. The gamblers, now, I've no use for them, though my husband was a gambler once, an' a gunman, too—years back in Texas an' New Mexico, where life was uncertain, I'll tell you."

"Raidy, one of my men, tells me life used to be pretty uncertain right here in Lineville, not so long ago," said Ben.

"Well, that depends upon experience," replied the woman. "Your man never seen any real frontier towns, such as old Dodge, an' Cimmaron, or Lincoln, or a hundred others. Not that there wasn't some real killers droppin' in Lineville now and then, years back. McPherson, a gambler an' a gunman, which was unusual for gamblers. An' Sandy Hall. He killed four men here once in a shootin' row. An' a miner named Hendricks. He was no slouch with a gun, either. Reckon, though,

Jim Lacy was the most dangerous man who ever struck Lineville."

"Jim Lacy?" said Ben, with interest. "I've heard of him, at least. What was he like? Did you ever see him?"

"See Jim Lacy! Why, he lived with me two winters," replied Mrs. Wood. "He used to set right there behind my stove an' talk for hours. Jim was only a boy. Somethin' like Billy the Kid, who I knew well. But Jim wasn't mean. He was just the quietest, nice, soft-speakin' fellar. Circumstances must have made Jim a gunman. He hailed from Idaho an' he was hell when he got riled. Jim killed several men here years back. The last one was a loud-yappin' coyote named Cawthorne. Link Cawthorne. He was the cheap notoriety-seekin', braggin' gunfighter. An' he was always tryin' to force Jim Lacy into a fight. Everybody knew Link'd get killed. But the fool himself couldn't see it. He beat a girl to death. Then Jim called him out an' shot him. After that Jim left for Arizona. I've never heard of him since."

"Arizona? That's where we are bound for," replied Ben, smiling. "We hoped to find the climate there beneficial. But if Arizona is full of Jim Lacys it might not be so healthy."

"Arizona or any other Territory would only be the better for men like Jim Lacy," returned the woman, rather brusquely.

"Reckon so. I was only joking," said Ben, as he arose. "We must be going. Thanks for a capital supper."

She received the money Ben proffered and led the way to the door, holding the lamp.

"Good luck to you, sir," she said. "It's a glorious country you're goin' to. But you'll lose this big-eyed sister of yours over there. . . . Good-by, little boy; you'll grow up on a horse in Arizona. Good-by, lady, an' you, miss."

Eight

The days multiplied until Hettie no longer could keep account of them. Endless leagues of Nevada, wastes of barren ground, plains of green, valleys between bleak ranges, ridge and upland ever heaving higher, lay back along the winding, rolling road.

"Boss, we're gettin' into the wild-hoss country," said old Raidy, one morning, when the caravan was about ready to start. "Yestiddy we seen herds of broomtails. An' the boys had their troubles. California Red had to be roped. An' I reckon, to-day, if you don't put him under a saddle we'll have to hawg-tie him."

"Fetch Red in," replied Ben, with a gleam of light flashing across his darkly tanned face. "I'll ride him and help drive the horses."

The road led over high country, where from every elevation the defiance of far-flung distances seemed to greet the travelers. A vast monotony like an invisible blanket covered the land. Gone were the towns, the mining camps, the lonely ranches of western and central Nevada. Away to the east and south stretched the desert solitude, day by day changing by almost imperceptible degree, gathering color and force, calling and beckoning toward some unseen yet promised infinitude.

Hettie Ide had come to touch happiness again, strangely, fearfully, as if these June days were dreams. The action and incident and life of such travel, day after day, with every mile bringing new scenes, with the future there beyond the purple ranges, satisfied a longing she had scarcely known she possessed. The dust and wind, the chill storms that blew down from the rocky heights, the rough descents and the slow uphill climbs, the rolling, rolling of the wagon wheels, the late camps and black nights, the work that it was imperative she share—all these did not pall upon Hettie. Rather they discovered some bond between her and the vague past and grew toward fulfillment of a need of her soul.

And in watching for and sighting the bands of wild horses she came at last to understand her brother Ben. His passion for wild horses that had almost been his ruin! But such conviction, so long her father's, and therefore accepted by family and friends, had begun to lose its hold on Hettie. Might not such love of horses and the open range, solitude, freedom, the hard fare and toil, the kinship with nature—might not these develop character to noble ends?

She saw the clouds of dust way out on the desert, under which dark moving bands of horses, with long manes and tails streaming in the wind, swept onward, to be swallowed by the gray obscurity. Black and sharp stood a stallion on a ridge top, silhouetted against the sky, to leap away and down, wildly instinct with freedom. On the cedar slopes, where the gnarled and stunted trees grew wide apart and the bleached dead grass waved over the outcropping green, wild horses grazed to start erect, lean heads high, ears and tails up, to stand like statues an instant, bays and buckskins, blacks and whites, with a pinto flashing like a zebra here and there, suddenly to bound into action and speed away.

"I know now why the boys call them broomies," Hettie told her mother. "Most of them have tails like brooms. Wild, ragged, scrawny horses! Yet some are sleek and graceful, long of tail and mane. And now and then I can pick out a beauty."

"I don't want to see any wild horses," replied Mrs. Ide. "I hope there'll be none where we settle down to ranch."

At times, on level plains or down long slopes, Hettie could see how Ben and the riders had almost to fight off wild stallions. How California Red glistened in the sunlight! He was in his element with the scent of his kind in his nostrils. Sometimes a piercing whistle floated back to Hettie.

The day passed as if it had flown, and Hettie recorded in memory pictures of lone stallions, and stragglers and strings and herds of wild horses numbering into the thousands. That night, far into the late hours, Hettie heard Ben's riders yelling and shooting, galloping in and out of camp. It was a hard night for them.

More wild-horse days, as Ben called them, passed and were added to the weeks. Then the colored rock walls of Utah rose above the long slopes of sage and greasewood.

Marysville at last! The Mormon town, far over the border into Utah, had been a Mecca for the riders. Here on the outskirts horses were rested, wagons were repaired, supplies were bought, and much-needed information secured.

"Yes, you can cross over into Arizona," an old Mormon told Ben in Hettie's hearing, while his keen eyes, like blue lightning, flashed over her. "Good road to Lund an' Kanab. Then you cross into the land of cliffs an' canyons. An' from there it's slow travel. Vermilion Cliffs, Buckskin, Rock House Valley, under the Paria Plateau, an' so on, down the Lee's Ferry an' the Canyon. When you reach there, stranger, you'll want to turn back. Better abide here with us, in this desert we've made blossom."

Hettie liked the black-hooded Mormon women, though she pitied them, and the unseen sealed wives the riders whispered about. The healthy happy children were most lovable. But when she saw the old white-bearded Mormons or the tall, still-faced, fire-eyed sons, she wanted to run back to the covert of her tent.

Then on again, rolling downgrade over a hard desert road, eating up the miles, the Ide caravan traveled, descending league-long slopes of red earth and green growths, with the red cliff walls keeping pace with them, and ever rising higher, as they wandered on down into the dim-hazed marvelous region of canyons.

Kanab was a lonesome Mormon settlement close to the Arizona line. Its white church stood out against the green background; orchards and fields encompassed log cabins and stone houses; irrigation ditches bordered the road on both sides. The sun smiled upon the fertile spot.

Arizona at last! Early the next morning Hettie heard that pealing slogan from Ben's lusty throat. What magic in a name! But as she gazed down the green-and-red hollow, thirty miles that looked like only three, up the purpling slope to the black fringe of Buckskin Plateau, where it flowed like a river of trees that merged into a lake of forests, and on to the grandly-looming Vermilion Cliffs, she marveled no more at the enchantment of that name. One long breathless look won Hettie Ide forever. After all the weeks of travel, the training of eye, the judgment of color and distance, she was confounded here on the border of Arizona.

"Oh, Ben," she called, "let us stop here!"

But Ben rode far ahead, ever thoughtful of his beloved horses. Hettie could see him gaze away down the wonderful valley toward the dim obscurity of the rock-walled fastnesses and again up at the vast frowning front of Buckskin.

At sunset the riders halted to camp in the edge of the pines, far above the valley which it had taken all day to cross. It had to be a dry camp, but the horses had been watered below. Hettie stood under the last pines and faced the west. She could not tell what it was that she saw. A glory of gold and purple cloud overhung a region of red rock, distant, broken, carved, where a lilac haze in transparent veils and rays spread from the sinking sun. She looked through that haze into an obscurity baffling and compelling, where shadows might be mountains and the purple depths beyond conception.

Then, as the pageant failed and faded, leaving her with a pang of regret, as if she had suffered actual loss, she turned to the forest and the camp. What magnificent pines! Black squirrels with white tails scurried over the brown-matted, bluebell-dotted ground. Marvie was to be seen prowling from tree to tree with his rifle. After so many camps on the desert, wide and open and windy, where camp fires were meager, and there was neither friendliness nor intimacy, how wonderful this temporary stand in the forest! Hettie had difficulty drawing her breath and the tang of pine seemed to clog her nostrils. Ben whistled as he brushed and combed his horse; the riders sang as they came in with bridles and nosebags on their arms; little Blaine, now like an Indian, gamboled about, and Mrs. Ide, as always, was bustling around the camp fire. Ina seemed busy at the back of her wagon. Hettie imagined they were nomads, gypsies on the march.

"Supper," sang out Mrs. Ide, cheerily.

"Come an' git it!" yelled Hank as if to outcall her.

"Marvie!" called Ben. His deep voice peeled down through the darkening aisles of the forest.

That night Hettie sought her bed early, exhausted in mind and body. But she did not at once fall asleep. Packs of coyotes surrounded the camp and kept up a continual howling, yelping, barking, whining. But what a wild, satisfying medley! Back on Tule Lake it had been an event for Hettie to hear one lonesome coyote, far off on the hills. On Buckskin Plateau it appeared the coyotes were many and bold. She was sure several ventured close to her wagon. At length they gradually worked away, until their wails and mourns died in the deep forest.

Hettie imagined she had prepared herself for Arizona. But next day, when riding horseback for a change, she emerged from the pines to the edge of the plateau, she was unable even to give an echo of Ben's stentorian long-drawn "WHOOPEE!"

Wild, beautiful, majestic, zigzagged the Vermilion Cliffs, towering over another and the vastly greater valley, softly, deeply purple, and sweeping away, widen-

ing like a colossal fan, out to the desert, where a ragged
rent in the earth, tremendous and awe-inspiring, told
Hettie she was gazing at the Grand Canyon.

From that moment time seemed to cease for Hettie
Ide. She let her horse follow the leaders, and rode
down and down, where neither dust nor heat meant
aught to her. The purple valley yawned and seemed to
swallow her. Lost was the sweep of the range and that
fascinating rent in the desert. The red wall towered on
the left, and on the right mounted the gray-sloped
black-fringed plateau.

Over the purple sage-flat strung out the cavalcade,
hour after hour, until another sunset halted the weary
travelers in a grass-green basin, where water salt to the
taste wound its gleaming musical way.

"Two more days, folks, and then the Rubicon!"
called out Ben, prayerfully, yet gayly.

"Wal, boss, what may thet there Rubicon be?"
asked Raidy as he wiped his grimy face.

"Lee's Ferry, man, where we cross the Colorado—
if we ever do."

"Son, we ain't crossin' any Rubies or ferries till we
come to them," relied Raidy. "I'm thinkin' luck is
with this Ide outfit."

"Not a horse lost yet, not a wheel slipped," returned
Ben, throwing up his head, like a lion tossing its mane.

"Wal, we ain't met any hoss thieves yet, or real bad
roads. But the Mormons say wait till we hit across the
canyon."

On the morrow, up out of the valley they climbed,
like snails; up out of the green to the dragging sand,
and toiled on ever nearer and nearer the grand jutting
corner of the red cliff that hid the desert beyond.

But at last they rode round under this colossal wall,
and Hettie Ide gasped. Desolation and ruin of earth
seemed flung in her face. Splintered and tumbled wall
of red wound down to a notch where the sinister red
river broke through; and on the other side, another
wall as red and ghastly, and lifting its rent and riven
front high to serrated crags, formed the far side of that

great Y-shaped pocket of the desert. No eye-soothing greens softened the glaring red and yellow. It was a pit of hell, from which the river gleamed through the split at the apex of the notch.

The sun beat down terribly hot. The red dust rose in clouds. Ever lifted the vast overhanging bulge of the plateau, from the ruins of which countless avalanches had crushed down, to litter the whole slope between wall and river with myriads of rocks, huge, sand- and wind-worn into grotesque shapes, adding to the ghastliness of this inferno.

Here the wagons crept along on slow-creaking wheels; here the horses lagged and the riders sagged in their saddles; here Hettie closed her eyes to shut out the glare, the dreadful decay and devastation, and the millions of glistening surfaces of rock, red and redder as the red sun sank to rest.

But before the afternoon light failed the travelers rounded the last corner of the wall, and Hettie opened her eyes upon a scene that seemed one of enchantment.

A rich dark green oasis lay deep down under lofty precipitous walls. On three sides these walls enclosed the oval acres of green, and on the other the sullen river swept by, as sinister as its surrounding confines, and slid swiftly on into the dark box-like canyon head, whence floated a bellowing roar of waters.

"Lee's Ferry," announced Raidy to the speechless onlookers. "An' the river's low. I was afeared of meltin' snow up in the mountains. There's the old scow we cross in. Wal, wal! if luck ain't settin' right in the saddle of this Ide outfit!"

Nine

It was late July and the long wagon-train journey had ended. The Ides were comfortably camped on a running brook in a grove of cottonwoods outside the little Arizona hamlet of Sunshine. Ben had secured a grazing permit for his horses on a ranch near by; and while his family rested, he scoured the ranges round about in search of a new home.

Hettie had never seen a man so full of zest and thrill over any project as Ben was in his search for a ranch in this amazing and glorious Arizona. His happy eagerness seemed reflected in all. But on the other hand, it turned out he had difficulty in finding a place which suited him.

"I want a thousand acres or more—five thousand if I can get them," he said. "Good water most important. Next I want grass and timber. Next a fine site for a ranch house, with a splendid view."

"Say, boss, you sure don't want very much a-tall," declared old Raidy, a little sarcastic. "Why, they hain't got all thet in this darned country."

Hettie shared Ben's enthusiasm, and encouraged him in his ambition. They had journeyed days up from the Colorado River to this high pleateau, where westward the gray-green range seemed like a vast ocean, waving away into purple distance. To the north and east it rose to dark red-banded mountains. Hettie loved the physical attributes of this bewildering Arizona, and so did Ina. But both of them were anxiously concerned about the wildness of the place, the aloofness of the few settlers, herders, riders whom they met, the fact that those mystic, forbidding mountains, seeming so close, were no other than the Mogollons, which Ben had been cautioned to avoid. Moreover, they were not so sure that he would make the wisest of business deals. Yet the buoyancy of his spirit, the change in him, and the undoubted improvement in Mrs. Ide's health, who had not been so active and happy for years, influenced Hettie and Ina not to discourage Ben and to resolve to stand by him, come what might. Added to this was the actual romance and appeal of this wilderness.

In the middle of the day it was very hot. The sun blazed down, burning face and hands. Yet it seemed to cast a dry heat that was bearable, even at its worst. Then, no matter how hot the sun, the shade was always cool. That seemed a strange property of this Arizona atmosphere. Anywhere in the shade it was cool. The sunshine was golden, the sky azure blue, the desert changeful at every hour, yet always dreamy, mystic, dim, and wonderful. At night the dark velvet dome of heaven burned with great white stars.

The little town, Sunshine, was on the railroad line and trains passed the Ide camp every day, to little Blaine's infinite delight. Hettie, too, found them a novelty and she never failed to watch them. Forty miles from Sunshine, down on a level bare reach of the desert, lay the town Winthrop. The Ides had stopped there a day. It was a stock-dealing and freighting town, with a main street on which saloons were remarkably numerous and prominent. Ben had preferred not to leave his family there, nor did he wish to advertise the fact that a rich Californian was looking for a ranch. They had stayed long enough in Winthrop, however, to ascertain that there were a number of good stores, two banks, a huge sawmill, workmen available, and a sprinkling of solid prosperous Westerners.

After an absence of three days Ben returned on the train late one afternoon, to descend upon his camp like a whirlwind.

Hettie, who first heard him, called out to Ina: "It's Ben. And you can bet we're settled now."

"Listen to him," replied Ina, in wondering gladness. "Well!"

They ran out to find him surrounded by his men, from whom, as Ina eagerly called, he broke away.

Whereupon she and Hettie and his mother were treated to bearish hugs, accompanied by various exclamations.

"Oh, gee! Oh, gee!" he continued, dragging them all to the camp table and benches under a cottonwood. "Give me a drink of water. I'm thirsty. And I've got to wash my hands and face. Hungrier than a wolf, too."

They waited on him, after the manner of loving women, plying him all the while with questions. Presently he flopped down on the grass and leaned back against the tree.

"I've bought my ranch," he said, with solemn finality, eying them.

Hettie and Ina regarded him in a momentous silence, but his mother spoke dryly: "Humph! we know that. I said you'd buy without even lettin' us women see the place."

"You'll all be crazy about it," he returned.

"Where?" asked Ina, slowly sinking on her knees in front of him.

"Sixty miles from Winthrop and about a hundred from here."

"How much land?"

"A thousand acres. Fine grazing all around. No other ranches near. Ten thousand head of cattle. Forty thousand dollars! Isn't that a bargain?"

"It remains to be seen. You've settled the deal, then?"

"I should smile," he replied, suiting the action to the words.

"Weren't you rather quick?"

"Yes. Had to be."

"Did you see all those ten thousand cattle? Count them?"

"Gracious, no! Ina, do you think I'm chain lightning? I took their word for it. The lawyer I engaged in Winthrop found the title of property okay. So I bought."

"Ben, I hope your ranch isn't out there—toward those Mogollons," said Hettie, breaking silence and pointing across the purple-hazed desert to the strange dark uplands.

"By George! Hettie, it *is*," he declared, smacking a hand on his knee. "It's right under the brakes of the Mogollons. But such a beautiful wild country. I couldn't resist it."

"Didn't you remember what your friend the sheriff said about the Mogollons?"

"I did, honest I did, Hettie," replied Ben, hastily. "But listen. I'll tell you all about it. . . . Day before yesterday I rode back to Winthrop after a hard and disappointing trip to half a dozen ranches. I was pretty discouraged and was coming back here pronto. Some horsemen rode up to the hotel where I was sitting out in front. They got off and tied up to the hitching-rail. I've gotten used to seeing these Arizonians. They're sure a rangy, hard-looking lot. But this outfit struck me as one to look at twice. Several of them packed two guns. They had fine horses and saddles. When they went in to drink I asked a cattleman sitting near me who and what they were. 'Wal,' he said, 'it ain't done in these parts—talkin' aboot your neighbors. Sort of on-healthy.' . . . Presently some one touched me on the shoulder. I turned round to see one of the riders, a tall fellow, blond and good-looking, not so young, but not old, either. He had eyes that looked right through you, but his manner was easy, friendly. 'Excuse me, sir,' he said. 'Are you the Californian who's lookin' for a ranch hereabouts?' "

" 'Yes, sir. My name's Ide,' I replied, 'and I'm not having much luck.' "

" 'They tell me you're hard to please. But I'm makin' bold to ask you personally just what kind of a ranch you want to buy?' "

"So I up and told him, elaborately, just what I was looking for. Then he laughed, sort of amused and, pulling at his long mustache, he said: 'My name's Burridge. I've got exactly what you want. Somewheres around ten thousand head. Lots of unbranded calves an' yearlin's. Cabins an' corrals not worth speakin' of. But water, grass, timber, an' range can't be beat in Arizona. It suits me to sell for cash. That's what they call me—Cash Burridge. Suppose you get a lawyer an' come over to the city hall an' see my title. Then if it strikes you right, I'll take you out to my ranch.'

"Well," went on Ben, reflectively, "Mr. Cash Burridge hit me about right. I liked his blunt way of putting the deal, and knew he didn't care a rap whether he sold or not. I consulted a lawyer recommended by the hotel man, and we met Burridge at the town hall. The title was clear. So I told Burridge I'd like a look at his property. We started right out in a buckboard behind a team of fast horses, I'll tell you. For thirty miles or more the road was good. Then we pitched off into what he called the brakes. Briefly, that part of the road was a terror. It was only a trail, up and down, narrow and rough. Burridge said there was a better way in, but longer. We reached his ranch before sunset. I'm only going to tell you that it was the most beautiful and wildest place I ever saw in my life. But the cabins were filthy, tumbledown huts. I slept out under the pines. This morning I was up before sunrise, and if I ever fell in love with anything, it is that place. It was on a high slope, with level benches reaching out, all covered with pines. I saw deer, wolves, bear, turkeys, antelope right from where I stood. Marvie will go crazy over the place. Also, everywhere I looked there were cattle. You can look out from the high pine benches down over the most beautiful valley of grass and sage and cedar, and then down into the red-and-gold desert, over a hundred miles away. Right there I asked Burridge how much he wanted. He said fifty thousand. On a venture I offered forty. He thought it over and took me up. We returned to Winthrop and closed the deal, at noon to-day. I had some hours to kill before train-time, so I strolled around into the stores and saloons. The last I saw of Cash Burridge was in a gambling hell, and from his look I gathered he was getting rid of some of his cash. I introduced myself to storekeepers as a prospective buyer and so gained their interest. But all of them were rather close-mouthed. They don't talk here in Arizona. One man told me Burridge probably had ten thousand head of stock. Then another man said Burridge didn't have so many, but it was hard to tell. The truth is I didn't get much satisfaction. I called to see a Mr. Franklidge, the largest cattle-owner in these parts, and also president of the bank. But he wasn't in. Now to wind up, I figured Burridge would be shy a lot of cattle on that number he gave—perhaps a thousand head or more. That is a wide margin for any kind of a cattle deal, and I'm more than satisfied. I'll make that the finest ranch in Arizona. We'll go out there at once and camp, and start the work of home building. If I don't miss my guess, you'll all fall in love with it as quickly as I did."

"I have already, Ben," was Ina's reply. "What you love I love. Your home is my home."

"Ben, am I in on this ranch deal with you?" asked Hettie, gravely.

"That's for you to say, my dear sister," replied Ben. "But I believe I'd rather you didn't come in, for it is a risk."

"Then if Ina has no objection, I'll take the risk."

"So will I. We'll share the risk, and together make a grand success of it," added Ina, happily.

Ben hired a guide from Winthrop to lead his horses and riders across country to the ranch. On the next day the wagons made Winthrop, where Ben expected to meet Burridge, as agreed. But Burridge failed to appear. Ben said this was strange, as Burridge was due to take his outfit over the better road and to make a count of the cattle, but it was not so strange, nor half so illuminating, as the glances Ben encountered when he mentioned Burridge casually to bystanders in Winthrop.

Whereupon Ben procured another guide, a Mexican

sheepherder, who guaranteed to pilot the heavily-laden wagons safely to their destination.

The four horse teams made good time over the open desert road, reaching the brakes some thirty miles out by sundown.

Hettie was enthralled by the sunset over the yellow sloping land and the weird mountains to the west. A storm had been gathering all day in that direction. The atmosphere had been sultry. Toward late afternoon the clouds coalesced and hung over the black ranges, so that when the sun set, the reds and golds and purples, heightened by the exquisite light, were lovely beyond compare. At dusk sheet lightning flared low down across the sky, and faint rumblings of thunder rolled along the battlements of the desert.

Next morning the travelers rode into rough forest land, where the main grade was uphill, but the apology for a road plunged down so often into dry hot ravines that the general ascent had to be taken for granted.

The forest consisted of cedars, oaks, piñons, and scattered pines, all of which grew more abundant and larger, sturdier as the caravan progressed. Travel was exasperatingly slow. In some places the road was not safe, and the women had to get out and walk. Ridges like those of a washboard sloped irregularly down from the south; outcroppings of limestone showed on the gully banks, pools of water gleamed in the shady washes. Open sandy flats, where the horses labored, had to be crossed. At length the cedars and piñons gave place to a heavier growth of pines. Here the real forest began, and except for the difficulty of travel, it was vastly satisfying to Hettie. She had her first view of wild deer and wild turkeys. Marvie reacted to sight of this game as might have been expected. For that matter, Ben leaped off his wagon, gun in hand. The progress of the train had to be halted while the hunters stalked the game. Soon shots reverberated throughout the forest. Ben returned empty-handed, but Marvie, with face glowing, exhibited a fine gobbler.

Only fifteen miles were covered that day, and everybody was wearied and glad to make camp. Before sleep came to Hettie she heard a blood-curdling cry of a wild beast unknown to her. It seemed a deep far-away moan, so sad and uncanny that she shuddered. Next morning Ben told her the cry had come from a timber wolf, a beast the guide called a lofer and said was plentiful in those parts.

Tedious travel began into an ever-increasingly wild and wonderful woodland. The trees hid any possible view of the country beyond. The air grew clearer, less oppressive, and the heat no longer made the shade desirable. Massed foliage, like green lace, dark-brown seamed boles of pines, patches of sunlight on the white grass, the red of a tufted flower, like a stiff brush dipped in paint, and golden aisles of needles up and down the forest, held for Hettie a never-failing delight.

About the middle of the afternoon the travelers rode to the edge of open light forest.

"We're here," shouted Ben, leaping down. "California to Arizona! . . . Ina—mother—Blaine—Hettie, get down and come in, as these Arizonians say."

"Gee! I see turkeys!" cried Marvie, leaping off his horse and tearing his rifle from the saddle sheath.

"Indian!" called Ben, after him.

Hettie sat under a great spreading pine on the edge of one of the level benches that sloped down into the open sage and cedar country.

She had tramped around until exhausted. A bubbling spring that gushed from under a mossy rock in a glen had held her only long enough to yield her a drink. She had passed by the long-unused and dilapidated corrals, and the ruined old log cabin which Ben had laughingly told the stricken Ina was to be their abode. The brook that came singing down from the dark forest slope above caused Hettie to linger and listen to its music. Across the brook on another bench stood another old log cabin, or in fact two small one-roomed cabins, with porch between, and all sheltered under one long sloping wide-eaved roof of rough moss-stained shingles. The picturesqueness of this woodland structure appealed to Hettie. Warily she peeped in, with vivid sense of the vacant speaking rooms and tumbled-down stone fireplaces, and the lofts that reached out over half the rooms. What had happened there? How dark, musty, woody!

"I'll make this my abode and mother's," she decided, with a thrill at the prospect of home-building. "Repairs, windows, floors, sheathing! Oh! I can see it! I'll not have a new house."

And so at last she had found herself on the edge of the wide bench, back against the last pine, with fascinated gaze riveted upon the view that Ben had raved about.

"No wonder!" whispered Hettie. "If there were nothing else, *that* would be enough."

Her position was on the edge of the irregular timber line, which stretched on each side of her, with fringes of the forest here running down to end in straggling lonesome pines, and there skirting the edge of the steep benches, as if the greatest of landscape gardeners had planted them there. And so he had, Hettie averred! What majestic pines! How the summer wind roared above and back of her, now low, now high, deepening upward with the denser growth of forest!

But it was the desert that enchanted Hettie. For she doubted not that the edge of the bench where she sat was the edge of the desert. Yet how soft, how marvelously purple and gray, how grandly the slope fell for league on league, widening, rolling, lengthening, descending, down to the blazing abyss of sand and rock and canyon.

Sage and grass in the foreground gave that vast valley its softest beauty, its infinite charms, its mistiness and brilliance, as if drenched with dew. How like troops of great beasts appeared the isolated green cedars and the lonely jutting rocks, some gray, others red. This valley was a portal down to the dim unknown. On each side it swelled to ranges of foothills, themselves like trains of colossal camels trooping down to drink. They were rounded, soft as clouds, gray and pink and faintly green, without a tree, a rock to mar their exquisite curve. From the dignity of low mountains these hills dwindled in size until they were mere mounds that at last flattened out into the desert.

Every time Hettie moved her absorbed gaze from one far point to another of the valley, the outlines, the colors, the distances, the lines of lonely cedars, the winding black threads of gullies—all seemed to change, to magnify in her sight, to draw upon her emotion, and to command her to set her eyes upon that sublime distance, that etheral blending of hues and forms, that stunning mystery of the desert, of that magnificent arid zone which gave this country its name.

"I can only look—and learn to worship," whispered Hettie, in a rapture. "It awakens me. What little have I seen and known! . . . Oh, lonely wild land—oh, Arizona! if you shelter *him* my prayer is answered, my cup is full!"

The Ides, imbued with Ben's spirit, set earnestly to work to wrest a beautiful home from this wilderness.

Two gangs of Mexican laborers, lent by the railroad, in the charge of capable men, were put to work clearing and grading a road, felling and hauling timber. Teamsters from Winthrop made a trip out every other day, bringing lumber, shingles, windows and doors, bricks and cement, pipe and plumbing, which were housed in a temporary shelter. Carpenters began to erect Ben's house, which was to be a long, one-story structure, with log walls, high peaked roofs, wide porches. Barns and corrals were planned, a reservoir from which the cold spring water could be piped into the houses and corrals, corn cribs and storehouses, and many other practical things Ben considered necessary.

Those were busy days. The work caused almost as much interest as a circus might have. There were many visitors, mostly sheepherders and cowmen from the surrounding range. Occasionally riders on high-gaited horses rode in, watched the work from a distance, looked long at Ben's fine horses, and especially California Red, and rode away without any pretense of friendliness. Old Raidy shook his head dubiously at sight of these men. Apparently they caused no concern to Ben. Hettie imagined that she alone divined what was going on in her brother's mind. She dared not voice it, but in her own secret thoughts she hugged it to her heart. She believed that Ben had deliberately chosen this wild spot in a wild range to develop a famous ranch, which would become a lodestone for cowboys, ranchers, cattlemen of all types, sheepmen, rustlers, outlaws, gunmen, through one of whom he might locate his lost friend Nevada. Hettie was convinced of this. It thrilled her very soul. What a reckless, yet grand thing for a man to do in search of his friend!

Hence, Hettie decided, Ben's intense interest in all visitors did not spring wholly from his desire to be neighborly. Yet, despite the good words that at once spread abroad his generosity and kindliness, and the fact that his coming meant much for this section of Arizona, the ranchers along the three hundred miles of the Mogollon Plateau were slow to call.

Nor did Cash Burridge come to count the cattle he had sold Ben. This omission caused Raidy and the riders from California much concern. They began to make dark hints round the camp fire, and were not particular about who heard them. Ben looked serious, but only laughed. Manifestly he was working and waiting, without worrying.

One hot midday, during the noon rest hour, when Ben and his family were having lunch in the shade of the pines, a rider appeared on the road. He came on at a walk and he was looking everywhere with great interest. Finally he took to the slope, and at length, arriving at the camp quarters, he dismounted and hailed the riders in a booming voice.

"I'm Tom Day an' I'm wantin' to meet Mr. Ide."

Raidy led him up to Ben, who rose expectantly, a smile on his sunburnt face.

"Howdy, sir!" said the visitor, extending a huge hand. "Are you Mr. Ide?"

"Yes, and I'm glad to meet you, Mr. Day," replied Ben, who evidently had heard of this man.

"I'm your nearest neighbor," said Day. "My ranch is over heah ten miles or so. Reckon I'm a little late in callin'. Shore we're pretty slow folks in Arizona."

"Better late than never," returned Ben, with his frank smile. "Meet my family, Mr. Day. . . . This is Ina, my wife . . . and this is my mother. . . . Hettie, my sister. . . . And this is my son Blaine, who's destined to be an Arizona rancher."

"Wal now, I'm shore glad to meet you-all," drawled the visitor, with an accent so surely Texan that it made Hettie's heart leap. He greeted them with a quaint courtliness that became him well, despite his rough soiled rider's garb. He made much of little Blaine, whom evidently he won at first sight.

Hettie, too, trusted him at first sight. This huge rancher was surely a Texan. He had a shock of fair hair, beginning to turn gray. His broad face was wrinkled like a brown parchment, recording the endurance, toil, and strife of a wonderful life. He had shrewd, penetrating, kindly eyes, light blue in color, and set under bushy brows.

"Reckon I'd like you to show me aboot," said Day to Ben, waving his hand toward the benches.

"I'll be glad to, and I'd like your opinion on some of my new-fangled ideas," replied Ben. Then he turned to Hettie. "Sis, have Hank fix us up something to eat and drink presently."

They strolled away in earnest conversation and did not return for an hour. Whereupon Hettie set lunch for them on the table under the fly; after which she repaired to her wagon-tent close by.

"Ide, the good looks of thet sister of yours has spread over the range," said Day. "Shore, she's a lovely lass."

"Hettie? Thanks. Yes indeed, and she's more than pretty," replied Ben, evidently much pleased.

"Girls are scarce in Arizona. Is she married?"

"No. Why, Hettie's only twenty!"

"Engaged to any lucky fellar?"

"No, I'm sure not."

"Wal, she'll shore have these long-legged punchers comin' around moon-eyed."

"If they don't they're not like my California riders," laughed Ben.

"Wal, I'll say if them riders of yours are as good at makin' love as they are at gossipin', our Arizona lads won't have much chance."

"I'm afraid my men do talk too much," observed Ben, seriously. "They brag, and I don't believe bragging will get very far in Arizona."

"Wal, only so far as makin' brag good," drawled Day. "Ide, I reckon I've taken a shine to you. It ain't Arizona ways, but somebody ought to give you some hunches. Reckon I never had such an idee when I rode over heah. I was downright curious, but reckon I expected to find you-all different."

"Mr. Day, I take that as a compliment and an offer of friendship," returned Ben heartily. "I was told in Winthrop to try to make friends with you. Lord knows I'm going to need a friend out here."

"Wal, heah's my hand," said Day, "an' I'm shore seein' you're not such a dam' fool as is bein' gossiped over the range."

"Maybe I *am* a damn fool, Day," returned Ben, grimly. "But at least I know what I'm going to do in the long run."

"Shore then you figger you're up ag'in a hell of a deal heah?" queried Day.

"You bet I know it. I expected it and I'm not going to be disappointed."

"All right. Thet's good talk to me. Fust off, are you goin' in for big cattle-raisin'?"

"Yes. And horses, too."

"Ahuh. You shore have some fine stock. Thet red

hoss! Say, he's grand! Reckon you'll have to keep him close or he'll be stolen. . . . Are you goin' to keep your family heah all the year round?"

"No. I'll take or send them back to California for the winter."

"Thet's good," replied Day. "The winters are bad some seasons. Not so cold, but it snows deep an' pens people up. Winter don't come, though, till late December. Why, I've seen Christmas heah the finest kind of weather!"

"That's splendid news. Now, Day, you encourage me to ask questions. Can you put me on to some crack Arizona cowboys? I'll keep Raidy and perhaps another of my riders, and send the others home."

"Shore I was goin' to advise thet. You'll have no trouble hirin' the best men out heah, because you can pay better wages. Our riders only get forty dollars, an' often not thet."

"But how am I to know riders who are honest, not to mention other qualifications?"

"Son, you're shore askin' me a question thet even Franklidge, the boss rancher of this country, cain't answer. I'm sorry to have to confess thet. But the honest Gawd's truth is this—nobody heah knows who's a rustler an' who's not."

"Good Heavens! Day, you don't mean that!" cried Ben, shocked.

"Wal, I shore do. I know for a fact I'm a square cattleman. I've branded calves in my day thet wasn't mine an' I knowed they wasn't. Every rancher has done thet, an' few there are in this neck of the woods who don't do it now. But I don't. Thet you can rely on, Ide, I swear. There are ranchers heah who suspect me, same as I suspect them. For this reason: Rustlin' cattle is a mighty big business along the three hundred miles of Mogollon range. The country grazes hundreds of thousands of cattle. They reckon Franklidge alone has a hundred thousand haid. Wal, it's great pickin' fer the rustlers. There's the Hash Knife gang, heah for many years. There's the Pine Tree outfit, which is newer an' wuss. An' no *honest* rancher can name the leader of thet outfit. He's shore some one of us ranchers, shore as hell. Then there's a host of lesser rustlers clear down to the cowboy who's startin' a herd of his own. . . . Thet, Ide, is the country you've come to ranch in."

"Well, I'm a son-of-a-gun!" ejaculated Ben.

"Shore you are. I wish I could have met you before you laid out so much money heah. How many cattle did Burridge sell you?"

"Ten thousand head," replied Ben. "I took his word. But at the same time I figured if he was a thousand head or so shy I'd be satisfied."

"Wal, you figgered good, but not good enough," said Day, gruffly. "Never take no man's word for a count of cattle. You want to see them brands. Burridge, now, had a half a dozen brands, but he never had no ten thousand, nor eight thousand, nor . . . Nobody could ever tell how many haid he ran. He was always sellin' cattle."

"What do you think of Burridge failing to make a count for me? He promised to do so at once."

"Wal, I don't like to say what I think. But if Burridge shows up soon an' makes a count, it'll be a good deal more than I have any idee he'll do."

"He'll not come," said Ben, decidedly. "Day, there's no doubt in my mind. Burridge has cheated me."

"Wal, don't you say thet to anyone else around heah," warned Day. "Be careful *what* you say, Ide. An' make your men keep their mouths shut. I'll let you have two of my boys, an' I can get you another. For all I know they're square, an' they're shore hard-ridin' an' hard-shootin' punchers."

"That's good of you, Day," responded Ben, with gratitude. "I sure appreciate it. I may be able to do you a favor now and then, since we're neighbors."

"I'm wonderin' about somethin', yet there ain't any sense in me doin' it."

"What?" asked Ben.

"Shore, Burridge didn't tell you thet I had a four-thousand-dollar lien on his cattle?"

"No, he sure didn't," returned Ben, shortly.

"Wal, I have. Soon after he come heah—let's see, about four years ago, I lent him the money. He paid interest for a while, then he quit, an' I was after him pretty hard when he sold out to you."

"That's bad news, Day," said Ben, soberly.

"Wal, I reckon, but don't let it worry you none, so far as I'm concerned. But there's wuss. The Hatts also have a lien on Burridge's stock."

"Well, well! this is getting thick. Who are the Hatts?"

"Father an' three sons. There's a girl, too, pretty young lass, the only decent one of a bad lot."

"Where do these Hatts live?"

"They're backwoodsmen an' live back in the brakes. Fact is all the rustlers an' outlaws hole up in these brakes, which are rough canyons runnin' down from the Mogollons. Rough they are, the hardest goin' in Arizona. It used to be Apache country."

"So Burridge palmed his debts off on me? Damn him! . . . What's the law in such a case as this?"

"Wal, I've knowed it come up in court more'n once. An' the buyer had to settle. You see, Burridge's property wasn't really his to sell."

"I appreciate that. I should have taken time to inquire. But he struck me right."

"Shore. He did the same to me, an' I'm an old timer."

"What the devil shall I do, Day? I don't mean about the liens. I'll have to settle them, soon as they are proven. But this deal shows up more complicated every day. How many cattle do I actually own? Where are they? How will I go about safe-guarding what I do own?"

"Son, the Lord himself couldn't answer them questions," replied the rancher, with his booming laugh. "But I reckon the case ain't so bad thet we'll have to take to drink about it. I'll ride over with these boys I'm gettin' you, say week today. Meanwhile I'll do a lot of thinkin'. Probably by thet time Elam Hatt will have seen you. I heerd he was comin', so look out fer him. We'll get your men an' we'll all put our haids together."

"Thank you very much, Day," rejoined Ben, most gratefully. "It's sure lucky for me that you came over."

"Wal, mebbe it's lucky fer me, too," said Day. "One more hunch before I go, an' I shore must be rustlin' home. There'll be other ranchers callin' on you, an' some of them will talk deals. Go slow. Don't offend, but don't go in anythin' without consultin' me."

"By George! you needn't caution me about that," returned Ben. "I'm too scared. Why, my wife and sister will have a fit when they find out how Burridge fooled me!"

"Wal, my advice is don't tell your wimmin-folks. What they don't know shore won't hurt them."

"But I should tell you my sister Hettie is in on this deal with me. She wanted a half interest, but I let her have only one third. Thank goodness!"

"Thet big-eyed lass! She must have a lot of money."

"Hettie is well off, yes. She's clever, too. I wish I had listened to her."

"Wal, wal! Thet lass—handsome an' rich! Golly! Some cow-puncher is shore goin' to fall into heaven. I wish I was a youngster. Reckon as it is I'll have to pick out the best fellar heahaboots fer her."

"I'm advising *you* now," laughed Ben. "Don't try that with Hettie, if you want her to like you."

"Thanks fer the hunch, Ide. . . . Wal, I said before I must be goin', an' heah I am yet."

"There's one thing—I—nearly forgot," said Ben, with hesitation and change of tone. "You must know everybody in Arizona?"

"Lord, no, son! Why, Arizona is most as big as the rest of the United States! But I'm pretty well acquainted all through heah."

"Did you ever know or hear of a—a fellow who—who went by the name of Nevada?"

Ben's voice shook a little, and that tremor was communicated poignantly to Hettie, who sat listening in her tent.

"Nevada?" queried Day, thoughtfully.

"Yes, Nevada. It was a nickname, of course. I never knew his—this fellow's other name."

"Humph! Somebody who did you a bad turn?"

"No indeed. I—reckon it was the other way."

"Wal, I'm sorry. Nevada? No, I never heerd thet handle on a fellar in my life. I've a good memory fer names. I've knowed a heap of Arizonie's in my time, an' Texas Jacks, an' Colorado somethin's or other. But no Nevada."

Ten

Some eighteen or twenty miles from Tom Day's ranch, Judge Franklidge maintained the last outpost of his extensive cattle range south of the railroad toward the Mogollons.

This property, called the Chevelon Ranch, as had many another, had come into his possession by the failure of a homesteader. At some time or other Franklidge had lent money or staked cattle to every poor settler in that part of Arizona. His kindness and generosity had for many years made him a mark. But though he had never been known to drive a hard bargain or force a payment, he had prospered through most all of his transactions. Chevelon Ranch, however, was a losing proposition so far as actual cattle-raising was concerned.

The hundred and sixty acres which comprised the ranch lay in a strip along the rim of Chevelon Canyon, one of the deep wild gorges that constituted part of the brakes of the Mogollons. Here the cedar piñon forest was at its thickest, and a little higher and farther south it merged into the belt of pines. Water was abundant, but it was down in the canyon and had to be pumped up. When the pump did not operate the water had to be packed up.

Cabins and corrals, built of logs, showed the weathering of years of storm and heat. The main cabin stood on the rim, and the wide porch ran to the edge of the gray rock wall. On this mid-August afternoon the porch was a shady and cool place to lounge and rest. The deep canyon was densely green with oak and cedar; a low roar of running water floated dreamily from the depths; the drowsy summer air was redolent with a sweet dry fragrance.

Judge Franklidge had just arrived on one of his rare visits to this margin of his vast cattle interests. The long hot dusty ride out from Winthrop had tired him, and with a great sigh of content he sank into one of the comfortable seats on the porch.

"Jack," he said to the cowboy who had driven him out, "I'm to meet Day here. Put the horses up. I'll stay all night. Then find Day if he's arrived, and come back yourself."

"Yes, sir. An' how aboot Stewart?" replied the cowboy.

"Stewart? Tell him I'll send word when I want him," returned the judge, somewhat impatiently.

"All right, sir," said Jack, and slapping the reins he drove away toward the barn.

"Humph! I'd forgotten about that foreman," muttered Judge Franklidge. "Damn the cattle business, anyway. . . . I'd like to forget it and enjoy the peace of this place."

This ranch was a favorite with Franklidge, owing to its wild beauty and solitude and the abundance of deer and turkey that ranged the forests. Every fall he came there for a few days of hunting.

"I'll invite young Ide to hunt with me in October," he soliloquized, "Fine chap that. Too bad about the rotten deal he fell into here. It sure doesn't speak well for Arizona. And what a lovely girl that sister of his! . . . If I were younger now . . ."

The Judge fell into a daydream that amused as well as made him sigh. Presently a jangle of spurs and thud of footsteps interrupted his reverie, and he looked up to see Tom Day and the cowboy approaching. Day had his hand on the younger man's shoulder and was talking earnestly. That reminded the judge of the strong friendship Day had always evinced for this young man the range called Texas Jack. How good to see two men he could swear by!

"Howdy, Judge! I'm shore glad to see you," said

Day, as he heavily mounted the porch with beaming smile and extended hand.

"How are you, Tom? Pull up that bench. We're in for a good long talk."

"Wal, it's aboot time," returned Day, as he deposited his huge bulk on a seat, with back to the porch rail. He threw his sombrero to the floor.

The judge laughed, and then glanced sharply at the cowboy waiting at the step.

"Jack, you've got something on your mind," he said.

"Yes, sir, but it can wait. No hurry, sir," replied the cowboy, hastily.

"Wal, Judge, if you'll take a hunch from me you'll not wait too long," interposed Day.

"Come up and sit in with us, Jack," was Frank-lidge's reply.

The cowboy did as he was bidden, but he made no reply. He sat near the porch rail and leaned over to gaze down into the green canyon. The judge's apprais-ing eyes took stock of the lithe figure, the service-worn garb, the lean bearded face that was half hidden under the wide sombrero.

"Stewart was in town last night, drunk," spoke Franklidge, casually. "Is he here to-day?"

"Yes, sir—an' he's all right now," rejoined the cow-boy.

"Judge, your foreman *may* be all right, as Texas Jack says, but I've my doubts," put in Day. "I cain't find anythin' ag'in' him, 'cept the drinkin'. But I've just come to distrust the man. Mebbe I'm wrong. It shore is a distrustful time."

"Mr. Franklidge, I hunted up Stewart, an' found him an' Dillon off under a cedar, talkin' deep an' quiet," said Texas Jack.

"Dillon? Who's he? That name's familiar."

"Dillon is young Ben Ide's foreman," replied Day, with interest. "He's held jobs all over the range the last two years. Fine cowman. Engagin' sort of chap. Everybody likes him. I shore do."

"Which ought to be recommendation enough for Ide or even me, sore old cattleman that I am. . . . Well, Tom, have you considered the offer I made you some time ago?"

"Reckon I have, Judge, an' I'm acceptin' with thanks. I know I'm gettin' the best of the deal," returned Day, heartily.

"We're not agreed on that. You're counting only the relative value of your ranch compared with this one. But I count your friendship and help. . . . It's a deal, then."

"Heah's my hand, Judge," said Day, reaching out his huge paw.

"We're partners, then," replied Franklidge, as he shook the proffered hand. "We'll throw these ranches and all the stock together. I'll have papers made out when I get back to town. . . . Now get what's troubling you off your chest."

"Wal, boss, the situation heah has grown from bad to wuss," returned Day, seriously.

"Where do you mean by here?" demanded Franklidge.

"All this range thet haids along the wild brakes of the Mogollons. Say, fifty miles in a straight line."

"Yes?"

"Reckon it takes in a good many ranches, countin' everybody, an' mebbe two hundred thousand haid of cattle. But Ben Ide's range an' this one of yours an' mine have come in fer the wust of the rustlin' this last month."

"We've always had rustlers to deal with. We always will have. What's the difference between say a year or five years ago and now?"

"Wal, Judge, fer a big cattleman you're shore poor informed."

"Tom, you know most of my holdings lie along the railroad and north in the open country. I know next to nothing about what goes on in this backwoods. That's why I wanted you for a partner."

"The difference you asked aboot I'd calkilate off-hand to stand you an' me an' Ben Ide around ten thousand haid."

The Judge's boots came down off the porch rail with a crash.

"What?" he demanded, incredulously.

"Boss, I said ten thousand, an' mebbe thet's conservative. Shore most of this rustled stock belongs to Ide. But we've lost a good deal, an' stand to lose more or all unless somethin' is done. You see, Ide proved an easy mark. He bought out Burridge, who had some stock, nobody knows how much. Wal, young Ide's cow outfit was green an' raw for Arizona. I gave him two of my best riders. One of them, Sam Tull, was found daid in the woods. Shot! We've never found out aboot it. The other cowboy, Rang Jones, had a quarrel with Dillon an' quit. I cain't see thet Dillon has changed matters fer the better. But I reckon no one man could at this stage of the game."

"So they've hit young Ide hard," muttered Franklidge, indignantly. "Funny he didn't complain to me. I've seen something of him lately."

"Ide's not thet kind, Judge," replied Day, warmly. "He's as game as they come. An' his sister—say, she's a thoroughbred. She stands to lose 'most as much as Ide."

The two men, warming to the subject, might have been alone for all the notice they took of Texas Jack. He leaned far over the porch rail, his face hidden, his long lithe form strung like a whipcord. It was the strained position of a listening deer.

"Tom, I admire Miss Ide very much indeed, and her brother, too," responded the judge. "I regret exceedingly the reception Arizona has given these two fine young people. I am ashamed. We all ought to be ashamed. We must end this damned wholesale cattle-stealing."

"Ahuh! . . . Boss, I reckon I feel it more than you, as I've come to be friends with the Ides. Why, he paid Burridge's debt to me. Four thousand! An' then I'm a son-of-gun if he didn't send for Elam Hatt an' pay the lien he had on Burridge. Don't know how much. But the Hatts were drunk fer a week."

"Well!" ejaculated Franklidge.

"Every since then the rustlers have been bolder than I ever seen them yet in Arizonie."

"Who are these rustlers, Tom?"

"Huh! If I said what I think it'd be old to you. But I reckon there is a new leader workin' now. Shore they're all workin'. But there's some big chief who's keen as a wolf."

"Where are these stolen cattle driven?" asked the judge, wonderingly. "I've been twenty years in this business. Yet this beats me."

"Reckon the stock gets drove everywhere," replied Day.

"Not to the railroad?" queried Franklidge, aghast.

"Shore to the railroad. Not to Winthrop. But, man, there's other stations along the line. Then I had a Mexican sheepherder tell me he'd seen herds of cattle drove over the Rim, down into the Tonto. Thet's a wild country. Shore no cow outfits are followin' rustlers down into the Tonto."

"Tom, the Hatts are a bad outfit," rejoined the Judge, thoughtfully. "Some years ago I had trouble with Elam Hatt. The Stillwells are another. Surely these backwoodsmen run with these rustler outfits."

"Shore they do," snorted Day. "But I reckon the Hatts ain't the ringleaders. Cedar Hatt is the wust of thet bad lot. He's dangerous. Bad *hombre* with guns! Ever' once in a while I heah of some shootin' scrape he's been in out there, among his own kind. The Mexican herders are afraid of Cedar. But they're close-mouthed. In the years I've lived heah I've known of several sheepherders bein' murdered."

"Cedar Hatt?" mused the Judge. "Yes, I know of him. Bad name; gun-fighter. . . . How many Hatts in the family?"

"I know the whole outfit," replied Day. "Elam an' me always got along pretty good. But I've no use fer Cedar. He's the eldest son. Then there's Henny an'

Tobe—packrats if I ever seen any in the woods. An' last there's a girl—Rose. Reckon she'll be aboot sixteen. Pretty slip of a lass, whose mother died when she was a baby."

"What a pity! No mother. No decent home. No schooling. There are many such unfortunate girls in this wild country, alas! Why don't some cowboys take this Rose away and marry her? She might turn out a good woman."

"Shore she might, An' so I've said often. But I ain't hit on any cowboy yet who cared to risk his skin down there in the brakes."

"What has Ide done in regard to the raids on his stock?" asked the judge, curiously.

"Aboot all any man could," replied Day, admiringly. "He has spent a lot of money hiring extra hands to trail stock. He took over this Dillon at a high salary. An' I reckon he puts a good deal of confidence in Dillon. Funny about Ben Ide, though. He gets sore when the rustlers make a raid. But he really don't care a damn aboot the cattle. He's shore afraid fer his horses, though, specially thet California Red. There's a grand hoss, Judge. I'll bet if the rustlers got thet stallion Ben Ide would hit the trail himself. Strikes me he's seen some wild life. He shore is a rider. Strange, wonderful sort of chap Ben Ide is. I'm just gettin' acquainted with him. He always struck me as a rancher whose heart wasn't in his ranch. There's somethin' he wants. But he worships his wife an' kid an' thet handsome sister. It ain't thet. I cain't explain what I don't savvy. But I've a hunch young Ide has been hurt. Mebbe he killed some one over in California an' had to get out. I've often wondered if thet could be it. Then it might be he's *lookin'* fer some man. Like a Texan, you know, who never *forgot*."

Before the judge could reply to Day's earnest statement the cowboy, Texas Jack, whirled round with a silent wrestling violence that indicated a suppressed and poignant passion. Under the shadow of his broad sombrero his eyes gleamed like clear coals of fire.

"I'm—heahin'—all—you say!" he burst out, pant-ingly.

"Suppose you are, Jack?" queried the judge, in kind-ly surprise. "If I'd minded about being overheard I'd have sent you away."

Tom Day stared, and it was evident he was not so surprised as expectant. He had lived with cowboys all his life.

"Wal, what the hell ails you, son?" he growled.

Jack whirled away in the same sudden violent ac-tion with which he had faced them, only now it seemed there was added a fierce struggle of mind over body. He bent over the rail. He sprang up erect and rigid. In a moment more he turned toward the men again, to present a remarkably transformed front.

"I'm shore beggin' pardon, Mr. Franklidge, an' of you too, Tom," he drawled, in slow, cool, easy speech. "I couldn't help heahin' all you said, an'—wal, it knocked me off my balance."

"No offense, Jack," replied the judge, kindly. "I think Tom's talk sort of locoed me, too."

"Wal, see heah, you long, lean, hungry-eyed Texan," spoke up Day, forcefully, "jest *why* did I knock you off your balance?"

"Tom, I reckon I happened to hit on a way to fix the rustlers," replied Jack, nonchalantly.

"The hell you did!" ejaculated Day. He accepted the statement without doubt or ridicule. He was pon-dering deeply. His sharp light-blue glance was riveted on the shadowy, half-concealed eyes of the cowboy.

Judge Franklidge sat up with a jerk, but his smile robbed his action of a convincing sincerity.

"Jack, we'd be grateful for any suggestions from one as well proven as you on the range."

"Wal, what is this heah idee you hit on?" added Day, sharply.

"Shore it's as simple as a-b-c," rejoined the cowboy, blandly. "Somebody has got to ride down into the brakes an' get thick with the rustlers."

"Oh-ho! I see!" quoth Day, almost derisively.

The cowboy's mild manner changed subtly, in a way to impress his listeners, though they could not have told how.

"Somebody has got to shoot up the Hatts an' mebbe the Stillwells. An' kill some of that Pine Tree outfit—in particular the *hombre* who's at the haid of it."

"Is *thet* all? My Gawd! Jack, I shore thought you'd hit on somethin' hard to pull off," returned Day, with infinite scorn.

"Shore it'd be hard enough," admitted Texas Jack, who refused to see the ridicule.

"Hard! Fly, cowboy, you're loco!" exploded the other. "Shore you hit on the way to fix the rustlers. Shore! But who'n hell's goin' to do it? Was you figurin' on us hirin' some fancy gun-slingers to do the little job? Kingfisher from Texas, huh? An' Wess Hardin? Or mebbe you had in mind some new Billy the Kid or Pat Garrett? Or more like, perhaps, Jim Lacey, who they say has been hidin' quiet in Arizonie for a long time!"

Texas Jack's tan appeared to become a shade less brown. He grew tense, steely-eyed.

"Tom Day, how long have you known me?" he demanded, in a voice that rang.

"Two years an' more, son," replied Day, surrendering to something compelling.

"Would you trust me?"

"I shore would. With my stock, my money, my reputation . . . with my life—so help me Gawd!"

"Judge Franklidge, how long have I worked for you!" queried the cowboy, turning to the other.

"About a year and a half, as I remember."

"An' what is your opinion of me—as a man?" flashed the cowboy, growing more piercing of eye and voice.

"Jack, you're the squarest and best man, the finest hand who ever worked for me!" responded the judge, feelingly.

"Thank you. Reckon you can have no idee what that means to me," returned the cowboy. "An' you'd trust me?"

"As well as I would my own flesh and blood."

Texas Jack removed his sombrero and sailed it against the wall. His brow was broad and pale, his clear light eyes seemed to burn with a steady flame; there were white hairs in the long locks smoothed back above his ears; under the thin bronze beard, cheeks and lips set hard.

"Wal, then, it's my job to fix the rustlers," he said, deliberately.

"You! Nonsense!" declared the judge. "You wouldn't tackle that alone?"

"It's got to be done alone."

"Nonsense! I say."

"Judge," interposed Tom Day, "it shore does look thet way. But wait. This cowboy has got somethin' up his sleeve. I always knowed it. . . . Come heah, Texas Jack. Spring it."

What shrewd, hard, comprehending yet wondering light flashed from the old rancher's eyes!

"Listen," went on Jack, bending to his hearers. "To serve Arizona an' you an' your good friends I've got to become a rustler. I may have to go a long way to find the leader of this heah Pine Tree outfit. I'll have to drink an' steal an' kill. Shore I may lose my life finishin' the job. An' I want my secret kept till it's ended. Then if I come back alive I want my name cleared."

"Who'n hell *are* you?" asked Tom Day, in low and husky voice.

"Man, you're forcing me against my will," said the judge, rising to his feet. "I don't want you to attempt this thing alone. It's a wild cowboy idea. You'd only be killed. But I admire you, Jack."

"Dead or alive, I want my name cleared!" exclaimed the cowboy.

"Of what?"

"Of the stealin' an' lyin' I'll have to do."

"Man, I have power to make you a deputy sheriff right here and now. And I'd do it."

"No. Shore I'll never be an officer of the law. What

I want is this. Your word of honor to keep my secret, an', if I come back alive, to clear my name."

"Jack, are you going to persist in this mad plan?" demanded the judge.

"Reckon I shore will, whether you stand by me or not," returned the other, grimly. "It's too late now. I've got a reason, Judge. But it'd only be fair for you to uphold me—to tell in court, if necessary, that you an' Tom Day were parties to the job I undertook."

"Jack you misunderstand," replied Franklidge, hastily. "Don't make me ashamed. I will give you any support and authority right here and now. In writing, if you want."

"Only your word, Judge."

"There! You have it. And here's my hand."

Texas Jack broke from the strong, earnest handclasp to make the same proffer to the other rancher.

"Tom, will you stand by me—when I come back?"

"Hell, yes," boomed Day as he pumped the cowboy's arm up and down.

Abruptly, then, with sharp husky expulsion of breath, Jack wrenched clear of the vigorous grasp and wheeled to a post of the porch, against which he leaned and clutched hard. Something long buried was being resurrected. Ignominy loomed out of the past to stain an honest name. There was sacrifice here, far greater than appeared plain to the two grave and expectant onlookers. Whatever the strife was, it passed as swiftly as it had come. Then the cowboy turned again, somehow different, so that the judge and Day had awe added to their surprise.

"Gentlemen, I shore hate to give myself away," he drawled. A smile outshone the strange, steely light in his eyes. "But I reckon it's got to be done."

"Wal now, who'n hell are you, anyhow?" queried Day as the other paused.

"Tom Day, the starved cowboy you once took pity on, happens to be Jim Lacy!"

Eleven

It was Sunday, and that hour of the afternoon when all the men off duty at the Franklidge Ranch would be anywhere except round the bunkhouse. The cowboy, Texas Jack, striding in, was relieved to find himself alone. He made for his bunk for the purpose of hurriedly packing his few belongings. An old pair of black chaps worn thin hung at the head of his bed, with a belt and gun. An instinct prompted him to throw out his hand. There, as if by magic, the gun whirled in the air.

"Reckon it was fate," he muttered as he sheathed the gun. "Somethin' never let me stop practicin' that old draw. Wal, wal!"

In a few moments he had tied his belongings into a small roll to fit behind a saddle. His movements were swift, but made as if he were in a trance. He rose from his knees to gaze around; then strode out into the rude yet comfortable living room. Something prompted him to step before the mirror.

"Wal, so long, Texas Jack," he said to the image reflected there. "Reckon I been almost happy with you. A shave an' hair-cut will shore say *adios* to you forever. . . . An' then there'll be men who'll recognize you as Jim Lacy."

A quarter of an hour later he rode briskly down a trail that led into the cedars. He had taken his own saddle, but the horse he bestrode was one long discarded by the boys at the ranch. Once under cover of the cedars, the rider pulled his mount to a walk. It was nineteen miles to Sunshine, and he wanted to reach that station after dark and board a night train without being seen.

A melancholy resignation had no power to cramp the slow-mounting exaltation in Jim Lacy's breast. Once free of the need to hurry, his mind reverted to the cause of this extraordinary adventure he had voluntarily accepted. Facts were cold, hard things. He had hidden his real identity; he had buried the past; he had risen on stepping-stones of his dead self to honest useful service; he had earned peace and victory, if not real happiness; and then, like a thunderbolt from heaven, an inevitable, irresistible fate had confronted him. What he had suffered during the moments when Tom Day had talked to Judge Franklidge about Ben and Hettie Ide! The old wound had not healed. The old love lived in his heart, stronger for the years of denial and repression. Jim Lacy rocked in his saddle. No eyes but those of hawks and prairie-dogs and perhaps a skulking coyote could see him surrender to his emotion. The old horse walked slowly down the trail; the west wind blew hot desert fragrance in the rider's face; the dust arose and the heat beat down.

"Aw, I shore knew it—all these weeks I knew," whispered Jim, huskily. "Ben come to Arizona to find me! . . . Didn't he comb California—didn't he send men to all the ranges in the West? . . . Didn't Tom Day tell me no more'n a month ago—how Ben Ide wanted to know if he'd ever met a cowboy called Nevada? . . . That was it—the name Ben gave me—*Nevada!* . . . He never forgot. An' at last he come to this wild land. He's married an' got a baby, they say. Old Amos Ide must have died an' left Ben rich. Shore it was Ina he married. Yet all that didn't hold him back."

How terribly sweet and soul-satisfying that knowledge, and yet somehow bitter! In one tremendous moment of decision it had flung him back into the past, once more to own an infamous name. It had destroyed all he had built up. Only through the power of his dreaded name could he ever bring to successful issue the task he had set himself. What irony of fate that the fame he hated must be his open sesame to the rendezvous of the rustlers who were ruining Ben Ide!

"Like as not in the long-run I'll stop a bullet," he muttered, harsh in his agitation. "But hardly before I get the job 'most done. . . . An' shore that'd be better so. Ben would never know I am Jim Lacy. An' Hettie —*she* would never know. . . . But I reckon that's not my kind of luck. Like as not I'll run plumb into Ben before it's over. An' Hettie, too! . . . O my God! How sweet an' terrible!"

He rode on through the hot waning afternoon, absorbed with the strife of his soul. A storm, passing in gray-black pall at a distance, cooled and cleared the atmosphere. Sunset came, a glorious gold and purple pageant in the west, where it vied with the wonder of a rainbow, receding with the storm. But Jim Lacy scarcely took note of these physical manifestations around him.

When darkness fell he had reached the outskirts of Sunshine, and he halted under a clump of cottonwoods. Here, removing saddle and bridle from the horse, he turned it loose. That act seemed to sever the last thread which bound him to the ranching life he had followed for long. It had, too, a singular effect upon the emotions which had beset him. The hour had come when he must plan his return to the old life. Wherefore he sat down beside his saddle and pack, and with bowed head and rending of his spirit, he slipped, as into a long-unused garment, back into the old personality. And it seemed that the instant this transformation was consummated his plan for the perilous adventure at hand was simple and complete. He had only to be Jim Lacy.

The whistle of an approaching freight train inspired him with an idea more satisfactory than the one of waiting for the passenger train. He would steal a ride on the freight, thus obviating any risk of being recognized at the station. To this end he shouldered his pack and saddle and, hurrying to the railroad track, which was only a few hundred paces away, he waited beside the slowly halting train, peering through the gloom for an empty car. At length it reached him, just as the train stopped. Jim threw pack and saddle aboard and climbed in.

Daylight found him across the Territory line, in New Mexico. When the train stopped outside of a town at a water tank, he threw his baggage out, down over a grassy embankment, and got off. He had some money, beside the considerable sum Judge Franklidge had forced him to take. And it was with something of an old familiar zest that he strolled into the town.

Before encountering any riders or cattlemen Jim entered a barber shop, from which he emerged a changed man. Next he purchased a complete new outfit of rider's apparel, the costliest he could find. Jim Lacy, he remembered, had once affected something near to dandyism. He retained only his gun and chaps, which were things more intimate than clothes and were not to be discarded.

His next move was to buy a good horse. This turned out to be easier than he had anticipated, and was accomplished without exciting any particular attention. Lastly he led the horse out of town, found his saddle and pack, and soon he was riding back across the line into Arizona.

Traveling leisurely, and stopping at ranches and stations convenient to the day's travel, Jim Lacy in due time arrived in Winthrop.

The day was a Friday, toward the close of afternoon. He made his way to Beacham's corrals, where overnight visitors to town usually left their horses to be cared for. The first corral appeared to be a little too crowded for Jim, so he led his animal out to another and smaller one. Several rangy, dusty-garbed riders had just ridden in, evidently behind a dilapidated old wagon drawn by a shaggy gaunt team. The driver, a lanky man, dark of face and bearded, clambered down with the cramped movements of one more at home in the saddle. Jim had seen him before, but could not place him. There was a young girl sitting on the driver's seat, and she appeared quite pretty, in a wild-rose way. Jim's quick eye also took in the stock of a rifle projecting from the side of the seat.

Jim led his horse somewhat closer to the wagon, and choosing one of the covered stalls adjoining the fence, he leisurely began to remove the saddle, while his eyes roved elsewhere. He noted presently, when the girl jumped down, that her slim brown legs were bare, that she wore beaded moccasins, and the rest of her apparel showed further indications of the backwoods. As she passed out of the corral with the bearded man, Jim had a closer scrutiny.

"Shore, I'll bet that'll be Elam Hatt an' his daughter Rose," muttered Jim. "An' if so, those three riders are the other Hatts. . . . Reckon the ball is openin' *pronto*."

By the time Jim had turned his horse over to the Mexican stable-boy the Hatts had gone into town. Jim got out just in time to see them turn a corner. He followed very slowly, not reluctantly in any sense, but ponderingly. Familiar as he was with Winthrop, it did not seem the same town. Turning into the broad main street, he strolled along, seeing everything while not appearing to be interested in anything. He passed several persons whom he knew well. They did not give him a second glance. The restaurant-keeper, standing in a doorway, did not recognize Jim. A cowboy came along on his horse, evidently going home. It was Jerry Smith from Franklidge Ranch. He saw Jim, yet did not look twice.

"Jerry! An' the son-of-a-gun didn't know me," soliloquized Jim, elated. "He owes me money I'll never get now. Wal, could I surprise him?"

The later afternoon hours were the busy ones in the stores of Winthrop, owing to the heat of midday. The saloons were always busy, all day and all night. Jim had never entered a saloon in Winthrop. He would break that record presently, but not just yet.

At the next corner he came abreast of three cowboys sitting on a stone step of a saloon.

"Look, Bill, do you see the same as me—somethin' awful pretty?" asked one.

"By josh! I do," was the jocular reply.

"Boys, anybody'd know there was a dance on to-night—huh?" said the other.

"Hey, stranger, yore sure steppin' high, wide, an' handsome," spoke up the third.

Jim wheeled round to face them, with amusement difficult to hide. These fine-spirited cowboys were far from being harmless, but it was only their way to extract fun out of every incident.

"Wal, are you boys lookin' for a fight or a drink?" he asked, smiling.

"Since you ask us, stranger, it sure must have been a drink," replied the first speaker.

Jim waved them into the saloon, followed them, threw money on the bar, and said: "On me, boys. Sorry I ain't drinkin' to-day. I just buried my grandma an' feel bad."

Loud guffaws greeted his sally, and as he walked out through the swinging doors one of the cowboys yelled, "You're all right, stranger."

Jim crossed the side street and went on down toward the center of the main block. He idled along, halting to gaze into windows, leaned against doorways here and there, watching the people. Presently he came to the entrance of a store and espied the girl he had taken for Rose Hatt standing in the door. She had a package under her arm and was evidently waiting for some one.

"Excuse me, miss," said Jim, doffing his sombrero and stepping up to her. "Don't I know you?"

She looked up at him with big hazel eyes that had not been long free of tears.

"You might, mister, but I sure don't know you," she replied.

Jim decided she was more than pretty and not such a child as he had first supposed. She had wavy brown hair, rather rebellious, red lips, and tanned rose-tinted cheeks.

"Aren't you Rose Hatt?" he asked.

"Sure."

Jim leaned easily against the doorpost, smiling down upon her. "Reckon I thought so. Shore that's not many girls as pretty as you in these parts."

"Put your hat back on, mister," she replied, tartly. "Standin' bareheaded don't go with such taffy. Besides, I ain't used to it."

"All right," returned Jim, good-humoredly. "Bad habit of mine. I'll get sunstruck some day."

"Say, you'll ketch worse if my dad comes along," she said, laughing. "Onless you tell me *pronto* who you are."

"Wal, Rose, I might be Samuel Snoozegazzer," drawled Jim.

"Only you ain't," she added, with interest, and she looked Jim over from boots to sombrero. She was not bold, but she certainly did not show embarrassment or shyness. Jim gathered that she was used to men.

"I'll tell you my name if I drop in on the dance tonight," he said.

"Mister, I knowed that was comin'," she returned. "An' I'll bet you never met me before."

"Wal, to be honest, I never did."

"Reckon it ain't no difference. But I'm afeared I can't promise to dance with you."

"Why not?"

"Dad says I can go, but Cedar—he's my brother—he says no. An' Cedar is boss of our outfit."

"Wal, if your dad's willin', why, go ahaid. He's your father."

"Say, mister, I reckon you ain't acquainted with Cedar Hatt," declared the girl, almost with scorn. "You're sure a stranger in these parts."

"Yes, I am, sorry to say," replied Jim, thoughtfully. "But what's so bad aboot your brother?"

"Cedar's just plain cactus an' side-winder rattlesnake mixed up with hell."

"Aw, that's a terrible thing to call a brother," rejoined Jim.

"He's only a half brother, same as Henny an' Tobe."

"Oh, I see! Your dad was married twice an' your ma was the second."

The girl's eyes grew somber and her red lips curled with bitterness.

"There're some folks out in the brakes who say my dad wasn't never married no second time."

"Shore he was, lass. Don't believe gossip of lowdown people. An' don't be so hard on your brother Cedar."

"I hate him," she burst out, with passion.

"Wal! Why do you hate your own kin, little girl? Shore it's not natural," went on Jim, in his slow, persuasive drawl, so full of interest and sympathy.

"Reason enough," she retorted. "It was his fault that Clan Dillon took to runnin' after me."

"Dillon!" flashed Jim, in an amaze too swift and deep to hide.

His tone, his look betrayed to the simple passionate girl that she had allowed her tongue too much freedom.

"Say, mister, here I am talkin' like an old woman," she cried, almost in affright. "I'm beggin' you to keep mum that slip of my tongue. Cedar would half kill me."

"Shore I will," returned Jim, in his former kindly tone. "Rose, you just happened to run into a man you can trust."

"You look it, mister. I like you," she replied, with relief.

"Thanks. I'm shore the lucky *hombre*. But I reckon now you're engaged to marry this Clan Dillon."

"Marry, hell!" she exclaimed, suddenly almost fierce again. "I wouldn't marry *him* to save his life, the handsome, smilin'-faced liar. Not even if he wanted to, which he sure don't. I'd be only a sheepskin rug to Clan Dillon."

Jim dropped his head, conscious of an inward shrinking of tingling nerves, to the coldness of ice. It had come again—that thing which had not frozen within his breast for years. How life tracked him down! Then he looked once more at the girl. She was recovering composure. Manifestly she was a primitive little girl, as much like a wildcat as a wild rose. Jim felt intuitively that she was good. The flame left her hazel eyes and the hardness around her lips softened. Jim did not need to be told more about her life.

"Rose, have you any friends?" he asked, earnestly. "Shore I mean women-folks who could advise a young girl like you."

"Me? Why, mister, didn't I tell you I lived down in the brakes?"

"Haven't you a man friend, then, or even a boy—who's good?"

"No. But I was makin' one fast enough," she replied, both with resentment and mischievousness in face and voice. "A boy from California! Say, he was nice. But Cedar caught me with him."

"Too bad. What'd Cedar do, now?" queried Jim, much concerned.

"Not much, for Cedar," replied the girl, demurely. "He drove my boy friend off into the woods, dodgin' bullets! An' he kicked me till I couldn't set down for days."

"Wal! . . . Look heah, girl, you're old enough an' you've sense enough to know a friend when you meet him. Aren't you?"

"Mister, I think so. But I—I'm afraid to trust myself," she faltered, swayed by his earnestness.

"Wal, you needn't be in my case. I'm going to trust you."

"How?" she asked, wonderingly.

"I'll tell you presently. I don't want you to run off scared before I say all I want to. . . . Now who's this California boy your brother caught you with?"

"Swear you'll never tell?" she returned, impulsively, drawn by his potent sympathy.

"Rose, I'll shore keep your secret, an' more. I'll help you to *make* a friend of him."

"Oh, mister, if that could be!" she cried, rapturously.

"Hurry. I see your dad comin' down the street."

"His name is Marvie Blaine," she whispered.

Jim Lacy drew a sharp swift breath that seemed to cut him like a knife as it swelled his breast. He leaned down to the girl.

"Listen," he whispered. "I will be your friend— an' this boy's—if you'll keep your mouth shut."

"Lord, mister, you needn't be afeared of *me*," replied the girl. "I wouldn't dare. Sure I don't know why I ever talked to you. But you're different. An' oh! How I need some one to talk to!"

"Shore you've found some one. Me! I'll be goin' down into the brakes."

"But who are you, mister?" she queried, aghast at his assertion.

"Did you ever heah of Jim Lacy?"

Her red lips parted to let out a little gasp and her brown face paled. "My Heavens—are you him?"

"Yes."

"Hear of you, Mister Jim Lacy!" she ejaculated, her eyes dilating. "Ever since I can remember I've heerd of you. Many men ride to my Dad's ranch, an' none but they speak your name. Some of them had seen you, an' two of them at least knowed you once."

"Rose, I'll tell you their names—Hardy Rue an' Cash Burridge."

"Yes—yes. Oh, you *are* Jim Lacy. An'—an' I'm not scared a bit," she whispered. "Why, it ain't so long ago that I heerd Cash Burridge tell of seein' you call out an' kill a man for beatin' a girl. . . . Oh, Mister Lacy, no one ever taught me about God, but I've prayed—prayed night after night—for some one to come an'——"

"That your Dad right heah?" interrupted Jim.

"Oh yes. . . . What'll I say?"

"Nothin', lass. He hasn't seen us. Don't forget. Keep mum. Good-by."

Jim strode out as if he were just leaving the store,

and he passed Elam Hatt so close he might have touched him. Hatt was walking with a man as rough in garb and hard of face as he was himself. Neither appeared to notice him. After a few steps Jim glanced back. The girl had disappeared and the men were passing on.

"Good!" said Jim, to himself. "That lass is game, but she's only a kid, an' I reckon it's better her dad didn't see her with me. Wal, wal! The old luck of Jim Lacy! Half an hour in Winthrop an' I'm on a hot trail."

Marvie Blaine! Marvie—the boy who had worshipped him and Ben Ide in those wonderful Forlorn River days! Jim had found the boy way over here in Arizona. Marvie would be eighteen now—quite a man as cowboys were rated on the ranges. But then Ben and his family had only arrived at Cedar Springs in July.

"Tall, freckled-faced, tow-haided kid, Marvie was," went on Jim. "Shore he's straddlin' mean hosses an' packin' a gun. . . . Reckon it's not the best country for a boy like him. But Ben could hold him in. . . . By golly! I'm forgettin' Rose Hatt. Shore as shootin' Marvie has fallen in love with her. No wonder. Reckon I would, too, if my heart hadn't been eaten up long ago. Wal, wal! A girl an' a boy I hadn't reckoned on. . . . How queer things come! Rose said it was Cedar's fault that Clan Dillon . . . Poor kid! She shore called Dillon. Handsome, smilin'-faced liar! An' she knows, if I ever saw truth. Wal now, I wonder, just *what* kind of a *hombre* is Ben Ide's foreman. Tom Day liked him. So does everybody I've ever heard speak of him, except this Hatt girl. . . . It's a hunch. I'll be damned if I don't back her against all of them."

Jim strolled the length of the main street, and crossing, sauntered back again, talking to himself in an undertone, and with his apparent casual observance taking cognizance of all visible persons. He had the pleasure of meeting Judge Franklidge face to face in front of the hotel. The rancher saw Jim only as a passerby. It would have been the opposite of pleasure, however, for Jim to have encountered Ben Ide face to face; and that was one reason Jim's keen eyes sighted every man first. But accidents could happen. It would be well for Jim, while in Winthrop, to keep under cover of the saloons or places not likely to be frequented by Ben Ide. At most, Jim's hours in town would be few and far between.

He went to a side-street restaurant to get his supper and engage lodgings for the night. As darkness came on he ventured into a store, where he made a few purchases, and then he returned to the corral for his pack. This he carried to his room.

"Reckon that'll be aboot all," he soliloquized, as he stood gazing around the dingy bare room.

He was thinking that he had walked the streets of Winthrop about the last time as an unknown man whom few people had noticed. Those swift moments— an hour or so at most—had seemed singularly sweet to Jim.

"Wal, I'm shore ready to pay all it'll take."

The small mirror showed his eyes piercing and light, like points of daggers gleaming out of shadow. He stood an instant longer, motionless in the chill lonely silence of the room. He knew that when he went forth again it must be into raw evil life of outlaws, gamblers, murderers—all that riffraff of the Southwest, which like a murky tide, had rolled into Arizona. He calculated coldly that he must be all he had ever been, all that his name had ever meant. He must add to these the intelligence which had sharpened in the years of peace. He seemed fitted for this task, and his motive had the strength of love and passion and the sanction of right.

"Reckon I ought to thank God," he said, to his pale image in the mirror. "Shore I never had no chance to do somethin' worth while. An' now I can use my evil gifts to a good end. For Ben—an' that means for *her*— an' then Franklidge an' all the honest people who're tryin' to civilize this wild country. Reckon, after all, they need such men as Jim Lacy. . . . I see clear now. Even if I'm killed, Ben an' Hettie will know the truth some day. It's got to come out, an' I reckon I'm glad."

Then before the mirror, with a grim smile on his face, he came at last to the practical business of the matter. Though the success of this enterprise depended upon his cunning and his knowledge of the outlawed men with whom he must throw his lot—and the more of such qualities he exercised the surer his chances—the cold hard fact was that all hung upon the deadliness of his skill with a gun. This job had to do with death. Such was the wildness of the time and the evil code of outlaws, that he could kill this one and that one, any number of them, and only add to his fame, only give himself greater standing among them. True, by so doing he must make bitter and relentless enemies; he must face the strange paradox that many an incipient gunman, or notoriety-seeking desperado, or drunken cowboy would seek to kill him just because he was Jim Lacy.

Whereupon, with deliberation he treated himself to a tense exhibition of his swiftness of eye and hand. In secret he had practiced all through these peaceful months while engaged in honest labor. An impelling force had exacted this of him. He understood it now. And with a dark satisfaction he realized that he had gained in speed, in sureness of hand. Beyond these he had in large measure the gift peculiar to all gunmen who survived long in the Southwest—and that gift was to read his opponent's mind.

"Reckon I might have bit off more'n I can chew," soliloquized Jim, as he sheathed his gun. "But from the minute I step out this heah door I shore won't be makin' many mistakes."

The Lincoln County war in New Mexico had ended recently. It had been the blackest and bloodiest fight between rustlers and cattlemen and many others who had been drawn into the vortex, that had ever been recorded in the frontier history of the Southwest. As such it had possessed an absorbing, even a morbid, interest for Jim Lacy. He had never lost an opportunity to hear or read something about this war. And once he had ridden into New Mexico on a cattle mission for Franklidge, during which trip he had seen at first hand some of the places and men who were later to become notorious. That war had in its beginning something analogous to the present situation here in Arizona. Jim did not believe there could ever again be such a fight as the Lincoln County war. But there was no telling. Arizona had vaster ranges and more cattle. Some of the characters prominent in the Lincoln County war had not been killed. They had disappeared. It was not unreasonable to suppose that one or more of them had drifted into Arizona. "No two-bit of a rustler is headin' that Pine Tree outfit!" ejaculated Jim, voicing aloud one of his thoughts. To be sure, Billy the Kid, the deadliest of all the real desperadoes of the Southwest, had fallen in the Lincoln fight, along with the worst of his gang. But they had not all bitten the bloody dust of New Mexico.

"Shore I'll run into some one from over there," muttered Jim. "When I do I'll shoot first an' ask questions after."

With that he opened the door, to step out into the dark, oppressive August night.

Twelve

Winthrop, the same as many other Western towns of the period, supported more saloons than all other kinds of business houses combined. It had a vast area of range land to draw from; and if there were a thousand cowboys and cattlemen in this section, there were probably an equal number of parasites who lived off them, from the diamond-shirted saloon-keeper and frock-coated gambler with all their motley associates, down to the rustler who hid in the brakes and the homesteader who branded as many calves not his own as he raised from his stock.

Once a month, if not oftener, the men of the range could be depended upon to visit town, "to paint it red" and "buck the tiger." These customs were carried out as regularly as the work of punching cows.

During the early evening hours Jim Lacy visited some of the main-street saloons, steering clear of the Ace High and others of prominence. He lounged about the bars and tables, agreeable and friendly to anyone who wanted to talk, willing to buy cigars and drinks, while he made some excuse or other for not indulging at the time. Cowboys were all friendly folk, except now and then one whom drink made mean. Gamblers and hangers-on, Mexicans and Indians, attracted by Jim's liberality and presence, added their little to the sum of information he was gathering.

"I'm lookin' for a pard," Jim would say to most everyone he met. "A cowboy who broke jail over in New Mexico." And then he went on with more of such fabrication, always to conclude with questions. Cowboys under the influence of a few strong drinks soon acquainted him with range gossip he had not heard. Several *habitués* of these dives accepted Jim's advances without telling him anything. These, of course, were the men who knew most and required cultivation. But they only eyed him covertly. Bartenders were mostly procurers for this or that gambling house, and from them he amassed much information. At length he left the last resort, intending to hunt up the dance hall.

"Shore, that wasn't so bad for a start," mused Jim as he summed up and sifted the bits of talk in which he found significance. "Cash Burridge, sold out an' gamblin' his fortune away, spends half his time heah in town. Thick with some Spanish girl. Same old Cash! . . . Clan Dillon one grand *hombre,* eh? Wal, wal! The Ides rich Californians who're bein' rustled an' sheeped off their range. Tom Day just as liable to be boss of the Pine Tree outfit as any one. That'll shore tickle Tom. The Hatt outfit, except Cedar, just no-good homesteaders, low-down enough for anythin' not really big an' dangerous. Cedar Hatt, though, is a plumb bad man. Not the even-break kind, but crafty as a redskin, treacherous as a Greaser. The Stillwells hardest nuts down in the brakes. Never come to town! Now that's shore worth rememberin'. Last an' perhaps meanin' most to me—what that half-drunk sheepherder told me. Strange riders often seen by herders passin' through the Mogollons. Wal, most of all this sounds familiar, as I think back. But now it comes close."

Jim, by following in the footsteps of hurrying young people, soon found where the dance was being held. It was out a side street, almost at the edge of town, in a low wide adobe building, very picturesque now with its hanging colored lanterns, its trailing vines over archways. Outside there was a crowd of Mexicans, Indians, white men in rough garb, noisy boys, all looking in through the archways at the couples walking down the long patio and the dancers inside, swaying to and fro with the music. There was something of the spirit of a *fiesta* in the air.

Upon entering the place Jim was aware that he came under the scrutiny of men who evidently were conducting the dance, or at least overseeing those who entered. One of these individuals was Macklin, the sheriff of Winthrop, an officer who arrested cowboys sometimes, and Indians and Mexicans, but who never had been known to jail a gambler or one of the more dangerous characters. Jim, however, was not questioned. He strolled up the wide steps to watch the dancers, and then moving from one vantage point to another, amused and pleased with the scene, he at length found a place that suited him, where he sat down to watch and listen.

Jim Lacy, in the old Texas and Idaho, even the Nevada days, had enjoyed dancing, but since his advent in Arizona he had never attended a dance. This had been one of the peculiar things about Jim that had puzzled his cowboy associates of the Franklidge Ranch. Failing to persuade him, they called him a woman-hater.

It did not take Jim long to appreciate that this dance was conducted on proper lines. He understood now why he had been so closely scrutinized at the entrance. There was no drinking permitted on this occasion, nor any obstreperous behavior. The cowboys and other young men present did not show any evidence of the bottle. Among the dancers, and promenaders in the patio, there were a number of dark-haired, flower-decorated Mexican girls, very bright and pretty in their festal array. It was indeed a gala occasion, full of color and life, and soft laughter and Spanish music. Jim had to admit that his calculations had fallen awry in this case. Rose Hatt might be in attendance, but it was a safe wager that Cedar Hatt would not be admitted, nor any of the men Jim wanted to watch, unless it might be Dillon. He, surely, would not only be welcome, but very probably the lion of the dance.

Presently Jim believed he had caught a glimpse of little Rose Hatt at the far end of the patio. So he arose to walk in that direction, and found it rather a running of the gauntlet, for as the music started up couples began gayly to hasten to the dancing floor. More than one pretty girl bumped into Jim's right side where his gun hung low. Finally another, dodging around a couple she evidently wanted to get ahead of, plumped into Jim's arms.

"Oh, goodness! Excuse me," she giggled, recovering her balance.

"See heah, lady, are you shore you didn't mean that?" drawled Jim, with a smile.

She could not very well have grown redder of face, so Jim could not tell whether or not she blushed. There was, however, a hint of coquetry in her merry eyes. Then a tall cowboy, very young in years, loomed over her and glowered at Jim.

"Hey, you dressed-up quirt!" he said. "You say 'lady,' but you don't know one when you see her. I've a notion to slap your smart-alec face."

"I'd hate to be slapped, so I beg pardon, sonny," replied Jim, and walked away.

The momentary halt had caused him to lose track of the dark curly head he had believed to be Rose Hatt's. At the end of the patio he turned, to espy the girl just stepping out upon the floor. It was indeed Rose, and a transformed little girl, too. She had on a gaudy, cheap, flimsy dress, with shoes and stockings to match, but these did not detract from her prettiness. She was young and radiant. Her partner was a cowboy not much older than herself. They stood a moment, holding to each other, self-conscious and awkward, before they began to dance. Rose did not know how to waltz, but she made a valiant effort.

Jim watched the couple until they were lost in the whirl of dancers. This end of the patio opened into a garden or yard where a walk wound between clumps of shrubbery. There were benches here and there, and some of these were overshadowed by vines. Jim watched the dancers, hoping to see Rose again, and perhaps catch her eye. But he missed her in the whirling throng, and when the dance ended he retreated to a seat on the adobe wall. Then again the dancers tripped to and fro, hurrying for refreshments and seats, and the wide aisle was filled with murmuring voices.

This scene roused in Jim Lacy a strange regret. The pleasure and life manifested here were things he had missed. "I can't see that it was my fault, either," he muttered. Young couples passed near, excited and gay, thoughtless, enchanted with the moment. There were older people, some with gray hair, and they did not seem beyond the magic of the hour. Jim's envy was short-lived. Happiness had eluded him. But it was not given to many men to serve as he could now.

Presently a couple approached out of the shadow. As they reached a point beyond, yet near where Jim sat, half concealed, the girl halted.

"Please—let's go outside," begged the man.

His voice prompted Jim to turn so that he could see better. The fellow had the build of a rider, lithe, tall, wide in the shoulders. He wore a dark suit and had a flower in the lapel of his coat. His face had a compelling attraction. But Jim, in his quick glance, could not decide whether it drew him because it was a handsome, unusual face, or for some other reason difficult to grasp at the moment.

"No, Mr. Dillon, I don't care to go farther," said the girl.

Jim started so violently that he almost fell off the low adobe wall. That voice! He would have known it among a thousand voices. His cool curiosity vanished in a rushing tide of emotion. His glance leaped from the man to his companion. She stood full in the soft rose light of one of the colored lanterns. Hettie Ide! His heart bounded, then seemed to become locked with a terrible pang. It was Hettie, grown into a woman. The face that had haunted Jim's camp fires in the lonely watches of the nights! The same rippling fair hair, the deep earnest eyes, the rich clear complexion that spoke of contact with the open, the strong full lips, more hauntingly sweet than ever for the sadness which had come!

So rapt, so agonizing was Jim's attention that he lost something of the words which passed between the two. It was the name Dillon that roused Jim from his trance.

"Mr. Dillon," she was saying, "the reason I can't marry you is that I don't love you."

"But, Hettie, you will—you must love me in time," he returned, passionately, seizing her hand and trying to pull her into the shadow. She resisted, broke away from him.

"I never will," she said, with eyes and cheeks flaming. "What kind of a man are you—that you persist so rudely? I liked you—even admired you until you forced such attentions as these on me. I've overlooked them because my brother Ben thinks so much of you. But no more, Mr. Dillon."

Her dignified yet spirited reply might as well not have been spoken, for all the effect it had to restrain Dillon. He burst into low impassioned appeal, and he backed her under the overhanging vines against the wall. Dillon was no young cowboy, mad with love. He appeared to be a man, masterful, adept at making love, absolutely indifferent to anything but his own desires. The way he confronted her in her several attemps to pass him, and without laying a hand on her crowded her back to the wall, proved how he was thinking about what he was doing.

"I—I thought you were a gentleman," she burst out.

"No man thinks of bein' over-gentle when he's in love," retorted Dillon. "I tried that with you. And to tell you the truth, I wasn't so natural then as I am now. I've plumb lost my head. I tell you I love you an' I'm goin' to have you. What do you say to that?"

"I say this, Mr. Dillon, we've all got you figured wrong," she retorted.

"Sure you have," he rejoined, with an exultant laugh. "An' here's how!" With that he attempted to seize her in his arms. But he had evidently cornered the wrong girl. Supple and strong, she wrestled free in an instant and wheeled away from the wall.

"What do you—think—Ben will do—when I tell him—you've insulted me?" she panted, backing into the aisle.

"If you've got any sense you won't tell him," replied Dillon, in a flash changing from an ardent lover to something almost menacing. "Ben Ide's in bad here. Arizona isn't California. There are rustlers here an' you can bet some of them are the ranchers he thinks his friends. I know this cattle game. I know these men. He's lost most of his stock. If he buys in more he'll lose that too. Hettie, I'm the only cowman in Arizona who can save him from ruin."

"Indeed! Are you aware that I have a share in the Ide ranch?" retorted Hettie, sarcastically.

"I've heard so, but I didn't believe."

"Well, it's true."

"Ahuh! What do you mean by share?" he queried, curiously.

"I own one third of the land and the stock. Besides, I have my own house apart from Ben."

"That's news to me," said Dillon. "But it sure makes my case stronger. What ruins Ben Ide will ruin you."

"The loss of a few thousand cattle won't hurt either my brother or me," she returned, almost flippantly, studying his face with steady, penetrating eyes. She was seeing the man as if he had suddenly unmasked.

"You must be pretty rich to talk like that," replied Dillon.

"Quite well off, thank you. I often wondered if that didn't interest you, and now I know."

He laughed in a way that would have been a revelation to an older woman, well versed in the life of the frontier. But Hettie did not grasp what seemed as plain as print to Jim Lacy, crouching like a tiger under the shadow.

"Thanks, you're very smart," he said. "But I'd be crazy about you if you were as poor as Rose Hatt. I tell you I love you—want you—need you so terribly that if I fail to get you it'll make a devil out of me."

"I'm beginning to imagine the process of *making* has progressed very far already."

"You've got cat in you—same as other women," he retorted. "Listen, we're wastin' talk. If you'll marry me I'll save Ben Ide. If you won't I'll quit him an' use my influence all over the range. I'll make ranchin' impossible for him in this country. An' I'll get *you* in the bargain."

Hettie Ide turned so pale that her eyes shone black.

"Mr. Clan Dillon! Popular fellow! Splendid cattleman! Best and squarest foreman in Arizona!" she exclaimed, with amazed and infinite scorn.

Dillon, whose back was now turned toward Jim, made a deprecatory gesture in reply.

"Mr. Dillon, weeks ago when you first came to us and began your—your attentions to me, I thought there was something queer about you," went on Hettie, deliberately. "You were too good to be true, as old Raidy said. Well, I think you're as bad as you seemed good. I think you're a contemptible, conceited ass. I think you're a deep, cunning scoundrel. . . . You need not return to Cedar Springs tomorrow. Marvie Blaine will drive me home."

"What do you mean?" demanded Dillon.

"You'll not get a chance to quit Ben. Right here and now you're discharged."

"Me! What? Who's dischargin' me?"

"I am."

"Bah! You're loco, girl. Ben Ide wouldn't listen to you. He can't run that ranch without me. Haven't you sense enough to see it?"

Hettie Ide abruptly turned her back upon Dillon and walked away, to disappear in the crowd of dancers returning to the floor.

"——damn the luck!" muttered Dillon. He lighted a cigarette and stood thoughtfully inhaling and expelling smoke.

Jim Lacy strode out from under the vines and the shadow.

"Howdy, Dillon!" he said, as he confronted the foreman.

A lightning-swift glance took Jim in from head to feet and back again.

"Howdy, yourself. Reckon you've got the best of me," returned Dillon, gruffly.

"Shore, I reckon I have," drawled Jim, with cool significance.

"Who are you?" queried Dillon, sharply.

"I might be Peter Punkins—only I ain't."

"Pretty smart, aren't you?" rejoined Dillon, feeling his way. He knew men; he knew the West. "Reckon you're more Simple Simon than Peter Punkins. I don't care. But I'm curious about where you just sprung from."

"Wal, I hail from New Mexico," returned Jim.

"The hell you do!" flashed Dillon. "That's nothin' to me. But where'd you come from just now?"

"Dillon, you're figurin' quick," returned Jim, in slow deliberation. "Wal, I was settin' right heah on the adobe wall."

Jim pointed to the spot in the shadow, but he did not take his gaze off Dillon.

The man cursed under his breath and flung his cigarette down so hard that the sparks flew from the stone pavement.

"You set there watchin'—listenin'?" he demanded, with sudden and powerful self-control.

"Shore did," drawled Jim.

"Stranger, where I come from men got shot for such offense."

"I reckon. That's why I'm not apologizin'."

Dillon seemed to accept this as confirmation of the suspicion which had evidently been growing with his thoughts. Abruptly his bullying manner changed. The swift retreat of his personality was almost as remarkable as the new one which took its place. He stood unmasked, as far as his pretense was concerned. Cautious, steady, cold, and hard he stood a moment, his strange green eyes trying to pierce Jim's mind. He was searching more for Jim's intent than for other knowledge of him.

As for Jim, he measured Dillon to be a Westerner vastly different from the character he enjoyed in the section of Arizona. He judged Dillon without recourse to the words of Rose Hatt. Jim did not recognize a kindred spirit, but he read in Dillon the depth, the courage, the desperate experience of a man used to the rawest and deadliest of frontier life.

"Ha! I see you pack a gun, stranger," coolly remarked Dillon, as he lighted another cigarette.

"Yes. I got sort of used to it."

"Reckon you see I don't?"

"Shore. I seen first off you didn't, an' then just now I read it in your eyes."

"Mind-reader, eh? Well, it's a helpin' trait for some men."

"Are you meanin' any particular breed?" queried Jim, dryly.

"Yes. Spies, gamblers, thieves, gun-throwers, an' the like."

"Thanks. I'm shore appreciatin' the way you speak. An' not wantin' to be outdone in compliments, I'll just repeat what Miss Hettie Ide called you—a conceited ass! A deep, cunnin' scoundrel!"

"You heard all she said?" snarled Dillon. Deep and crafty as he was, he could not help the risk of passion, though he controlled it.

"Shore. An' I never heard a low-down man called more proper. Tickled me more because only to-day some one called you a handsome, smilin'-faced liar."

"Aho! You happened to hear a good deal, now didn't you, stranger?" returned Dillon. "Well, I don't care a damn."

"Shore you don't. A skunk stinks so bad that nothin' but bullets can get to his hide."

"You're a brave man, stranger, shoutin' that way above your gun. But I'm tired listenin'. Are you from New Mexico?"

"No. I was lyin'."

"Ahuh? An' you've got a hunch that's where I come from?"

"I reckon."

"You see I don't deny it. What do I care what you know or think or do? You pose for a dandy cowboy. But you're not ridin' for any outfit around Winthrop. You excite a little suspicion yourself, mister, considerin' this country is full of outlaws an' rustlers."

"It shore is. That's why I come over," returned Jim, meaningly.

For the first time the dark red showed in Dillon's face.

"I'll have you put out of here," he said. "An' I'll tip Macklin off that you need watchin'."

"Wal," drawled Jim, with his glance cold and set, "go ahaid, but be sure to tip him off that I'm Jim Lacy."

Dillon's stalwart frame jerked with a perceptible tremor. A slow pale shade began to blot out the brown of his face.

"Jim Lacy, eh! Say, I've had that dodge worked on me before. Paradin' under a dead man's name! It's an old trick of four-flushers."

But Dillon was not so cocksure as his bluster was intended to indicate. His iron nerve had been pierced. Here was a name to conjure with. For a moment the revelation of it unmasked him as had nothing else. Honest men seldom had anything to fear from Jim Lacy or any other of his class. It was only a sudden, instinctive fear at that, a weakening at once controlled. Dillon might have been afraid of a name, but not of any man.

"You expect me to believe you're Jim Lacy?" he demanded, hoarsely.

"Wal, I'm tellin' you, but it's nothin' to me what you believe," returned Jim, icily. This interview was about to conclude.

"All right," went on Dillon, breathing hard. "But I still figure you a liar."

Jim sprang forward and knocked Dillon down.

"Wal, shore it may take more'n that," he said, in

slow accents. "But I told you who I am. An' that's somethin' you didn't tell me."

Dillon cautiously arose on his hand, lifting a dark face to his assailant. But he made no response.

Jim, wheeling away to go, found himself confronted by Rose Hatt. The girl had seen at least the last of Jim's encounter with Dillon.

"Oh—mister!" she cried, in a comprehension bounded by fear.

The dancers were trooping off the floor. A tall youth, with features strangely familiar to Jim, appeared behind Rose. She clasped his arm, while she stared from Jim to Dillon, who had not attempted to get up. Without a word Jim hurried on.

"My—God! Who was that?" called out some one Jim took to be the youth with Rose. The voice added to the stirring of Jim Lacy's memory. It also urged him faster through the throng of dancers and out into the street.

"That was Marvie Blaine, God bless him!" whispered Jim, as he gained the darkness. "Shore a close shave for me."

It was eleven o'clock when Jim Lacy entered the Ace High Saloon, at the period one of the noted gambling hells of the southwest.

John Brennan, its proprietor, had two unique characteristics that stood in his favor. He had the reputation of being a square gambler and he would not have a woman about the place. Consequently he was not so prosperous as most men of his business and his house was without costly and gaudy fittings. He did not bar any man from his tables, so long as that man played fairly. More than one crooked gambler had been carried out of the Ace High, feet first. This fact was reported to have had its effect upon the intent-eyed, still-faced sharps who frequented the rooms.

Jim Lacy bolted into the barroom like a man who was being pursued. He was, indeed, though not by any visible thing.

"Cowboy, what you runnin' from?" queried a tall man. He happened to be standing nearest to the door, his back to the bar, his high hat tipped back, to expose a weatherbeaten face. A brass shield, with letters printed upon it, stood out prominently on his vest.

Jim recognized this individual almost instantly.

"Howdy, Macklin!" he said, nonchalantly. "I was just runnin' from a sheriff."

"Wal, you run right into another," growled Macklin, surprised and annoyed. "Who air you?"

"I'm foreman of the Coffee Pot outfit," drawled Jim.

"What's your handle, smarty? It jest happens there ain't any Coffee Pot outfit at this particular time. . . . I've a notion to clap you into the jug. You look kinda pale round the gills. What have you been up to an' who air you?"

"None of your damn business," returned Jim, with abrupt change of tone and manner. "But if you hang around I reckon somebody'll tell you."

"Hyar, you come right along with——"

"Lookout, Mack!" interrupted some one behind Jim. A glass went crash on the floor, and the rasp of heavy boots followed. Then a man strode in front of the sheriff, facing Jim. "Excuse me, stranger, but I believe I know you. If I'm wrong, say so."

"Howdy, Cash!" returned Jim, extending his hand.

Cash Burridge looked a full ten years older than when Jim had last seen him. Drink and hard life and evil passion had broken the man. His lined dark visage lost its set expression of uncertainty, almost alarm, and worked convulsively into a broad smile.

"Jumpin' steers!" he ejaculated, grasping Jim's hand in both his and wagging it vigorously. His smile kept on expanding. His eyes lighted. "If it ain't you!"

"Shore is, Cash. Just got in, an' am lookin' for trouble."

"No! *Who?*" queried Burridge, with a sudden check to his almost boisterous welcome. He had bent forward and lowered his voice.

"Wal, nobody in particular, Cash. I just feel mean."

"I'm a son-of-a-gun! It's you—changed a lot. Most in disposition—if it's true. You're *lookin'* for trouble."

Here the sheriff interposed by placing an ungentle hand on Burridge's shoulder and turning him somewhat.

"Friend of yours, hey? Thet's no guarantee to keep him out of jail."

"Hell!" exploded Burridge. "I'm tryin' to keep *you* out of the boneyard. My Gawd! if I told you who this man is you'd sweat blood."

Macklin's jaw dropped and he swayed back against the bar, dominated by Burridge's fierce sincerity. Then Burridge drew Jim aside from the gaping, grinning bystanders at the bar and the gamesters at the tables.

"It's you—really *you,* Jim?" he whispered, huskily.

"Shore, Cash. Cain't you see?"

"But we heard you were dead."

"That was terrible exaggerated, Cash."

"Dropped from the sky! Jim Lacy, just down from heaven, huh? Well, I'm damned! . . . An' I never was so glad to see a man in my life. Honest, Jim."

"Wal, I'm glad to see you, Cash, though we was never very thick."

"Where you been, Jim, since you left Lineville? Lord! I never forgot that night you shot Link Cawthorne's eye out."

"Wal, Cash, never mind where I've been."

"Sure, that doesn't matter, only I always had my idea, an' I was curious. I had a hunch you went to New Mexico an' got mixed up in that Lincoln County war. *Some* of those *hombres* got out of that fight alive. I know one of them did. Close-pard of Billy the Kid."

"Who?" queried Jim.

"I'm not givin' any man away, Jim. Sure wouldn't have said as much as that to anyone else. When'd you drift in?"

"To-day."

"You'll be recognized here."

"Shore. I expect to be an' I'm not carin'."

"Lord! Jim, have you grown reckless with the years? You look older, but fine, healthy, an' prosperous."

"Who's goin' to recognize me, Cash?"

"You remember Ace Black? He's the gambler we knowed at the Gold Mine back in Lineville."

"Shore I remember Black."

"He's upstairs playing faro. Reckon Black will know you, but he'd never give you away. Hardy Rue, though. He will. He never cottoned to you. Always had a hunch you'd killed Less Setter. Rue has dogged me all these years. An' I'm layin' it to him that I'm down on my luck now."

"Wal, what come of your ranchin' deal heah, Cash?"

"Jim, you had me figured. I couldn't stand prosperity," returned Burridge, heavily. "But I swear I went straight till I got in need of money. I'd made poor deals. I could steal cattle an' make money, but not by tradin' or ranchin'. I began to borrow. Then I had a chance to sell out to Ben Ide, a Californian. I did him dirt, an' I've lived to be sorry. There's a man, Jim. . . . Well, when I was flush again I began to drink an' buck the tiger."

"An' now you're aboot broke. Who got all that money, Cash?"

"Aw, everybody. Brennan some, but then I don't begrudge it to him. Hardy Rue beat me out of most of it. I fell in love with a Spanish girl here. She an' Rue double-crossed me. Got my pile!"

"Wal, why didn't you kill him?"

"I couldn't try an even break with Rue. An' I never had a chance to shoot him in the back."

"Is Rue heah now?" asked Jim.

"Reckon he's with that black-eyed hussy. It's a little early for him to drop in. Lord! it'll tickle me to have him see you with me. Rue was afraid of you, Jim, an' you need to watch him."

"Where do you hang out, Cash?"

"I've been most here in town," replied Burridge. "I've a cabin down in the brakes."

"Are you acquainted down there?"

"Sure am, Jim. Know everybody except the new-comers. An' I'm givin' you a hunch there's some hard customers driftin' in. It's a hell of a rough country an' big as all outdoors. I sure learned to love Arizona."

"Wal, Cash, when you was rich an' high-handed I didn't have much use for you," said Jim, with a smile. "But now you're broke an' down on your luck, I reckon I'll chip in with you."

"Jim Lacy! You always was a queer one," returned Burridge, feelingly. "Reckon, I know you've got somethin' up your sleeve, an' whatever it is, I'm sure with you."

"All right, Cash. Suppose you tote me round to look 'em over."

Thirteen

Hettie Ide had attended the dance at Winthrop as a guest of Alice Franklidge, a girl of nineteen, daughter of the judge's second wife. She was a frank, breezy, Western girl to whom Hettie took a liking, and they were on the way to become real friends.

They left the dance before midnight, to be driven out to the Franklidge house by Alice's escort. The night was cold and clear, with myriads of blinking stars overhead. Hettie removed her hat to let the cool wind blow her hair.

"Did you enjoy your first dance in Arizona?" asked the young rancher.

"Yes indeed I did, Mr. Van Horn—in spite of a—a rather unpleasant incident," replied Hettie.

"Sure, we're awful glad. Sorry, too, somethin' annoyed you. But honest, the dances now are Sunday-school affairs to what they once was. Isn't that so, Alice?"

"It is. I used to be afraid to go," replied the girl. "Fights were common. One for each dance! They're really nice now. Dad and some of the town men have seen to that. . . . Hettie, it mortifies me that you were annoyed by—by Clan Dillon. I know it was he. You danced with him—then came back to us all flushed and nervous."

"Yes, it was Mr. Dillon. He—he insulted me."

Van Horn cracked his whip over the horses in rather abrupt and forceful action.

"I'm not surprised," returned Alice, thoughtfully. "Dillon is a handsome, fascinating man. Very agreeable, winning. But I always thought him a little common and bold."

"Who was the pretty girl Marvie paid so much attention to?" asked Hettie.

"I didn't notice her. But I saw he was having a grand time."

"He had her with him just before we left," went on Hettie. "She wore a white muslin dress, cotton stockings, cheap slippers too large for her feet. She hung back as Marvie came up to me. I think she was afraid to meet us. I thought her very pretty. Big staring dark eyes. Red lips. Curly brown hair."

"That was Rose Hatt," replied Van Horn.

"Rose Hatt? She couldn't belong to that notorious Hatt family we hear about?" asked Alice.

"There's only one family of Hatts, Alice, an' Rose is the only girl," explained the young rancher. "I'd seen her before. Charley Moss danced with her. Pretty kid. An' she seemed modest an' quiet. Young Blaine sure acted smitten with her."

"Indeed he did," corroborated Hettie, seriously. "Marvie is such a fine boy. But he's going a little wild. I've remonstrated with Ben, who lets Marvie run around too freely."

"Hettie, love affairs in Arizona go like fire in the dry desert grass," said Alice, with a little laugh. *"You* want to watch out, doesn't she, Frank?"

"Sure won't do her any good to watch out," returned Van Horn, gayly. "One of our Arizona lads is goin' to get her."

"Mr. Van Horn, that's the second time to-night I've heard such prediction," replied Hettie, pleasantly. "I'm sure I feel flattered."

Soon they arrived at the Franklidge home, which stood on a bench of high ground, among stately pine trees. The girls went in to find Judge Franklidge smoking beside an open fireplace. He greeted Hettie warmly.

"Did you meet your brother?" he asked, as he placed a chair for her.

"No. Did he come in, after all?"

"Yes. He was here for an hour," replied the judge.

"Came in to talk over a cattle deal. I advised him not to buy more stock just now."

"Was Ina with Ben?" asked Hettie.

"Sure was, and she looked powerful handsome. I wanted them to stay here overnight. But Ben said he'd rather go to the hotel, so he could be in town early. Left word if he didn't see you at the dance that you were to meet him tomorrow at noon sharp. At Brydon's."

"Goodness! I'm glad we got away from the dance before Ben arrived," exclaimed Hettie, with a rather unmirthful laugh.

"Well now, you don't say?" queried the judge, lowering his head to gaze at her over his glasses.

"I'm afraid it's going to be embarrassing for me when I see Ben. I'll have to tell him I—I discharged Dillon."

"Dillon! Clan Dillon? Did you fire *him?*" asked the judge, sitting up abruptly.

"I sure did," rejoined Hettie.

"I'll be darned. What for, lass?"

"I had reason enough, though I'm afraid Ben may not see it that way. He swears by Dillon. In fact he trusts Dillon implicitly and entertains a very high opinion of him. Well, Mr. Dillon has made it rather hard for me out at the ranch. He waylays me whenever I go outdoors. At first he didn't do me the honor to offer marriage. But finally he got that far along, and despite my refusals he kept at it. I did not know he was to be at the dance to-night, or I wouldn't have gone. But I danced with him, and walked with him, on the terrace—and—well, to make it short he insulted me."

"Dad, I'm not surprised. I never liked Dillon," interposed Alice.

At that juncture Frank Van Horn entered.

"Lass, now just how did Dillon insult you?" asked Judge Franklidge, with fire in his eye.

"He declared he was going to have me whether I wanted it or not, and I had to fight him!"

"You don't mean he dared to lay a hand on you?" demanded the old rancher.

"Both hands, and arms, too," laughed Hettie, though she blushed as she admitted it. "In fact, he was a ruffian. I imagine Dillon has had his way with a certain kind of women. I think he expected me to squeal, or beg—then flop into his arms. But I'm strong and I broke away from him."

"Damned hound! Somebody ought to use a quirt on him," ejaculated the judge, growing red in the face.

"I'd suggest a gun," added Van Horn, with a compression of his lips.

Hettie held back a revelation of Dillon's threat to ruin Ben and herself. Upon cool reflection she had not been sure of how Ben would react to her taking upon herself the authority to discharge Dillon. Unfortunately, Ben was used to Hettie's complaints about the attentions his men bestowed upon her, and he had come to take them with a grain of salt.

"So I discharged Dillon," concluded Hettie.

"You did right, lass, but how in the devil is Ben going to take that?" queried Franklidge, seriously. "He thinks a heap of this Dillon. Only to-night he was bragging about Dillon's recovery of a bunch of cattle that'd just been rustled off into the brakes. . . . Still, come to squint at the offense, Ben can't overlook it. He's bound to stand by your dismissal of this foreman."

"You don't know my brother very well yet," returned Hettie, shaking her head. "If he had *seen* Dillon insult me he'd have horsewhipped him. But Ben scouts my statements. He's tired of hearing about these lovelorn cowboys who annoy me. He thinks I'm—well, a little too sensitive. Once he said, 'If I was that cowboy I'd throw you on a horse and ride off with you.' And another time when I went to him in distress he said: 'Of course he tried to kiss you. Why shouldn't he? You were made to be loved and kissed.' . . . Sometimes I believe Ben is only in fun. He doesn't mean that as it sounds. But he hasn't so much patience with me as he used to have. I declare I don't know how he will take this Dillon affair."

"I'll tell you, lass, now that you've expounded the situation," replied the judge. "He'll not uphold you. Dillon will get to him first and soften his offense, and Ben will keep him on."

"That would be dreadful," said Hettie. "I'll actually be afraid of Dillon."

"Well, the only solution to your problem, Hettie Ide, is to fall in love with some fine Arizona lad," declared Judge Franklidge, with both kindly conviction and teasing good humor.

"Indeed!" returned Hettie, trying in vain to look haughty. Then she thought it might be just as well to drop a hint to these new friends. "I'd take your advice, Judge Franklidge—if it wasn't for an insurmountable obstacle. . . . I can't fall in love with a fine Arizona lad, because I'm already in love with a fine— *Nevada* lad!"

As the beloved name sounded off her lips Hettie felt the swift blood rise to tighten and heat her face.

The judge laughed heartily, but Alice, intuitively grasping the import beneath Hettie's rather flippant speech, crossed over to Hettie and put an arm around her.

"Dad is as bad as Ben, dear. Come, it's late. Let's go to bed," she said.

"Well, Hettie," added the judge, in the same mirthful vein, "if I were forty years younger I'd contest this mysterious Nevadian's right. Where is the confounded lucky jackass?"

Hettie looked back from the doorway, through which Alice was leading her.

"I do not know," she replied, sadly.

When the door closed she heard the judge burst out: "Did you hear that, Van? It explains a lot. . . . Well, doggone me for a thick-headed fool! And I'll gamble Ben Ide is the same."

At breakfast next morning Judge Franklidge seemed to have undergone a subtle change. His interest in Hettie had increased, but he dispensed with the mischievous bantering. Hettie felt that in his estimation she had grown into a woman overnight, and that she had found a friend in him.

"Hettie, I'm going to be sort of a dad to you," he said, at parting. "I'm ashamed of the way Arizona has treated you and Ben. But listen, lass. Have faith in us and this grand country. Have patience with your brother. Try to persuade him not to spend more money just now. We may have a year or two, or more, of hard times. But take the word of an old cattleman who has been through more than one rustler war. We will come out of it. These outlaws destroy themselves. I've a hunch some hard-shootin' gunman will come along and do for the ringleaders. It's happened here before. It happened lately in New Mexico. So do not lose your nerve and come to hate this beautiful country. We want you Ides to love it. We need such fine people. We are pioneers, Hettie. I've lost a million on cattle. But it'll come back. And so will your losses. Likewise your happiness."

"Judge Franklidge," answered Hettie, smiling through her tears, "despite my weakness for *Nevada* —I reckon I'm Arizona's for life."

"Whoopee! That's the game lass! . . . Come to see us often, Hettie. *Adios.*"

One of the Franklidge stable hands drove Hettie into town, so that she had time for thinking how best to approach Ben. It had not occurred to her that Ben might get a warped version of the affair from Dillon. She felt grateful to Judge Franklidge for his kindly counsel and advice. Indeed, she had felt, too, with a woman's keenness, something in regard to the judge's attitude toward Dillon—something he did not confide. Yet she sensed his friendship. He would very likely take her side, if the issue came to an argument. She decided to wait and see if Dillon had approached Ben.

Hettie, upon arriving in town, went about buying the supplies usually ordered twice a month. She and her mother had preferred to keep house in their own little cabin, a proceeding that Ina and Ben had opposed. But Mrs. Ide vowed she would never be a mother-in-law to anybody.

After she had finished her ordering, Hettie passed on down street, presently to encounter Ben. He did not look in a very good humor. There was a dark shade on his face which Hettie had learned to regret, long ago back at Tule Lake Ranch. Her heart sank a little, despite her fortitude. What if she had offended Ben?

"Ina is at the dressmaker's," he said, after greeting her. "Reckon it's a good time for you to go to the bank with me."

"Bank. What for?" she queried, as she yielded to his hand and turned back up the street.

"I'm having a certified check made out for your interest in the ranch."

"Ben!" she cried, in amazed reproach.

"Yes, Ben," he returned, a little testily. "Hettie, I can't have you doing things without my knowledge. Besides, to be honest with you, I don't want to see you lose that money. And I'm pretty certain I'll lose all I put in cattle."

"But, Ben, it was an investment. I played to win or lose with you," she protested.

"I know, dear, an' you sure are a thoroughbred. But this was a crazy deal of mine. I don't regret it," he added, hastily. "But I can't feel right to have you in with me. Maybe some day, when these bad times are over."

"Ben, something has happened since I saw you," said Hettie, quickly.

"Reckon it has," returned Ben, dropping his head so she could not meet his eyes. "California Red is gone!"

"Gone? Oh no, Ben!" she cried, poignantly.

He nodded disconsolately. She saw his lips quiver.

"Stolen?"

"We don't know. He disappeared from the pasture. Raidy swears Red was stolen, that he couldn't jump the fence. I know he could jump over the moon if he took a notion. Dillon agrees with me that Red just got away."

"But you don't *know?*" queried Hettie, sharply.

"That's the rub, Hettie. We don't. And there isn't a man in my outfit who could track Red. Sure disgusted me. I tried to track him myself. Had to give up. . . . Reckon there never was but one horse hunter who *could* have done it."

"Ben, you'll get Red back," replied Hettie, earnestly, and forthwith she launched into an eloquent speech, drawing upon the judge's advice and optimism, and adding considerable of her own hopeful and persistent opinions as to their ultimate success and happiness in the future.

"You're game, Hettie," he returned, squeezing her arm. "With you and Ina and the kid I can an' will beat this rotten deal. Reckon it'll help some if you consent to withdraw from it."

"I'll consent to anything that will relieve or help you."

They reached the bank, where presently Hettie received a certified check for her share in the transaction. She immediately deposited it to her account.

"For the time being I'll leave it there," she said.

"Yes, do. I might have to borrow from you," he laughed, then with serious brow he drew her to a seat and said in a low voice, "Dillon just told me you'd discharged him."

"Yes?" queried Hettie, lifting her chin, while the tingle and heat of battle ran along her nerves.

"Hettie, I had to countermand your order," he went on, gravely. "Now we won't argue about it. Dillon is the best man available. I can't get along without him. He knows it, too. I had some trouble conciliatin' him."

"Oh, indeed!" retorted Hettie, biting her lips. "May I ask what Mr. Dillon told you."

"Not much. He was sore, but he laughed, at that. Said he loved you an' had been coaxin' you to look upon him favorably. Then last night—at the dance—he asked you to marry him. Said you weren't very encouragin'. Then he tried to kiss you, an' you made a fuss an' took it upon yourself to fire him."

"If you believe him, Ben, why, there's no need in my bothering you with my side of the story," rejoined Hettie, finding her self-control.

"Reckon there's no call to think Dillon's a liar," went on Ben. "The truth is, Hettie, you're a little of a man-hater. Oh, I know—I remember, an' I sure don't blame you for bein' true—to—to *him*. . . . But you're hard on all these poor devils who fall in love with you. That's the way I see it."

"Ben Ide, I am not a man-hater," protested Hettie.

"We won't argue the question," said Ben, wearily. "You an' Ina always beat me. But please don't misunderstand. I don't want you to marry Dillon. He seems a fine fellow who'll make a big man in Arizona some day. Just the same, I'd want to know him better before I'd let him have you."

"Thank you, Ben. I can forgive you now," murmured Hettie.

"I'd like to ask you somethin'," went on Ben, with both concern and mirth in his look. "Did you strike Dillon last night—when he tried to kiss you?"

"Strike him? No, I certainly did not," declared Hettie, vehemently. "I wouldn't soil my hands on— But why do you ask that?"

"Well, he had a beautiful black eye," replied Ben, ponderingly. "He told me he had stumbled in the dark —in his room—an' hit a chair. Sure it could have happened. But it looked to me like a beautiful black eye that had come from a good swing an' a hard fist. I've been wonderin' if he lied to me."

"Well, I'm wondering who gave him just what he deserved. But, Ben, if you have such faith in this Dillon, why did you wonder at all?"

"I happened to run into Dillon talkin' to Stewart, who is Tom Day's foreman," replied Ben. "I heard Dillon say somethin' about bumpin' into a chair. Then Stewart, who'd been drinkin', gave Dillon the horse laugh. Struck me funny, that's all."

"Brother dear, I hope you won't be struck by anything funnier," said Hettie, as she arose. "I've got more shopping to do, and time flies. You wished me to meet you at twelve?"

"You bet; *pronto*, too," he returned. "It's a long drive home, you know. I've got a lot of things to see to. But reckon I'll make it."

"How about Marvie?"

"He'll be there. Marvie hunted me up an' asked for money. I'd just given him some, before we left. The kid was intoxicated, all right."

"Ben! You don't mean he was drunk?" burst out Hettie, in horror.

"No. I was goin' to tell you he was intoxicated over some girl. Wanted to buy her candy an' presents. But, by George! I forgot I promised not to give him away. Don't you dare give *me* away. . . . So long, till twelve. I'll pick you up at Brydon's store."

"What a fright you gave me!" complained Hettie. "You should choose your words more carefully. As to Marvie—I think he's in love. I saw the girl. Tell you more later."

Hettie's thoughts reverted to Marvie and lingered dreamily and anxiously around him until she reached the dry-goods store, where she forgot everything except the important shopping at hand.

It lacked five minutes to twelve when she labored to the front of the store, burdened by bundles, and vastly satisfied with herself that she had finished in time to meet Ben. He was punctuality itself and appreciated the same in anyone. Hettie deposited her bundles on a window seat beside the door, and looked out for Ben. He had not yet arrived.

Suddenly a man, hatless and coatless, dashed by, yelling, *"Keep off the street!"*

"What's the matter with him?" asked Hettie, amused.

Several clerks came hurriedly to peep out.

"Looks like another fight," said one of them, excitedly.

Shouting and trampling of feet followed. Across the

street pedestrians hurriedly ran into the first open door-way they happened upon. The noise ceased. Then a man entered the door where Hettie stood transfixed and thrilling.

"Hello, Matt! What's doin'?" queried the clerk.

"Darned if I know," replied the man. "I seen people run off the street, so I ducked in here. Just before I heard Jim Lacy was in town."

"Who?" shouted his questioner.

"Jim Lacy. Don't know how true it is. But some-body's in town, you can gamble on that."

Faces appeared at all doors and windows. Some peeped down the street, then jerked back. How ridicu-lous it seemed to Hettie! Yet there she stood likewise, her heart throbbing, her whole being in a state of sus-pense.

A shot pealed out, deep and ringing. Then *bang!* Another followed, almost like an echo. Silence ensued, palpitating, stifling to Hettie. What had happened? A fight! Guns! A single shout came from far down the street.

The man beside Hettie peeped out.

"By Gawd!" he ejaculated, in husky accents.

The clerk, frightened as he was, also had to look. He jerked in his head, with pale face and eyes staring, and he began to jabber.

Hettie obeyed an irresistible instinct. She peeped out. The street appeared empty. No, there was a man lying face down, not fifty feet from the door. His arms were outstretched.

"It's Jim Lacy. I never saw him, but I know them who has," said the man beside Hettie.

"Oh—how dreadful! . . . the dead man—there in the road—Jim Lacy?" whispered Hettie, beginning to shake and grow sick.

"No. Jim Lacy is the one comin' up the street. . . . See his gun. It's smokin'!"

Then Hettie, looking farther, espied a man in rider's garb, gun in hand, stalking toward his victim. He passed him, with only a downward glance. He sheathed the gun. He strode toward the sidewalk.

His walk! His shape! A terrible piercing sensation attacked Hettie. Had she been horrified out of her senses? Was she mad? What flashed so swiftly in memory? But this man—this Jim Lacy! He was coming. He would pass the door.

Hettie drew back with the last of failing strength. She reeled. Her mind had halted. The quivering of her body ceased as if paralysis had set in. Cold, numb, awful suspense held her upright, waiting, as if for death itself.

The man in rider's garb passed the doorway, erect, stonefaced, with eyes of lightning set ahead.

Nevada! Hettie's faculties leaped out of terror and stupefaction to recognize him. Nevada! Jim Lacy? . . . *Nevada!*

She had a sense of sinking down. All went blank—then slipped into black oblivion.

Fourteen

Hettie recovered consciousness before she had strength enough to open her eyes. She was lying down, with some one supporting her head. Cold water had been dashed in her face. She felt it trickling down her neck.

"It's Miss Ide," said some one. "She fainted. . . . Fell right down!"

"No wonder!" returned another speaker, evidently a woman. "I'm sort of sickish an' weak myself. Hadn't you better call a doctor?"

Whereupon Hettie opened her eyes, to whisper weakly, "I'll be—all right."

She lay on the window seat, with her head supported by the young clerk. Several persons, one a woman, stood around sympathetically.

"There! She's come to."

A bewildering complexity and whirling of thought suddenly left Hettie with her mind clear.

"Is my brother here?" she asked, trying to sit up. With the aid of the young man she managed it, and slipped her feet to the floor.

"No," was the reply.

"First time—in my life—I ever fainted," said Hettie.

"Better set still a little, miss. You're awful white yet," said the woman kindly. "Let me help you put on your hat. It was here on the floor. You must have had a tumble."

The clerk smiled and got up. "No. She just sank. Like a limp sack. So she couldn't have hurt herself."

"Indeed, I'm not hurt," returned Hettie. "You're all very kind. . . . It was silly of me to—to keel over like that."

While she talked there seemed to be an awful question hammering at her consciousness. When Ben and Marvie entered, at that moment, she understood what the question was. Neither of them knew what she knew. Her relief was so great that it overcame her, and when she tried to rise she only sank back again.

"Why, Hettie!" cried Ben, in sharp concern, as he sat down to grasp her. Then Marvie knelt on the seat at her other side. Hettie smiled wanly at them and closed her eyes. She felt dizzy, and then feared to look at them.

"It's nothin' serious, Mr. Ide," spoke up the clerk, hastily. "She just fainted. It was the shootin'. She peeped out—an' then when I seen her again, there she lay on the floor."

"Whew, Hettie! You gave me a scare," said Ben, as he hugged her and shook her a little. "But you're all right. It was only you went flooy over a street duel. Why, I'm surprised at you. Anyone would think you'd never heard a gun back in California. . . . Come, brace up, Hettie."

"Take me home," replied Hettie, opening her eyes again. "I—I want to get out of this town."

"Wal, I should smile! Me, too," joined in Marvie, squeezing her hand. Hettie had never seen the lad look quite as he did then. The freckles stood out on his pale wet face. His eyes held a bright stare. She did not dare ask him if he had seen the participants of the street duel. She feared he had.

"Marvie, you fetch these bundles," requested Ben, as he lifted Hettie to her feet. He had to support her, or she could not have walked just yet. He swore under his breath, then, scornfully, "This Arizona's a nice place for women! . . . Never mind, honey; maybe we'll get over it. I'm thankin' my stars Ina didn't see."

Ben helped her into the back seat of the buckboard. "There, you're all right. . . . Marvie, put the bundles under the seats. Then get in beside Hettie an' hang on to her. I've got some drivin' to do. Soon as I pick up Ina, I'll sure leave this town in a cloud of dust."

Hettie did not look to right or left, yet she saw and heard the excited people passing, talking down the street. Ben drove rapidly. Soon the center of town lay behind. The streets were quiet. Hettie lost the cold dread of seeing a lithe stone-faced man in rider's garb. Ben halted the horses before a house set well back in a green yard, and as he leaped to the ground Ina appeared.

"Hello, you-all!" she called, merrily. "See, Ben, I'm right on the dot. Now, sir." As she reached the buckboard she suddenly halted aghast. "Why, Hettie! . . . You look terrible. Are you ill? Oh, what has happened?"

"Ina, I'm a poor pioneer," said Hettie, with rueful smile.

"Nothin' to upset you, wife," replied Ben. "Hettie had a scare. There was a shootin' fray downtown, an' she fainted. Climb up, an' we'll be off *pronto*. These ponies are sure rarin' to go."

As soon as Ina had climbed up she turned solicitously to Hettie and reached for her hand. "You poor dear! I never saw you look like this. Fainted! That's strange. You never fainted in your life."

"I did this time, all right," returned Hettie.

"Why? What happened? Did you see a fight?" queried Ina, excitedly.

"No. I didn't see—the fight," replied Hettie, shutting her eyes tight. "But I heard it. . . . Then I peeped out—to see a—a dead man lying in the street."

"How dreadful! Oh, this wild Arizona! It's worse than Forlorn River when we were girls."

"Worse?" laughed Ben, grimly. "Say, Ina, California in our day could never hold a candle to Arizona."

"Did you see this fight?"

"No. I missed it."

"Did you, Marvie? Oh, I hope you didn't."

"All I saw of it was the dead man. I walked by him. He had a bloody hole in the top——"

"Shut up, you infant gun-slinger," interrupted Ben.

"Did you know the fighters, Ben?" went on Ina, curiously.

"No. Some one told me Jim Lacy had come to town, lookin' for trouble. He gave a rustler named Hardy Rue choice of leavin' town or throwin' a gun. Rue chose to stick, an' it cost him his life. Had no chance on earth, some one said. They met in the street. Even break, of course, as these Arizonians call a fair fight. But Rue was fallin' when his gun went off."

"Terrible," said his wife, shuddering. "But a rustler cannot be a very great loss to the community."

"Ina, I sure hope Mr. Jim Lacy sticks around for a while," replied Ben, laconically. "Tom Day told me Hardy Rue might be the leader of the rustlers who've been pinchin' me so hard. But Dillon scouted the idea."

During this conversation Hettie was glad to have the support of Marvie's arm and shoulder. She had not opened her eyes. But her ears rang acutely with the words she heard.

"Ben, I reckon you an' sis might shut up, yourselves," declared Marvie, significantly, "or talk about somethin' else."

"Sure, sonny," agreed Ben. "It's no pleasant subject."

The spirited team drew the light buckboard at a rapid pace over the smooth, hard road. The breeze stirred by this pace was cool and pleasant to Hettie's throbbing brow. After a long rest, she opened her eyes and sat up again. Already the dark line of cedars was in sight, and beyond them the uneven timbered ridges that ran up to the black frowning Mogollons. How vast and wild that range! Hettie's heart seemed to come to life again. It had been locked, clamped, frozen. What was it that had stricken her, almost unto death? If she were only alone in her room, so that she could face the catastrophe, so that she could give way to her agony! But many miles and hours lay between her and seclusion. She essayed to make conversation with Marvie.

"Your girl is very pretty, Marvie," she said, close to his ear.

Marvie actually blushed and squirmed in his seat, and gripped Hettie's arm so hard under the robe that it hurt.

"You had met her before last night," whispered Hettie.

"Ahuh!" he replied.

"Marvie, you are no longer a boy. You're a young man with prospects. And she—forgive me—she belongs to that notorious Hatt family. I don't blame you for—for admiring her; she's like a wild rose. But say it's not serious."

"I wish I could," whispered Marvie, swallowing hard.

"Marvie! Tell me."

"Not now. I can't, Hettie," he said, huskily. "But I will when we get home."

"I'm on your side, Marvie," concluded Hettie, pressing his arm.

For a while she was able to concentrate her thoughts upon this lad and the girl, Rose Hatt, and the unhappiness that might accrue for both. Marvie was under probation. Yet it would not be long until he was of age and his own master. It seemed altogether unlikely that he would ever return to California. The rich acres of Hart Blaine had no hold upon Marvie.

Soon Hettie's will succumbed to the tremendous pressure of recurring thoughts and emotion. She gave up. She had to let herself go. Then while her gaze strained out over the yellow and green prairieland, and the rolling ridges with their slopes of sage, and the miles of white grass where herds of cattle grazed, and on and on, and ever upward to the purple ranges lost in the rosy pearly clouds of hot afternoon, while she saw these beautiful characteristics of Arizona, she was confronting herself with the staggering truth.

She had seen Nevada. She could not torture herself with a thought of doubt—that she might have been mistaken. Sight and heart and mind, her whole being had recognized him in one terrible instant. He was in Winthrop. He was Jim Lacy. Jim Lacy, whom range rumor had long made mysterious, famous, ruthless. Jim Lacy was Nevada. Back in those Forlorn River days, when she and Ben and Ina and Marvie had loved him as Nevada, even then he had been Jim Lacy. Why was she stunned? Ever since Nevada had killed Setter and ridden away never to be heard of again Hettie had realized he had borne a name he could not endure for her or Ben to know. That was not so astounding. Nevada might have been any one of the noted desperadoes of the West. The overwhelming thing was that Nevada was here in Arizona, alive, virile, stone-faced as she had seen him but once, here in Winthrop, close to the home she and Ben had chosen almost solely in the hope that they might find him some day.

What if she had seen him? A sickening helpless impotence assailed her. All the longing of years wasted! All the hope and prayer and faith wasted! Vain oblations. Nevada had been false to her, false to the best she had helped to raise in him, false to the blessed conviction she had always entertained—that whoever he was and whatever he had done, out of love for her and assurance of her faith, he would go on to disappear from the evil roads of the West and turn to an honest life. Hettie would have gambled her soul on that. And now the soul she would have staked grew sick with horror and revulsion. Nevada was a consort of rustlers, a bloodthirsty killer, a terrible engine of destruction.

But perhaps he had only killed another man! A bad man—a thief—even as Less Setter had been! The insidious small voice beat at the gate of her consciousness of faithlessness. And she listened, she clutched at it with the hope of a drowning woman, she hugged it to that soul which seemed to be freezing. So with unseeing eyes on the rolling, darkening desert, she admitted more and keener anguish into this strife of love and faith. How could she be faithless in hope, in trust? Had she not sworn, with her lips close to his, that she would die before she ever failed him? What if he had used his deadly gun again? He had killed, as before, perhaps more than once in his life, a worthless wicked man, whose death must serve some good purpose. Nevada had once saved Ben and Ina and her, all of them, from grief and misery. Who could tell what the killing of Hardy Rue might be to some one? No! Nevada had not sunk to the companionship of evil men and women, to drinking, gambling, rustling, to the vile dregs of this wild West.

Over and over again this stream of consciousness eddied through Hettie's mind, like conflicting tides, now rushing, again receding, now full and devastating.

Through the waning afternoon, sunset, twilight, dusk, on into the night Hettie acquired deeper insight into the gulf which yawned beneath her.

The swift horses had swung into the home stretch, over the short-cut road that had been one of Ben's achievements. How the night wind moaned in the lofty pines! It seemed the moan of the world. The fragrance of sage filled the air. Down through the pale aisles of the forest moved shadows, unreal, grotesque, things as strange as shadows of the mind.

Marvie now leaned against Hettie's shoulder, sound asleep. Ina had not spoken for hours. Ben, tireless and silent, kept the horses at a steady clip-clop, clip-clop. He always took pride in driving to town in eight hours and home in nine. A good road, a stanch fast team, a light vehicle, had conquered the one drawback to Ben's wilderness ranch.

When at last they arrived Hettie crept exhausted to her room, and falling upon her bed, she lay quiet, wanting to rest and think before she undressed. But she fell asleep.

When she awakened the sun was shining gold in at her window, and the fresh sweet cool fragrance of the forest blew over her. Instead of being beautiful they seemed dreadful. She dreaded wakefulness, the daylight, the many duties to be met, the imperative need of action, the facing of her family and of life. But she could not keep them back. And with the truth there surged over her the catastrophe that had fallen.

"Maybe it's not a catastrophe," she whispered to the faithful, waiting silence of her room.

Hettie sensed then that her greatest trial was yet to come, and a faint intimation of what it might be appalled her. It roused her to battle. Dragging her aching body off the bed, she undressed, and bathed her hot face, and brushed out her tangled hair, and put on her outdoor clothes.

Then she slipped out without awakening her mother in the adjoining room. What was it that she must do? Find him, save him, or perish! All that she faced in the golden morning light seemed to mingle in one subtle whisper. There was no deceit, no blindness, no vacillation in the nature that spoke to her.

Only the birds and the wild game, and the calves in the pasture, the roosters in the barnyard, the burros out on the range shared with Hettie those perfect uplifting, clarifying moments of the sunrise.

Golden gleams of light crossed the brown boles of the stately pines; low down through the foliage shone patches of pink sky; to the north and west opened the vast slant down to the desert, illimitable and magnificent in the rosy, shadowy soft dawn. Deer and antelope grazed with the cows in the pasture. Squirrels barked from the trees, hawks sent down their shrill piercing cries, wild turkeys gobbled from over the ridge. Joy of life, radiance of creation, peace and solitude, wholesomeness and sweetness of nature, the exquisite beauty of woodland and wasteland at the break of day, and a marvelous, inscrutable, divine will pervaded that wilderness scene.

Hettie absorbed it. She lifted up her head to the one black dome of the Mogollons. The misery of the night faded away like a nightmare. She had been a coward. She had failed to be grateful for the very thing that had been the beginning and end of her prayers. Could she be so slight and shallow a woman as to succumb to heartbreak? A terrible ordeal faced her, the outcome of which she could not divine. She could only endure and fight whatever fate had in store.

"Oh, if I can cling to this blessed strength!" she cried. "To hold it fast when I'm distracted! To have it in hours of gloom!"

That day Hettie did not cross the picturesque log bridge that spanned the brook between her cabin and the beautiful rambling residence of her brother. She plunged into her work, which consisted of the housekeeping she shared with her mother, her dressmaking and other personal tasks, and all the bookkeeping necessary to the running of a large expensive ranch.

She did not see Ben all day. Late in the afternoon, when she went out to walk a little in the open air, she espied Marvie sitting on the porch, a most abject-looking lad.

"Hello, Marv, old pard! Come and walk with me," she said, brightly.

"Aw, I want to die!" replied Marvie.

"Goodness gracious! Well, don't do that on my porch. It'd be a perpetual reminder of you."

She dragged him to his feet and locking an arm with his led him off into the woods, until they were out of sight of anyone at the house. Then Hettie bade him sit with her under an old pine where the fragrant brown needle mat looked so inviting.

"Now, Marv, I'm through teasing," she said, with a gravity that suited his mood. "What's the trouble?"

"I had a run-in with Ben," replied the lad. "First one we ever had."

"You did? Well, I've had a thousand. When Ben gets sulky and cross a good run-in clears him up, as a thunderstorm does a sultry day. Where did Ben go to-day?"

"He finally rode off to a deserted homestead over here, five miles or so. Some one found tracks of California Red, and that news upset Ben. Then he waited round hours for Dillon, who didn't come. Raidy, who's on the outs with Dillon, said some things that made Ben sorer. You know Raidy. Well, doggone it, Ben pretty soon pitched into me."

"What for?" queried Hettie, practically.

"Nothin'. Not a darned thing. 'Cept I moped along at a job he gave me. Fixin' fence. If there's any job I hate it's that. He swore at me. Then I told him to go to the devil—I'd quit and go home."

"What did Ben say?" asked Hettie.

"He said, 'Go ahead, you bull-headed, lop-eared little jackass.' . . . So I rode off home. And I reckon I'll quit. I'm goin' to be a rustler."

"All right. You want to become a rustler," returned Hettie, accepting the statement. "What for?"

Marvie did not reply for a long while, during which his head sank lower.

"Hettie, I'm turrible—in love," he said at last, with an effort.

"Rose Hatt?"

"Yes. It couldn't be nobody else."

"Does Rose love you?" asked Hettie, softly, her hand going to Marvie's.

"I thought she did, at first," replied the boy, writhing. "She let me kiss her—kissed me back. But last night, when I asked her to meet me again, she said no. I got mad. But she stuck to it. When I accused her of flirtin', and me dead in earnest, she said: 'Marvie, I've a bad name. I belong to the Hatts. You've a lovely sister' (she'd seen *you*) 'and a proud family. I'm only a backwoods girl. It won't do. I'll not see you no more.' She ran away from me then an' I couldn't find her. She'd hidden or left the dance. In the mornin' I tried again. No luck."

"Marvie, I admire Rose for that," said Hettie, earnestly. "I think she's a square girl, even if she is a Hatt."

"Now, Hettie, don't you go talkin' like dad or mother," burst out Marvie, warningly.

"Oh, Marvie, I won't," declared Hettie, ashamed of the fact that she had been about to do so. By Marvie's warning she estimated his regard for her.

"I don't care a damn about myself—even when I do love her turrible," went on Marvie, passionately. "But what's to become of Rose?"

In the sincerity and inevitableness of youth he had hit upon the thing that mattered most.

"I understand, Marvie," said Hettie, gravely. "You make me ashamed. Rose is not to blame for her family, for her surroundings, for—anything."

"Now you're talkin' like Hettie Ide," returned Marvie, fervently. "And I'm givin' you a hunch. If Rose really loves me I'll stick to her. In spite of dad or Ben or anyone!"

Hettie dropped her head. Here was a problem. What should she say? Marvie's confidence in her suddenly meant more than ever before. He needed something from her.

"What knocks me flat is—I'm afraid she doesn't love me," went on the lad. "I'm goin' to find out, though, if I have to ride right under Cedar Hatt's nose. . . . Last night I believed she didn't. This mornin' I thought she did. If not—if she was only a little hussy—why'd she say she had a bad name and wouldn't meet me no more?"

Hettie had no quick reply to his passionate query. Owing to her own stress of emotion during the last twenty-four hours, she was far from being her old logical self. But she was fighting a conviction that Rose Hatt had shown nobility and sacrifice in her attitude toward Marvie's advances. If those attributes did not spring from love, Hettie did not know what to call it.

"Tell me, Hettie," begged Marvie, with soul-searching eyes that hurt her, "don't you think Rose cared really? Wasn't that good in her—givin' me up? Wasn't it because she—she liked me too well to go on with what she thought might disgrace me an' you an' Ben?"

"Marv, I can't be sure, but I think so."

"Thanks—Hettie," choked the lad, sitting up

straight and facing ahead. A light crossed his somber youthful face. "You hit me right here." And he put his hand to his breast. "Sure I couldn't tell nobody else but you. It's helped a lot."

"Marvie, how in the world did all this come about?" asked Hettie, in wondering sympathy.

"Like a story, Hettie. I met Rose over a month ago. Went huntin' on a Sunday. Rode a long way, then walked. I got after some turkeys. They were awful wild. I followed them a long ways, down into a big grassy canyon where a stream ran. Most beautiful place. Deer, elk, beaver all along. But I wanted one of them big old gobblers. So I kept on. And I run plump into a girl. She was cryin'. I spoke to her—sat down with her. After a while she began to talk. First she was sore an' hot at her brother, Cedar Hatt, who beat her. Showed me black-and-blue marks on her bare legs. I said somebody like Jim Lacy ought to come along and kill him. Funny, wasn't it—me sayin' that? Well, we got real friendly. She said she'd meet me again, but farther away. That place was too near home. So she told me where a trail ran and how I could find it. I never told her who I was that time. Forgot. Anyway, I kept the day she set, and sure enough she came. . . . It was different that day. I reckon I fell in love then—not the first day. And she —but never mind. . . . I met her three times more. And last time, night before last at the dance. That's all."

"It's quite enough, isn't it, Marvie?" said Hettie.

"It sure is. I forgot to tell you. At the dance, when she said first she wouldn't meet me no more, I said I was goin' to our place Wednesday at the same time as before. I'm goin', too."

"Marv, if what I know of girls holds true—if she really cares—she'll come. Rose is too young to stick to a hard decision like that, if her heart's involved."

"Hettie, you're a comfort," cried Marvie, gratefully, almost hugging her. "I'll hope she'll come. I'll believe it. Maybe that'll let me eat and sleep."

"You'll tell me everything?" asked Hettie, earnestly.

"You bet I will. Now I'll go and crawl to Ben."

Several days passed. Hettie took to horseback-riding again, venturing perhaps farther away from the ranch than Ben would have allowed, had he known. But Hettie seemed driven. On Wednesday she rode with Marvie for five miles back into the forest toward the brakes, and that was the greatest ride she ever enjoyed. Ridge and canyon, the aspen thickets, the wonderful swales where the turkeys and elk lived, the beaver dams and bee trees, the first coloring of vines and sumach in the open spots, the deep dark thickets where the horses scented bear and reared to turn back, the roar of water over boulders and the wind through the pine tops—these things enchanted Hettie and won her more than ever to the wilderness of Arizona.

On the last stretch back home, where the trail was fairly level and open, she urged her horse to his best speed. That race satisfied, for the time being, a restlessness and need of violence. Her blood danced hot; wind and sun burned her cheeks; the tang of the woods acted like wine. Thus she rode down into the clearing and on to the barn and corrals. And she ran pell-mell into Ben, Raidy, Dillon, and Tom Day, scattering them like quail.

"Hey there, you Indian!" yelled Ben, and he climbed a corral fence, the better to tease her.

Hettie reined her mount and, wheeling him, trotted back, and slid from the saddle.

"He's a—fine horse, Ben," she declared, patting the wet neck.

"Wal, he suits you, lass," said Tom Day, admiringly, as he took her in from boots to sombrero.

"Miss Hettie, strikes me this hyar Arizonie has got into your blood," added old Raidy, shaking his head dubiously. "Reckon I don't like it. Day says it ain't safe for you to ride out alone. So does Dillon."

"What do *you* say, Ben?" queried Hettie, archly.

"Not a darn thing. I quit long ago tryin' to run you," returned Ben.

Dillon leaned against the corral, in the background, without entering into the conversation. The discoloration round his eye had not wholly disappeared.

"Miss, can't you be happy ridin' on the ranch, without headin' off into the woods?" asked Raidy.

"Do you think I'd ride inside a fence? Not much."

"Wal, Hettie Ide, I sure know what you need," declared Tom Day.

"To be spanked, I suppose," laughed Hettie. "But seriously, what's the danger?"

"Wal, lass, mebbe there ain't any real danger," replied Day, thoughtfully. "But we're sort of locoed these days. Reckon it's far-fetched to think hoss-thieves an' rustlers might take a notion to steal you."

"Kidnap me for ransom?" queried Hettie, incredulously.

"Wal, yes, an' for other reasons, too," rejoined the old cattleman, significantly. "You don't 'pear to know it, but you're a mighty handsome girl."

"Thank you, Uncle Tom. That's a fine compliment. But it's not scaring me."

"Hettie, look here," interposed Ben, gravely, stepping to her with a piece of paper in his hand. "Read this."

Hettie took the coarse dirty paper and read:

Ben Ide
Sir.
Fire your foreman Dillon or dig a grave for him.
X.

Without a word Hettie returned the slip to her brother.

"We found that nailed on the bunkhouse door," he said, angrily. "It's a threat. Dillon recovered another bunch of my cattle yesterday. Only a few head, but enough to make these rustlers sore. To-day we found where they'd been camping in an old cabin, on my own land. Of all the nerve! I've been reasonable about this cattle-stealing. I expected it. But when these thieves grab my best horse and camp right under my nose—it's time for me to get sore."

"See, Miss Hettie," added Raidy. "That's why it ain't safe for you to ride out so far."

"I'll be careful hereafter," replied Hettie, soberly, handing her horse over to Raidy. "Mr. Day, won't you stay for supper?"

"Sorry, lass, but I've got to be goin' home."

"Good-by then. Come soon again," said Hettie, turning away. She was proceeding up the lane, revolving in mind that threatening note Ben had showed her, when he caught up with her and fell into her step.

"Hettie, on the square now—did you write this note and stick it up on the bunkhouse?" he asked.

"Ben Ide! Are you crazy?" Hettie cried, incredulously. Then she burst out laughing. "Of all things! . . . Brother, I fear the loss of your cattle and California Red has caused you to lose your head."

"Forgive me, Hettie," returned Ben, contritely. "I imagined you might have done that, just to plague me. And honest, I wish you had."

"Ben, why in the world can you wish such a thing as that?"

"Because if you had I wouldn't worry. I hoped you'd done it. Reckon I am loco, as these riders say. But, Hettie, I don't like this situation I'm in."

"Neither do I, Ben," retorted Hettie. "But nobody can tell you anything."

"Aw now, Hettie, that's not nice of you," said Ben, reproachfully. "I told Ina about your affair with Dillon —*your* side of it, mind you. She pitched into me like sixty. I can't stand havin' both of you against me."

"We're not against you, Ben," returned Hettie, earnestly.

"Yes, you are," he said, doggedly. "An' I'm getting sore at everybody. I'm going against your advice and Ina's, even Tom Day's. I've offered a reward of one thousand dollars for the return of California Red. Posted notices along the trails. Tom didn't like that. Said some one would bring the horse back, then steal him again."

"What did Dillon say?" asked Hettie, curiously.

"He approved my offering the reward. You know Dillon said he could get Red back. And he was away two days, after he returned from Winthrop. I don't know where he went. He's worked with most of these outfits along the Mogollons. He knows them all, anyway, and no doubt some of them are clanny with the horse and cattle thieves. That's the worst of this country. You really don't know who is honest. Well, Dillon came back and said he couldn't find out anything about Red. So I decided to offer a reward. And Dillon himself took the notices out on the range."

"You'll get Red back," returned Hettie, hopefully.

"I've got another idea," he went on. "I want to send for several well-known sheriffs and put them on the track of these rustlers. Pat Garrett, of New Mexico. If I could get him, and a couple from Phoenix, and hire a gang of hard-shooting cowboys, I'll bet they'd clean out the rustlers. But Tom Day yelled murder at the very idea. And Dillon, he hit the roof. Swore they'd burn me out instead of just rustling a few cattle. Few? By George! I'd like to know what Dillon would call a lot of cattle."

"Ben, you should listen to Tom Day, at least," replied Hettie. "He knows the country."

"I'm listening, Hettie. But I want some action," he retorted. "If I don't get Red back inside of ten days there'll be hell to pay by somebody."

Marvie did not return to the ranch till late. Hettie sat up waiting for him, trying to read, but mostly gazing into the wood fire with dreamy, sad eyes. She heard his swift step on the porch, and a jingle of spurs, then a quick knock.

"Come in, Marvie," she called expectantly.

In he rushed, like the wind, but quietly, and he

startled her with his pale face crossed by black smudges, and his piercing, radiant eyes. He carried a rifle and quirt and gloves in his hands; and altogether he appeared a striking, thrilling figure. Hettie knew before he spoke what had happened.

"She was there!" he whispered, dramatically.

"Marv, I knew that the instant you entered," said Hettie, with a smile. There was a contagion in his spirit.

"Hettie, I'm sure the happiest an' miserablest man in the world," he added.

"Sit down, Marvie, and tell me all about it."

"Not a great deal to tell, but what there is of it is turrible," he returned, coming to the seat beside her. Then in a low voice, full of suppressed emotion, he went on: "Rose was there. She'd been there for hours, waitin', cryin', fearin' I wouldn't come. She said her heart broke. She'd found out she loved me. I was the only one who'd ever cared for her—been good to her. She said she could give me up—to save me disgrace—but she'd have to kill herself. I swore I'd stick to her —marry her. I talked an' talked. An' then I told her I'd fetch you down the trail next Wednesday. She was turrible scared at that. But I told her you'd help us. An' finally she agreed. She's to ride down a trail we know, till we meet her. . . . That's all, Hettie. An' for God's sake——"

Marvie broke off huskily, his voice failing.

Hettie impulsively kissed him. "Marvie, I think you're pretty much of a man," she said. "I'll go. And I'll find some way to solve your problem."

He mumbled something incoherent and rushed out of the room, neglecting to close the door. Hettie watched him stalk away in the moonlight, then shutting the door she drew her chair nearer the fire and fell into grave and sympathetic pondering over Marvie's love affair.

Fifteen

Hettie, early riser as she was, outdid herself on this Wednesday morning, which was the day on which she had agreed to ride down into the brakes with Marvie.

There were tasks to see to, some of which she performed before her mother called her to breakfast. Hettie was still at the table when whoops outside alarmed her. Then she recognized Marvie's "Whoopee!"

"Gracious! Is the poor kid celebrating the arrival of this day?" ejaculated Hettie, mirthfully.

Nevertheless, she ran out on the porch, followed by her mother.

"For the land's sake!" cried Mrs. Ide. "Has Marvie gone daffy!"

They saw him running wildly bareheaded, up the walk toward Ben's house. Once up on the ridge, Marvie espied Hettie, and waving to her he yelled:

"Look down in the pasture!"

Hettie did so, at least toward the near pasture, but as her view was most obscured by pine trees she did not see anything unusual.

"Whoopee!" yelled Marvie again. "Hey, Ben!"

Hettie realized now that something was up, so she started to run across the log bridge. When she got halfway she saw Ben rush out on the porch, in his shirt sleeves, rifle in hand.

"What's the matter, Marv?" he shouted.

"CALIFORNIA RED'S BACK!" bellowed Marvie, coming to a halt.

Hettie saw Ben start as if struck. Then he ran to meet Marvie. Hettie lost little time getting over the bridge and across the grassy bench. Breathless and excited she arrived in time to see Ben sink down on a log, as if overcome. Ina came running in her dressing-gown.

"Oh, Ben—who—what is it?" she cried, in alarm.

"Glory be! Ina, Red is back."

"That all? I thought we were attacked by rustlers. Marvie, you can yell like a demon."

"Ben, I'm—so glad," panted Hettie.

"Boy, you're not playin' a trick on me—because I was sore on you?" implored Ben of Marvie.

"Nope, I saw him sure. An' I was tickled to death."

"Aw! . . . Reckon Dillon fetched him back," sighed Ben, in unutterable gratitude.

"Dillon, hell!" exclaimed Marvie, evidently provoked out of his radiant pleasure of being the first to inform his boss about the return of his beloved favorite. "Dillon is in bed. There's nobody up but me."

"Ahuh! By George! Did you see anyone?"

"Not a soul."

"Well! That beats me. Let's go down. Ina, get some clothes on if you're comin'. Tell the kid. This'll sure tickle him."

Ben and Marvie, with Hettie trying to keep beside them, stalked down off the ridge, into the lane, through the courtyard, and on to the corrals. Three times during that swift walk Ben asked the same question and three times Marvie made the same reply. Raidy appeared on the bunkhouse porch and he carried a rifle.

"Boss, what's the bellarin' about?" he queried, as he joined the trio. Marvie led the way through two corrals, and then across the wide square to a high pasture fence, up which he scrambled like a squirrel.

"There!" he shouted, pointing.

Ben surmounted the fence ahead of Hettie, and his wondering exultant cry prepared her.

California Red stood not far distant, down along the fence. Nervously he jerked up at Ben's cry, and wheeled with head high, ears up, eyes wild. How sensitive, splendid he looked to Hettie!

Ben whistled and began to call: "Red—Red, old boy, come here, Red!"

The stallion lost his alarm, and laying down his ears he approached slowly, step by step. Ben kept calling. Red knew the voice and showed increasing gladness. He whinnied. Then he trotted straight to where Ben straddled the fence. He looked the worse for his absence. Ragged, scratched, muddy, somewhat thinner, he showed the effect of hard travel and probably harsh treatment.

"Ben, somebody's been mean to him, else he wouldn't come hankerin' to you thet way," declared Raidy.

"By Heaven! if that's true!" cried Ben, fiercely, and reaching out his hand he called again. "Come, Red. Come, old boy. Don't you know your boss?"

But Red would not come all the way. He halted uncertain, pawing the ground. His dark eyes shone softly. Again he whinnied. Ben guardedly got down off the fence, speaking all the time, and slowly went up to Red, finally encircling the noble neck with his arm. Then he buried his face in the red mane.

Hettie's thoughts went back to the Forlorn River days when California Red had roamed the sage hills, free and proud, when Ben had been a lonely, outcast, wild-horse hunter, and when Nevada had come so mysteriously into their lives. Hettie's eyes dimmed. She could not understand Ben's great and passionate love for that grand horse, but she felt sympathy for him and rejoiced in his happiness.

Meanwhile the cowboys had arrived on the scene. Raidy had opened the pasture gate. Presently Ben led the stallion through to the square.

"Look him over, Raidy," said Ben.

While the cowboys crowded around and Hettie still stayed on the fence, the better to see, the old horseman walked round Red, feeling him, examining him, lifting his hoofs one after the other.

"Wal, boss, he's as sound as a bullet," declared Raidy, gladly. "Ganted up a little an' got a couple of bad cuts. An' he's lost a shoe. Nervous an' skittish. But

you can bet he's glad to git home; an' far as I can see
he's no wuss for bein' stolen."

"Raidy, do you still hang to that opinion?" inquired
Ben.

"I sure do. They ain't anything else to it. Why, man,
don't you know hosses? Can't you see he's been haltered an' hobbled?"

"Aw, no!" said Ben.

"Sure. Look thar. Use your eyes, boss. You got him
back an' I reckon you'll keep him this time. But don't
let your love for the hoss blind you to facts."

Raidy kept running gentle, skillful hands over Red,
ruffling up the silky hair, looking with the eyes of
long experience to marks and signs by which he read
something of what had happened to the horse.

"See for yourself," went on Raidy, with vehemence.
"Look hyar! . . . By Gawd! he's been roped, too!"

At this point Hettie espied Dillon stalk around the
corner of the high fence, which had obscured the men
and horse. Abruptly he halted. Swift amaze and consternation leaped across his expression of curiosity,
blotting it out. Then as swiftly his face changed,
smoothing to a smile. What a handsome, pleasant man!
Hettie marveled at his consummate control and acting.
But he could not fool her again. The return of Red was
actually as startling to Dillon as it had been to anyone
else there.

The circle of cowboys opened to admit Dillon.

"Ha! So, boss, what'd I tell you?" he broke out, and
vigorously shook Ben's hand. It was strange for Hettie
to see how much pleasure that gave Ben. But just then
he was up in the skies. "The old red son-of-a-gun has
come back. Jumped the pasture fence goin' an' comin'.
. . . Red, I take off my hat to you. But you never had
me guessin'!"

"Dillon, I had it figured the same," declared Ben.

Raidy snorted his disgust. "An' you once a wild-
hoss hunter! Say, if Red had *run* off he'd never have
come back. I asked you to take a peep at them marks

on him. But you keep huggin' the hoss an' you won't look."

"Old-timer, I'm so happy to get him back that I don't want to do anythin' else. Besides, Raidy, on the square, I'd hate to have it proved he'd been stolen."

"Stolen? That's nonsense, I tell you," interposed Dillon, testily. "Red took a little run an' come home. I've had many a hoss do it."

"Not wild hosses, Mister Dillon," snapped Raidy.

"What do you know about hosses, Raidy?"

"Wal, I reckon I've forgot more'n you ever knew," retorted the older man. "I ain't doubtin' you've *had* a lot of hosses, Dillon, but you didn't *raise* them—you didn't *catch* them—an' you didn't *keep* them long."

This was pretty plain speaking, as was evinced by Ben's stepping between the men, and the dark flash that wiped out Dillon's geniality.

"What're you hintin' at?" he queried.

"I'm not hintin'. I'm tellin' you, that's all. An' you can like it or lump it."

Ben raised a hand to silence Raidy. "That'll do. You're both privileged to your opinions, but don't get nasty."

"All right, boss," replied Raidy, in an aggrieved tone. "But my word is sort of ridiculed hyar. An' I'm askin' thet you look at these marks on Red. If you won't I reckon I'll take it as a slap at me, an' I'll quit you cold."

"Raidy!" exclaimed Ben, astounded.

"You know me, boss," returned the old horseman, sturdily.

Ben wavered. It was plain to Hettie that he hoped to keep peace between the old and new hands, so valuable to him now. But Raidy had thrown down his gage and he looked formidable.

"Ben," called Hettie, from the fence, "you've known Raidy all your life. He taught you how to ride. It's only fair that you listen to him."

"All right, Raidy, if you feel that bad about it," replied Ben, resignedly.

Again the old horseman ran his gentle, skillful hands over Red's supple body, down to the wonderfully muscled legs. "Look hyar," said Raidy, as he stooped. "He's been hobbled. See! He's been gone *ten* days. Thet mark was made no more'n yesterday."

"Reckon you're right," admitted Ben, as he slowly arose. "I apologize."

"No apology wanted," said Raidy. "All I want is for you to come out of your trance. . . . Now look hyar. Look at Red's nose. He's been roped."

"By thunder! There's been a hackamore on him," ejaculated Ben.

Dillon was not to be outwitted, and he had swiftly followed Ben's examination of the horse.

"Damn if Raidy isn't right boss," he exploded, evidently regretful. "I hadn't even looked at Red. But there are the marks, plain as print. . . . I apologize, too, Raidy. My mistake."

"Wal, Mister Dillon, I'm acceptin' your apology," drawled Raidy, his keen old hawk eyes on the handsome foreman.

Hettie was riding beside Marvie, across the western end of the sage flat, toward the fence which marked the limit of Ben Ide's ranch land.

Marvie dismounted to open the gate for them, and when he vaulted to the saddle again he grinned. "Nobody but Raidy saw us, an' he won't tell. But Ben would stand for anythin' to-day. Gee! how he loves that red horse!"

"He does indeed. Well, I love California Red, too."

"Ben's daffy over him. Gave me a hundred dollars, just for seein' Red first!"

"Early to bed, early to rise, makes a boy healthy, wealthy, and——"

"Gee! I do feel rich!" interrupted Marvie. "An' I'd like to fly to town an' back. But it'll keep."

"Marvie, were you looking at Dillon when he first came on us and saw Red?" inquired Hettie.

"No, I wasn't. Why?" returned Marvie, turning to eye her.

"He struck me as being more amazed than any of us, and *not* so happy."

"Ahuh!" replied Marvie. It was evident that he chose to be noncommittal. Hettie, however, did not fail to catch the glint in his eye.

"Raidy and Dillon are at odds," she continued. "That's plain."

"Wasn't Dillon the slick one, though, when he turned the tables on Raidy?" rejoined Marvie, as if impelled.

"Yes. He's too clever for men. It takes a woman to see through him."

"I'll bet *daylight* will show through him—presently," returned Marvie, in dark significance.

"Marv, you are absorbing a lot of Arizona."

"Here's where we turn off, Hettie," said Marvie, as he left the road. "Narrow trail, but good. Look out for the brush an' duck the branches. Ride now!"

He spurred his horse into a lope and Hettie did likewise. Soon they entered the forest, where the shade was welcome and no dust arose. Hettie had been on this trail several times, though not to go very far. It led west, toward the brakes and the frowning dark notches of the Mogollons, dim and purple in the distance. Soon they passed the limit of Hettie's experience in that direction, a fact which gave her a thrill. She scarcely had a chance, however, to look at the scenery, for Marvie was making time, and she had to watch her horse and the low branches.

They rode perhaps five miles before the trail began to penetrate deeper into the forest and to ascend into rockier and rougher country. They climbed high, and Hettie had a glimpse now and then of the red desert far to the north, and the black slopes beneath her, falling away to the west. She soon gathered what the brakes of the Mogollons meant. The brakes were canyons, running like the ridges of a washboard, walled with brush and rock, choked with dense thickets, above which the lofty pines and spruces towered. Ridge after ridge Marvie climbed and descended, until coming to a deeper, clearer canyon he turned off to follow a willow-bordered stream.

As they progressed, again riding at a lope, the canyon widened and deepened, the walls grew rugged and unscalable, the fringe of pines on the rims lifted higher, and every aspect of the wilderness seemed likewise intensified. The time came when the horses had to walk again, down and down, under narrow gray shelves of stone, under the massed foliage of maple, oak, aspen, all beginning to show a tint of autumn, especially the fluttering aspens, just turning to gold. The stream grew larger, swifter, deeper, and its mellow roar filled the dreamy solitude.

At corners, where the trail turned, Marvie always exercised a caution which added more than romance to Hettie's feelings. This adventure grew with the miles. How dark, still, lonely some of the constrictions in this brake of the Mogollons!

Turkeys ran fleetly from the open grass patches into the thickets; deer walked up the steep wooded slopes; elk stopped their browsing on the willows to gaze at the disturbers of their solitude; beaver slipped off their muddy dams to make swirls in the still green pools; squirrels chattered; jays squalled; ravens croaked; hawks sailed across the blue strip of sky overhead.

"Somewhere along here we'll meet her," whispered Marvie, fearfully. "It always scares me. That Cedar Hatt might be prowlin' along the rim to spy us. Rose is cute, though. I've waited half a day before she came."

They wound along the crooked trail, and if it were possible, Hettie imagined every vista wilder and more hauntingly beautiful than the last. The white bleached grass, the green willows, the amber rocks, the rushing foaming brook, the thickets of oak and aspen, russet and gold, the wonderful walls rising sheer, stained and mossy, gray and purple, up to the ragged fringed rims —all these aided the movement of leaves, the flash of birds, the fragrance of pine, the utter solitude, into working an enchantment upon Hettie's senses. No wonder Marvie had fallen in love with his wild Rose.

"I see her horse," whispered Marvie, as he halted. "She'll be near. We'll get off now. I'll hide our horses in the aspen thicket."

Hettie got off to hand her bridle to him, and waited while he led their mounts out of sight. How noiselessly he moved! Marvie had become a woodsman. Soon he returned and led her off the trail into the grass.

"Anyone ridin' along behind us would sure see our tracks," he whispered. "But that's a slim chance. You see it's an old unused trail here. The Hatts live over in the next canyon."

"She's a brave kid, to meet you this way. And you're not such a coward, Marvie, boy," returned Hettie.

He led her up a gradual grassy slope, into the protecting shelter of low pines and silver spruces. "Look at the elk beds," he whispered, pointing to round places where grass and moss had been flattened.

Hettie espied a ragged red pony, without a saddle, haltered to a sapling. Then she saw a dark curly head rise above the tall grass. Next moment Marvie was speaking low: "Hettie, this is Rose Hatt. . . . Rose, I've fetched her. This's Hettie Ide, my best friend an' sort of sister."

As Hettie sank down, smiling, with hands outstretched, the girl rose to her knees, her eyes dilating, her face without color.

"Rose, I'm glad—to meet you," whispered Hettie, pantingly, and she kissed the girl.

"Oh, Miss Ide—you're good to come," faltered Rose. She was trembling all over. This child of the wilderness was nothing less than terrified at meeting one of Marvie's kin.

Marvie knelt beside Rose, and it was evident this was a torturing moment for him, too. The romance and excitement had passed. Ben Ide's sister was now face to face with the daughter of rustler and backwoodsman Elam Hatt, with the sister of notorious Cedar Hatt.

"Hettie, I reckon Rose won't be so scared an' shy if I leave you alone with her," said Marvie. "So I'll keep watch below. An' don't forget we haven't lots of time."

Then with a bright and reassuring look at Rose he slipped off under the low-spreading trees. Hettie turned to the girl, trying to think of words to put her at ease. How like a woodland wild flower! Rose wore a buckskin blouse fringed and beaded, a ragged brown skirt, and boots without stockings. She held a sprig of tiny aspen leaves, turning gold.

"Rose, since Marvie loves you, I must love you, too," said Hettie, speaking not what she had intended, but the words that welled from her heart. She did not need to be told that Rose Hatt had never had love of mother, sister, or friend. The girl gave a little gasping cry of wonder and pain, then fell into Hettie's arms, where she burst into tears.

This made the ordeal easier for Hettie, and she held the girl in silence until the paroxysms of weeping had subsided. Then she began to talk, kindly, soothingly, as if to a child, saying she hardly knew what, until the moment came when she felt she might venture a question. But before she could ask it Rose sat up, wiped her wet face, and smiled through her tears.

"Marvie was right," she said. "It's sure good to see you, hear you, now I'm over my scare. I'll never forget you till my dyin' day."

"Rose, you love Marvie, very much?" said Hettie, venturing to open the serious interview.

"Yes," replied the girl, simply. "I couldn't help it. But I didn't know at first. Not till the dance."

"Then you two have pledged your troth?"

"If you mean told our love, yes—Miss Ide. But I didn't promise to marry Marvie."

"He asked you, of course?"

"He begged me to," replied the girl, lifting her head with pride.

"Why did you refuse?"

"I love Marvie too well to hurt him with you an' all his family."

"Do you mean you think you'd disgrace him and us because you're a Hatt?"

"Yes, an' a good deal more I haven't told Marvie," she went on, steady of voice, though her round breast heaved. "Cedar would come down on Marvie an' you an' your brother Ben for money. An' so would another man whose name I daren't tell. He—this man—has got a hold on Cedar—an' me. He'd ruin us all."

"Rose, that's a strong statement," said Hettie. "But even if it isn't exaggerated it doesn't change the fact that you and Marvie ought to wait. You're both very young."

"I'm not exaggeratin'. I could tell you more. An' about marryin'—Marvie's reason for hurry is to get me away from the life I live. It's turrible, Miss Ide. I have to cook, wash, scrub for an outfit of rustlers an' hoss-thieves. Look at my hands! Look at the black marks —here—an' there. I get kicked an' beat. Marvie knows an' he can't stand it any longer."

"Could you not leave this home?" queried Hettie, earnestly.

"I've thought of that. Yes. I could. My dad wouldn't care. But I'd have to be a servant—or worse."

"No, indeed. Rose, you could come to my home."

"Oh, how—wonderful!" gasped the girl, rapturously clasping her hands. "But that'd be 'most the same as marryin' Marvie, so far as Cedar an'—that other man are concerned. . . . No, it'd never do. But thank you— bless you!"

"Rose, we mustn't despair," continued Hettie, touched to the heart by this girl's sincerity. "Time will help us. If you could only escape this—this drudgery and shame."

"That's the hope which keeps me up, Miss Ide. If I could only tide over a little time! Cedar is goin' to hell fast. He's rustlin', gamblin', drinkin' harder than ever. He's under the thumb of—the man I daren't squeal on."

"But why daren't you?"

"Because if he didn't kill me, Cedar would. I'm the

only one outside of this Pine Tree outfit who *knows*.
An' my life ain't worth much."

"Pine Tree outfit!" echoed Hettie, her eyes lighting.
"That's the mysterious gang of rustlers."

"It sure is. I'm trustin' you with my life, Miss Hettie.
But I daren't tell more. Nobody knows how secrets slip
out. You might talk in your sleep."

"Naturally. But I think you could risk it, considering
I sleep alone," said Hettie. "Rose, this *is* a plot. We're
all involved. Your people and mine. What a tangle! It
must have been fate that brought you and Marvie together. Oh, if I only knew how best to advise you."

"Reckon I wish so, too. But I've got a hunch. It's
my job to stick home—to fool my people—to learn all
I can—to fight that devil off who—who . . . I must see
Marvie very seldom an' be sure we're never ketched.
Somethin' will happen, Miss Ide. You've made me feel
it. You made things different. Neither Cedar—nor *him*,
can last long in this country. Not now. I heard my dad
say so. . . . Oh, this is the second time my hopes have
risen. Oh, I wish I could tell you of another friend I
found lately. I forgot. . . . But he came to my house an'
there was hell. I listened at night through the chinks of
the logs. Cedar was wild. Cash Burridge was there.
'We've got a big deal on,' says Cash. An' that pleased
all the gang except Cedar. They set to whisperin' an' I
heard no more."

"Rose—isn't your friend—Jim Lacy?" whispered
Hettie, haltingly, with dry lips.

The girl caught her breath and drew back sharply,
wonder the most predominant of her varying emotions.

"There, you have betrayed it," continued Hettie,
forcefully, trying to command her voice. "Call Marvie
now. We will plan another meeting, then hurry home.
I've enough to think of—this time."

Rose silently slipped away under the pines, and Hettie, staring at the green-walled foliage, seemed to see a
ghost. "Oh, my God!" she whispered in agony. "Nevada belongs to this thieving, vile crew!"

Sixteen

Frost fell early in September on the high rims of the Mogollons. Soon after the sun set the rarefied air became cold and sharp, making a campfire something to draw the riders and hunters, and other men of the woodland.

A group of five dark-faced, dark-garbed campers sat around a beautiful opal-hearted cedar fire, at the wild edge of Black Butte, where it fell sheer into the brakes. Three of the men were playing cards, cross-legged in front of a saddle blanket, intensely intent on the greasy bits of colored pasteboard and the piles of gold coin and rolls of greenbacks. They were gambling—the absorbing pastime of all dyed-in-the-wool rustlers.

The other two men occupied a position on the opposite side of the fire. One had his back and his outspread palms to the blaze, while the other sat against a log.

"Hell, Jim," swore the standing man, flicking a hand toward the gamblers, "they couldn't hear the crack of doom. They'll gamble there all night or till one of them has all the money. An' what difference would it make now—if they did hear what you say?"

"Wal, Cash, the fact is I'm not used to crowds," replied the other. "It takes long to get acquainted. An' you know I can never be shore of any man."

"That's the price you pay for leadership. Reckon it's the same among honest businessmen in the world as among rustlers an' gunmen. But I didn't mean to split hairs over it. I was just complainin' because you're so close-mouthed."

"What of it, Burridge?" queried Jim, somewhat acidly. "I shore talk plenty to you, don't I, when we're alone?"

"Course you do, Jim," answered Burridge. "All I want to get at is this. If you'd loosen up a little more, drink an' gamble a little, especially when we run into other outfits, it'd facilitate our plans."

"I reckon, Cash," returned Jim, wearily. "But how can I have a quick eye an' hand if I drink? I'll agree, though, to be more friendly an' set in a game now an' then."

"Good! Reckon that'll do. Lord, Jim, don't get me wrong! Ever since you called Hardy Rue out an' killed him I've been ready to crawl an' wear my fingernails off scratchin' for you. I mayn't have been your friend back in Lineville, but I sure love you now. You've put me on my feet again."

"Wal, Cash, that's plain talk," replied Jim. "An' I don't mind sayin' I like you better than I used to. But I can't love any man or even be pards."

"Sure, sure I understand," returned Burridge, hastily. "An' I'm damn glad for small favors. But you needn't tell that to our gang or any of these outfits we meet. They all think you were my pard back in California an' are yet. Burt Stillwell would have shot me, surer than the Lord made little apples. But he was afraid of you. He was undecided. He couldn't be himself, an' I'm tellin' you he was a bad *hombre*."

"Aw, bad, yes, in a sense of dirty yellow behind-your-back viciousness," agreed Jim, flashing a quick eloquent hand. "I hate to throw a gun on such fodder. But he forced it. He kept still till he got a few drinks. Then he r'iled up aboot Ben Ide's red horse, an' he put in that ridiculous claim for his pard, Cedar Hatt. Wanted a share of the divvy for the cattle—for this Hatt fellow."

"The hell he did! Well, I wondered what it was about. But I was so glad I didn't feel no curiosity," returned Burridge; he turned round to kick the fire-logs. Then again he faced his companion. "Maybe you don't know it, Lacy, but you made a lot of friends by pluggin' Stillwell, an' one sure-enough enemy."

"Who's that? This Cedar Hatt?"

"He's the bird. A red-tailed buzzard, an' no mistake. He's a backwoodsman, Jim, like an Indian, who knows the woods. Cedar wouldn't ever try you out, unless, like Burt, he'd been lookin' at the bottle. All the same you'll be in more danger from Cedar than from all the gun-throwers in Arizona. He's killed shepherds an' cowboys enough, believe me. He'll trail you—ambush you in the woods."

"Much obliged, Cash," drawled Jim, yawning. "Reckon I'd better look out for this heah Cedar Hatt."

"I'm givin' you a hunch of hunches," declared Burridge. "I'm most damn honest an' selfish about it, too. I've other reasons beside affection not to want Jim Lacy killed. Cedar Hatt will be sore enough when he hears you put Stillwell over, but, say, when he learns you got that red stallion an' sent him back to Ide—my Gawd! brother, he'll be hell's fire!"

"How soon is he goin' to find out?" queried Lacy, with more interest. "Stillwell cain't very wal tell. An' that pard of Stillwell's—Babe Morgan, some one called him—he'll be runnin' yet."

"Cedar'll find out *pronto*," declared Burridge. "If not from some one outside our outfit, then from some one inside. For you were playin' a queer high hand, Jim, when you took the stallion away from Burt an' Babe an' sent it back to the Ide ranch. They'd stolen it. Your argument sounded good to me. Ben Ide would raise more hell over the loss of California Red than a hundred thousand head of stock."

"Huh! I'll bet he would," declared Lacy, dropping his head. The twig he had been twirling in his fingers snapped sharply.

"Well, to go on, your argument looked good to me. Now I've got brains, an' most of these rustlin' *hombres* haven't nothin' but spruce gum in their heads. That deal looked queer to all our outfit. Still, only Hubrigg opened his trap to say so. Hubrigg likes you, though, an' I think you can gamble on him."

Here Burridge leaned over toward Jim to whisper: "If our gang seem a little standoffish yet, it's only your reputation. Since you helped us to steal cattle an' drive them an' sell them, why, they're sure you are one of us, even if you are Jim Lacy."

"Reckon that ought to be aboot enough," returned Lacy.

He turned his ear to the faint cold wind that breathed up out of the black void below.

"Hear anythin'?" queried Burridge.

"Rollin' stones. Might be deer on the trail."

"Might be Stagg, too, an' I'll gamble it is. For he's overdue."

"Listen," rejoined Lacy, holding up a sensitive hand.

Both men turned their heads sidewise to the wind and waited. Fitfully the faint wind mourned through the forest. From far below floated up a soft murmur of tumbling stream. Solitude and silence seemed to be emphasized by these wilderness factors. The campfire cracked; the gamblers slapped their cards and clinked their gold.

"Heah anythin'?" asked Lacy, suddenly relaxing.

"Sure. A lot of night sounds, includin' our gamblin' pards here, but no hoss," returned Burridge.

"Wal, I heah a hoss," said Lacy.

"Good! That'll be Stagg, unless it might be one of our hosses. I'll take a look an' then I'll unroll my bed."

Burridge stalked away in the gloom of the forest, while Lacy, left alone, attended to the campfire. Once or twice he glanced at the absorbed gamesters, with something curious, strange, and menacing in his eyes. Then he fell to contemplation of the opal heart of the campfire. He watched it, the glow and sparkle and white shade and pearly red. And the moment arrived when he forgot the wild environment, the gambling rustlers, to become like a statue, cold-faced, with haunted eyes. He must have seen a ghost in the radiant embers, for not till a thud of hoofs sounded close at hand did he rouse out of his trance.

Presently two dark forms entered the circle of light, and approached, talking low. Lacy got up to meet them.

"Howdy, Jim!" greeted the newcomer with Burridge. He was a swarthy-faced, beady-eyed white man with a strain of Indian or Mexican blood.

"Howdy, Stagg! Did you make a good job of it?" returned Lacy, with apparent carelessness.

"Wasn't no job a-tall," said Stagg, reaching bare grimy hands toward the fire. "Soon as you-all left, the red hoss quieted down, an' I coaxed him out of thet measly leetle corral. He din't like thet. An' after he found out I was leadin' him home he didn't make no more fuss. An' we made fast time. Reckon it was nigh on midnight when we got down on the sage. I tied up both hosses, pulled off my boots, put on my moccasins, an' led the stallion five miles through grass an' sage. When I run into Ide's fence I kept goin' along till I come to a gate. I opened it an' let him in."

"Much obliged, Stagg. I—reckon it was no fool move of mine—though some think different," replied Lacy, turning his face away from the fire.

"Lacy, it was the slickest piece of headwork I ever seen on this range," declared Stagg. "I hadn't time to tell you I was at Burton's ranch the next day after Stillwell stole the stallion. Ide's cowmen came rarin' over the country. Thet Raidy, he's an old hand, an' he was mad as a hornet. An' to-day as I was climbin' the Hogback I run into a sheepherder I know. Greaser named Juan somethin'. He said Ide had plastered the trees along the trails, offerin' reward for Red."

"There, Jim—you see, it was a wise move," declared Burridge, with satisfaction. "Young Ide would have spent a fortune gettin' back that stallion. Well, he sure was grand hoss-flesh. I only looked at him once. If I'd looked twice I'd been a hoss-thief, too."

Lacy stared out into the gloom of the forest.

"Reckon you're hungry?" asked Burridge of the arrival.

"Had a bite at Hatt's to-day," returned Stagg. "But a chuck of deer meat an' a cup of coffee wouldn't go bad."

"We got roast turkey. Young gobbler that Jim shot the head off as we was ridin' along."

"Wal, friend Jim must pack a shotgun," replied Stagg, with an attempt at facetiousness.

"Nope. Only that old six-shooter."

Lacy turned from the darkness to the firelight. "Stagg, did you see any of the Hatts?"

"Sure. They was all home, an' had company, too. Strangers to me."

"Did you tell them about takin' Red back to the Ide ranch?"

"Sure. Thought it a good idee. An' I rubbed it in, too. Elam's no hoss-thief. He said hoss-stealin' was a low-down bizness. But Cedar swore there was somethin' crooked about a gunman an' rustler who returned stolen property. Also he swore he'd steal the red stallion again, jest to spite you."

"Ahuh. Wal, what did Cedar say when he heahed I'd shot his pard, Burt Stillwell?" inquired Jim, in a dry, caustic tone.

"What?" queried Stagg, with a start.

"You heahed me, man."

"Sure. But it—I . . . An' you shot Burt?"

Lacy nodded coldly, eying the fire.

Stagg stiffened a little, and after a stultified pause glanced from Burridge to Lacy, and then out into the forest. A silence ensued, broken only by the gamblers.

"Burt's dead—then—of course?" asked Stagg, presently, with an effort.

Cash Burridge broke the strange spell of the moment.

"Burt's under the sod an' the leaves, waitin' the Judgment Day. An' it was a damn good job, Stagg."

"No arguin' ag'in' thet," returned Stagg, recovering to grin. "Wal, Lacy, fact is Cedar Hatt hadn't heerd no more'n me. But if you're curious, I can sure tell you—Cedar will be hoppin' mad."

"I told Jim that," said Burridge, impatiently. "What's it amount to, anyhow? There'll be a Hatt less *pronto*."

"Wal, pards, the population of this hyar Arizonie is sure deterioratin'," returned Stagg, with a guffaw.

One of the gamesters, disturbed by the loud laugh, looked up to say, "Bill, shet your loud mouth, an' come set in this game. Hubrigg an' Brann ain't very much to stack up ag'in'."

His bold face and rolling eyes expressed exceeding gratification while he clinked his pile of gold.

"I'm on," replied Stagg, eagerly. "Wait till I swaller some grub."

"How about you—Lacy?" inquired Brann, with marked hesitation. "We ain't slightin' you. It's an open game."

"Thanks, Brann," drawled Lacy. "I'd hate to win your pile. You see, I've got uncommon good eyes, an' it shore hurts my feelin's to see you men slippin' aces around. I'm a caird sharp. I'd break you. Like as not, then, you'd get sore an' pull a gun—which would be bad for this outfit."

Long and loud rolled the mirth of Burridge and Stagg down the aisles of the forest. Brann appeared a droll and good-humored rustler. He stared hard at Lacy, finally grinning.

"Jim, I'm recallin' thet invite for you to set in," he said, meaningly.

"Gamble your heads off," spoke up Burridge. "We needn't break camp till late to-morrow. But I'm turnin' in."

"Same for me," said Lacy, and strode out of the lighted circle. Presently he had to feel his way to the black tent-like spruce tree under which he had spread his tarpaulin and blankets. Sitting down, he pulled off his boots. Then he sat motionless, peering back at the ruddy campfire. Presently he removed his coat and made a pillow of it. Next he unbuckled his gun belt, took it off, and laid the gun under the edge of his coat. After that he gazed a long time out into the spectral forest. The wind had risen, and sang through the pines. A deep wild bay of a wolf rang out. How lonely, hungry, mournful!

"Reckon that poor lofer is like me," muttered Lacy,
and rolled in his blankets.

The ring of a cold ax on hardwood awakened Jim
Lacy from his slumbers.

There was a white frost on his tarpaulin and his
boots and his sombrero, also his nose, from the feel of
it. Hubrigg, who appeared to be an agreeable and help-
ful chap, was chopping wood for a campfire.

"Nifty mawnin', Hub," said Jim, by way of greeting.
"I'll pack some water."

"Hullo! I reckon your conscious never lets you
sleep," said Hubrigg. "Look at them stiffs there. Dead
to the world. Now watch."

With that he snatched up a bucket, pounded it with
the ax handle, then tossed it to Lacy. The rustlers,
rudely disturbed, leaped out of their beds, wild-eyed,
hair on end, every one of them holding a gun or
reaching for one.

"Haw! Haw! Haw!" roared Hubrigg. "Wake up, you
sour-dough eaters, an' help at the chores."

All of his roused hearers, except Burridge, cursed
him roundly, and Burridge, when he realized what had
happened, said, "Lord, I thought my day had come!"

Jim Lacy went down the trail for a pail of water.

Whenever such duty as this, or other opportunity,
afforded, he always took advantage of it, seeking ever
a moment away from the rustlers with whom he had
cast his lot. That time, however short, was a blessed
relief. He need not then be perpetually on the *qui vive,*
watching, listening, reading the minds of his companions. In those stolen moments or hours he reverted to
his old character, Nevada, lover of the open, of desert
and forest, of the life and color and mystery of nature.

The sun had not yet arisen. To the east the sky, over
the long arms of the Mogollons, reaching, sweeping
down black and wild, had begun to flush rosily. The
forest seemed awakening from its slumber with the bark
of squirrels and screech of jays, the bugle of bull elk,
and the sweet, plaintive twittering of canaries. Rocks

and grass showed the hoary coating of frost. The air nipped, and the water at the spring felt like ice to his face. There was a thin edge of crystal ice along the margin of the little pool.

Upon climbing back to the rim he paused a moment to gaze down into that marvelous black basin called the brakes of the Mogollons. They were really not black, though black predominated over the rich gold of aspens, and the scarlet of maples, the russet of oaks, and the vivid cerise of vines for which he had no name. A ragged pine-speared slope fell almost perpendicularly to the ribbed and ridged lowland below, and here and there outcroppings of gray crags and yellow shafts added to the effect of an exceedingly broken country. His experienced eye wandered down to the brakes, over what from that height appeared undulating ridge and swale. Its vastness amazed Jim Lacy. Here was a wilderness country as large as the northern California he knew so well. And to increase the effect to one of staggering conception, there stretched the desert, grand and illimitable. He had a moment of silent ecstasy of appreciation, followed by a melancholy longing for a time when he might be free to love Arizona, to have a ranch of his own, a few horses and cattle, a home in the wilds where he could hunt and ride, free to live peacefully, dreaming of the past. Melancholy longing because he knew it could never come true!

Returning to the campfire, he arrived in time to hear Brann exclaim: "What'n hell Columbia for do we want to ring the Hatts in on this deal?"

"Say, man, there's brains back of this deal," replied Burridge, derisively.

"Meanin' yours, eh? Wal, all right, but I'm from Missouri."

They ceased the argument at the approach of Jim Lacy.

"Somebody rustle the hosses," called out Burridge.

An hour later the six men, with as many pack horses, started over the rim on the trail down into the brakes.

It was a trail that would cause even the most expert and daring rider to hesitate before attempting it on horseback. Moreover, it was seldom used. Lacy decided it must be a rear outlet from the rendezvous of desperate men. Many a time axes had to be brought into requisition to enable pack horses to pass down. Jumble of rocks, weathered slides, narrow slanting ledges, fallen trees and thick brush, made this Hatt trail one to remember.

But though very steep, it was not long. It let out into the head of a canyon where the stream gushed forth from under an amber-mossed cliff, and went singing down through a winding defile, surely the wildest and most beautiful that Jim Lacy's eyes had ever beheld.

"Cash, tell me," said Lacy, at an opportune time, when they rode abreast, "is Cedar Hatt the haid of this Pine Tree outfit?"

"Hell no!" ejaculated Burridge, in ridicule. Then as an afterthought he continued: "But, Jim, I don't *know* he isn't. I mean I've sense enough to figure he couldn't be. There's a real man at the reins of that gang."

"You're square now? You honestly don't know?"

"So help me Heaven!" returned Burridge, raising his gloved right hand. "If I knew I'd tell you—even though the man was my pard. But I don't know. I never met a man who did. Of course no one is goin' to brag about that. The Pine Tree outfit is only three years old. It's got a brand, but sure no one ever seen it on a steer or a calf. I never seen it on anythin'. I hear it's cut on aspen trees. Sheepherders will tell you that."

"Cedar Hatt might belong to it?" queried Lacy.

"Sure. But he'd be a bad *hombre* to trust, unless you had some hold on him. My idea of the Pine Tree outfit is this. Some slick rustler from other parts has ridden in here, either with a few choice men or picked them carefully after he got here, an' he has the money an' the brains to control a small outfit. Some cowboy found a stray steer on the range. It had its brand painted out. Painted! That's new. But how the devil could they paint out the brands on a big bunch of wild steers?"

"Not very practical," observed Jim, thoughtfully.

"It's no trick to steal cattle in this country, an' it's a heap sight easier to sell them," declared Burridge. "But to do it on a big scale an' not be found out—I call that brains."

"How far to the Hatt ranch?"

"Round this next bend. Wonderful place to hole up, don't you think?"

"Shore is. Are all these canyons like this?"

"Like it? Yes, only rougher. Some of them are so thick you can't get a hoss through."

When they rode around a high green corner Jim gave vent to an exclamation of utmost pleasure. The brake opened into an oval valley surrounded by gray-cliffed, green-thicketed walls, rising high. A level meadow, where horses and cows grazed in deep grass, ended in a low bench of land, upon which huge isolated pines and spruces towered halfway to the rim. Two log cabins stood picturesquely at the edge of this rise of ground. In the background a corral and barn, with logs awry and roof caved in, showed half hidden in a blaze of golden aspens.

"Here's where the Hatts hang out," remarked Burridge. "It's like a fox den, with two holes. The one we just came down, an' a pass below where a couple of good shots could stave off all the cowboys in Arizona."

"Beautiful!" ejaculated Jim, charmed out of his usual reserve.

"I've been here often. Once tried to buy the place from Hatt. Not much."

"What do these Hatts live on?" queried Jim, gazing round.

"Meat an' beans an' corn meal. An' they make their own whiskey. If you take a swill of that it'll knock you flat."

"How many women-folks?"

"Only the kid—Rose. There was a woman here, a while back, wife of one of the boys, I heard. But I never saw her. . . . Well, old sharp-eyed Elam sees us already. He's comin' out with a gun."

The riders in advance drove the pack horses up on the bench, and followed to dismount. Burridge, arrived a little in advance of Jim. The old mountaineer, Hatt, stood shaggy-headed, with a smile of welcome on his craggy face.

"Howdy, Elam! Did you get word I was comin'?"

"Yep, but never expected you so soon."

"Shake hands with Jim Lacy," went on Burridge, laconically.

"Howdy, sir! Reckon you ain't no stranger, by name," responded Hatt, offering his hand.

Lacy leaned off his horse to accept Hatt's advance. "Shore glad to meet you, Elam," he drawled. "Reckon I fell in love with your homestead, heah. An' I'll hang around till you kick me out."

"Welcome you air," said Hatt, genially. "We keep open house fer our friends. Git down an' come in."

Burridge made no offer to introduce Jim to the other Hatts present, though he called them by name, Tobe and Henny. Cedar Hatt did not put in an appearance, nor did Lacy's quick eye sight the girl—Rose.

"Throw yer packs back in the grove," said Hatt. "Jest turn your hosses loose. Never yit had a hoss leave hyar."

While pack and saddle horses were led back toward the aspen grove Elam Hatt walked with Burridge, while the two sons followed. Lacy did not need more than a casual glance at Elam to define his status. He was a rough, sturdy backwoodsman who had, no doubt, lived by hunting until an easier vocation had presented with the ranging of cattle along the Mogollons. The two sons, however, exhibited nothing to impress favorably. They were uncouth, unshaven louts with bad teeth and pale eyes, and faces that indicated very low mentality. Lacy's advent manifestly did not cause them either apprehension or interest. Tobe was barefooted. Henny leaned on a short carbine, worn shiny from long service.

"Where's Cedar?" inquired Burridge, casually.

"He's hyarabouts somewhere," replied Elam. "He seen you fust."

"Hope Cedar won't take exception to our comin'."

"No tellin' what Cedar'll take," replied Hatt, with a grin. "But I'm right glad to see you. I'm wantin' news. Make yourself to home. I'll go an' see about grub. . . . Tobe, whar's your sister?"

"I dunno," replied the son.

"Find her, you terbaccer-chewin' cub," returned Hatt, and strode away toward the cabins.

Tobe Hatt might never have heard his father, for all the attention he paid to the order. Instead he gravitated toward Lacy.

"Got any smokin'?" he asked.

"Shore. Help yourself there in my saddlebag," replied Lacy.

The other young Hatt, Henny, now moved out of his tracks, and dragging the rifle butt over the ground, he joined Tobe in a search of Lacy's saddlebag. Finding the tobacco, they availed themselves of Lacy's offer. They took it all.

"Cash, where you goin' to bunk?" asked Lacy, presently.

"Right here in the aspens. Good a place as any. Elam will offer the loft of the big cabin, but I'd just as lief be out."

"Wal, I'd a good deal rather," drawled Jim. "Cabin lofts are full of dirt, spiders, centipedes an' smoke. I'll throw my outfit somewhere aboot."

"Make it within call, Jim," replied Burridge, not without significance.

Jim sat down, ostensibly to mend one of his stirrups, but as a matter of fact he did not care to pick out his bed site under the pale eyes of these degenerate Hatt boys. He could peer through the eyes of men to their minds. Either Tobe or Henny would commit murder for a sack of tobacco. Jim decided he would carry his bed to a secluded place in the brush and change that place every night. With covert glances he watched the Hatt boys and also kept a lookout for Rose.

"Wal, fellars, what about goin' on with our little game?" inquired Hubrigg.

"Sure," replied Brann.

"I should smile," added Stagg, cheerfully.

Cash Burridge shook his head dubiously, but did not voice his opinion until the Hatt boys had ambled off out of hearing.

"Say, men, I don't want to be a kill-joy, but honest I question the sense of showin' all that money here."

"Why not?" asked Hubrigg.

"It might not be safe. We don't belong to this Hatt outfit. They could have this canyon 'most full of back-woodsmen in no time. There's only six of us."

"Wal, listen to him!" ejaculated Brann. "You got it wrong, Cash. There's five of us, an' Jim Lacy!"

"I just don't think it's wise," added Burridge, stubbornly, ignoring the sarcasm.

"We may have to hang around here for a week or more," spoke up Stagg. "What'll we do? If we can't gamble we might as well not have any money."

"Jim, what do you say?" asked Burridge, in perplexity.

"Wal, seein' that money changes hands so often, I reckon nobody'd miss it if the Hatts did get it," chuckled Jim.

"Haw! Haw!" roared Cash, slapping his knee.

"Miss it!" ejaculated Brann, evidently affronted with catastrophe. "Say, I look on thet pile as mine."

"Jim, you seem a nice fellar, with fun in your talk, but I'm sort of doubtful about you," said Hubrigg, dubiously.

"How so?" queried Jim, pleasantly.

"Wal, I can't exactly explain. But when you talk lazy an' easy, like all you darn Texans, an' look some other way, I always feel queer."

"Right you are. Our new member makes me feel like a fellar who's runnin' like hell an' knows sure he's goin' to get the seat of his pants slung full of buckshot."

This from Brann indicated the slow progress of the

rustlers toward amity with Jim. They all laughed uproariously.

"Shore I must be a likable cuss to have round," declared Jim, presently. "I've a notion to get sore."

"Wal, for Gawd's sake, don't," burst out Brann. "Be a good fellar an' set in the game with us."

"I'd like to, for pastime, anyhow. But suppose I catch one of you manipulatin' the cairds?"

"Huh! Manip-oo-latin'? What's thet?"

"Brann, our friend Jim means slippin' aces off the bottom, holdin' out, stackin' the deck, an' a few other tricks gamblers have."

"Aw, I see. Wal, Jim has a right to holler when he ketches us, same as we when we ketch him doin' the same."

That sally elicited a yell from Brann's comrades.

"Jest so he hollers only with his mouth," shouted Stagg.

"All right, I'll set in a few hands," said Jim, goodnaturedly. "Anyway, till I'm broke."

"Jim, your credit is good in this outfit," interposed Cash Burridge. "An', anyway, you'll have a gunny sack full of money before long."

Whereupon the rustlers, in high spirits, owing to being well fed and flush with money, repaired to the shade of a pine in front of Elam's cabin, and squatting round a blanket, emptied their pockets of coin and bills. Jim joined them, choosing a seat from which he could watch the cabins and the approach of anyone.

Bantering ceased abruptly the instant gambling began. And the cares of rustlers, if they had any, vanished as if by magic.

The game was draw-poker, the stakes any amount a player chose to wager, provided he produced it. Jim knew he could hold his own with these gamblers, but he preferred to lose the ill-gotten gains Burridge had forced upon him as his share of their first rustling deal together. So Jim played recklessly, making his losses more than discount the ridiculously lucky cards he held at times. His apparently casual glances at the cabin, however, were not few and far between.

The Hatt boys came to watch the game, soon growing equally absorbed with the gamblers; and it was noticeable to Jim that they gravitated round the circle of players, wherever the gold coin went. Old Elam came presently, and likewise fell to the attraction of the game, but it seemed the playing itself rather than the sums of money lost and won, that held charm for him.

Elam Hatt's house was one of the picturesque double-cabined structures under one roof, with wide porch space between. The logs had been peeled. They were old and brown, rotting in places; the sloping roof of split shingles had a covering of green moss and pine needles; the rude stone chimney, built on the outside of the right-hand cabin, had been repaired many times with yellow clay and red adobe mud. The porch ran all along the front of both cabins, and one end was littered with saddles and packs. Deer and elk antlers on the walls supported rifles and bridles. A bearskin hide, not yet dried, hung nailed flesh side out, on the wall of the left cabin. This was smaller than the other, evidently consisting of only one room. The window, without glass or shutter, opened toward Jim, who had been quick to see a face peer from the darkness and draw back again.

When he caught sight of it again he knew at once that it belonged to Rose Hatt and that she had espied him. She stood far back in the gloom of the cabin, her face only a vague oval, but with staring eyes like black holes.

"Elam, do you know draw-poker?" asked Jim, presently.

"Tolerable. I wisht I hed stake enough to set in this hyar game. I'd bust somebody," replied old Hatt, to the amusement of the gamesters.

"Play a few hands for me," said Jim, rising. "Change my luck, maybe. I want a drink."

"Whiskey?"

"No. Water. Where'll I get it?"

"Thar inside the kitchen door at the end of the porch," replied Hatt, rising with alacrity to take Jim's place. "My girl jest fetched some fresh from the spring. Snow water, an' thar's none better."

As Jim neared the porch, Rose came out of the cabin where he had seen her, and crossed to enter the other. She wore buckskin. He caught the flash of brown bare legs and feet. Jim went down the porch and entered the door mentioned by Hatt. As he expected, he encountered Rose. Despite excitement manifest in her face, he thought she looked clearer of eye and skin, somehow prettier.

"Howdy, Rose! You see I've come," he said.

"I saw you first thing," she replied.

"I want a drink, please."

She filled a dipper from a pail and handed it to him. Facing her and standing in the door, Jim drank thirstily. It was good water.

"Will it be all right if I talk to you?" asked Jim.

"Sure. 'Cept when Cedar's around."

"Where is he?"

"Reckon he's hidin' somewhere, watchin' you-all. So we can't talk now. . . . But, oh! I've so much to tell you!"

"Yes? Tell me a little—quick," said Jim.

"Marvie's to fetch Hettie Ide—to meet me," whispered the girl, fearfully, yet with eyes full of glad light. "Oh, she must be an angel! He says she will give me a home—if I can ever get away from here."

"Wal, now, that's fine," sympathized Jim, vibrating to this news. "*Three* friends now—Marvie an' Hettie Ide an' me. Lucky girl!"

"I can't thank God enough," she breathed from a full breast.

"Keep on thankin', an' fightin'," said Jim, with ring of voice and meaning smile. Then he set down the dipper on the bench and backed out of the door, eyes still intent on Rose. She was flushed of face now, eager, hopeful, yet still fearful.

"I will. They can't stop me now—unless they kill

me," she answered, resolutely, with a wonderful blaze in her eyes.

"Who're they, Rose?"

"Cedar, for one. I told you," she replied, haltingly. But there seemed to be tremendous impelling power working on her—greater, Jim sensed, than could come through him just then.

"Tell me the other man."

"Oh, I daren't—I daren't," she faltered, losing courage.

"If you love Marvie—an' if *she* will stand by you —you can dare," he shot at her, relentlessly.

She showed then a struggle over fear that had out-lived childish years.

"Rose, that other man is Clan Dillon?"

"Yes—yes," she whispered, in unutterable relief, as if she had been spared betraying him. "Are—are you to be here long?"

"Days, maybe weeks."

"Keep watch," begged the girl, finding courage. "Cedar will drag me off in the woods—to meet Dillon. If he does—follow us, for God's sake."

"I shore will, Rose. Don't lose your nerve."

"But be *careful*, Cedar's an Indian in the woods."

Jim Lacy leisurely turned, and with glance on the ground, apparently idle and lax, he strolled back to the gamesters.

"How comes the luck, Elam?" he asked.

"My Gord! Won three hands straight runnin'," ejaculated Hatt. "An' one a fat jack-pot."

"Wal, shore reckoned you'd change my luck. Play 'em for all you're worth, Elam, an' if you break this outfit I'll divvy with you."

"Ha! he's got no chanct on earth, Jim," said Cash. "Better set back in before we break you."

Old Elam held his own, however, evidently to his immense gratification. Jim watched for a while, much amused, until his ever-roving glance fastened upon a newcomer to the scene.

A man had come out of the aspen thicket. He

carried a rifle, which he held by the barrel over his shoulder. His gait, his build, betrayed him to Jim Lacy. This was Cedar Hatt.

Jim had been kneeling on one knee behind Elam, and now, leisurely rising to his feet, he stood at ease. Upon nearer view Cedar Hatt turned out to possess only the walk and the shape of the Hatt family. He was darker than any of them, with beardless face of clear brown tan, small glittering eyes set close, black as coal, and of a strange intensity, sharp nose and sharp chin, with a slit between for a mouth. He wore his hair long and it curled dark from under an old slouch hat full of bullet holes. His garb was greasy buckskin, from head to toe. There was a knife in his belt, but no shells for the rifle.

Cedar Hatt stood across from the circle of gamblers, and dropping the muzzle of his rifle upon his moccasined foot he leaned on it, and gave his restless sloe-black eyes scope of all present. If the players saw him they gave no outward show of it. At length Cedar put the toe of his moccasin against his father.

Elam looked up with a start.

"Hullo! You back, Cedar?"

The son made an almost imperceptible movement with his right hand toward Lacy.

"Cedar, say howdy to Jim Lacy," went on Hatt, a little hurriedly. Nevertheless, he was not greatly concerned. "Lacy, this hyar's my son Cedar."

Jim nodded civilly, without speaking, and he received even less in response. A look, like a streak of black lightning, flashed over him from head to toe—then Cedar Hatt deigned him no more attention.

It was a singular thing for Jim Lacy to meet men; and in a case like this, when he knew before he had seen Cedar Hatt that he was going to kill him, the incident seemed extraordinarily potent and strange. If there was an instinct to act almost involuntarily in such a meeting, there was also an intuitive searching that followed. Lacy needed only the slightest glimpse at Hatt's eyes to know that he had not yet learned of the killing of Burt Stillwell. After that instant the meeting became only ordinary for Jim, inasmuch as Hatt could never again be formidable face to face. Jim knew him now. It was the unfamiliar that men of Lacy's caliber always reckoned with.

The game progressed, with luck shifting from one player to another, and manifestly what seemed a long, tedious, irritating waste of time to Jim was only a fleeting of precious moments to the gamblers.

Finally Cedar Hatt, without ever having uttered a word, shouldered his rifle, and stalked away with the spring of a deer-hunter in his stride. He went up the canyon to disappear around the green bend.

Whereupon Lacy strolled away himself, into the golden shade of the aspen thicket, and on through darker shade to the lichened base of the cliff. He flung himself down here and leaned against the wall. Above him the quivering aspen leaves fluttered with the marvelous noiseless movement peculiar to them. All around in the brush the lizards rustled. Nature was alive and full of treasure for the watcher, the seeker. But Jim Lacy's eyes were focused inward; his ears were attuned to a beating within. He had come there into the obscurity and loneliness of the thicket to think, to plan, to plot, to work out a course he could inevitably follow. But how useless that was! The slightest accident or incident might change the best of his plans. If he decided on a definite thing his mind would be set. His task demanded more than that; and it involved infinite patience and sacrifice, incredible command of geniality and good-fellowship with these rustlers, sight and sense that must grasp every little clue which might lead to the success of his venture. All this when his spirit revolted and his nature demanded quick, hard, fierce action!

After supper, which was served about sundown, on the porch between the two cabins, Elam Hatt scraped his rude seat back and arose.

"You-all who want to gamble air welcome, but I

reckon some of you will want to set in to a confab with me."

He went into his cabin, followed by Burridge and Lacy. The large room was dark, except where breaks in the chinks between the logs let in light. Hatt stirred the slumbering embers in the huge yellow stone fireplace and put on chips of wood.

"Reckon they'll want the lamps, an' we don't need none," said Elam.

The door opened to admit Cedar Hatt, who advanced with his sliding silent step, to seat himself on a bench in the shadow besides the stone chimney.

"Burridge, if thar's a lead weight on your chest, shove it off," invited Elam, bending down to lift a fiery ember with which to light his pipe.

"Are you open to a big deal?" queried the rustler, bluntly.

"Always open to anythin'. But I'm careful not to change the minds of ranchers about Elam Hatt," replied the backwoodsman, shrewdly.

"Which means they think you do some two-bit brandin' of mavericks, like any cowboy, but you never tackle a real rustlin' job?"

"Reckon thet's the size of it, Cash."

"An' that's exactly why I'm goin' to spring this deal on you. No one will ever lay it to you an' everyone will lay it to the Pine Tree outfit. Savvy? The time's just ripe. The trap's set. We can't do it half so well without you an' your sons. We don't know the country. Otherwise you bet we wouldn't let you or anyone else in on it."

"Sounds good. I'm listenin'."

"Tom Day an' Franklidge have throwed a big herd of stock together. Some of it's workin' with Ben Ide's big herd, the last of his stock, in what the sheepherders call Silver Meadows. They're high an' won't be comin' down before the fall roundup. That'll come anywhere along first of October. Now while them cattle are high up we plan to drive them—*on up over the Rim*—an' down into the Basin, where we could sell a hundred times as many head, with never a question asked. I've already got the buyer. To do the job right an' quick we need more riders, an' particular some who know how to find fast travelin' through them bad canyons up to the Rim. That's all. I leave it to you to call the turn on that deal."

"How do you know Ide's stock air runnin' on Silver Meadows? Thet's Day's range."

"I know because I saw them an' they used to be my cattle."

"You're calculatin' thet if Ide does rare, he'll lay it onto the Pine Tree outfit?"

"Exactly. The deal is ready-made for us."

"How much stock thar now?"

"We can bunch three or four thousand head in half a day, an' land them over the Rim in less'n two days."

"An' you've got a buyer?"

"Waitin' an' willin'. He's drivin' ten thousand head to Maricopa. How easy to run in a few more thousand!"

"Looks too powerful easy to me," returned Hatt, as if sagging under an overpowering weight.

"Easy an' safe. An' listen, Elam. . . . Twenty dollars a head. In gold! One yellow old double-eagle for every steer!"

Elam Hatt paced the rough-hewn logs that constituted the floor of his cabin. He seemed to find strength in their solidity. His legs were the first part of him to weaken. His collapse came suddenly, with a crash to the bench before the fire.

"Cedar, what'd'ye say?" he asked, in a hoarse low voice.

"Burridge, swear them steers air in Silver Meadows," said Cedar Hatt, his moccasined feet coming down with padded thuds as he leaped up and leaned out of the shadow.

"Sure I swear. Three days ago. An' the grass an' water are fine. They'll work higher for several more days. . . . Ask Jim Lacy here. Reckon you'll not be intimatin' he's a liar."

"Talk up, Jim Lacy, if you're a rustler," called the younger Hatt.

"Wal, I was with Burridge. I saw the cattle," replied Lacy.

Cedar Hatt glided into the light of the fire, to lean over his father and strike out with lean dark hand, like the claw of an eagle.

"Papa, with ten riders I can run them cattle over the Rim in one day," he declared. How grotesque and striking the epithet he gave his father! He seemed the epitome of lawlessness, of the hardened rustler, yet acknowledged the endearing claim of blood.

"Thet settles it, then," returned Elam Hatt, throwing up his hands as one whose price had been met.

"Hold on! Thar ain't no Greaser herder in these brakes who'd lead thet drive. An' I'm the only white man who kin."

"Wal, what's makin' you yap so? It's settled, ain't it, 'cept the workin' out?"

"I want my pard, Burt Stillwell, in on this."

"Reckon I see no kick to thet. But it ain't my deal."

Cedar Hatt faced round with the swift, sinister action peculiar to him.

"Anythin' ag'in' Stillwell?" he queried.

"Wal, not any more, Hatt," drawled Jim. "I shore had a little grudge, but it's gone. When I saw Burt last, I shore had a friendly feelin' for him."

"Burridge, you had no use for the Stillwells. How're you standin' on this hyar deal I want?"

"Cedar, all I say is, sure—ring your pard Burt in— if you can get him," returned Burridge, with something unnatural in his tone. And it was noticeable that he stepped more into the shadow.

"Papa," hissed Cedar Hatt, and that word inspired awe as well as mirth, "I'm double-crossin' the Pine Tree outfit to make us all rich on this big job."

"Air you drunk, son?" asked Hatt, slowly rising to his feet. "How'n tarnation can you double-cross them —onless you mean beatin' them to the deal?"

"Me an' Burt belong to the Pine Tree outfit."

Seventeen

A week later to the day, about the middle of the afternoon, Jim Lacy stood with Cash Burridge on the Mogollon Rim, facing south over the magnificent wilderness of southern Arizona. The black timber of the basin merged in the grassy parks and flats, growing hazy in the distance, and all that wild lowland led to the bleak colored desert ranges.

"My Gord! listen to that!" ejaculated Burridge, with red sweaty face wrinkled ecstatically. "Grandest music on earth."

"Cash, they'll greet you in Hades some day with that music," drawled Jim.

"Bawlin' bulls an' whoopin' cowboys! I'll be glad to hear it, providin' it don't come too soon," returned Burridge.

Yellow dust palls hung over the steep Maricopa trail, where it jumped zigzag off the Rim and wound down into the green depths. A mighty roar of trampling hoofs, and bellowing cattle, and crashing brush, and whooping riders waved up from that hot slope. It seemed an avalanche of sound now softening and again swelling, wild and free, harmonious with the country which made it possible. From the look of the trail, trampled and dug and widened by thousands of hoofs, it appeared that a river of live beasts had poured over the Rim.

"Lacy, it's all over but the fireworks," said Cash exultantly.

"*Quién sabe?* It might fetch some fireworks you're not figurin' on," admonished his companion, moving over from his heaving, foam-lashed horse to get in the shade of a pine.

"Not much. We're shakin' the dust of the brakes. Say, won't Ben Ide an' Tom Day bite nails? Biggest drive I ever had a hand in. An' all so easy! All like clockwork! All in a couple of days despite that—yellow traitor, Cedar Hatt!"

"Shore we didn't need him," responded Lacy, thoughtfully.

"Jim, I've seen some mad *hombres* in my time, but that Cedar Hatt beats them all to hell," declared Burridge, aghast at the memory.

"Shore he was mad. Didn't I warn you to keep your outfit from givin' it away aboot Stillwell?"

"Yes, you did, an' I talked myself hoarse. But it couldn't be kept. They *hated* Cedar, an' the minute somebody got two drinks aboard he up an' blows that Burt Stillwell was dead. It sure made a hydrophobia-coyote out of Cedar. But he didn't know *who* shot Burt. When he spit questions at you, like a snake with a hunch, why didn't you lie?"

"Wal, Cash, I reckon you don't savvy me."

"Why didn't you kill him, then?" went on Burridge, sharper of tongue.

"I just aboot did," returned Lacy, reflectively. "But I saw he didn't have the nerve to draw—so I waited."

"Ahuh! Waited? I get your hunch. Cedar knows somethin' you're keen to find out. Bet it's that Pine Tree outfit."

"Cash, you're figurin' fair. But on the daid square now—rememberin' the favors I've done you—cain't you tell me somethin' about that outfit?"

"No more'n we all know, Jim."

"Shore you have some suspicion aboot who leads them?"

"Honest to Gawd, Lacy, I haven't even an idee!" returned Burridge, with truth in look and voice. "It might be Judge Franklidge himself."

"Holy Moses! Cash, that's a wild guess!" ejaculated Lacy.

"Sure. An' it's only a guess. But you can gamble all the coin you're goin' to get *pronto* that the Pine Tree boss is not hidin' in the brakes, like the rest of us rustlers. He's an honest member of range society. Ha! Ha! Yes he is! . . . Jim, there might be a combine of homesteaders an' ranchers in cahoots with an outfit of great riders like Burt Stillwell an' Cedar Hatt."

"Reckon I've thought of that."

"What's it to you, anyway, Jim?" queried Burridge, curiously.

"Reckon I've got to put my brand on the boss of the Pine Trees," said Lacy.

"Ah! Is *that* all? Hell! I thought you might have some interest in him," retorted Cash sarcastically. "Jim, on the square, if you hadn't done so much to straighten me out again, I'd have suspicions about you."

"Wal, keep them in your haid."

Burridge laughed, and gathering up his bridle swung into the saddle.

"Come on. I don't want the outfit to get far ahead. You'll be hearin' the clink of gold before sundown."

"Not me, Cash."

"What?"

"I'm not goin' any farther with you."

The rustler exhibited profound concern and amaze.

"You're not goin' any farther—what——?"

"Say, Cash, are you out of your haid?" queried Jim, testily.

"Sure I am, if you're not."

"Wal, I'm not, old-timer."

Burridge studied his companion for a long moment, his face working. Regret began to erase the incredulity.

"What the hell are you goin' to do?"

"That's my concern now. I'm through."

"Through! . . . But, Jim——"

"Didn't I help you out of a bad hole—the worst you was ever in?"

"You sure did, Jim. An' I——"

"Didn't I rustle cattle with you?"

"Yes."

"Didn't I come out in the open—so everybody on

this range will know I helped steal Ben Ide's cattle?"

"By Heaven! you did!" declared Burridge, with redder face. "An' I hold that against you, Jim. I just can't figure why you did that. We could sure have laid that onto the Pine Tree outfit."

"Wal, neither Ben Ide nor any other honest rancher will know *you* had the high hand in this big cattle steal. But my name an' my hand in it will be known. I saw to that. They'll think *I* am the boss of the Pine Tree outfit."

"I'm damned! . . . Jim Lacy, you're too deep for me. But I'm gettin' a hunch. . . . How about your share in the divvy for this deal?"

"You're welcome to it. Take it an' go out of this country. Try bein' honest again. You might succeed next time. But don't ever come back heah!"

"Why not, Jim?" queried Burridge, strong and hard.

"Because if you do I'll kill you," flashed Lacy, in a voice that cut like a whip.

The ruddy heat left Burridge's face, and he began to nod his head, slowly, with increasing motion, while his eyes fixed in a startling comprehension.

"Jim—Lacy!" he said, huskily.

"I reckon," replied Lacy, grimly, as he turned to his horse.

"You been a pard to me, whatever your reasons," went on Burridge, with feeling. "I don't care a damn what they were. . . . I'll leave this country. Here's my hand on it. . . . Good-by an' good luck!"

"Same to you, Cash," replied Jim, as they gripped hands.

Burridge wheeled his horse so violently that it reared and plunged, and then slid to its haunches in the soft ground where the trail broke over the Rim. Burridge hauled it up and used his spurs. The animal snorted and took the first descent on a jump, then steadied to a quick walk. At the first bend of the trail into the timber the rustler looked back up to the Rim.

"I'll send my compliments to Cedar Hatt an' his boss in hell!"

Lacy strode into the level shady forest, leading his horse. He had prepared for this separation from Burridge, and had tied a light pack behind his saddle. There was a spring in his step and a light on his face. The deep forest land, beginning almost at once to slope north from the Rim, seemed to receive and absorb Lacy as a transformed man. How sweet and enchanting the silence, the solitude! He listened for the last ebb of that tide of hoofs, roaring down into the Basin. Gone! The air had cleared of the dust, the heat, the din, the smell of a cattle drive.

It still wanted an hour to sunset, and the time was approaching the most wonderful of all hours on the Mogollons. Birds and game had roused from the midday Indian-summer heat; the long black shadows of the trees were slanting down across the open swales and dells, where the white grass furnished contrast to the reds and purples and golds of the autumn leaves. The tracks of man and horse showed dark through the thick covering of gold and green that carpeted the ground.

Lacy descended winding ravines and aspen hollows until one opened into the head of a canyon where the murmur of water invited him to camp.

"Reckon you're plumb tired," he said to his horse, laying swift hands on the ropes. "Wal, it was a day. But we're through now—through with that kind of work. . . . An' I'm hatin' to hobble you, old boy."

Jim kindled a little fire, and while he heated water in his one pot he gathered ferns for bedding. The frost had seared the long leaves, making them brittle and easy to break off. He piled a great bundle in his blanket and carried it to the edge of an aspen thicket, where, as was his habit, he made a bed under cover of the foliage.

"I'll be cold as blazes along toward mawnin', but I cain't keep a fire goin' . . . not with that Indian Cedar Hatt roamin' the woods!"

The sordid atmosphere common to the rustler gang was lacking here. Lacy did not realize it until he grew conscious of his alacrity, of his zest with the old camp tasks, in the pause to see and feel and hear and smell the forest which seemed now his alone, in his habit of talking to himself.

"Wal, now, won't there be hell around the Ide ranch some of these heah mawnin's, when riders come in with the news? Last of the Ide cattle! . . . Jim Lacy takin' to rustlin'. . . . It will be funny. I'd like to be hid an' heah Ben cuss. This'll be the last straw. He'll get as many gun-toters as he can hire, an' set out to land me in jail."

Jim seemed immensely pleased with the thought. The hard, morose intentness of the past weeks did not inhibit his natural geniality.

"Ben is shore goin' to get the shock of his life one of these heah days," went on Jim. "The doggone old wild-hoss hunter! . . . What's he goin' to say to me first off—an' then after? . . . Lordy! . . . An' Hettie! . . . She'll call me a low-down yellow faithless . . . Say, meetin' her will be about as funny as dyin'. I can feel myself cavin' in right heah!"

Jim Lacy, with his plans well in mind, had on the whole journey across country from Elam Hatt's ranch to the head of the Maricopa trail, taken careful account of the lay of the land.

It served him now. His intention was to return to Hatt's ranch, if possible without encountering even a sheepherder. Hatt had left his daughter Rose alone, unless the mysterious woman consort of Henny or Tobe Hatt, of whom Jim had heard vaguely, might be considered as company. Elam, of course, with his two sons, could be expected to get back home from the cattle drive in two days from the time Jim had left them, or even less. As for Cedar Hatt, who had deserted Burridge and Elam after the revelation of Stillwell's death, no doubt he had rushed to the secret rendezvous of the Pine Tree men, wherever that was, there to betray to them news of the impending drive of the Ide stock. It was Cedar Hatt whom Lacy had greatest interest in, at the present stage of the game; and Cedar was most likely to be found at or near home.

There was reason, too, for Lacy to have an interview with Rose Hatt, from whom he expected to force more about the man who dominated her brother and whom she feared. Moreover, Rose was to be considered on her own behalf.

Jim Lacy did not think it wise to go near Silver Meadows, where the cattle had been collected for the great drive; and therefore he made a wide detour, hoping to strike the trail he and the rustler band had made coming from Hatt's ranch. But he had to go into camp the second night of his journey without having come to this trail. The forest was exceedingly rough, he had only a general direction to go by, and often windfalls and impassable brakes threw him off. On the third morning, however, he struck the trail he was looking for, and he back-tracked it all day. On the following day it failed on high ridges, on hard ground, rocky flats, and pine-needle mats, over which Elam Hatt had led the rustlers for the express purpose of hiding their tracks.

Lacy wasted no time trying to recover them, though he believed he could eventually have done so. Sure of his direction now, he pressed on rapidly, and the next afternoon struck the deep canyon east of the one in which Hatt lived. During his sojourn with the Hatts, Lacy had hunted turkey and deer up and down these brakes, with the sport of the hunt not at all his prime motive.

Jim took the precaution to ride well back from the Rim, peeping over whenever opportunity offered from behind foliage or rock covert. He did not really expect to see anyone, but that did not influence his actions. Lacy was always cautious, watchful, alert; and in this instance he might have been on a scent, so instinctive was his progress along that Rim.

Presently, down in an open bend of the deep canyon Lacy caught a glimpse of a rider. He was riding slowly up the trail, leaning down from his saddle, evidently with eyes on the ground.

"Trackin' somethin'," muttered Jim. "Now I wonder who that is an' what he's trackin'."

Lacy rode back away from the Rim, and urged his horse to a lope, careful to avoid rocks and brush. There were places where he had to go slowly, but in the main he covered a mile or more in short order, then again approached the Rim.

This time he dismounted and cautiously stole to a vantage-point, from which he could peer unseen. As luck would have it, there was an open grassy meadow, narrow and long, just beneath his position. The canyon was five hundred feet deep at this point, green-walled, precipitous, and unsurmountable.

Lacy watched so long without seeing the rider that he believed he had been too late to catch him crossing this open flat. But as Lacy had about decided to hurry on again, the man emerged from the lower end.

Horse and rider grew strangely familiar as they came nearer. Lacy's iron nerves were not beyond a tiny burning thrill.

"Am I drunk or loco?" he muttered.

On the rider came, his horse at a trot, and still he bent over to one side, studying tracks in the trail. He would have had an ominous look to any experienced eye. This rider was not tracking a lost horse or deer or turkey. He was a manhunter.

"*Cedar Hatt!*" whispered Lacy, his head lowering with the motion of a striking eagle. "Talk about luck! I'm shore smothered with it. . . . Jim Lacy's luck! . . . But bad for you, Cedar—you treacherous soul!"

Lacy watched the man with a strained, piercing gaze, as if it were possible to divine his motive.

"This might be the trail Marvie Blaine rides when he comes to meet Rose," soliloquized Jim, ponderingly. "Shore it is. She said the brake east of where she lived."

Cedar Hatt rode on, directly under Jim's position,

and once he halted his horse, to lean far down from his saddle. How like an Indian! Then he swung up again to peer ahead, as if calculating on something. He made a dark wild figure, suiting his ragged horse and the background of tangled brush and rugged wall. Then he rode on, more slowly.

"By God!" burst out Lacy. "That *hombre* is sure trackin' Marvie Blaine!"

Lacy crawled back from the Rim, then rose to run for his horse. He would head off this rustler. Luckily, the lower part of the canyon was miles below the locality where Rose was in the habit of meeting young Blaine. Lacy had time to get ahead and find a place where he could descend to the floor of the canyon. Working still farther back from the Rim, he put his horse to a gallop and made a hard fast ride for several miles. Then he slowed down and headed for the Rim again. No break in sight where he might descend! The wall grew more precipitous and higher. Lacy rode on, close to the Rim now, risking detection in his search for a descent. But he had no concern that Cedar Hatt might be the one to espy him.

At length Lacy came upon an interesting canyon, a narrow crack which ran off into the woods. He rode back to where it headed in one of the thickest ravines, so common to the country. He descended as far as possible, then dismounting, he tied his horse and hurried on. This gorge deepened into a split between toppling walls, so rough that there was not even a deer trail. But Lacy, sparing no effort, traversed it, to reach the main canyon hot and bruised and out of breath.

Under cover of the oak thicket that lined the slope from the wall he rested a few moments, listening like a pursued deer. Only the distant murmur of a stream, a dreamy hum, and the moan of wind up on the timbered ruins came to his ears.

"Reckon I'll slip down to the trail an' hold Cedar up," soliloquized Jim. "But I'd shore like to know what he's aboot."

The east side of the canyon was a gentle slope, covered with white grass, brown ferns, and low pines and oaks, affording perfect cover for anyone hiding. Lacy worked gradually down toward the level of the canyon. He did not snap twigs, or scrape brush, or make any sound. At each little opening he peered out before advancing. Often he stopped to listen. Once an elk bugled—wonderful piercing note of the wild.

It was through this extreme caution and the eye of a woodsman that Lacy came upon Marvie Blaine and Rose Hatt.

They were locked in each other's arms, lost in the enchantment of their dream. But they had chosen a secluded nook, halfway up the grassy pine-dotted slope, from which they could see, by peering under the low-spreading branches, both up and down the trail. At this moment, however, they would not have become aware of the approach of an army.

Lacy seemed struck to the heart by their rapture and the poignant pang that rent his own breast. He understood. He had lived that. He knew the sweetness and glory of love. Lacy sank to his knees, feeling that he had no right to interrupt their sacred hour. Marvie bent over Rose, whose head lay back upon his breast, with her face upturned to his, eyes closed, heavy-lidded, rapt and dreamy. If they were whispering Lacy would not hear, though he was close. But he doubted that they were whispering. Both bliss and tragedy seemed to hover over these youthful lovers.

Suddenly Lacy heard a sound that cruelly disrupted both the pain and the joy he felt. In a flash he found his equilibrium. What was that sound? It had been faint, and therefore hard to locate. It could have come from either near or far. He listened, while his eyes roved everywhere. Marvie was deaf to sounds. No doubt there was a beautiful bell ringing in his soul. Rose lay entranced.

Again Jim heard a sound, which he calculated to be a swish from the tail of a horse. Of course Marvie and Rose had their horses tethered somewhere near.

But the first noise had not been like the second. It was not a thud of hoof, nor a step of foot. It seemed to have been a slippery gliding sound, as of a soft substance in contact with one rough and hard. All at once an idea flashed to Jim—buckskin over rock! Cedar Hatt always wore buckskin. Close at hand there were corners of cliff, ledges, huge slabs of rock. The instant that thought stood clear in Lacy's mind he grew stiff, intense in the grasp of a sensation for which he never found an adequate name. It mounted almost to a power of divination. It always brought the icy steadiness to his nerves.

Then from the dark shadow of pines behind Marvie a lithe figure glided. Silently Jim Lacy drew his gun. The situation was clarified, and a dread of something he could not see or control faded away.

Marvie never looked up from the beloved face until Cedar Hatt halted. It was clear to Jim that Cedar's sudden violent check came from the surprise of seeing Rose in Marvie's arms.

Marvie likewise started, so suddenly and rudely that Rose rolled off his shoulder into the grass. She screamed. She swayed up to her knees, and with hands out she backed until the pine tree stopped her.

"So hyar's why you run off from me to-day?" he shouted, fiercely. The muscles of his neck swelled, his lean jaw protruded.

"Don't—don't hurt me—Cedar!" cried Rose in terror.

"I'll beat you half to death. So hyar's why you played sick to-day an' then run off. You lyin' hussy! Answer me!"

"Yes—yes, Cedar. I—I did," replied Rose, sagging back against the tree. Her open hands fell to her sides. A paralysis of surprise began to leave her.

"This hyar ain't no accident?" he demanded, with a forceful gesture toward the stricken Marvie.

"No. I come—on purpose."

"How long's it b'en goin' on?"

"Weeks. I—I've come eight times."

"Who's this hyar young buck?"

"I'll never tell," flashed Rose.

Marvie stumbled to his feet and stepped forward, livid of face, but resolute.

"I'll tell you," he said.

"Don't—don't!" cried Rose. "Never tell him!"

"Who'n hell air you?" queried Cedar, in amaze, as if the factor of Marvie's participation in this treachery of Rose's had just dawned upon him.

"I'm Marvie Blaine," answered the lad.

"Blaine! Huh! thet means nothin' to me."

"I live with Ben Ide. We're related."

"Ben Ide! . . . Oho! You belong to them rich Ide folks, huh, as wouldn't wipe their feet on sich as us Hatts? Wal, damn your white skin, what you doin' hyar with my sister?"

"I—I love her," answered Marvie, manfully.

Cedar knocked him down.

"I'll kick your guts out," he snarled.

Marvie rolled out of reach, leaped to his feet, and came back, with fight struggling to master his consternation and distress for Rose.

"I seen you huggin' an' kissin' Rose. An' you got nerve to say you love her. Playin' with my sister, huh? An' you belong to them Ides!"

"Cedar, it's not—what you think," burst out Rose, with the scarlet dyeing her face.

"Git out, you lyin' little devil. If you'll lie about one thing you'll lie about another. . . . All the time you been meetin' this young buck. Layin' hyar in his arms, huh?"

"You skunk!" retorted Rose, passionately. "He loves me honest. . . . You're too low-down to understand what that means."

"Didn't I ketch you layin' in his arms?" demanded Cedar, harshly, yet with a hint of wonder in his query.

"Yes, you did. An' you might have ketched me there often," cried the girl.

"Ed Richardson will kill you fer this!" hissed Cedar.

"Let him kill an' be damned!" returned Rose, with

an equal passion. "I don't belong to him. I hate him. Did he ever talk honest love to me? Bah! But Marvie Blaine did. An' he's made a woman out of me."

"Hatt, I've asked—Rose to marry—me," interposed Marvie, beside himself with emotion.

"Yes, an' Miss Ide is goin' to give me a decent home till I'm old enough," added Rose.

"Oho! Double-crossin' Ed an' all of us, hey? You black-eyed cat! . . . Git your hoss, an' soon as I take the hide off this kid lover of yours, we'll——"

"Cedar Hatt, you'll have to pack me dead—if you take me one single step. . . . You'll never drag me alive to your Pine Tree——"

"Shut up!" interrupted Cedar, and he struck her down.

Marvie, with furious imprecation, wildly swinging his arms, rushed at Hatt, only to be sent staggering against the tree.

"I'll blow your insides out!" yelled Cedar, reaching for his gun.

But before he could draw, Marvie closed with him, and as Hatt dragged the gun out they began a swift struggle for possession of it. Here Jim bounded out of his covert and down the slope, his gun half leveled. Neither of the contestants was aware of his presence, but Rose saw him, and she shrieked.

Jim tried to get a bead on Cedar. But he had to be sure of his aim. He did not want to risk injuring Marvie. As they whirled and wrestled, Cedar pulled his arm over his head, his hand clutching the gun. Marvie clung desperately to that arm.

Jim took a snap shot at Cedar's gun hand. Missed! He snapped another and the bullet almost tore Cedar's hand off. The gun went flying, while Cedar, backing away from Marvie, cursing hideously, suddenly froze stiff at sight of Jim.

Marvie had not yet seen his savior. No doubt he thought the shots had been fired accidentally in the struggle, wounding Cedar. Quick as a flash he snatched up Cedar's gun and, leveling it with both hands, he worked the trigger. Bang! Bang!

Cedar Hatt clutched at his breast. An awful blank surprise rendered his expression once more human. With gasps his mouth opened to emit blood. Then he reeled and fell at Marvie's feet.

Marvie began to sag, changing his crouching position. The smoking gun dropped from his limp hands. Rose, on her knees, with a red stain on her lips, rocked to and fro, mute with terror.

"Wal, Marvie, that wasn't so bad for a youngster," said Jim, stepping forward. "I was just about to plug him myself."

As if a giant arm was grinding him around the lad turned.

"Who're—you?" he whispered, wildly, almost maudlinly.

"Reckon I'm your old pard, Nevada, of Forlorn River days," replied Jim, and then he grasped Marvie as he collapsed. He embraced him and half carried him toward the trees, where Rose now clung, trying to get to her feet. "Brace up, boy. It's all over. There. . . . An' you, Rose, buck up. Why, you're both showin' yellow after as game a fight as two kids ever made! . . . That's right. Let him lean against you. Wal, wal!"

Marvie, with eyes starting, cried out: "O my God— it's you—*Nevada!*"

"Shore is, boy, an' glad to meet you again."

"Mister Lacy—do—you—know Marvie?" faltered Rose.

"Wal, I should smile. Me an' Marvie are old pards."

Marvie suddenly seemed to revert to a consciousness that recalled Cedar Hatt. He stared in terror at the prone rustler.

"Nevada, you—you shot him," he said, huskily.

"Me? Nope. I only shot his hand off. You see, you was dancin' around so I couldn't bore him."

"He—he's *dead?*"

"Wal, I reckon so. Has that sort of limp look,"

replied Jim. "But I'll make shore." And Jim rose from his kneeling posture to walk over to Hatt. "Daid as a door nail! Marvie, he was roarin' a minute ago aboot blowin' out your insides. An', lo!—there he lays with his own insides blowed out. His own gun! Funny aboot things. . . . Don't look so sick. Wasn't he tryin' to kill you? Wouldn't he have murdered Rose—or worse?"

Marvie sat up, pallid and wet, with his lower lip quivering and his eyes losing their fixed horror.

"Nevada! You were here—somewhere?"

"Shore. I was watchin' you an' Rose make love when Cedar sneaked up. Reckon I ought to have shot him *pronto,* but I wanted to heah what he'd say."

"Marvie, it's turrible," interposed Rose. "My own brother! But I don't care. I'm glad. He was a devil. . . . Did he hurt you? Oh, there's blood on your hands!"

"I'm not hurt. It come off the gun. I felt it—all wet an' sliddery."

Jim studied these two brave young people and thrilled to his heart. What had guided his steps on this eventful day?

"Rose, I reckon you can never be scared by Cedar again," he said.

"No, Mister Lacy. I'm free—saved," replied the girl, in agitation.

"*Lacy?*" cried Marvie, starting up incredulously. "But you're Nevada!"

"Son, the Nevada you knew was Jim Lacy."

"My Heaven! what will Ben say? . . . An' Hettie," exclaimed Marvie, overcome.

"Reckon they'll say a lot—when they know. But promise me you won't give me away."

"Aw, Nevada, if you only knew how Ben——"

"Marvie, I'm not askin' you to keep it secret forever," interrupted Jim hastily. "But for a little while. Promise, old pard."

"I—will," replied Marvie, choking.

"An' you, too, Rose?"

"I can keep secrets. An' I mustn't let slip that you're Marvie's old pard Nevada?"

"Shore. An' now, Rose, let's get this confab over. I reckon my hunch is correct. But I need to know more."

"I'll tell anything," she replied, under her breath.

"You told me Dillon is haid of this Pine Tree outfit?" queried Nevada, bending down to the agitated face.

"Yes, sir," replied Rose. "Some of his men called him Campbell. But he told Cedar his real name was Ed Richardson. He's from New Mexico. He figgered in the Lincoln County war an' was close to Billy the Kid. He fetched rustlers here with him. An' he got hold of Cedar, an' Burt Stillwell, an' Stewart, an' other Arizona riders whose names I never heard."

"Rose, how'd you happen on this?" asked Nevada, seriously.

"Cedar fetched Clan Dillon to our ranch, an' he tried to make up to me," went on Rose. "I liked him first off. But I soon saw what he was up to an' I had no use for him. Wal, one day Cedar threw me on a horse an' rode me off to a cabin over here in Piñon Brake. Dillon was there. He tried makin' more love to me. But I bit an' kicked an' clawed him. Then he manhandled me bad, with Cedar grinnin' by. He'd have ruined me, too, but the men they was expectin' rode up an' I got thrown in the loft. Some of them were drunk. They all had money. An' they gambled an' stayed up all night. In the mornin' they had a powwow. Then Cedar fetched me back home an' swore he'd kill me if I squealed."

"Clan Dillon, then, is Ed Richardson—haid of this Pine Tree outfit," said Nevada, "an' Ben Ide's foreman."

"Yes, sir," replied Rose, bravely, with lips that trembled.

"Good Lord!" ejaculated Marvie. "Ben swears by Dillon. He's gone against Raidy, his oldest hand. . . . Gee! I wouldn't want to be in Dillon's boots when Ben finds out!"

"Wal, Marvie, it's likely that Dillon's boots will be stickin' out straight when Ben heahs the truth. . . .

Rose, is there any particular reason why you'd like to go back home again? Clothes or anythin' you care for?"

"All the duds I own are on my back," replied Rose, ruefully. "Cedar burned my pretty dance dress—that I bought to look nice for Marvie. My pony's all I have. An' he's here."

"Marvie, get your horse an' put Rose on hers an' leave heah *pronto* for the Ide ranch. Look sharp an' don't run into any riders. When you reach home turn Rose over to Hettie, an' both of you keep your mouth shut."

His compelling force wrung mute promises from both Marvie and the girl.

"My horse is on top, an' I cain't get him down heah. Rustle now."

Marvie started to lead Rose away, when he espied Cedar Hatt's gun lying on the brown pine needles.

"Nevada—can I take it?" he queried, haltingly.

"What? Oh, Cedar's gun? Shore you take it."

The girl turned with lips parted. "Mister Jim—Nevada—we'll see you again?"

"I reckon. Remember, I trust you to keep mum. Look sharp now, an' hurry along."

Nevada did not linger to watch them find and mount their horses; however, as he started up the slope he heard them, and felt that now all would be well with them. He climbed as one with wings. How strange that the rough gully presented no obstacles! Reaching his horse, he tightened the cinches, leaped astride, and rode up to the level, where he faced north with a grim smile.

The afternoon had not far advanced. At a steady lope he covered the miles of forested ridge, downhill and easy going until he descended into the brakes. Here his horse toiled for an hour, at last to crash out into the trail. One glance at the bare ground showed him that Marvie and Rose had not yet come so far. He preferred to reach the Ide ranch before they did.

His mind clamped round one thing and set there, cold and sure.

Five miles of travel, now slow, now swift, and then a hard climb took Nevada out of the brakes into the beautiful stately forest, where the pines thinned and straggled to the desert sage. How sweet the fragrance! He had once viewed from afar the Ide ranch, with its slope of sage and cedar leading up to the black benches.

The trail grew broad and sandy, so that his speeding horse thudded almost noiselessly on. Clumps of spruce and low branches of pines obscured the bends.

Nevada rode around an abrupt green curve almost to run down a horse coming toward him. He pulled his mount to a sliding halt. He heard a cry. The rider was a woman. Hettie Ide!

Eighteen

"Hettie," said Ben Ide as he stood on the porch and spread his arms to the glorious beauty and color of the Arizona landscape, "I once thought Forlorn River in the fall was pretty close to heaven. But Cedar Springs Ranch has it beaten a mile."

"Ben Ide! You going back on Forlorn River!" exclaimed Hettie, in surprise.

"Well, hasn't it? Look around. What do you think, yourself?"

"Long ago, before this wonderful autumn came, I was faithless to California," murmured Hettie, regretfully.

"Hettie, not faithless. I don't love the old home country any the less because I've learned to love this more. Lord knows I've reason to hate Arizona. But I can't. It grows on me. Here it's way in September. Frost an' ice every mornin'. Indian summer days. Look at the sage. It's purple. Look at the foothills. Anyone would think they were painted. Look at the patches of gold an' scarlet back up in the woods."

"It's very beautiful," replied Hettie, more dreamily.

"Sister, we mustn't forget that mother is to be taken to San Diego for the winter months."

"I've not forgotten, Ben, But there's no hurry. This weather is perfect. Mr. Day claims it'll last till Christmas."

"Well, if it does, I could ask no more," said Ben. "Then I'll send mother with you an' Ina an' the kid to San Diego till spring. But I'll stay on here. I'd be afraid to leave."

"It wouldn't be wise, Ben. Things have grown from bad to worse. I fear you are in for more shocks."

"Tom Day says they must grow worse before they get better. Heigho! . . . Well, I'm not lettin' disappointment sour me, anyhow."

"Disappointment? You mean—about ranching in Arizona?"

"Between you an' me, Hettie, I wasn't thinkin' of cattle at all," replied Ben, sadly.

Hettie suffered a contraction of her heart. If Ben knew what she knew! She prayed that he never would. And she gave no sign that she divined the undercurrent of his words.

Marvie Blaine sat on the porch step, morosely cleaning his rifle, which evidently he had used that day. The lad had grown taller, thinner, more of a man these last few weeks.

"Marv, you don't ride far away when you hunt, do you?" queried Ben.

"Lots of turkey an' deer right in our back yard," answered Marvie, evasively.

"Humph! Much good that does you. I've yet to eat the venison you killed."

"Ben, I've killed some turkeys," insisted Marvie, stoutly. "An' to-day I had a shot at a buck."

"Seems to me you take a lot of time off," went on Ben, "an' I'm supposed to pay you a cowboy's salary."

"I do the work given me. Dillon sure slights me on every job he can."

"Weren't you pretty smart-alec?" asked Ben.

"I wasn't until he got mean."

"An' when was that? Are you sure you don't imagine things? Dillon is the kindest of foremen."

Marvie looked up deliberately and fastened unfathomable eyes upon this friend of his boyhood.

"Dillon used to like me. But he changed after the cowboys told him how I'd made up to little Rose Hatt at the dance in Winthrop."

"Rose Hatt! That child of Elam Hatt's? I saw her once. What on earth could it be to Dillon if you did flirt with Rose? As a matter of fact, he was merely worried about you. Rose was no girl for you to get friendly with."

"Say, did Dillon tell you that?" queried Marvie, flushing.

"Yes. An' he advised me to put a stop to it. Said you might get in trouble."

Marvie jumped up as if he had been stung by a hornet.

"Ha! Ha!" he burst out, striding away with his head back. "Ha! Ha! . . . Ha! Ha! Ha!"

He kept it up until he went out of sight around the house.

"Well, I'll be doggoned," ejaculated Ben, gazing at Hettie for confirmation of his fears. "Was that boy givin' me the horse-laugh?"

"He was surely giving you some kind of a laugh," replied Hettie, striving to hide her own amusement.

"Hettie, am I growin' old, thick-headed, absent-minded?" inquired Ben, wistfully.

"No, Ben," returned his sister, dropping her head. "You've only the worry of the ranch on your mind."

"By George it is a worry," he sighed. "But, old girl, you've not been so bright and happy as you were here at first. Neither is Ina. I'm afraid I've done bad by both of you."

"Ben, it will all come right," spoke up Hettie, forcing a smile. "We must take our medicine. It's Arizona medicine, which your friend, Tom Day, says is powerful strong."

"Hettie, do you still think of—of—*him?*" asked Ben, in lower tone.

"Always," she replied, quaking inwardly. If only she had the courage and the wit to keep her secret hidden!

"I'm afraid I've given up hope," went on Ben, somberly. "An' it's taken the sap out of me. Don't tell Ina. But I'm fallin' into the same rut as I was in last spring, over home on Tule Lake."

"Given up hope of what?" murmured Hettie.

"Of ever findin' Nevada," he replied, simply, as if

the name was not one he never mentioned. "That's why I came to Arizona. Once at Forlorn River, when I asked Nevada what he'd do if anythin' separated us, he said he'd go to Arizona an' take to hard ridin'. I never forgot. . . . Well, I reckon every cowboy on these ranges has hit me for a job. But sure not one of them was Nevada, nor had they ever heard of him. I reckon he's dead. Don't you ever think that, Hettie?"

"Yes. . . . Dead to us, surely," she returned, with dry lips.

"How could Nevada be dead to us if he were alive?" queried Ben, sharply. Then he lifted his head to some interruption of his thought. "I hear a horse . . . comin' lickety cut! Hello! it's Dillon! . . . Damn the luck! There's somethin' up!"

Hettie sustained a sharp quickening of her pulse. A horse and rider bobbed up over the bench. At the moment Ina came out of the house, to begin some speech to Ben, which did not materialize. Ben strode off the porch to meet Dillon, who rode up like a whirl-wind, scattering gravel all over the porch; and he leaped out of the saddle with the lithe grace of one to whom such action was a habit.

"Mornin', boss," he said and tipped his sombrero to Hettie and Ina. "You're late. So I rode up."

"Bad news?" asked Ben.

"No, it ain't bad, but it's disturbin'. Cowboy just in from Tom Day's range. Name's Laskin. He rode a hoss to death gettin' here. I gave him another hoss, an' soon as he'd swallowed some drink an' grub he rode off for Franklidge's ranch."

"Yes. Well, what was he ridin' so hard for?" queried Ben, as if prepared.

"Yesterday he was in camp near Silver Meadows," went on Dillon. "Another rider with him—whose name I didn't get. Some men rode down on them. Las-kin said they wasn't drunk. Just keyed up over a big deal. They made no bones about the deal—at least their leader didn't. An' he was no other than Jim Lacy."

"Jim Lacy bobbed up again!" ejaculated Ben, with irritation. "Go on, Dillon."

"Lacy said he was goin' to rustle the stock at Silver Meadows an' sent you his compliments."

"Well, I'm a —— ——!" broke out Ben, choking down the last of his utterance.

"Pretty nervy, wasn't it?" asked Dillon. He appeared excited, which was a striking exception to his usual genial and imperturbable mood. Hettie gazed spell-bound at him.

"Nervy? Yes, if it's true," retorted Ben. "But I don't believe it."

"It's as straight as shootin', boss," rejoined Dillon. "I happen to know the rider who tipped us off."

"But Jim Lacy or anybody else would be a fool to tell such a plan, before pullin' it off," said Ben, incredulously.

"Reckon that seems so," replied the foreman, smoothly. "But sometimes these desperadoes like Lacy do queer things. It's not braggin'. Such men don't brag. It's just sort of a cool defiance of law—an' honest ranchin'. . . . Well, Lacy has twenty-four hours' start. There was a big bunch of cattle at Silver, so Laskin said. The last of your stock, an' some of Day's an' Franklidge's. We were figgerin' on a big roundup *pronto*. But we're too late, boss."

"Too late! Why, man, if it *is* true, we can stop that drive before it gets down to the road," declared Ben.

"Stop nothin'. Lacy's outfit won't drive this way. They'll drive up over the Rim, an' I'll gamble there's a bunch of five thousand head on the way now."

Ben sat down as if suddenly weighted.

"Boss, I'm sure kickin' myself for not figgerin' that very deal," went on Dillon, and his smile was something to conjure with. Hettie caught it, but Ben saw nothing. "You see, the cattle were workin' high up. An' grass an' water's so good at Silver that they bunched thick. Laskin swears it's only a half day's drive up the canyon which opens into Silver. . . . An' there you are."

A hoarse intolerant resentment rang in Dillon's voice. To Ben Ide he must have seemed a masterful and experienced foreman, angry at this coup of the latest recruit to Arizona rustlers.

"If it's true I'll—I'll run down this Jim Lacy an' jail him. I don't care what it costs," declared Ben. "But I reckon we're gettin' all r'iled up over cowboy guessin'."

"Give me a couple of days off, boss?" asked Dillon, in strange eagerness. "I'll find out."

"You want to ride off alone?" queried Ben.

"Sure. That's the best way."

"No. Some of the rustlers will plug you, an' then I *would* be out of luck," replied Ben, decisively.

"But I want to go," declared Dillon, with the blood rising under the tan of his handsome face.

"I appreciate the risk you'd take for me, Dillon. But, no, I'm givin' you orders to take Raidy with six cowboys an' go to Silver Meadows. Hurry back to report. Then we'll see."

Dillon had difficulty in repressing some kind of agitation that did not owe its source to respect and regard for Ben Ide. What an intent, almost derisive glance he gave Ben! Then without another word he mounted and rode furiously down toward the corrals.

"Girls, did you hear all he had to say?" asked Ben, appealing for sympathy.

"We couldn't very well help it," replied Ina, putting a hand on Ben's shoulder. "Dear, I—I haven't confidence in this man Dillon."

"Huh! Nor in me, either," retorted Ben, shaking her hand off.

That action hurt Ina's sensitive feelings and she drew away haughtily.

"Very well, Ben Ide," she declared. "But when the crash comes, don't you look to *me* for sympathy."

With that she went back into the house. Ben gazed helplessly up at his sister.

"There! Can you beat that? My own wife gone against me!"

Hettie subdued her own impatience, not without effort, and then set herself the task of meeting her brother's morbid irritation, and by agreeing with him and bidding him hope on and fight on forever, if need be, she made some little impression upon his mood.

Then Marvie appeared again, this time black in the face. Alas for Hettie! Her heart sank.

"Ben Ide, I've a bone to pick with you," he burst out.

"Pick away, you young rooster," returned Ben, wearily; but he was interested. Marvie had never before bearded the lion in his den.

"Did Dillon tell you a cowboy named Laskin rode in with news about a cattle drive?"

"Sure he did."

"Ha! That's what he told Raidy. He's a damn liar!"

"Marvie, take care! You're no longer a kid. Would you say that to Dillon's face?"

"Would I? Huh! I DID an' I cussed him good," rejoined Marvie, hotly.

"Why did you? Marv, I'm losin' patience."

"An, I'm losin' patience with you, Ben Ide. Listen. I saw that cowboy. He wasn't no rider named Laskin. He was Cedar Hatt!"

"What?"

"Cedar Hatt, I tell you. I *know* him."

"Marvie, you're not only loco, but you're ravin' sore at Dillon. You'll go too far. Take care."

"Care, hell!" shouted Marvie, beside himself with rage. "It's you who's loco."

"Marvie Blaine, you're fired," replied Ben, curtly. "You can't ride for me any more."

Marvie underwent a sudden disastrous change of mood.

"Fired?" he said, poignantly.

"Yes, fired. Now get out of my house an' go over to Hettie's till I can decide what to do with you."

"Aw—Ben!" gasped Marvie.

"Don't aw—Ben me," said Ben, furiously. "Get

out of here now—you round-eyed, freckle-faced four-flush of a cowboy!"

Marvie started as if he had been lashed.

"Ben Ide, you'll be sorry for that," he declared, solemnly, and stamped away.

Ben stared at the erect retreating figure of the lad.

"Marvie, too!" he said, huskily.

Hettie felt something of a sneak herself as she stole away, back to her own cabin and the seclusion of her room. Was she not betraying Ben by withholding facts she alone knew? Yet how impossible to crush him utterly! Jim Lacy was Nevada! She would never have the courage to tell him.

As for herself, the last hope had fled, the last doubt, the last shred of stubborn faith. Nevada was a rustler. He had fallen so low that he could steal from the friend who had once succored him. The thing was so base that Hettie writhed under the shame of her seemingly indestructible love for this impostor Nevada—this fugitive horseman who had won her under another guise—this Jim Lacy, killer and thief. But though everything else seemed dead, hope, faith, interest in life, will to go on fighting, she knew her love survived. It was the very pulse of her heart.

A long hour she lay there on her bed, until collapse and tears came to her relief. And when she again rose to face herself in the mirror she shrank aghast. But there was her mother to live for, and poor blind Ben, who had loved this traitor Nevada, even as she.

Two days went by, with the Ide households under considerable strain of uncertainty.

Raidy and Dillon, with their riders, returned about noon of the third day. The news reached Hettie while she was in the kitchen, with her sleeves rolled up and flour to her elbows, but she did not lose time on account of that.

Ben was somber, nervous, silent, and he paced the living-room, oblivious to the importunities of little

Blaine, who toddled here and there, as if he were playing a game.

Presently Raidy entered the open door, sombrero in hand, dusty and unshaven.

"Howdy, boss!" he said in greeting, and bowed quaintly to Hettie and Ina.

"Took you long enough. Where's Dillon?" replied Ben, gruffly.

"Wal, you know Dillon always leaves the bad reports for me to make."

"Did he return with you?"

"Not exactly. He left us at daybreak this mornin' an' beat us in."

"Is he here now?"

"Sure. I told him he'd better come along with me. But he said he'd see you later. . . . Boss, Dillon is in purty bad humor. I never seen him like this. He's another fellar."

"Drinkin'?" queried Ben, sharply.

"No. He's just black as thunder an' sore as a kicked pup."

"That'd be natural for anyone who had my interests at heart, as Dillon has. But it's odd he didn't come to report. . . . Well, out with your bad news."

Ben squared himself as if for a blow and frowned upon his old foreman.

"I'm sorry, Ben. It couldn't be no wuss."

"Oh, Ben!" cried Ina, who had evidently worried more about her husband than the impending loss.

"Reckin you an' Hettie better leave us alone," returned Ben.

Neither of the women moved a step, though Ina subsided into a chair. Raidy appeared to have lost his usual taciturnity.

"Boss, you're rustled off the range. The last of your stock, except some stragglin' steers an' yearlin's, is gone—along with a thousand head of Tom Day's."

Ben Ide made a flashing violent gesture, as if to strike. He paled. His eyes shot fire.

"They've cleaned me?" he demanded, fiercely, as if still doubting.

"Yes, boss. I made sure, because I wasn't trustin' Dillon to give a full report."

Hettie, standing back of Ina's chair, felt both hot and cold; and she stared at her brother fearfully, expecting him to break into an ungovernable rage. For Ben had not been himself in weeks, and lately he had been hard to live with. She had reckoned without her host, however, for although Ben turned white to the lips he suddenly became calm and cool. With uncertainty gone he changed radically.

"Ahuh. So your hunch has come true," he said, almost with sarcasm. "Wal, I reckon you'll get a lot of satisfaction crowin' over me an' Dillon."

"No, boss, I won't even say I told you so," returned Raidy.

"Give me the facts, short an' sweet," said Ben.

"Wal, Tom Day an' his riders were at Silver Meadows when we arrived. A sheepherder had tipped them off to the drive. We split up an' rode all around the Meadows. Only a few cattle left. Them rustlers made a slick job of it. Day an' Franklidge lost over a thousand head, an' you lost all you had left. A matter of three thousand head. We took the trail up the canyon. An' say, it was a bowlavarde clear to the Rim. . . . I was for trailin' the rustlers to finish a fight. But Day wouldn't let any of us go down in that hole. We'd have been ambushed an' some of us killed. Besides, he said we could never have recovered the cattle. Once turned loose in that jungle of scrub oak, manzanita, an' cactus, them cattle would have vamoosed like ticks shook off a leaf. So we turned back."

"You told Tom Day, of course, that Jim Lacy made this drive?" queried Ben.

"Tom knowed all about it from the sheepherder. Seems thet Lacy sent Tom word he was goin' to make this big steal. Sent his respects to Tom an' Judge Franklidge an' said he'd drop in to Winthrop some day."

"By Heaven! this Lacy is a cool one!" exclaimed Ben, as if admiration was wrenched from him.

"Cool? Wal, boss, you might call Lacy thet, but I reckon he's a mixture of hell's fire an' chain lightnin'!"

"I'll hang him," said Ben, with deadly calm.

"No, Ben, if you'll excuse me, I'll say you'll never put a rope around Jim Lacy's neck. He couldn't never be jailed, either. He'll die in his boots, with a gun spoutin', an' Gawd help the men frontin' him!"

"Bah! You talk like Marvie Blaine," retorted Ben, curtly. "An' you Raidy—a grown man!"

"Boss, it grieves me thet I've lived to disagree with you," returned Raidy, with dignity.

"This Jim Lacy is the leader of the Pine Tree outfit," asserted Ben, positively.

"Wal, me an' Tom Day reckoned so. An' for once Dillon agreed with us," replied Raidy. "Tom said Lacy jest got tired of layin' low an' bein' mysterious. So he comes out in the open. I'll bet you he'll ride right into Winthrop."

"Raidy, I'm glad Lacy cleaned me out. I'm through waitin' around to see what's goin' to happen next. I've sent for Sheriff Macklin an' a posse. This mornin' I got word from Struthers, the Phoenix sheriff who's made it so hot for rustlers in southern Arizona. Struthers is in Winthrop at my request. They'll arrive here not later than to-morrow. I'll have Dillon get twenty-five of the hardest men he can gather. I'll offer ten thousand dollars reward for Jim Lacy, dead or alive. I'll spend every dollar I have to run down Lacy an' his Pine Tree gang."

"Wal, boss, you're talkin' high, wide, an' handsome," replied Raidy. "But it's not for me to offer opinions. This ranch—an' for that matter, this whole range—ain't big enough for me an' your man Dillon. I jest have to quit."

"Very well, Raidy. I'm sorry you see it that way," returned Ben, coldly, and with a wave of his hand terminated the interview.

Hettie fled. As she ran out she heard Ina deliver a

stinging rebuke to her husband. Then a door slammed. Hettie hurried home in a state of mind bordering on a breakdown. She finished her work in a mechanical way, while slow torment consumed her.

"What's all the row over at Ben's?" her mother inquired, placidly, from her comfortable chair.

"Rustlers, cattle, foremen, sheriffs, and Heaven only knows what," replied Hettie, distractedly.

"Well, daughter, don't be upset. You know Ben."

"I thought I did, mother. But I'm doubtful about it now. He fired Raidy."

"No! Why, that's dreadful! Raidy taught Ben how to ride a horse. Oh, this dreadful Arizona! . . . But I don't mean that, Hettie. I love this quiet, sweet wild country. The men, though—they're—they're loco, as Marvie says. And Ben has got it, too?"

"Mother, have you seen Marvie to-day?" asked Hettie, suddenly remembering that she had not.

"Marvie went away yesterday and hasn't come back. At least he didn't sleep in his bed."

"Oh dear! That wild boy! Here's more to—to worry over. . . . Mother, I didn't tell you that the reason Marvie came to us is because Ben discharged him— drove him out of the house."

"Reckon we'll have Ina next," said her mother.

"I—I wouldn't be surprised at anything," returned Hettie, tearfully.

Hettie went to her room, with the motive of indulging her grief. But sight of her riding-boots acted powerfully upon her and she decided to take a ride. Not for days had she been on her horse. Perhaps a long hard gallop would be good for her; and moreover, she might meet Marvie on the trail. Could something have happened to him? It might very well have, Hettie concluded, with a tremor. He and Rose might have been discovered by that Cedar Hat, of whom Rose had such great fear. The very air round the Ide ranch seemed congested, heavy, sultry, ominous with menace.

Hettie passed the quarters of the riders at some distance, not caring to be accosted by Dillon or Raidy.

She saw some saddled horses, dusty and tired, that had evidently just come in. There were a number of men bunched in a circle, conversing so earnestly that none espied her. Gaining the stables, she found Pedro and had him saddle her horse. Soon she was riding fast with the wind in her face.

But neither a gallop nor a run sufficed to change Hettie's mood. She rode into the woods, and let her horse walk at will down the shady trail in the direction from which Marvie always returned.

And here, alone, under the impelling influence of the forest, Hettie realized that she was a most miserable and heartbroken girl, with a terrible sword hanging over her head. How hopeless her situation! What use to think? There was not a thought nor an action that could help her in her extremity. Courage and intelligence had gone with the loss of hope.

A purple haze like smoke hung in the aisles of the forest; the only sound was the faintest of breezes murmuring in the pines; the thickets were on fire with golden and scarlet flame of autumn leaves; the westering sun caught the glint of falling leaf and pine needle.

Nature seemed so pitiless this day. It went on, calm, sweet, beautiful, inscrutable, unmindful of the poor little lives of human beings. Hettie could not derive any solace, any strength, from either forest or range or desert.

Arizona had killed her dream, as it had ruined her brother. And the horror of Hettie's state seemed that the climax of this infernal paradox, the dénouement, the worst, had yet to come.

Suddenly she caught the rhythmic beat of swift hoofs ahead round a green curve of the trail. That must be Marvie's horse. A rush of relief swept over her. The pine boughs spread. A big black horse was upon her before she could pull a rein. She cried out. But the rider hauled back to his haunches, and that rider was Nevada.

Nineteen

Hettie clutched the pommel of her saddle. An awful stunning shock suspended, for an instant, all her faculties, and every sensibility except the physical animal instinct of holding her equilibrium. Then emotion burst the dam.

When Nevada's horse plunged up, his head came abreast Hettie's horse.

"You!" Hettie felt the word leave her stiff lips, but she heard it only as a whisper.

Nevada swept off his sombrero and bowed low to the mane of his horse. And as he rose erect he remained bareheaded.

"Wal, shore it's Hettie Ide," he drawled, in the cool, leisurely, Southern accent that cut into her heart like blades.

Then they gazed at one another, as if sight was trying to reconcile the face of dreams with the reality. The face Hettie looked into had the same lean outline, the dark blue-black shade of beard against the clear brown tan, the intent light hazel-flecked eyes, like level piercing points. But it did not have the soul with which her imagination and memory had invested it.

"I—saw you—in Winthrop," began Hettie, as if to find relief from oppression. Silence was impossible.

"Shore. I reckoned you might," he replied. As he spoke he rolled a cigarette with steady fingers. No surprise, no emotion that Hettie could read, manifested itself in look or manner. "Too bad you had to run into me heah!"

"Too bad! . . . It's terrible. But I'm glad," exclaimed Hettie, quivering, shaking all over.

"Thank you, an' I'm shore sorry I cain't return the

compliment," he said, and bent his head to light the cigarette.

His cool nonchalance, that she remembered so poignantly, seemed now to inflame her.

"*Jim Lacy!*" she cried, in scornful, sad haste to acquaint him with her knowledge of his infamy.

He thrust his sombrero on, tilted back, and as he blew a thin column of smoke upward his penetrating, inscrutable eyes studied her face.

"Why didn't you trust me? Oh, why?" she went on, slipping farther toward an emotional outbreak.

"Hettie, there was a time, long ago, when I'd rather have been daid than let you know I was Jim Lacy."

"You were ashamed?"

"I shore was."

"Long ago, you said. . . . Then you're *not* ashamed now?"

"Wal, it cain't matter now," he rejoined, with a gleam of a smile.

"Why can't it matter now?" she queried.

He made an expressive gesture, and then gazed down through the open forest to the colorful desert. His horse rubbed noses with Hettie's, and gradually backed it across the trail.

"Ben doesn't dream his—his old friend Nevada is you—the notorious Jim Lacy."

"I reckon not. . . . Too bad he's got to find out pretty soon!"

"Must Ben—find out?" asked Hettie, huskily. Thought of Ben augmented her weakness.

Nevada dropped his head. His horse, nosing Hettie's, brought Nevada closer to her, so that she might have touched him. This proximity bore upon her with incalculable influence. She pulled her horse aside, to no avail, for the big black followed with eager whinny. His rider did not seem to be aware of this proceeding, or of the proximity that again ensued.

"How can you be so cool—so hatefully cool?" burst out Hettie, "Ben loved you. I—I . . . What did he care who you were? Why didn't you always stay Nevada?

. . . Ben left no stone unturned to locate you. Failing that, he came to Arizona because he hoped you might turn up. . . . You have turned up. But as Jim Lacy—as a rustler who stole from him. Stole from a friend you once saved and succored and loved! Did you know those cattle were Ben's?"

"Shore—I did," replied Nevada, showing a faint pallor.

"Oh, it was a terrible thing to do!" cried Hettie, covering her face with her hands. "Your pard? It will cut him to the quick—embitter him forever. . . . And it'll kill *me!*"

His silence, his imperturbability in its unnaturalness roused her to a sudden furious passion that burned away her tears and waved her face scarlet.

"Wal, you're a mighty healthy lady after so many years of dyin'," he drawled, tossing away his half-smoked cigarette. "Hettie, you always was pretty, but you've grown into a plumb handsome woman. . . . Reckon the cowboys are sweeter'n ever on you."

"That must have meant a lot to you," she flashed, breathing hard.

"Dillon, now. *He* was."

"Yes. He has made love to me. Begged me to marry him," returned Hettie, in fiery flippancy, hoping with a woman's strange coquetry to make him jealous.

"Wal, you don't say. He's shore a handsome *hombre*. Devil with the women. I heah. . . . Why don't you marry him?"

"I—may yet," replied Hettie, somberly. He baffled her. In his cool, inscrutable presence she felt like a child. And a deep unplumbed emotion seemed to swell at the gates of her self-control.

"Hettie, if you do you'll be changin' your mind considerable from what it was that night at the dance in Winthrop."

"What do you know about that?" she queried, wonderingly.

"Wal, I happened to heah you tell Dillon a few things, an' I seen him try to get you in his arms."

"*You!* You were there?"

"Shore. An' after you flounced off I introduced myself to Dillon an' most polite invited him to draw. But he didn't have the nerve, so I took a punch at his handsome face."

"You struck Dillon on my behalf!" murmured Hettie softening.

"Wal, yes, partly. But I had it in for him before. . . . By the way, is he at the ranch?"

"Yes. I saw him at the corrals as I came out."

"Good! I'm shore a lucky *hombre*—since I took up with Jim Lacy again."

"You were going to our ranch?" queried Hettie, quickly.

"I *am* goin', Miss Hettie Ide."

"What—for?"

"Wal, reckon my prime reason is to shoot out one of Dillon's handsome eyes. But I've another—"

"Oh! . . . You've something against Dillon?"

"Huh! I should rather smile I have, Hettie."

"You'll—you'll *kill* him?"

Nevada's flashing eye and sweeping gesture were the first indications of passion he had evinced.

"Reckon if you hadn't held me up heah he'd be daid now. An' that stands for me, too."

"Ah! Then Dillon is—a—a dangerous man—as you—"

"Hettie, *he's* a bad *hombre*. Come from New Mexico. Name is Ed Richardson, once with the Billy the Kid outfit. . . . I'll kill him, shore, but he might return the compliment."

"You—you bloody gunman!" returned Hettie, as if those few words expressed her infinite amaze and contempt for men who lived by such a creed.

"Hettie, if he does kill me you can tell Ben the truth, then come an' smooth back my hair an' wipe my bloody face. Ha! Ha!" he said, in bitter mockery.

"Hush!" Hettie reined her horse closer, so that her stirrup locked with Nevada's. "Do not do this terrible deed. For Ben's sake, if not mine. Be big enough to abandon your blood feud. Give up this outlaw, rustler, gunman life. . . . Take me away with you to some far country. I have money. You can start anew. I will cleave to you—live for you."

"For Gawd's sake, Hettie Ide, are you crazy?" he returned, stridently.

"Not yet. But I will be soon—if this—goes on," she panted, and slipped her gloved hand to his shoulder. "Nevada, I—I still love you. I've always loved you. . . . I forgive all. I surrender all. I don't care who you are —what you've been. All I ask is that you save Ben the horror so near—that you take me away and give up this life. . . . We can plan quickly. I will meet you at some point on the railroad. . . . Say you will."

"No," he said, hoarsely.

"Nevada! . . . Don't you love me—still?" And she leaned to him, overcome, betraying all her woman's soul of love, and hope for him, for Ben, for herself.

"Love you? Ha! Ha!"

"Don't stare. Don't laugh. This means life or death to me. Say you love me. Say you'll take me."

"Yes, I love you, mad woman. But I cain't accept your sacrifice. I cain't ruin you. . . . Good Gawd! Hettie, you forget I'm Jim Lacy!"

"It's because you *are* Jim Lacy."

"Heavens! This heah is awful! . . . Hettie, I cain't—I won't."

"You lie, then. You do not love me. *I* am proving mine. But you—you are false. You have taken some— other woman. You don't love me!"

Hettie, dim of eye, saw him loom over her. She felt herself seized in iron arms and dragged from her horse. Then she was lifted over the pommel and crushed to his breast, and bent backward, blind and breathless, a victim of terrible devouring lips. He kissed her mouth, her cheeks, her eyes, her brow, her hair, and then again her mouth.

Hettie's senses reeled and almost failed her. When his violence ceased she felt herself held closely for a long moment, then let down from the horse until her feet touched the ground. She was falling when he leaped from the saddle. He set her on the grass with her back against a tree, and there, presently, her eyes opened.

Nevada knelt before her, his face convulsed. Slowly it smoothed out and a wild darkness faded from his eyes.

"There. You've come to. I reckon I must ask you to excuse me for bein' rough. But I shore couldn't stand that talk aboot not lovin' you."

"I will not believe—unless you prove it," returned Hettie, unsteadily, as she reached for her sombrero.

Nevada rose to his feet. "I cain't prove it your way," he replied, and his features set stone-cold and gray.

"Oh, what have you done to me?" cried Hettie, wildly, as again passion rose strong and regained the ascendancy over her.

"Reckon nothin' compared to what you've done to me," he responded, with somber gaze upon her. "Dillon will just aboot beat me to a gun."

Hettie stood up, holding to the tree trunk. "Nothing. . . . I've loved you since I first met you. I've been true. I trusted you. I cared not for your past. I believed in your future. I prayed for you. My faith in you was as great as my faith in God. I believed you loved me. That when you rode away from Forlorn River— to escape the consequences—when you killed Less Setter to save Ben—I believed you would be true to me, to the higher self you found through Ben's love and mine. . . . But you were too little. You went back to the old life—to the old comrades. Rustlers, gamblers, gunmen! You killed just because you wanted to keep that name hated and feared. You are a bloody monster. . . . No doubt you sank to the embrace of vile women—the consorts of thieves! O my God! it would be my death if I could not kill my love. But I will. It will lie dead as my faith. . . . You are a liar, a failure, a weakling. Basest of all is your ingratitude. You stole from my brother—who loved you."

Nevada's eyes held a blaze like black lightning.

"Reckon that'll be aboot all I want to heah," he said, in tones she had never heard before.

"That is—all."

He gathered up the reins and vaulted into the saddle, then turned to gaze down the trail.

"Horses comin'," he said, briefly. "It's Marvie with his girl, Rose Hatt."

"Yes, I see," returned Hettie, with a start. "Oh, I'm —glad."

"Wal, Miss Hettie Ide," he said, "you might heah somethin' from Marvie an' Rose. Anyway, don't rustle back home too quick."

Her lips framed a query she could not speak.

"It's aboot sunset," he went on, with strange gaze upon the west. "Sunset for Dillon! An' shore sunset for me!"

Then he spurred the big black, and clattering into the trail soon vanished from sight toward the ranch.

Twenty

Nevada approached the Ide ranch from that side closest to the forest, where the pines and cedars trooped down the gentle slopes of the benches, clear to the most outwardly of the cattle sheds.

With his brain on fire and his heart like lead, his whole being crushed under the burning weight of Hettie's outspoken love and terrible scorn, he halted under cover of the last clump of cedars, and dismounted, answering to an instinct, true even in that hour of utter catastrophe, to the instinct which had preserved him so long as Jim Lacy. Not now, however, was it an instinct of self-preservation, but one to meet and kill Ed Richardson, alias Campbell, alias Clan Dillon, late member of the few surviving Lincoln County war desperadoes.

Wedging this purpose into his stunned brain, Nevada kept driving it deeper, while he removed saddle and bridle from his horse and turned it free. He would have no more need of a horse. Then he crouched in the cedars, under tremendous strain, driving himself to the exclusion of all thought, of all emotion, of all faculties except those few cardinally important for the issue at hand.

When he emerged from under cover of the cedars he might have been an automaton, with guidance of some grim-strung spirit.

He glided behind brush to the sage and through this to the pole fence. It led to the back of log cabins, which he marked as the bunkhouses. The sunset hour was near. Silver-edged purple clouds hung over the soft rounded foothills. Soon the sun would sink from behind the broken mass of cloud and slide down into that golden space behind the ranges. Cowboys, riders, range hands, foreman, all would be waiting the call to supper. The day had been hot. Just now, with the first cool breeze breathing down from the hill, all the men would be outdoors.

There was a fate in many meetings of life, and singularly in all those that involved Jim Lacy.

He swept his magnified gaze to the left, over pasture and field, which were open to his sight. A few horses and colts, cows and calves, a burro, and some black pigs dotted the gray-green pastures and the brown fields. No rider in sight!

Nevada stole swiftly along the fence to the first high corral. It contained a number of horses, with saddles and packs stacked in a corner. He would have to cross this corral, and go through the others, to reach the rear of the bunkhouses. Climbing to the top log of the high fence, he peeped over. No man in sight! He climbed and ran and climbed and ran, quickly gaining the open gate of the last corral. The two small log cabins and the long one stood across the open space, with barns to the left and courtyard on the right, leading up to the Ide homes in the edge of the forest.

A Mexican boy appeared leading horses to a watering-trough; a rider came trotting down the long lane between the fields; some one was driving cows in from the pasture. From behind the cabins came the loud rollicking laughter of cowboys.

Nevada did not hesitate a moment. Leisurely he strode from the corral toward the long cabin, making for the nearest end, where cords of firewood were stacked high. That end, where blue smoke curled from a stone chimney, would be the kitchen. There would be a porch on the other side.

Nevada gained the woodpiles. They had been stacked, seemingly, to furnish him perfect passageway and perfect cover, for the fruition of this long-planned moment. It never crossed his mind that Dillon might not be there. Dillon would be there. For the men who had wronged Jim Lacy or incurred his enmity there existed a fatality which operated infallibly. Or else

Lacy never made a mistake. It was something that he felt.

He glided between the high stacks of wood. Before he peeped out he saw horsemen riding down the dusty road which wound away to the north and Winthrop. Then Nevada put his eye to an aperture between two billets of cedar that protruded from the stack.

A dozen or more men lounged and sat and stood in plain sight. Cowboys in shirt sleeves, faces shiny and red, hair glossed and wet, sat on the ground, backs to the cabin. Nevada recognized Macklin, the Winthrop sheriff, leaning against the hitching rail, in conversation with two other men, not garbed as riders. Facing Nevada was a tall man in black and he had a bright badge on his vest. He was another sheriff, a stranger to Nevada.

"We sure want to get off by sunup," he was saying to a man near him.

This man stood with his back toward Nevada. His powerful supple shoulders showed wonderfully through his white clean shirt. Nevada recognized that lithe stalwart build, the leonine neck, the handsome head, with its clustering fair hair.

Dillon! A slight cold thrill ran over Nevada. Following it came an instinct like that of a tiger to leap.

Nevada swiftly ran his glance over the other men, standing near and in the background. Ben Ide was not present!

Then Nevada drew back behind the woodpile, loosened his gun in its sheath, and stood there an instant while the waiting forces of brain and muscle vibrated into a tremendous unity.

"Come an' get it," sang out the cheery voice of the cook inside.

"Whoopee! Whoaboy," shouted the cowboys, scrambling up.

At this instant Nevada bounded out swiftly and ran to a halt.

"HOLD ON!" he yelled, with all the power of his

lungs. His piercing voice made statues of all, even the cowboys stiffening in half-erect postures.

In the instant of silence that ensued Dillon was the only man to move and he wheeled swift as a flash, so swiftly that the receding trace of mirth had not yet left his handsome face.

"Howdy, Dillon!" drawled Nevada, slow and cool.

Macklin shuffled erect in great alarm.

"That's Jim Lacy," he shouted, hoarsely.

"Shore is. Careful now, you outsiders!" warned Nevada, yet with eye only for Dillon.

Every man in line with Dillon plunged off the porch or darted into the cabin. The cowboys sank back to the ground, sagging against the log wall.

Dillon stood on the porch, facing Nevada, scarcely thirty feet distant. His reaction from careless mirth to recognition of peril was as swift as his sight. But there followed the instant when his faculties had to grasp what that peril was and how he should meet it.

Nevada had gambled on this instant. It was his advantage. He did not underrate Dillon. He read his mind in those dilating eyes.

"Wal, you know me," cut out Nevada, icily. "An' I know you—Dillon—*Campbell!*—ED RICHARDSON!"

That was the paralyzing challenge. The rustler turned a ghastly white. The frontier's bloody creed, by which he had lived, called him to his death. His green eyes set balefully. He knew. He showed his training. He had no more fear of death than of the swallows flitting under the eaves above. But he had a magnificent and desperate courage to take his enemy with him.

Richardson never uttered a word. Almost imperceptibly his body lowered as if under instinct to crouch. His stiff bent right arm began to quiver.

Nevada saw the thought in Richardson's eyes—the birth of the message to nerve and muscle. When his hand flashed down Nevada was drawing.

Crash! Nevada's shot did not beat Richardson's draw, but it broke his aim. Boom! The rustler's gun went off half leveled. He lurched with terrible violence and his gun boomed again. The bullet scattered the gravel at Nevada's feet and spanged away into the air.

A wide red spot appeared as if by magic on the middle of Richardson's white shirt. How terrible to see him strain to raise his gun-arm!

At Nevada's second shot one of Richardson's awful eyes went blank. His gun clattered to the floor. He swayed. His arm hooked round the porch post. Then it sank limp, letting him fall with sodden thud.

Nevada was the first to withdraw his gaze from that twitching body. He flipped his gun into the air and caught it by the barrel.

"Heah, sir," he said to the sheriff with the star on his vest, and extended the gun butt foremost. "I reckon that'll be aboot all for Jim Lacy."

The strain on the watchers relaxed. A murmur of wonder ran through them, growing louder. The sheriff came to a power of movement and speech.

"What? Lacy, are you handin'—over your gun?" he queried, hoarsely.

"Wal, I'm not pointin' the right end of it at you," replied Nevada, and tossed the gun at the sheriff's feet.

"What—the hell?" gasped a weatherbeaten old rider, Raidy, staring hard at Nevada.

Here Macklin came rushing up, to get between Nevada and the other sheriff.

"Jim Lacy, you're my prisoner," yelled Macklin, beside himself with the strange opportunity presented and a terror of the enormity of his risk. He drew his gun. "Hands up."

"Shoot an' be damned, you four-flush officer of the law," retorted Nevada, wearily, and turning his back to Macklin he strode to a seat on the porch steps.

"Run for the boss," shouted Raidy to the cowboys. "Tell him there's hell come off. Fetch him an' Judge Franklidge."

"Hyar comes Tom Day with his outfit," yelled a cowboy, excitedly, pointing to the horsemen entering the square. "The whole range's hyar. Haw! Haw!"

Nevada experienced a weariness of soul and body. It was over. He did not care what happened.

"Say, give me a smoke—one of you punchers," he said, removing his sombrero to wipe his clammy brow.

Twenty-one

Marvie Blaine came swinging down the trail at a gallop, with Rose Hatt riding close behind.

Eager excitement lent Hettie the strength to mount her horse. Nevada's strange eyes and words! What might not Marvie and Rose have to tell her?

"Hey there, Hettie!" shouted Marvie, when still some rods distant. "Look who's comin' behind."

Hettie complied, with emotions changing, rising again in a flood, new, bewildering, looming darkly to threaten her with panic. Marvie rode right upon her before halting.

"Say, you look like the devil!" he ejaculated, with anxious concern.

"Marv, that's the way I feel," replied Hettie.

Rose joined them, to crowd her pony close, eager yet shy, with eyes alight and lips parted. "Oh, Miss Hettie!" she cried, rapturously. "Marvie's brought me to you. I—I'll never go back—to the brakes."

"My dear, you're welcome to my home," returned Hettie, warmly, leaning to kiss the flushed face.

"Hettie, you've seen a ghost—the same ghost I seen," declared Marvie, shrewdly.

"Oh, Marvie lad—a ghost indeed!" moaned Hettie. "Nevada! . . . He just left me—to—to kill Dillon!"

"No news to me," shouted Marvie, fiercely. "I've got to see that. . . . Fetch Rose. But go round. Keep away from the corrals."

The last he delivered over his shoulder as he urged his horse into the trail and beat him into a run. In a moment he passed out of sight among the pines. The swift patter of hoofs died away.

"Come, Rose—ride," suddenly cried Hettie, with a start, striking her horse.

The spirited animal, unused to that, broke into a gallop, and then a run. Hettie looked back. The girl was close behind, her hair flying in the wind, her face flashing. Her pony was fast and she could ride. Hettie turned her attention to the trail and the low branches of pines and the obstructing brush. Soon she was flying at a tremendous gait through the forest. The speed, the violence added to her agitation.

Where the trail emerged from the pines, to drop down on the sage and cedar slope adjacent to the ranch land, Hettie turned her horse and kept to the top of the slope. Soon she passed Nevada's big black horse grazing on the sage. Her heart took a great bursting leap. *"An' shore sunset for me!"* Nevada's words of resignation and sadness rang in her ears like bells of doom.

Suddenly she imagined she heard a shot. She turned her ear to the left. Another! A gun-shot—then two sharp cracks, clear on the breeze. She reeled in her saddle. Almost she put her horse at the ranch fence. But she kept on in wild flight, forgetting Rose, clutching with left hand at her breast, where uncertainty augmented to supreme agony.

Her fast horse, keen at the freedom afforded him, swept on as in a race, on by the corrals and gardens, up over the low bench, and through the woods to her cabin, where her mother stood waving frantically from the porch. Hettie rode on, over the swaying bridge, into the shady green glade before Ben's house.

Here she pulled her iron-jawed horse to a snorting halt. She saw men running. She heard Rose's pony come clattering over the bridge. Then Marvie's horse appeared over the rise of ground toward the corral. What breakneck speed! How he thundered up the drive!

One sight of Marvie's flashing face answered Hettie. She could have screamed in her frenzy. Marvie reached her at the moment Rose came up. His horse reared and pounded. Marvie jerked him down with powerful arm, and closed with Hettie.

"Nevada's down there—handcuffed!" he whispered, pantingly. "Dillon's dead! . . . Oh, there'll be—hell now! . . . But not a word from—you an' Rose!"

The boy's heated face, the horses, Rose so white and rapt, the running riders, the houses and the pines—all blurred in Hettie's sight. She had to fight fiercely to recover. She felt the girl's strong hand on her, steadying her in the saddle. The deadly faintness passed. Her eyes cleared and her breast lifted to give rein to a tumult there.

Ben and Judge Franklidge were striding out to meet the running cowboys.

"Judge, I told you I heard shots," Ben was saying. "Somethin's happened!"

"Seems like. But don't let it upset you," replied the judge.

"There's Marvie. . . . Has he gone loco?" exclaimed Ben, in amaze, as the boy, riding wildly, scattered the men coming up the slope.

"By thunder! Ben," replied Franklidge, suddenly espying Hettie and Rose, as they rode in upon the lawn.

At that juncture the first cowboys reached Ben to blurt out:

"Boss, Jim Lacy's here! He just killed Dillon."

"Wha—at?" shouted Ben, incredulously.

As the cowboy repeated his news Raidy arrived at the head of three more of Ben's hands, and all began to jabber pantingly.

"One at a time," ordered Ben, harshly. "What the hell's wrong? Raidy!"

The old foreman drew himself up steadily, though with heaving breast.

"Boss, I have to report—Dillon's been killed—Jim Lacy!"

Ben Ide leaped straight up in sudden ungovernable

fury. His face turned dusk red. He clenched his fists high above his head.

"On my own place?" he thundered.

"Yes, sir. Right on the cook-house porch."

"Dillon dead?"

"He is indeed, sir," replied Raidy. "Lacy shot him through the middle—then put out his right eye."

"Murder!" gasped Ben.

"Not much! . . . It was an even break. Lacy dropped out of the clouds, seems like. Dillon was game, sir, an' quick—but not quick enough."

"Killed! My best man," rasped out Ben, stridently. "Where's this Jim Lacy?"

"He's sittin' on the cook-house porch," replied Raidy. "Handcuffed, sir. . . . The sheriffs put him in irons."

Ben cracked a hard fist into his palm. "They got him, then. . . . Judge Franklidge, I knew we'd land that gunman-rustler."

"Ide, it's a little embarrassing to know what to do with this—this Jim Lacy—now we've got him," replied the judge, dryly.

"Damn him! I'll show you."

"An', boss," interrupted Raidy, "Tom Day has rid in with his outfit. They wanted to lynch Lacy. But Tom roared at them like a mad bull. Reckon you'd better hurry down."

Ina came running from the house. "Ben, what—in the—world's happened?" she asked, in alarm.

"Ina, it's all over, so don't get scared," returned Ben. "Dillon has been shot by that bloody devil, Jim Lacy. Why, the man must be insane! Comin' here to carry out his queer feud! Right at my back door!"

"Dillon? Is—is he dead?" asked Ina, fearfully.

"Yes, ma'am," interposed Raidy, touching his sombrero.

"Oh, how dreadful!" Then Ina caught sight of Hettie and Rose. She ran to them. "Hettie, isn't it awful? That Dillon! I wonder. . . . You look sort of wild, Hettie. Who's this girl with you?"

"Rose Hatt. Marvie's friend," replied Hettie, bending down. "Oh, Ina, I've——"

Ben, striding away with his men, turned to call out, "Ina, stay back, an' keep those girls with you!"

"But why can't I come, too?" burst out Ina.

"No place for women," he returned, curtly. "There's one dead man now an' soon there'll be another."

Ina halted with a revulsion of feeling too strong for curiosity.

"Hettie, we mustn't go," she said.

"Listen, old girl. Chucks for Ben Ide. There's not enough men in Arizona to keep me away," declared Hettie, wildly. Then she bent down over Ina to whisper. "Jim Lacy is Nevada!"

Ina put a hand over her mouth to stifle a scream. Then she gasped, "No!"

"Yes! I've known it for long. And I *met* him to-day. . . . O God! . . . But I—I can't talk now. Come."

Hettie, with Rose on her left, rode at the heels of the striding men. Ina ran beside Hettie, clinging to the stirrup, looking up now and then with dark bright eyes.

They traversed the short lane to enter the wide square, on the other side of which stood the quarters of the ranch hands. There were ten or more saddle horses standing bridles down. Hettie's startled sight included a dark group of men massed in front of the cook-house. There! Nevada must be there—soon to be confronted by Ben. How terrible for Ben—for both of them! Hettie's state became one of palpitating suspense, of nerve-racking torture. Yet an overwhelming, incomprehensible curiosity consumed her.

They reached the crowd of cowboys and men strange to Hettie, some of whom faced around.

"Open up here," shouted Ben, in a loud hard voice. "Spread out. . . . Let me see this man."

The crowd split in a hurry, leaving a wide V-shaped space, at the apex of which sat the prisoner on the edge of the porch. The dead man lay on the ground, covered with a blanket.

Hettie recognized Nevada, though his head was bowed and his sombrero hid his face. His hands, in irons, hung over his knees. What a strange, pathetic figure! Hettie's sore heart failed her. What mystery was here? The moment seemed charged with indefinable and profound portent.

Macklin, the Winthrop sheriff, beaming and bristling with his importance, advanced a stride, with pompous gesture.

"Wal, Mr. Ide, here's your man. I've got him in irons," he boomed.

Ben advanced, his gaze passing from the dead man on the ground to the slumping prisoner.

"Jim Lacy," he called, sternly.

There was no movement from Nevada, except that he seemed to contract. Nobody else stirred. The air was fraught with tragic suggestion, with inscrutable meaning that yet transfixed the onlookers.

"Lacy, I'm goin' to hang you!" rang out Ben Ide.

Still no response from this notorious gunman, whose daring, whose cold nerve, had long been a subject for campfire gossip.

"Stand up. Let me look at you," ordered Ben, suddenly.

With a violent wrench the prisoner jerked out of his dejected posture, to slip off the porch and stand erect. He ducked his head, removing the sombrero, which fell to the ground. Composed and pale then he faced his judge.

Ben Ide seemed struck by lightning.

"My God! . . . Who—is this—man?" he faltered, almost inaudibly.

There was no answer. The crowd of onlookers gazed spellbound.

"Who are you?"

"Wal, Ben, I'm shore sorry we met this heah way," came the reply, in the old slow cool accents. "But I reckon it had to be."

"NEVADA!"

With the hoarse wondering cry, Ben leaped forward to clasp his old friend in a close embrace and hold him so a long moment.

Hettie saw Ben's face in convulsion, his eyes shut tight, his expression one to bewilder the staring bystanders. To her it was beautiful and somehow soul-satisfying. Her eyes were dim, her heart pounding.

"My old pard! Found at last! . . . Thank God!—I feared you were dead. . . . All these long years! But I hoped an' prayed. . . . An' here you are. It's too good to be true. I reckon it's a dream. Say somethin' to me— you old wild-horse-huntin' pard. Nevada!"

Ben held him back, hands on his shoulders, oblivious to all but that lean stone-gray face.

"Yes, Ben . . . Nevada to you—but to all the world —only Jim Lacy," replied Nevada, sadly.

"What?" cried Ben, with a violent start. Then his nervous quick hands ran down to Nevada's irons. "God Almighty! . . . You Jim Lacy?"

"Yes, to my shame—pard."

Ben's transition to reality was swift and passionate. Suddenly white, with blazing eyes, he tore at Nevada's handcuffs. "I don't care a damn who you were. You're Nevada to me—my friend—my pard. An' so you'll be forever."

"Wal, Ben—it's shore good to heah you," replied Nevada, his voice trailing off.

"Macklin, unlock these irons," ordered Ben.

"What? . . . But, Mr. Ide—he's my prisoner!" protested the sheriff, aghast. "He's wanted for rustlin'. He killed your foreman. The law——"

"To hell with your law!" interrupted Ben, fiercely. "Unlock his irons!"

"You hired us to ketch this man!"

"Quick. Before I throw my gun on you!"

His hand went to his hip. The crowd stirred with restless feet and whispered exclamation. Tom Day stepped out to get between Macklin and Ben.

"Easy now, Ben. Let old Tom have a word," he said, in his big voice, now full and resonant. "We've had enough gun-play for one day. . . . Macklin, give me the keys to these irons."

The sheriff, red of face, flustered and intimidated, complied with poor grace. Day unlocked the irons, removed them, and somewhat with contempt cast them at Macklin's feet.

Nevada rubbed his wrists and then looked up to smile at Day.

"Put her thar, Texas Jack," boomed the old rancher, with a wonderful smile wreathing his rugged face. "We're shore from the old Lone Star State. Let me be the first to shake the good right hand thet did for Dillon."

"Wal, Tom, shore you needn't rub it in," drawled Nevada, as he yielded to the vigorous onslaught of the older man.

"Come heah, Franklidge," called Day, beckoning to the judge. "I reckon it's aboot time."

Ben Ide stood motionless, his jaw dropping, his eyes expressive of an incredulous wonder that he could not voice. His feeling was surely shared by others there. As for Hettie, she seemed to feel her blood and brain whirl madly. Texas Jack! That warm, splendid smile of the old rancher! Judge Franklidge moving forward with dignified step and grave, kindly face!

But the other black-garbed sheriff intercepted him.

"Mr. Ide, these are sure most extraordinary proceedings," he said, authoritatively.

"Hell, yes!" burst out Ben. "But it's an extraordinary case."

"The law must take its course. Even if this Jim Lacy was an old pard of yours, he's now a criminal. Reckon his gun-play was always on the level. But he's a cattle an' hoss thief. We set out to hang the leader of this Pine Tree rustler outfit. Sure Lacy is him. His killin' of Dillon proves that. If this is no hangin' case, it sure is one for jail."

"Struthers, I hired you to come up here," returned Ben, deliberately. "I admit I wanted Jim Lacy shot or hanged. But I've changed my mind. He's my friend. I owe my life, my fortune, my family, all to him. There's some mystery—some mistake here. That's for me to learn, an' not for you."

"All right. But I'll take Lacy to Phoenix for trial," replied Struthers.

"If you do, it'll be over my dead body. Take care, Struthers. This isn't Phoenix. You're up in the brakes."

Thus Ben Ide answered to his few months in Arizona. The situation looked grave again. But Judge Franklidge interposed to push Struthers back.

"You have no jurisdiction here unless I give it," he said. Then he turned to Ben with courtly kindness. "My son, don't distress yourself further. Just have a little patience."

"Patience!" ejaculated Ben, as if he had not heard aright.

Judge Franklidge advanced to place his left hand on Nevada's shoulder and extended his right, which Nevada quickly met.

"Jack, you may be from Texas, as old Tom here brags, but you sure belong to Arizona," he said, heartily.

"Wal, I should smile," corroborated Day, heartily.

Judge Franklidge turned to indicate in slight gesture the dead man on the ground.

"Dillon, of course, was the leader of this Pine Tree rustler gang," he asserted. "Otherwise you would not have risked revealing yourself here?"

"Wal, reckon I wouldn't," replied Nevada, with a smile that held no mirth.

"Dillon!" boomed Tom Day, his eyes rolling at the dead man. "Who was he, Jack?"

"Ed Richardson, late of New Mexico."

"Richardson? I know aboot him. Lincoln County war *hombre*? Billy the Kid outfit?"

"That's the man, Tom."

"Wal, I'm a son-of-a-gun!" ejaculated the old rancher. "I begin to see light. Dillon was thick with Stewart. An' Stewart never worked the same for me after Dillon became foreman heah at Ben's. This mawnin' he was gone. An' he knowed where we was bound for. . . . Jack, what you make of thet?"

"Stewart was one of the three Arizonians that Richardson took into his New Mexican outfit."

"Ahuh! Who's the other two?"

"Burt Stillwell an' Cedar Hatt."

"Stillwell! . . . Jack, didn't you—meet thet *hombre* just lately?" queried Day, his eyes glinting.

"Yes. It was Stillwell who stole Ben's horse, California Red. I made him send Red back. Reckon that r'iled Stillwell. . . . An' Marvie Blaine shot Cedar Hatt to-day. So the Pine Tree outfit is shore broke."

Ben Ide, in bewildered state, crowded closer to the speakers.

"Marvie Blaine shot Cedar Hatt?" ejaculated Judge Franklidge.

"Good Lord!" added Day in his booming voice. "What next? Ben, you listenin' to all this?"

"Tom—I'm stumped," replied Ben, hoarsely.

"Spill it, Jack. Tell us about Marvie. Heaven help us now!" went on Day.

"I happened on Cedar Hatt to-day," replied Nevada. "He was ridin' down in one of the brakes an' I was on top. Wal, I soon saw he was trailin' some one. So I worked ahaid an' got down off the Rim. There I happened to run on Marvie an' his girl, Rose Hatt. They were spoonin' under the trees an' never saw me. I was lookin' for Cedar an' I knew Cedar was lookin' for them. So I kept quiet. Pretty soon Cedar slips up, right on to them. An' he begins to rave. Rose talked back an' shore Marvie showed spunk. Cedar knocked him down, an' then Rose, too. That riled Marvie an' he tore into Cedar. It looked bad, with Cedar pullin' at his gun. He got it out, but Marvie fought him for it. . . . An', wal, in the fight Cedar dropped the gun an' Marvie quick as a cat snatched it up. Usin' both hands, he throwed it on Cedar an' shore bored him twice."

"Whoop-ee!" yelled one of the cowboys at the back of the crowd.

"By thunder! I'd whoop myself if I had any voice

left," returned Tom Day. "Where's Marvie? Come heah, you gunslingin' kid!"

"Rose Hatt is heah, too," said Nevada. "An', Tom, it'd be wal for you an' Judge Franklidge to talk to her. Rose is a good honest girl. Dillon was after her. An' Cedar Hatt had dragged Rose away from home to meet Dillon. That was how Rose found out aboot the Pine Tree outfit. An' she confessed to me."

"Wal, I'll be darned!" replied Day, feelingly. "The lass looks a little scared an' white, Judge. I reckon we needn't heah her say now, in this crowd. But that kid Marvie—he shore don't look scared."

"Come here, my lad," called Judge Franklidge, beckoning.

Marvie slipped off his horse and stalked forward to confront the three men. Hettie thrilled at sight of him, yet she could have wept and screamed with mirth. Marvie, if he were any character at all, was surely Nevada. In look, in walk, in manner! He had a big black gun in his chaps pocket, and another smaller one in his belt. What a moment for Marvie Blaine!

"Son, what's this we heah?" asked Day, bluntly. "Did you shoot Cedar Hatt?"

"Reckon I did," replied Marvie. "Here's his gun. It happened just about as Nevada told you."

"Who's Nevada?"

Marvie laid a hand on his friend.

"Oho! You mean Jim Lacy heah?"

"No, I mean Nevada," replied the lad, stoutly. "That Jim Lacy handle doesn't go with me."

"Marvie, you speak for me," interposed Judge Franklidge. "He may indeed be Nevada and Jim Lacy. But for me he will always be Texas Jack. He has worked for me for two years. And before that for Tom Day. We found him to be the best cowboy who ever threw a rope for us. And more—a splendid honest man whom it is my privilege to call friend—and whom I would be happy to take into my cattle business."

"Hey, you sheriff rustlers," boomed Tom Day, with loud satisfaction, "did you heah that? Wal, listen to some more. Texas Jack volunteered to clean up this Pine Tree outfit. He had my backin'. He had Judge Franklidge's office behind him. He had free hand to become a rustler an' thief, to drink an' gamble an' shoot his way into the secret of the Pine Tree outfit. Do you savvy? Or are you wearin' your hair too long? There won't be any arrest. There won't be anyone danglin' on a rope."

Twenty-two

Hettie lay upon her bed, face to the open window, with the cool sweet sage-laden wind blowing in upon her. Dusk had fallen. The last rose and gold of the afterglow of sunset lingered in the west. She never knew how she had gotten from Ben's courtyard to her room. Dimly she remembered faces and murmuring voices that had no meaning for her.

The door opened—closed. Ben knelt beside her bed —took her hands—kissed her face.

"Hettie, I came as quick as I could get away," he said, with deep agitation. "I was knocked off my pins. But happy—oh, girl, never so happy before, except on the day Ina married me! . . . When I could think I remembered you. So here I am."

"Oh—Ben!" she whispered, and clung to him, her slow overburdened heart lifting painfully.

"Hettie dear—joy never kills," he replied, tenderly.

"If it were—only joy," mourned Hettie.

"Child, there's nothing *but* joy," he rushed on. "It was a terrible shock. To find out old Nevada—was Jim Lacy. But we always knew he was somebody bad. No, not bad. But somebody wild an' great. You knew— Hettie. . . . An' now he's turned up. The wonder of it is that he had hidden the old identity. He had given up the old wild life. He had found honest work an' had lived clean an' fine. As we knew him in those happy days at Forlorn River. So you see all your love an' faith an' hope were justified. He *was* worth it. Thank God I never lost——"

"Hush! You're killing—me!" gasped Hettie, writhing from his embrace.

"Hettie! Why, sister, this isn't like you," he expostu-

274

lated, in anxiety. "You're overcome. It has been too much for you."

"Not the joy—not the excitement," she returned. "I've been a poor miserable creature! . . . A coward! A selfish, headstrong woman! Jealous, little! . . . Oh, so poor in love—in faith!"

It came out then, gradually, sometimes incoherently, the story of her meeting with Nevada; and Hettie, in her self-abasement, magnified all the shame and ignominy—all the bitter invective and scorn which she had flung into his face.

Ben drew her head back to his shoulder and smoothed her disheveled hair.

"Well! . . . I understand now. Too bad! But there are excuses for you. Didn't you believe in him—love him—keep yourself for him all these years? Some things are too much for anybody."

"He—will—never—forgive," she sobbed, with the relief that came through his sympathy, his championship.

"Nevada? Why, that fellow would forgive anythin'."

"I—can never—forgive myself."

"Hettie, it will all come right. Don't you remember how you harped on that? Beat it into my poor thick head! . . . An', lo! it has come right. . . . Nevada could not hurt you."

"I have—hurt myself. I've lost something. My ideal has failed me."

"No—no. You're just overwrought by this sudden crash. Please, Hettie. I don't mean cheer up. But brace up an' see it through. Where's your Ide spunk?"

"Gone—gone."

"Well, then, get it back. I swear to you Nevada will be just like I am now. On my knees to you!"

"Where is he?"

"I left him in the livin'-room, playin' with Blaine. The kid took a shine to him *pronto*. An' Nevada. Lord! no one would ever dream of him bein' what we've learned to understand by the name Jim Lacy. . . . Hettie, there's somethin' so simple an' great about Nevada.

He's just himself now as we remembered him. He's Nevada, that's all."

Hettie lay awake many hours, with anguish slowly wearing away to a regurgitation of something quite as full of pangs. The night wind moved through the pines, sweeping, swelling, lulling. Coyotes added their lonesome chorus. White stars shone from the dark blue sky. When she fell asleep she dreamed vague, unreal, distorted dreams, in which she seemed the central shadow among shadows of Nevada, Marvie, Rose, Ben, and that mocking handsome Dillon. But she awoke to a new day—new as the bright morning, and with a dawning hope, like the gold and blue of the Arizona sky.

She had no time for her own thoughts. Marvie rushed in upon her, in the kitchen, to be followed by Rose, shy, sweet, modest as the wildflower for which she was named. Already they had been out in the woods and now they were as hungry as bears. Mrs. Ide looked upon them with wonder and favor. They wanted to go to Winthrop. Would Hettie go? Rose must have clothes and books and things. How Marvie's face glowed under his freckles! And Rose was in a transport. Had she forgotten that sordid home down in the brakes?

"Not to-day," replied Hettie, to their importunities. "To-morrow, maybe, if Ben consents."

"What has that Ben Ide to do with my affairs?" demanded Marvie, loftily. "I'd like to have you know *I* can ride for Franklidge or Tom Day or any other big rancher in Arizona."

Hettie sensed trouble for Ben when he came to attempt reconciliation with Marvie. Ben would surely need her aid.

"Marv, boy, of course I know," she said. "But you must use some sense. Rose is to have a home with me. And I shall take her to San Diego for the winter. I should think you would want to be near her this fall, and also go to San Diego, at least for a while."

Marvie wilted under that. What a master-stroke, thought Hettie.

"Well, if Ben crawls to me I'll consider comin' back," replied Marvie, condescendingly.

After breakfast Tom Day came over to pay his respects to Hettie and her mother. How bluff and genial and substantial he was!

"Wal, lass," he said at parting, "I reckon the Ides an' the Days can go back to ranchin' again, thanks to thet Texas Jack of ours. Shore, we'll have rustlin' bees again an' mebbe for years to come. But there'll be a spell now, like these Indian-summer days. Folks can sleep an' be happy. An' you youngsters can make love. Haw! Haw! . . . Hettie lass, I've been a-wonderin' aboot you. I'm shore a keen old fox. Wal, *adios,* an' God bless you."

Later in the morning Ben came to her so utterly abject that he was funny.

"Now what?" queried Hettie. "You needn't come to me for sympathy."

"Aw, Hettie, that's what Ina said, an' she stuck to it," said Ben. "But I've got to tell somebody. An' Nevada is moonstruck or somethin'. He never heard me."

"All right, Bennie," smiled Hettie, relenting.

"You know I fired Raidy—well, of course I had to go to him an' ask him to come back. Reckon the old fellow was hurt deep. He didn't rub it in, but he was sure cold. For a long while I apologized, made excuses, swore, an' did about everythin' before he would take back the old job. But at that he was nothin' compared to Marvie Blaine."

"Indeed! Yes, I remember you fired Marvie, too," said Hettie.

"You would have died laughin' to see that kid," went on Ben, ruefully. "I sent for him. Did he come? Not much. He sent word back by my messenger that if I wanted to talk to him I could hunt him up. So I had to. An' I'm darned if I don't believe he watched me an' kept dodgin' me. Well, anyway, I found him at last an' asked him to forget our difference. Whew! . . . Say, he's expanded in this Arizona air. He had an argument that floored me. It *was* logic, though I wouldn't admit it. He made me crawl. By George! You know I love Marvie an' I could never let him leave Ina an' me till he's grown up. He had more dignity than Judge Franklidge an' more conceit than any cowboy I ever saw. He swelled up like that Sheriff Macklin. Well, after he got his job back at a higher salary he put on the screws some more. He actually hit me for the reward I offered for any clue leadin' to the apprehension of the Pine Tree outfit. That reward was a thousand dollars. Marvie claimed Rose was his clue. The cheeky little rooster! But Nevada backed him up. An' as a matter of fact, 'most everythin' came through Rose. So I promised it to him. . . . Now what do you say?"

Hettie leaped up gladly. "Good for Marv! Now, Ben, run over and crawl to Ina. Then we—*you* all can be happy again!"

"Ahuh! I get the hunch that 'you' aren't included. I'll bet before this day ends you'll be as crazy as Marv an' as mum as his little wood mouse, Rose."

Still Hettie was not to have any of the solitude she craved. No sooner had Ben gone than Judge Franklidge appeared.

"I've come over to bid you and Mrs. Ide good-by," he said, in his kindly way. "It has been a rather staggering time. But we're on our feet again, and 'ridin' pretty,' as the cowboys say."

Then leaning closer to Hettie he continued in lower tone: "You recall one day at my home—when you said somethin' mysterious to me then, but pertinent now. It was about—*Nevada*."

"I remember—Judge Franklidge," murmured Hettie, trembling.

"Well, would I be correct if I—sort of put two and two together—or perhaps I should say one and one? . . . Nevada and Hettie, for instance?"

His persuasive voice, deep with understanding, and his linking together the two names, quite subdued her poor and rebellious resistance. She dropped her head, murmuring a faint affirmative.

"I'm glad I hit upon the truth," he said, with eagerness. "I watched you yesterday and I believe I saw then something of your ordeal. And I see now in your face the havoc that tells of your pain. It is my earnest hope to soothe that pain, Hettie Ide, and I know I can do so. Listen. It has been a terrible shock for you to find in your Texas Jack—or Nevada, as you call him—no other than the infamous or famous Jim Lacy. This is natural, but it is all wrong. There need be no shame, no fear, no shrinking in your acceptance of this fact. I've met and trusted no finer man than this same Jim Lacy. But I did not come to eulogize him. . . . I want to make clear in your mind just what such men as Jim Lacy mean to me. I have lived most of my life on the frontier and I know what its wilderness has been, and still is. There are bad men and bad men. It is a distinction with a vast difference. I have met or seen many of the noted killers. Wild Bill, Wess Hardin, Kingfisher, Billy the Kid, Pat Garrett, an' a host of others. These men are not bloody murderers. They are a product of the times. The West could never have been populated without them. They strike a balance between the hordes of ruffians, outlaws, strong evil characters like Dillon, and the wild life of a wild era. It is the West as any Westerner knows it now. And as such we could not be pioneers, we could not progress without this violence. Without the snuffing out of dissolute and desperate men such as Dillon, Cedar Hatt, Stillwell, and so on. The rub is that only hard iron-nerved youths like Billy the Kid, or Jim Lacy, can meet such men on their own ground. That is all I wanted you to know. And also, that if my daughter cared for Jim Lacy I would be proud to give her to him."

"Thank you, Judge Franklidge," replied Hettie, lifting her head to look straight into his eyes. "But you misunderstand my—my case. I do not mind—that Nevada has been Jim Lacy."

"For Heaven's sake! Then, why all this—this—I don't know what?" burst out the judge, in smiling amaze.

Hettie glanced away, out into the green black-striped forest.

"I scorned him. I believed him lost to—to . . . I failed in faith. And I fear he will never forgive."

"Hettie Ide," returned Franklidge, with solemn finality, "this Texas Jack won't even know he has anything to forgive."

Before Hettie could recover from this ultimatum Marvie waylaid her. Full of importance and authority, added to something of mystery, he hauled Hettie off the porch and out under the trees.

"Hettie," he whispered in her ear, "I fixed it for you."

"Marvie! . . . Are you—— Oh, if you——"

"Keep in the saddle," he interrupted, shaking her. "Nevada just told me he was dyin' of love for you. . . . There now, Hettie, don't look like that. I'm dead serious. Honest to God! Cross my heart! . . . Didn't you make my Rose happy? Why, I'd go to hell for you. An' Nevada knows it. He's sufferin'. He thinks you ought to send for him, if you can forgive him for bein' Jim Lacy."

Hettie could only cling mutely to this glad-eyed boy who was torturing her.

"So I fixed it. You run out there across the bench," he went on, pointing with eager, trembling finger. "You know. There among the pines where I always find you. Go now. Nevada is watchin'. He'll come. I swore I'd get you there if I had to pack you. An' I will."

Hettie kissed his brown lean cheek, then ran wildly into the shelter of the pines. First she meant only to escape Marvie and all of them. But an irresistible magnet drew her to the secluded nook where she went so often alone to gaze out under the low cover of green to the purple sage and the changing radiance of the desert.

Nevada was there—somehow the Nevada of old. Hettie ran into his arms.

"I—love—you! I love you!" she cried, imploringly. "Forgive me. It was my one failure. I was the weak one—not you."

Hours passed and sunset again widened its golden effulgence down over the sage hills to the rolling slopes. Purple clouds like ships sailed in a sea of gold and rose.

Hettie and Nevada sat with their backs to the great pine tree, their cheeks together, their hands clinging.

"Ben sprung somethin' on me," Nevada was saying. "Why not all of us rustle down to San Diego! Shore, it floored me. . . . But I'd like you to get away from heah just now, for a little. . . . So, darlin' Hettie, would I be askin' too much if—if——"

"No. Ask me anything," murmured Hettie.

"If I'd ask you to marry me?"

"If! . . . Do you?"

"Shore. I reckon I'm darin' to."

"No," said Hettie.

He accepted that in startled silence.

"I mean no—you are *not* asking too much. . . . Oh, Nevada! Yes! Yes!"

The last golden flare of sunset burned from over the darkening range.

"Arizona is smilin' at us," said Nevada, gazing at the sunset glow upon her rapt face.

"Nevada is smiling down upon me," she replied, dreamily.

ABOUT THE AUTHOR

ZANE GREY, perhaps America's most popular author, started out to be a dentist. Born in 1872 in Ohio, he attended the University of Pennsylvania and there made a name for himself as a baseball player. Upon graduating, he went to New York to practice dentistry, but the itch to write overcame him and he holed up in a furnished room to begin his literary career.

He had little success until 1908 when he went west on a hunting trip with Colonel Buffalo Jones. Riding after antelope, mountain lions and wolves, Grey got the feeling of the land and the rugged men and women who tamed it. He promptly put this feeling to use and in 1912 his novel, *Riders of the Purple Sage,* was published. It became an immediate success, with an eventual sale of a million copies, and is still being issued.

In the next twenty years, Zane Grey wrote twenty-five novels, with a total sale of seventeen million copies. At least three readers to each copy gave him an audience larger than any American author before him. His name is familiar to everyone. It is unbreakably linked with the romance of the old West.